PRAISE FOR

KASEY MICHAELS

"Using wit and romance with a master's skill,
Kasey Michaels aims for the heart and never misses."
—*New York Times* bestselling author Nora Roberts

"Kasey Michaels creates characters who stick with
you long after her wonderful stories are told."
—*New York Times* bestselling author Kay Hooper

"If you want emotion, humor and characters you can
love, you want a story by Kasey Michaels."
—national bestselling author Joan Hohl

"Sparkling with Michaels's characteristically droll
repartee and lovable lead characters, this Regency-set
romance enchants with its skillful treatment of a
familiar formula."
—*Publishers Weekly* on *Someone To Love*

"Michaels demonstrates her flair for creating likable
protagonists who possess chemistry, charm and a
penchant for getting into trouble. In addition, her
dialogue and descriptions are full of humor...."
—*Publishers Weekly* on *This Must Be Love*

Coming soon from Kasey Michaels

SHALL WE DANCE?

Available from HQN Books in March 2005

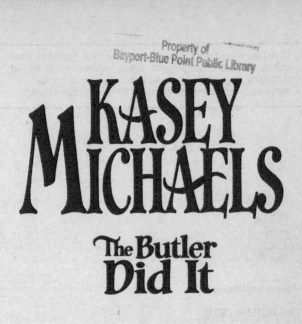

KASEY MICHAELS

The Butler Did It

HQN™

ISBN 0-373-77006-5

THE BUTLER DID IT

Copyright © 2004 by Kathryn Seidick

To Michelle Van Norman Tirpak.
Always missed, forever loved.

One, Two, Three, Etcetera...

As I was going to St. Ives,
I met a man with seven wives,
Each wife had seven sacks,
Each sack had seven cats,
Each cat had seven kits:
Kits, cats, sacks, and wives,
How many were there going to St. Ives?
—Anonymous

TO BEGIN WITH ONCE UPON A TIME would be, perhaps, a tad facetious. Rather to simply begin at the beginning, or at least as nearly as possible to that part of the beginning where it becomes interesting.

Picture England during the Regency. Such a time, such a varied generation. War, civil upheaval, opulence, indulgence, genius and cruelty. Great literature, great inventions, great deeds, great injustices. The English Regency has all of that.

Those who live there, happily, also manage to squeeze in a little silliness, a little fun. There are a few, in particular, who might be mentioned now.

Who are these people?

Why not commence with Morgan Drummond, Marquis of Westham, a gentleman who has been blessed with fine good looks, great wealth and high intelligence…and cursed with a quick temper that, five years earlier, ended in a duel that nearly cost another man his life.

Shameful.

And Morgan *was* ashamed, devastated by his actions. What was the matter with him? he asked himself. Did an insult to his latest light-o'-love (what was her name again?) really necessitate a trip to Lincolns Inn Fields and dueling foils drawn at dawn?

Was he that mad? Hadn't he learned anything through his father's death at the hands of another duelist when he, Morgan, had been only a toddler in leading strings? What had that fight been about anyway? If Morgan couldn't recall the story, and he was the son of "Mad Harry," obviously the reason had been insufficient to the result—his mother a widow, his father's body moldering in the family mausoleum at Westham.

What he did know was that he did not wish his epitaph to read: "Mad Morgan, laid low by his own wretched temper."

So the chastened and repentant Morgan swore to shun his former hey-go-mad ways and had fled London, retreating to his estate in Westham, to lick his own wounds and examine his life.

And he had been exceedingly boring.

He had drunk deep and long, then thought, hard and long, and finally decided that he could control his temper. He worked diligently during those five years of self-imposed isolation, remaking himself less in his father's image and more in what he believed to be his own. He did not, however, metamorphose into Mellow Morgan, as he never quite overcame his inborn arrogance, his penchant for sarcasm, or his most definite disdain for fools.

Alas, ho-hum, he was still boring.

But at last Morgan, having just passed his thirtieth birthday, and admittedly weary of his reclusive life, believes himself equipped to rejoin civilization once more. Sure of himself, confident in his self-control, he even feels prepared to bear the silliness of a London Season, because yes, indeed, it is time Morgan marries and sets up his nursery, begets himself an heir to carry on the line.

He has thought long and hard (and boringly) about this as well. What he needs is a complacent wife, a calm and never ruffled wife, a woman of breeding and some wit, but with a temper as sweet as a May morning—for the sake of their unborn children, naturally.

So off he goes, to London.

NEXT UP, WE HAVE ONE Miss Emma Clifford who, as it happens, is also on her way to London.

Dear Emma. Was there ever a more beautiful female?

Poor Emma. Was there ever a more beleaguered female?

Emma Clifford is the older child and keeper of the Clifford family, which explains the beleaguered portion of her description.

Emma's mother is lovable, but a bit of a twit. Her brother is a complete loss. Her irascible grandmother is forever reliving her not quite proper past. And they're all constantly in need of funds.

The Cliffords do have one hope. Actually, they harbor quite a few hopes. Emma, however, has just one. She is not a silly girl; she knows she is quite beautiful. And, in London, beautiful is often the key that opens the door to an advantageous marriage.

In other words, a good marriage equaled solvency for the entire family. Ah, a financially comfortable existence; always considered A Good Thing To Have, and eternally prized as a cure-all to any woe by Those Who Don't Have.

Although her grandmother keeps telling Emma that, ideally, marriage shouldn't have anything to do with lining one's pocket at the expense of being stuck with a belching, scratching buffoon who probably ingests cabbage for breakfast.

Her grandmother's advice to one side, the determined Emma has sold her mother's diamonds, hocked the family portraits, and traded the services of a fairly good stud horse for the use of an ancient traveling coach and some showy if not quite prime carriage horses.

So the Cliffords, like Morgan Drummond, are off to London for the Season. In the Cliffords' case, it is to cut a dash, to shop the marriage mart (already the marquis and the questing young miss have something in common), to trade on Mama's grasstime friendship with Lady Sally Jersey in order to secure vouchers to Almack's, and be introduced to the Very Cream of Society.

Daphne Clifford, Emma's mother, can barely contain herself. Daphne, never to be spoken of as The Widow Clifford, is a faded beauty, yet still quite attractive. The years have brought a few lines, a few extra pounds…and not a whit more intelligence than when, a quarter century earlier, she'd tossed herself away on the handsome spendthrift, Samuel Clifford.

She agrees that dearest Emma should find herself a wealthy husband. She sees no reason why such a beautiful girl should have the least trouble in Snatching Up the Catch of the Season. Daphne certainly doesn't expect any difficulties in her own quest for—ta-da!—True Love.

Daphne does quite a bit of her thinking in capitals.

Fanny Clifford scoffs at her daughter-in-law's hopes, which she considers as likely to be fulfilled as Daphne's wish to have Mother Clifford retire to Bath with her elderly cousin Maude, and For Goodness' Sakes Leave Everyone Alone.

Fanny is a trifle…well, it could be said that she is very much her own woman. She lived a different London life than debutantes coming to town during the namby-pamby and oh, so proper Regency. A product of a freer, bawdier age, Fanny speaks frankly, behaves just as she wishes, and believes missish girls and milksop gentlemen should be locked up somewhere so that the world shouldn't have to wince as they mince.

Fanny's hoping for adventure in London, not a wedding ring. After all, she'd been married, and doesn't quite see the appeal of being legally bracketed to another man who could very well gnaw at his toenails in bed.

Definitely unknown to her granddaughter, Fanny has big plans. Or as Daphne might think it: Big Plans. Besides having herself a little fun before she's too aged to recognize fun even if it toddled up and pinched her on the bottom, she has conjured up a plan to convince at least one of her old lovers to offer up a solvent, handsome, hopefully appealing grandson to wed Emma.

One thing Fanny knows for certain is that she will not, for any amount of money, for the possibility of any grand title, allow her dear Emma to wed anyone in the least like her grandson.

Clifford Clifford (Daphne had *so* little imagination), better known as Cliff, is younger than Emma, still two years shy of reaching his majority, but he is old enough to believe he, too, can go cut himself a dash in London Society.

To Cliff, this means attendance at mills, bearbaitings, cockfights, and visits to any gaming hell where green-as-grass country bumpkins can be assured that they will leave the establishment with empty pockets.

In short, in long, Cliff Clifford is the sort of knock-headed young fool Morgan Drummond could never learn to suffer gladly, even if he had remained at his estate until his blood had cooled enough to form ice chips in his veins.

Also traveling to London this Season is one Edgar Marmon, Adventurer.

Not to put too fine a point on it, Edgar *used* to be an Adventurer. Now, at the ripe old age of seventy, he *thinks* he's an Adventurer. A man who lives by his wits, and the lack of wits of his victims, the man has run many a rig, usually unsuccessfully, and has more than a few enemies he hopes are older, and slower, and cannot outrun him.

Edgar is coming to London with a Grand Idea. A Brilliant Scheme. A Grand Plan sure to line his pockets one last time so that he can retire to Brighton or some such comfortable spot, and prey on rich widows at his leisure.

Oh dear, someone else who thinks in capitals.

At the moment, Edgar is masquerading as Sir Edgar Marmington, inventor and gentleman…a man who really, really discourages investors from believing they'll become even more wealthy than they were by lining his pockets with blunt for the privilege of coming in on the ground floor, as it were, of his most ambitious invention to date: converting lead to gold.

Of course Edgar discourages investors. And pretty pink pigs are frequently observed orbiting around Parliament in the noonday sun.

Already in London but hoping for a change of address is one Mrs. Olive Norbert, the "Mrs." being a courtesy title, although no one numbered in Olive's former acquaintance had found it necessary to live within any such rules of courtesy.

Olive is a seamstress of two and fifty, now happily retired, who has even more happily come into a moderate fortune by way of an inheritance from her last client, a fairly dotty woman who dearly loved clothing and definitely disliked her relatives.

With no plans to marry, even if someone should ask, Olive is intent only on looking at London through a different window than the small, dusty one in the single cramped attic room she'd inhabited above her former employer's shop in one of the less fashionable neighborhoods just outside Mayfair.

In short, Olive, newly solvent, is intent on having herself a small holiday. Right smack in the center of London Society.

She knows she'll have a splendid time. After all, she's psychic. How else would she have known that Mrs. Hartford would perish in a nasty fall down the stairs and leave her seamstress five thousand pounds?

As Daphne would have said: Mrs. Norbert Could Be Trouble.

Perry Shepherd, the Earl of Brentwood, has already been "trouble" to Morgan Drummond. His lordship had been one of the marquis's chums in school, and during his one Season in London. Right up until the moment, as a matter of fact, that the marquis had challenged him to that infamous duel over the affections of a comely young Covent Garden dancer (What *was* her name?).

Yet, the duel to one side, the earl still likes the marquis. Really. After all, the scar on his cheek is actually rather dashing. The ladies seem to fancy it, and the earl certainly fancies the ladies, so he's rather well pleased with the whole thing, even if the scar gives his valet the very devil when he shaves him.

Perry also would be happy to take up his friendship with Morgan once more when that man returns to London, sort of help ease the man's way back into Society. Besides, London has been sadly flat without Morgan there to comment on the foolishness and frailties of the *ton* and, as Perry well knows, where Morgan goes, it is many things, but it is never, never dull.

Yes, the earl will call on his friend Morgan as soon as he learns that the man has arrived at his home in London.

There is a staff in residence year-round at the marquis's Grosvenor Square mansion in Mayfair.

Mrs. Hazel Timon, for one, is housekeeper of the marquis's London domicile. But not for long, as she has a nice little nest egg growing in the trunk at the bottom of her closet.

Mrs. Timon rides herd on Claramae, the young, comely but vacant-headed maid of all work on the skeleton staff. Claramae also acts as ladies' maid when needed, and spends as much time as possible flirting with the rascally Riley.

Footman, under-butler, groom, coachie, Riley does

whatever is needed. He's happy to be of service. This is obvious by the way his hand is always out whenever he is of service.

The Grosvenor Square staff being quite small in the absence of its owner, that leaves just one more servant: the estimable, and quite inventive Thornley.

For years, Thornley has played the role of butler to the Drummond family, father and son.

He is loyal. He is as proper as one can get without having an actual pole thrust up one's…suffice it to say, he's quite proper.

Thornley is two more things. He is ambitious, and he is a practical sort who can't abide waste.

Thornley rules the mansion as butler, as majordomo, as the most important, elevated servant, during good times and bad, including the past five long years, while the young master sulked in the country and the London mansion stood empty.

But ruling a skeleton staff that does little more than occasionally polish some silver and swipe cobwebs from the corners, while eating their heads off, is not much of a challenge for the man.

At least it wasn't. For the first two Seasons the mansion stood empty as the city came to life from late March through the King's birthday.

For the past three Seasons, including this one, Thornley, acting on his own initiative, has found a way to keep the staff busy. He has been leasing rooms in the mansion to those who need accommodations while in town for the festivities.

Because a house, even a London mansion, needs people. Needs life.

And the profits aren't too shabby, either.

So, HOW MANY WERE THERE going to Saint Ives…er, who all will be gathering at that Grosvenor Square mansion? Ticking them off on one's fingers would get:

One small but inventive staff.

One Interesting Family.

One old friend.

One slightly illegal adventurer.

One possible killer.

Lastly, arriving late and without notice, one dedicatedly mild-tempered Marquis of Westham.

Perhaps he should have sent a note….

They Gather Here Together...

If possible honestly, if not,
somehow, make money.
—Horace

TRAFFIC BECAME BOTH more frequent and slower as Morgan Drummond, Marquis of Westham, neared the metropolis of London atop his favorite mount, Sampson.

The stallion took exception to nearly every coach, wagon and curricle that approached them along the roadway, and Morgan was kept occupied in restraining Sampson from breaking into a gallop that could only end in disaster—at least according to Wycliff, Morgan's valet, who rode along just behind him, shadowing him like a damp gray cloud on an otherwise sunny day.

It was a cloudy day, in point of fact, but Wycliff could make anything feel worse than it actually was. It was his particular gift.

"There he goes again, my lord!" Wycliff exclaimed in clear (and expected) horror as a dray piled high with empty cages lumbered past. "Hold him, my lord! Hold him!"

Morgan, a top-o'-the-trees whipster who would have no trouble commanding six highly strung and definitely randy stallions while tooling a coach through a field filled with flirtatious mares, merely gritted his teeth and danced Sampson carefully past the dray wagon.

"Remind me, Wycliff, if you will, precisely *why* you have chosen to accept my invitation to ride with me today," the marquis drawled as the valet, his face ashen, drew his aged gelding abreast of Sampson.

"You put forth a wish to ride ahead of the coaches, my lord," Wycliff said, employing both hands on the reins of his persecuted mount. "I could not in good conscience remain safely in the coach. There…there could well be brigands about, my lord."

"Too true. Tell me, what had you planned to do if any attacked us? *Faint* on them?" the marquis asked, casting a short glance at the valet, just long enough to be reminded of the man's tall, reed-slim and rather badly proportioned body, his bald pate that looked so naked even beneath the man's low-crowned, broad-brimmed hat (held up mostly by Wycliff's astonishingly protrudent ears), and the fellow's narrow, pasty face that must have been turned to the wall when lips were being handed out. "That said, and considering your truly humbling loyalty to my person, you won't mind overmuch if I toss you to the first ones we meet, will you?"

The valet laughed. Giggled, actually. Nervously. Partly because he was a nervous sort, but mostly because he was one of those unfortunate souls born without the ability to recognize sarcasm, although he did laugh at odd moments, as if he sometimes had inklings that he should. "You are so droll, my lord, I always say so. Brilliant wit, my lord! I am so proud to be in your employ. Indeed, sir, I exist only for the pleasure of serving you."

"My, aren't I the lucky one." Morgan smiled thinly, and urged Sampson ahead once more. "Do try to keep up, Wycliff."

"Yes, my lord, indeed, my lord. Keeping up, my lord," Wycliff answered, digging his heels into the gelding's flanks, which served to break the patient horse into a slow and rather bumpy trot.

Wycliff was in the way of a test, and the marquis had employed the man three months earlier because, and not in spite of, the valet's grating effect on his lordship's nerves. It wasn't the man's features that annoyed him; he wasn't that shallow. It was the nervous, always inappropriate giggle, and the perpetual doomsaying, and, mostly, the man's creepily subservient ways that set Morgan's teeth on edge.

The way Morgan saw it, if he could make it to London without pummeling the man heavily about the head and shoulders before sticking him skinny-shanks-up in a trunk in the boot of one of his two traveling coaches, he should be able to handle any provocations being in the metropolis for the Season might toss at him.

Because he was about to become one of the most sought-after bachelors of the Season, Lord help him.

Morgan knew he cut a fine figure atop the bay stallion, dressed in his best hacking clothes, finely polished Hessians, and his favorite curly brimmed beaver. A five-caped dusky gray driving coat fell in neat folds from his shoulders and cascaded over Sampson's twitching flanks.

A fully loaded and ready brace of pistols nested in special pockets built into the saddle in case any of Wycliff's feared brigands dared approach, and the gold-tipped sword cane had been slid into its holder, also incorporated into the saddle.

He wore dove-gray gloves on his hands, covering the gold-and-ruby signet ring that had been his father's, and had tucked a fine wool scarf beneath his coat, knitted by his mother and handed over two days ago with the admonition to wear it or Catch His Death Of Cold (A pity Lady Westham's health did not support a sojourn to London; she would have had Kindred Spirits waiting for her there).

A handsome man, in his prime at thirty, the marquis could lay claim to startling blue eyes, a thick mop of blacker-than-black hair, a truly glorious, aristocratic nose, a firm, strong jaw, and the physique of a true Corinthian: broad shoulders, narrow through the hips, long, muscular legs.

He knew he turned heads; he had always turned heads, even in the nursery. He had always been lucky, and popular with the ladies, and having a title and not inconsiderable wealth had done nothing to diminish the high regard in which he had been held during his first and only London Season.

There were even those who had congratulated him on the outcome of his duel with Perry Shepherd, the truest friend one man could have.

Fools. Sycophants. Morgan was not looking forward to meeting any of those people this time around, or in following any of the pursuits that had engaged him for most of that first Season.

He would not drink to excess, he would not play cards for any but tame stakes, he would avoid mills, and Gentleman Jackson's Boxing Saloon. These were all occasions of sin for a man with a volatile temperament.

Instead, he would frequent the balls, the soirees, the Italian breakfasts for six hundred of one's closest friends. He'd even force himself through the doors of Almack's, perish the thought, and in general, he would behave as what he was, a man on the lookout for a wife.

When he thought of his plan, he knew it to be a recipe for boredom, and that seemed like a good thing. No temptations, no pretty Covent Garden ankles vied for by all the young bucks, no provocation more than having to deal with Wycliff when the man wrung his hands over the fact that Morgan often preferred to shave himself.

Confident, sure of himself, Morgan Drummond, Marquis of Westham, rode on toward London, into the dense, yellow, odoriferous fog that hung over the city, and straight for his destiny.

EVEN AS MORGAN RODE toward his destiny, Emma Clifford, along with her mother, Daphne, all but stumbled into the foyer of the marquis's Grosvenor Square mansion, followed hard on their heels by the maid, Claramae. It was noticed immediately that the maid was weeping, an action, to Claramae, that was as natural, and as frequent, as exhaling.

"Good afternoon, ladies," Thornley said, for he, as butler, was already present in the foyer. He made it a point to always be present where he was needed, leading to the whispered rumor that he was, in reality, triplets. This seemed to explain to the staff how the man could appear to be in three places at once, with all three watching to make sure the servants missed not a speck of dust on the library shelves, didn't overlook polishing the doorknobs, or ever dare to sample meals meant for abovestairs.

Thornley, his spine rod-stiff, his chin lifted high, took a moment to assess his lodgers. Well, all right, the Marquis of Westham's lodgers, if one wished to nitpick.

He doubted Miss Emma Clifford would have much trouble bagging at least a reasonable husband in the next few weeks, with only her all but nonexistent dowry standing as an impediment to a more brilliant match.

The young lady was a beauty, a diamond of the first water. Petite, dark haired, and with stunning gray eyes, she had a look of liveliness about her, not at all a milk-and-water miss. She had conversation, she had wit, she moved with a natural grace, and she must possess the patience of a saint in order to put up with the menagerie that had come to Town in tow with her.

Mrs. Clifford the Elder, thankfully not present at the moment, was Imminent Disaster rolling on wheels, and Thornley, with his highly developed sense of self-preservation, had dedicated himself to not watching what Fanny Clifford did, hearing what she said, or speculating on what she might do or say next.

Mr. Clifford Clifford, Thornley had decided within five seconds of meeting the boy, was a dead loss, and he refused to think of him, either.

Although the mother, the Widow Clifford, held a certain nerve-shredding appeal. Thornley believed in an armful of woman, and Daphne Clifford could fit that bill very well. She had dimples, not just in her plump cheeks, but at her elbows as well, and Thornley had scolded himself mightily when he'd found himself cogitating the odds of dimples also decorating the lady's knees.

All in all, Daphne Clifford had a look of faded glory, gray eyes like the dust of roses, and hair once red but now streaked with silver. A woman of some beauty, for all her short stature, and quite beyond Thornley's touch. Everyone above a housekeeper was beyond Thornley's touch; he had accepted that long ago, and had resigned himself to bachelorhood without many regrets.

He would not even speculate upon how very comforting warm, dimpled knees might be, pressed up against him, spoonlike, on cold winter nights.

"Good afternoon, Thornley," Emma said, stripping off her gloves. "And see if you can turn off that watering pot behind me, if you could, please. It was no more than a simple walk in the Square. You'd think I just led a forced march to Hampstead Heath and back. Mama," she added, "Riley will be happy to take your things for you."

Daphne Clifford, who had been staring at Thornley, and smiling rather dreamily, quickly pulled off her gloves, mumbling, "I...I was just doing that, dear."

"Yes, miss," Thornley said, bowing to Emma, then glaring at the sniffling Claramae in his practiced, penetrating way, which quite naturally served to instantly silence her, mid-snuffle. "If you'll forgive her, miss, Claramae has quite a fear of fog such as we've been enduring these past three days. She once became lost for more than two hours, as I recall, not ten feet from the kitchen door."

Being a proper butler, and loyal to his staff, Thornley refrained from adding that Claramae could also most probably become confused and misplace all sense of direction in a small linen closet. While carrying a blazing lamp. And while gripping a length of stout string tied to the doorknob.

Daphne Clifford who, after giving over her gloves, bonnet and pelisse, had been doling out a lint-dusted penny to Riley, snapped her thin purse closed and added her mote to the conversation: "Why the child thinks we needs must take the air for a full hour every day, even when that air tastes of coal dust and we can't see our own fingers in front of our faces...why, I sometimes wonder for her mind."

"Yes, Mrs. Clifford," Thornley said, bowing once more, even as he shuddered inwardly at this clearly too-intimate conversation with the woman. Wasn't it enough that he was attracted? Did she have to make matters worse by smiling at him? Showing him those dimples? "It is my understanding that all social events have been postponed again for this evening due to this pea soup, as we here in London call it."

Thornley would bow and agree with anyone, even the devil himself, if it would get these two ladies out of the foyer and upstairs before the tea grew cold (or his libido grew any warmer). Thornley liked an orderly household, one that ran to his schedule, and Miss Clifford's daily walks around the Square at three o'clock pained him, and that schedule, dearly.

With a sharp look to Riley, and then to the door, the footman jumped to, pushing a rolled-up carpet firmly against the bottom of the door, to keep the yellow fog in the Square, rather than allow it to seep into the mansion. Similar measures had been taken at every door, every window, and the lack of aesthetics bothered Thornley, but not as much as waist-deep fog in the mansion would do. Mrs. Timon had already developed a hacking cough and had been ordered to her bed.

"Is there—" Daphne began, and Thornley ended, "Tea and fresh, warm biscuits await both you good ladies in the main drawing room. I do believe there is also blueberry jam, your favorite I noticed, Mrs. Clifford. If I might lead the way, madam?"

Thornley realized at once that he had made a verbal mistake, adding that bit about the jam in some absurd thought of puffing himself up in Daphne Clifford's eyes. She immediately grabbed hold of his arm at the elbow, as if they were man and woman, not butler and well-born tenant. A lesser man would have felt a jolt of hope, but Thornley was not a lesser man. He knew his place.

"You're so good, so kind, Thornley," Daphne trilled, batting her remarkably lush eyelashes at him. "La, I fear we must be quite the burden to you, new to London as we are."

"Not at all, madam," Thornley assured her as Miss Clifford, whom he had instantly recognized as the wits as well as the anchor of the entire Clifford family, turned to pat Claramae's arm.

"We'll take no more walks until this fog is dissipated, I promise. I was foolish to insist, but I do so hate being cooped up inside, ever, no matter how pleasing my surroundings. And I'm very sorry you were frightened out there, Claramae," she apologized in her pleasing voice.

Indeed, all of Miss Emma Clifford was pleasing, to

the ears, to the eyes. Even to the mind, unless one was the sort to be frightened by an intelligent female. Still, for all her perfection, she hadn't got her mother's dimples, which at least Thornley could only consider a pity. A bleeding pity.

"Yes, miss," Claramae said, stuffing a soggy handkerchief back into her apron pocket even as she dropped into a quick curtsy. "'Tis just that robbers and murderers lurk in the fog. Everyone knows that."

"Possibly, Claramae, but if those cutpurses and cutthroats encountered the same problems we had in seeing even two feet in front of us, I imagine they're all still out there, bumping into each other, cutting each other's noses off, and no worry to us."

"Yes, miss. I'll take your things, miss? Everything will need a good brushing, as it's so dusty out there."

Emma handed over her bonnet, gloves and pelisse, and Claramae scuttled off toward the baize door under the stairs, leaving Emma to follow in her mother's wake.

She could hear Daphne Clifford still nattering nineteen to the dozen to Thornley.

Emma sighed, shook her head and mentally attempted to compose a small homily that would convince her mother that, while Thornley was admittedly a well-set-up gentleman, he was their butler, not their host.

Not that this would matter a whit to Daphne, Emma realized on yet another sigh. She had never before noticed her mother's proclivity to gush, to eyelash bat, to simper and giggle. At home, Daphne concentrated on her embroidery. At home, Daphne still spoke well of her husband, dead these three years. At home, Daphne *behaved* herself.

Here, from absolutely the first moment her mother had set eyes on Thornley five short days ago, the woman had been afflicted with some strange mental aberration that had her believing she was a young girl on the flirt.

It was embarrassing, that's what it was, and that Daphne's old chum, Lady Jersey, seemed to encourage her was only to be considered criminal. Emma knew that Sally Jersey was laughing behind her hand at Daphne, but Sally Jersey had also issued them all vouchers to Almack's, so Emma had steeled herself to overlook the woman's rather perverse humor. But only until she had snagged herself a suitable husband. After that, she would cut Sally Jersey dead, and hang the consequences, no matter how much her mother seemed to admire the woman.

Emma entered the large main drawing room just as her mother was asking Thornley to please "play Mother" for them and pour the tea. She'd stopped short of asking the man to sit down, spread a serviette over his knee and join them in their refreshments, and Emma could only be grateful for that small favor.

The butler, his ears rather red, cited his inability to linger, as he had pressing duties, and avoided Emma's gaze as he walked, stiff-backed, from the room.

"Mama, you really mustn't do that," Emma said, sit-

ting down on the facing couch, the silver tea service between them.

"Really mustn't do what, dear?" Daphne asked
vaguely, making a great business out of attempting to lift
the teapot before sitting back, sighing. "Much, much too
heavy. You know, Emma, this is a very pretty place, by
and large, but I don't understand opulence if it's too
heavy to use."

Emma bit her bottom lip, reached forward to place a
cup beneath the spout of the teapot, then tipped the pot
on its cradle to pour the tea…as the pot was designed to
do. "Here you are, Mama. You must be chilled. Drink
up."

"Oh, my," Daphne said, giving the teapot a little push
with her spoon. "Would you just look at that, Emma?
What will they think of next?"

"I have no idea, Mama," Emma said, straight-faced,
then looked up as her grandmother entered the room.

She resisted sniffing the air for the scent of mischief,
because she didn't want to know, and because she was
a well-bred young lady. Which didn't mean she could
overlook the rather shrewd look in her grandmother's
lively eyes. Living with Fanny Clifford was rather like
being in charge of maintaining the night fire in a forest,
so that it didn't go out and wolves were able to approach.
One could not rest easy, ever.

"Fresh from your nap, Grandmama?" Emma asked,
her voice deliberately vague, only mildly and politely in-

terested in whatever answer her grandmother might offer.

Because Fanny Clifford never napped, and Emma knew this. What she didn't want to know was where her grandmother had been the past hour, or what she'd been doing. No sane person would. It was better to pretend to believe a lie, and much easier than trying to explain any of her grandmother's activities to Daphne Clifford.

"A lovely rest for these weary old bones, yes, dear," Fanny lied smoothly as she lowered her small, paper-thin self onto the couch beside Daphne. "And you two were out mucking about in the fog again, I suppose? You've a smut of coal dust on your nose, Daphne."

Daphne quickly raised her serviette to her face, exclaiming, "Oh, no, no! No wonder he looked at me so oddly. I could just Expire. I'm So Ashamed."

"Twit," Fanny Clifford muttered, winking at her granddaughter. "There's no smut, Daphne. I was merely checking to see if you're still so arsy-varsy over Thornley. And you are. And still making a cake out of yourself, I have no doubt. My wastrel son must be spinning in his grave, that you'd think to replace him with a servant. Of course, Thornley is butler to a marquis, could even be called a majordomo, so that might have Samuel not rotating quite so fast. The boy always was hot for titles."

"I am not making a push for Thornley, Mother Clifford," Daphne protested, but she did not look the older woman in the eyes. "Doesn't he have the loveliest posture? Samuel always *slouched* so."

Emma added two sugars to her tea. "Grandmama, remember, we are not to specifically mention the marquis in public unless forced to do so, and then just to say that he is our unfortunately absent host. Thornley was adamant about that. I think the poor man must be strapped for cash, which is the only explanation I can find as to why he leases rooms to perfect strangers for the Season. We were even quite vague with Lady Jersey on her single visit here, as you might remember, although she is much too interested in herself to notice where she is when she's telling all and sundry how very wonderful she is. But we must protect the man's reputation."

"Humph. If it's his reputation he's worried about, you'd think he'd at least vet whom he leases to better before allowing them to run tame in his household."

Emma put down her spoon very carefully, trying to hang on to her composure. She had two choices: ignore what her grandmother just said—hinted at—or ask the woman what she meant. She must be feeling daring, or else the fog had muddled her mind, because she then took a deep breath and asked, "What have you done this time, Grandmama? Waited until either Mrs. Norbert or Sir Edgar went out and about, and then pored through their belongings?"

"Oh, don't be silly, Emma. Your grandmother would

never do any such thing. It would be unladylike, and too shabby by half," Daphne scolded, brushing pastry crumbs from her skirt. "Would you, Mother Clifford? Sneak about, that is, and poke into drawers and such?"

"Here's a lesson for you, Daphne. You, too, Emma. Never ask questions you wouldn't want to hear answered." Fanny shook off Emma's silent offer of tea (a move meant to shut the woman up, at least for a few moments), stood, and headed for the drinks table. She picked up the decanter of sherry, made a face at it, then poured herself two fingers of port.

Daphne looked to her daughter, her eyes wide. "She wouldn't…she couldn't go poking about in…she—oh, Lord, she did, didn't she? No, don't tell me. I don't want to know. *Tell* me!"

"She did," Emma admitted to her mother. Why hadn't she waited until she and Fanny were alone, before opening this particular jar of worms? "But," she added quietly, "I believe that was yesterday."

Emma looked at her grandmother as that tiny, always energetic woman sat herself down once more, and decided she had to know everything, now. "What was on today's agenda, Grandmama? Waiting until one of them fell asleep, and then prying open his or her mouth, to count teeth?"

"A good hiding, Emma, I've always said you should have had at least one during your formative years. Don't badger an old lady, all right? If you behave, I may make you happy and tell you that I have been badly served for my inquisitive nature."

"You got no reward for your nosiness, you mean," Emma interrupted. "Good."

"A dozen hidings wouldn't have been enough," Fanny said, sipping at her port. "But I tell you, I'm extremely disappointed. Mrs. Norbert, after a careful investigation of her belongings—oh, Daphne, close your mouth before a fly lands in it—is a seamstress."

Emma blinked. "Well, yes, she said as much, Grandmama, that first night at dinner. A seamstress who came into some inheritance or another. She doesn't wish to enter Society, but only to be treated like a lady for a few months, being waited on, eating well. She hasn't tried to hide her past. What of it?"

Fanny rolled her still bright-blue eyes. "A *seamstress,* Emma. You know what that means. Or, what it usually means, not that old hatchet face would have been more than a penny-a-poke gel, up against some slimy warehouse wall."

Daphne dropped her teacup—it shattered against the edge of the table—before slapping her hands over Emma's ears. "Mother Clifford! I'll not have you saying such things with my innocent daughter here. Or with me here, come to think of it. Samuel always said you had a mouth that needed a good scrubbing with strong soap."

Emma calmly reached up and removed her mother's hands, unfortunately just in time to hear Fanny go off on one of her favorite jaunts—that of riding up and down her daughter-in-law's tender sensibilities.

"Oh, stubble it, Daphne. You knew what I meant, which shows you to not be as pure and ladylike as you wish you were. You couldn't have been, living with Samuel and his constant peccadilloes with various bits of the muslin company. That, dear girl," she ended, looking to Emma, "would be whores, lightskirts and, once, when he was particularly flushed from a win at the tables, a kept woman he lost in the next run of his usual bad luck."

"You never liked him. Your own son." Daphne sighed deeply. "And to that, Mother Clifford, I can only say For Shame."

Emma had enough of her mother in her to be at least marginally horrified, and enough of her grandmother in her to have to remind herself not to laugh out loud. Suddenly, Mrs. Norbert seemed a safer topic of conversation. "How…" she asked at last, "…how do you know Mrs. Norbert is a seamstress, Grandmama, rather than a…a *seamstress?*"

Fanny sniffed. "Her sewing basket, for one. Packets of pins and needles, a well-worn darning knob, a full set of workmanlike scissors. That basket isn't for show, I tell you. It has been *used*. That," she said, "and the fact that her underclothes and nightwear are of sturdy, oft-mended spinster quality. Meaning," she ended, looking to her daughter-in-law, "they were never meant to see a man, just a long, cold winter."

"So you *did* sneak into her room and look in her drawers," Daphne said, slowly catching up.

"Looked at 'em, picked 'em up and inspected 'em," Fanny said (as Emma gave in and began laughing), then downed the remainder of her port. "I had so hoped she'd been a streetwalker, even a kept woman. But she's a demned seamstress, which makes her about as interesting as the mud fence she so greatly resembles. But I have hopes yet for Sir Edgar. There's something about that man that screams out to be investigated."

Emma sobered. "Grandmama, you will *not* be looking at his drawers, understand? I won't have it."

"And I'm not interested in his drawers. He's older than dirt," Fanny shot back. "I've got bigger fish to fry, gel. I just want to know our fellow tenants. Or are you looking to get murdered in your bed?"

Emma sighed in the midst of picking up shards of very fine china cup and looked to her mother, who was going rather pale. "She doesn't really mean that, Mama."

"Yes, she does," Fanny said, winking at her granddaughter. "There we'd be, dreaming sweet dreams, and *bam*, eternal rest, with sewing scissors sticking out from between our ribs. Or maybe a pillow over our heads, pressed there by Sir Edgar, who is really a bloody murderer who, even as we lay there, cold and dead as stones, spends the rest of the night going through *our* drawers."

"She doesn't really mean that, either, Mama," Emma

said as Daphne clutched an embroidered silk pillow to her ample bosom. "Grandmama, you're impossible."

"And I pride myself on it," Fanny said, standing up to go refill her glass. "Except, of course, you're so *easy*, Daphne. I really wish you'd give me more incentive to tease you. But, then, I've got other fish to fry here in London, don't I? And them I'll tease to much better effect."

Emma laid the pieces of broken china on the tea tray and sat back once more, to stare in her grandmother's direction. "What are you planning, Grandmama? We've got some funds left, but probably not enough to bribe your way out of the local guardhouse. And, come to think of it, we'd first need to take a family vote as to whether or not we'd wish to spend our last penny saving you. I'd consider that, Grandmama, as I know where my vote would go, and Cliff still hasn't quite forgiven you for making him ride all the way here inside the coach with us."

"You should both thank me for that. You know what would have happened if he rode up with the coachman. He'd have found some way to take the ribbons, and we'd all be dead in a ditch right now."

"Dead, dead, dead," Daphne lamented, still clutching the pillow. "Have you no other conversation today, Mother Clifford?"

"I do, Daphne, but you don't want to hear it. Now, Thornley told me that all social events have been postponed again because of this fog, which leaves us at loose ends this evening, again. I'm bored to flinders, frankly, so what I thought was that we could corner Sir Edgar, all three of us, and press him for a bit of his history. You know. Where he was born, who his father was, why he keeps several extremely large, heavy trunks hidden behind the locked door of his dressing room. I saw them go up the stairs when he arrived, but they're sitting nowhere they can be seen. He has to have locked them up for a terrible reason."

"Let's talk about locking you in your dressing room," Emma said succinctly, ringing the small bell on the tea tray, at which time Thornley appeared in the doorway, just as if he'd been standing right outside all along, waiting for the summons...and hearing every word the ladies said.

"You rang, Miss Clifford?" Thornley inquired, already picking up the tea tray, and not appearing at all surprised to see that one of the marquis's priceless china cups was now in seven uneven pieces.

"Yes, thank you, Thornley," she said, laying her damp, tea-stained serviette on the tray. "I was wondering—" she looked straight into the man's eyes "—do you happen to know the whereabouts of Mr. Clifford?"

Thornley, eyes quickly averted, looking somewhere in the vicinity of the portrait of the late Marquis and several of his hounds that hung over the mantel, said, "I believe he is resting, Miss Clifford."

"He's still in *bed?*" Emma sighed. "It's nearly gone

five, Thornley. What time did my brother get in this morning?"

"I couldn't really say, Miss Clifford," Thornley said, still avoiding her gaze, even as she stood—which didn't come close to putting her on eye level with the man, but she'd hoped to at least be able to read his expression.

But Thornley *had* no expressions, other than Proper, and possibly, Prudent.

"Very well, as I know he accompanied my brother, I'll ask Riley," Emma said, brushing past him as she headed for the stairs. She stopped, turned back toward the pair of sofas. "Mama? Do you have another penny?"

"That won't be necessary, Miss Clifford," Thornley said stiffly. "Riley escorted Mr. Clifford to a…a sporting event last evening, and they returned here at approximately six this morning, Mr. Clifford rather the worse for wear. Riley has been reprimanded, Miss Clifford."

"A sporting event?" Fanny asked. "What was it? Mill? Cockfight? Oh, wait. A sporting *event,* you say, Thornley? Or a sporting *house?*"

Emma watched as Thornley's ears turned bright red. Poor fellow. He could keep his spine straight. His expression never betrayed what he might be thinking. And she hadn't really needed to see his eyes. Those ears of his were a dead giveaway.

"Ah!" Fanny crowed, punching a fist into the air. "Good for him, and about time, too!"

Daphne, who had come within Ames Ace of swooning into the cushions at the thought of being murdered in her bed, now gave way to the blessed darkness that swam before her eyes.

DARKNESS WOULD HAVE BEEN swimming in front of Morgan's eyes, save for the fact that the fog wouldn't let it. The entire countryside had turned a thick, ugly gray-yellow, slowing the progress of the pair of coaches to a crawl.

They should have reached London hours ago, he knew, snapping shut his pocket watch after checking the time. He'd returned to the coach at the last posting inn, to rest Sampson, and because he did not much care for the feel of the gray-yellow damp on his face, but it was now past his usual dinnertime, and he was hungry. Damn early country hours, where he'd become accustomed to eating his main meal long before six.

"We still should arrive before eight, don't you think?" he asked a morose and rather pale-looking Wycliff, who didn't seem quite at his best riding backward in the coach. "In plenty of time for supper."

"I...I really hadn't thought much about...about food, my lord," the valet choked out, somehow able to speak without really opening his teeth.

"Really? And here I am, famished. As I recall the thing, Mrs. Timon always had a way with a capon. Gaston will be in charge of the kitchen while we're there, but for the most part, Mrs. Timon does just fine. Except for the eel. Don't care for eel, Wycliff," Morgan said, watching the man closely.

"I…I also don't care for…for eel, my lord."

Morgan was being perverse, he knew it, but he had cause. Wycliff had made a cake of himself after departing that last posting inn, insisting almost to hysteria that the three harmless-looking farmers who had shared the common room with them were sure to follow the coaches, intent on slitting their throats.

Morgan would consider a figurative crawl inside Wycliff's head, just for a moment, to see where the man's brainbox had been wound up incorrectly, except he'd first have to fight his way through the maggots that doubtless collected there.

"No? Then, at last, we're agreed on something. The thing about eel, Wycliff, is that rather rubbery texture when it isn't cooked just right. Do you know what I mean? It can be swimming in the best, most creamy parsley sauce, but if you put it in your mouth and it sort of *bounces* off your back teeth, well—"

God was both testing him and punishing him, Morgan decided, as Wycliff tossed up his accounts all over his lordship's shiny Hessians.

THIS WAS IT, the final test of his resolve. Edgar Marmon, Adventurer, and currently known as Sir Edgar Marmington, counted to ten to calm his queasy stomach as he stood just outside the tavern at the bottom end of Bond Street. He was getting too old for this, and knew that, if he hesitated, he would be in danger of losing his nerve.

But, as he was also in no monetary position to turn tail and run, and too aged to contemplate employing the sweat of his brow in an honest day's work—probably because he'd never used the words "work" and "honest" in the same thought—he screwed himself up to the sticking point and soldiered on.

Once inside, his gaze roamed the place, seeking into the darkest corners, on the lookout for anyone who might see through his disguise of now snowy-white hair, a bushy white mustache, and the cane he used to support his limp, a leftover of his valiant service against the French, years earlier.

If one could count tagging after the army valiant as, for the most part, he had hidden himself in the rear during the day and left his visits to the battlefields to the dark of night, when he scavenged for any bits of loot he could find and carry away. If, not to make too fine a point on it, one could even call it a limp, as Sir Edgar, just to be sure he'd keep favoring the correct leg, placed a few pebbles in his left boot each morning, to remind him.

Sir Edgar selected the perfect small table in the corner, and carefully sat down in the chair that positioned his back to the wall. He ordered a bottle and two glasses, and announced very clearly to the disinterested barmaid that he was waiting for his good friend, the Viscount Claypole, to join him.

He'd wait a good long time for that, too, as Sir Edgar had made it his business to send the viscount a missive in the middle of the night, telling him he needs must hie himself home at once, as his father, the earl, was on his deathbed. As Claypole was located nearly thirty miles above Leicester, and the viscount was looking hard at finally inheriting his earldom, Sir Edgar was not disappointed in the man's alacrity in obeying the summons, and waved him on his way from an alley as the viscount's coach set north at first light.

Two or three days to Claypole. More, if this fog had drifted to the countryside. A few days' rest as the viscount asked his father, repeatedly, "Are you *quite sure* you're not dying?" A few days for the return trip.

And, by then, nobody would remember that Sir Edgar had even mentioned the man's name.

"Oh dear, oh dear, where can he be?" Sir Edgar said several times over the next hour, as he consulted his pocket watch, as he looked anxiously toward the door to the street, sighed.

He only needed one. Two could be a problem, and three were definitely too many. More than one meant enough for a conversation, some shared contemplation, even an opening for a modicum of sense to overtake boundless greed. No, just one, that's all.

He was considering if he should give it up as a bad

job, and head for another tavern where the gentlemen of the *ton* thought it wonderful to rub elbows with the *hoi polloi*, select another target, when his last "oh, dear" finally caught the attention of the well-dressed, and fairly well into his cups gentleman at the next table.

"A problem, sir?" the man asked. Then, without waiting for an invitation, he picked up his glass and his bottle and joined Sir Edgar. "You're waiting for someone, right? So am I, but I've got the feeling old Winfield is still probably hiding his head under the covers. We drank fairly deep last night, and the man doesn't have the liver he should." He stuck out his hand. "John Hatcher."

Yes, Sir Edgar knew that. John Hatcher. No title, but a family that went back to the Great Fire (and may even have started it, if all his ancestors were as inept as this particular member of the Hatcher clan). Money that went back ever farther than that conflagration. Brains that had got misplaced somewhere along the way.

Oh, yes, Sir Edgar knew all about John Hatcher.

"It is a pleasure, sir," Sir Edgar said, allowing his thin, trim hand to be half crushed in the bearlike grip of the much larger man. "Sir Edgar Marmington. I'm new to the city, never been here before, but my old school chum, Claypole, promised to…um…show me the sights. Can't imagine where he is."

"Claypole? Bit of a dry stick, that, don't you think? I mean, maybe you wouldn't know, not if you haven't seen him since your school days, but he's dull as…as a clay pole. Har! Har! That was a good one, eh? No, friend, you don't want him. Claypole's idea of seeing the sights would be a tour of all the churches, Lord help you. You're better for him gone."

Sir Edgar smiled, all attention. "Really? Not that I'm the hey-go-mad sort myself, understand. Sadly bookish, actually. But we've been corresponding, the viscount and myself, and he'd seemed so interested in my work…my travels through the ancient lands, my discovery of that old tome that told all about…"

Now Sir Edgar sighed. "I had so wanted to tell him in person that I'm wonderfully close now…at the very brink of discovery. He's been so generous, subsidizing me monetarily in my research all these twenty years or more, you understand, for the greater end, the final reward. All I need are a few more things to complete my duplication of the monks' experiments, the alchemist's notes, and he'd promised—but, no, this is of no interest to you."

"Probably not," Hatcher said, tossing back the contents of his glass, and then pouring himself another measure of wine even while calling for a full bottle. "Don't think I ever read a book, God's truth. Pride m'self on that. Monks, you said? And what the devil's an alchemist?"

Sir Edgar sat back, looked around the room nervously, then leaned in close, to whisper to John Hatcher….

"WHAT'S THIS MESS?" Olive Norbert whispered to Daphne Clifford in her booming voice (which is to say, she was probably heard in Tothill Fields, by little old ladies with brass ear trumpets), as she employed her fork to poke suspiciously at something on her plate. "It don't look right. Looks sick."

"More than sick, Mrs. Norbert," Fanny said, winking at Emma. "It's dead. And, as it's escargot—that would be a snail, Mrs. Norbert—a snail, minus its shell, it demned well better would be dead, or I'll be marching into the kitchens myself to ask why not. Oh, and because you're looking as if you don't believe me, please allow me to state this very firmly—it's *food*."

"Not on my plate, it ain't," Olive Norbert declared, pushing the serving of genuine French snails away from her with the tip of her fork. "Slimy things, leaving trails up the wall in the damp. Here now, you. Cart this mess off," she commanded to Riley, doing duty at the table this evening.

"Bring me some meat, boy. Bloody red with juice. And a pudding. Go on, hop to it! I'm paying down good money for snails? In a pig's eye, I am. Oh, and some ham, while you're about it. It's meat I want, and meat I will get or know the reason why."

As Mrs. Norbert was twice Riley's size (width-wise), and a paying guest, Riley hopped to, ready to serve, although it grated on him something awful, it really did. Mrs. Norbert was a pudding herself, a short, fat prawn with tiny, mean green eyes glinting out of a lumpy face, and with piss-yellow hair that frizzed here, curled there, but didn't quite cover the shine of skin on the top of the behemoth's head. She was no better than him. Maybe a whole lot worse.

"And it's not me wanting you to try to cudgel that ugly brainbox of yours to think up a reason why, no, ma'am, it's not," Riley muttered under his breath as he turned to walk away.

Emma heard him, however, and kept her head down, to hide her smile. Mrs. Norbert might be crude, bordering on obnoxious most times, but she also had a point. When pinching the purse strings tight, the first thing to be sacrificed was meat. There had been many a meatless evening in the Clifford household until the next quarter's allowance arrived from her father's small estate.

"Um, Riley?" Daphne called timidly. "If…if I could also have this taken away? I…I think there may be *eyes* in it."

"Oh, all right," Fanny said, waving her hand. "We all want these snails gone, Riley. Might as well own up to it. Fancy is as fancy does, and I don't really fancy chewing on these things. What's up next?"

"I'll check straightaway, madam," Riley said, gathering up the "snail course" and piling the plates on his arm. "Just nip belowstairs to ask Mrs. Timon."

"Evening, all. Started without me, I see. Riley, you rotter, you look better than me, and I consider that an insult, I truly do."

Riley, and the rest of the company, turned in the direction of the sound, to see Clifford Clifford lurching into the room like a man who has been at sea for months and was just now touching down on dry land, holding on to chair backs until he could collapse into his own chair, beside his sister.

"About time you showed up, you pernicious little weasel," Fanny said from her position at the bottom of the table. "Shameful, a man who can't hold his spirits. You look terrible."

And he did. Other than the lurching from chair to chair, Cliff's dark hair appeared faintly greasy, and one lock hung down unflatteringly over his normally light gray but at the moment quite bloodshot eyes. His cravat was askew, his waistcoat misbuttoned, and his jacket still resided in his room rather than across his shoulders.

Daphne gasped at her beloved son's disheveled appearance and rose from her seat, grabbing up her serviette and dipping it into the floral arrangement in the middle of the table. "Here, darling, cool water for your aching head," she said, after racing around to the other side of the table, trying to dab her son's forehead. "Mama will fix."

Cliff fought his mother away by turning his head this way and that, and finally by grabbing the serviette and tossing it to the floor. "Don't *do* that, Mama, I'm not a child," he said, and Daphne, accustomed to taking orders from anyone in breeches, promptly returned to her chair and sat down. And proceeded to sulk. Over the course of her marriage, she had quite mastered the injured sulk.

"If you're not a child, Cliff, I propose you stop behaving like one," Emma said, resigned to her role as her brother's keeper.

Cliff took great exception to his sister's mild rebuke. "Child, am I? I'm head of this household, remember? I'm the *man*. So what's *he* doing, sitting at the head of the table?"

Sir Edgar looked up from his plate—the one that now held three servings of escargot, because he was one, hungry, and two, sitting closest to Riley as he'd tried to leave the room with the rejected dishes.

"Forgive me," he said, smiling at the ladies. "In an attempt to render myself politely deaf during a domestic upheaval that I, as a gentleman, have chosen to ignore— have I missed something? Oh, hallo there, Clifford. Mind if I pretend I didn't see you join us?"

"Ha! Very good, Sir Edgar," Fanny said approvingly. "Now, if you can say you likewise didn't notice my daughter-in-law's silly outburst, I'd say you were kin to my late husband, who could blissfully ignore me if I entered the room with my hair on fire if he thought I might ask him to put it out."

"My thanks, madam, for being compared to your beloved husband. I am honored, at least I think I am," Sir Edgar said, smiling as Riley laid a plate groaning under the weight of roasted beef in front of him.

"Not if you knew him," Fanny said, winking at Sir Edgar. "Cliff, over there, puts me in mind of him most, after my late son. None of the three of them cared a jot save for their own comfort. Luckily, my late husband paid so little attention to me that I was free to find my own pleasures. Greatest pity of my life has to be that my son turned out to be his son as well. Could have gone either way, you understand. Several ways, actually."

"Mother Clifford!" Daphne exclaimed, looking straight at Emma with a look meant to say "in heaven's name, Do Something."

"We missed you at luncheon today, Sir Edgar," Emma broke in gamely, smiling at the man as she leaped toward the first thing to jump into her head. "Were you out, in this horrid fog?"

"Only for a few hours, Miss Emma," Sir Edgar said, "and I chanced to meet a delightful man. Mr. John Hatcher. Is the name familiar to anyone?"

"No, I can't say that it is," Fanny said, sitting back in her chair, sorry to have the subject changed, just when she was having so much fun.

"I fear not," Daphne apologized, still looking at Cliff and mentally rebuttoning the boy's waistcoat.

"I knows him," Mrs. Norbert said, her mouth full of beef. "Sent his latest fillies to our shop, to dress 'em out. Great fondness for red satin he had, John Hatcher. Paid his blunt on time, sometimes with a little extra for us in the sewing room. A real toff."

Thornley, who had decided it was cowardly to completely avoid the dining room, heard this last bit of wisdom from Olive Norbert as he pushed open the swinging door…and immediately retreated to the kitchens. And he'd tried so hard to fit together a comfortable group for the Season. Next year, he promised himself, he would require *extensive* references!

JOHN HATCHER STOOD in the middle of the enormous study holding the extensive library his family had collected over the years, and frowned as he approached the wall entirely devoted to blue and green covers.

"Anderson?" he called over his shoulder to his man of business. "Be a good fellow and find me a book on alchemists. We must have one. Lord knows we have everything else."

Anderson put down the newspaper. "Alchemists, sir? I know what they are, or what they were purported to be."

Hatcher snatched up his snifter of brandy and plunked himself down in the facing chair in front of the fireplace. "Purported? Is that good? Tell me."

"Well, sir, the most venerable practice of alchemy is believed, by most scholars and devotées, to have been originally generated in—" He hesitated, realizing his life would be made immensely easier if he employed as few large words as possible. "That is, alchemists began their work a very long time ago, in a faraway country. Very wise men."

His employer leaned his elbows on his knees, and grinned. "Wise, eh? How do you know?"

Anderson hadn't kept his position for fifteen years without learning how to please his employer. "I…I think they wore pointy hats, sir."

Hatcher nodded eagerly. "Yes, they would, wouldn't they? With stars on them, I'll wager. So where are they now? These alchemists?"

"Unless there are a few more recent adherents to the tenets, I think it would be safe to say that they're all quite dead, sir. Although there are those who say that, before succumbing to their mortal ills, they may have succeeded in discovering a way to turn base metals into gold."

"Ah-ha!" Thatcher said, thrusting his fist into the air. "And they probably wrote it all down somewheres, how they did it. I mean, you'd write it down, wouldn't you? How to do it?"

All right, so now Anderson was interested. "Yes, sir. I'd write it all down. Why do you ask?"

"None of your business, boy, none of your bloody business," Thatcher bit out, and quit the room.

As was customary in all the great houses, the females gathered in the drawing room after dinner, taking their tea there while the men remained in the dining room, tossing back brandy, gnawing fruit and blowing a cloud with their cheroots.

"There's something havey cavey about Sir Edgar," Fanny pronounced, sipping brandy—not a lady's drink, but Fanny had her own definition of what a lady does, which had a lot to do with what that lady wants.

As Daphne had picked up her embroidery and was busy counting stitches, and Emma was pointedly ignoring her grandmother, it was left to Olive Norbert to ask, "Like what? Seems all right to me."

Fanny rolled her eyes. "And, if I but valued your opinion, Mrs. Norbert, that would weigh heavily with me, I assure you. The man is too clever. Too clever by half."

"You're just saying that because you prefer your men stupid," Emma said before she realized that, yes, her mouth could move before her brain was fully awake to what it was saying.

"Not true, my dear. I can't abide Cliff. Couldn't stand his father, or his father before him. And if you want to find three more stupid men, I suggest you take a lantern and have Mrs. Timon pack you a lunch."

"My Cliff is not stupid, Mother Clifford," Daphne said, putting down her embroidery. "His last tutor told me he's quite inventive."

Emma refused to meet her grandmother's eyes, but just waited for that woman's comment.

"Inventive, is it? Of course. That would explain how the idiot child was sent down last term for throwing his lantern at a mouse he saw peeking at him from a corner of the room. I say the boy's just lucky his eyebrows grew back."

"More tea, anyone?" Emma asked, trying not to look at Mrs. Norbert.

"It was an accident, and I would take it as a kindness, Mother Clifford, if you were not to speak of Cliff any more this evening," Daphne said, picking up her embroidery once again, as counting stitches was less stressing than listening to her youngest child's less-laudable exploits trotted past her.

Olive Norbert shoved another pastry into her already fairly full mouth, and said, "You know, I'm ponderin' this, what you said. Sir Edgar says he's never come to London before, but I asked him to pick up some number-three lacing for me at m'old shop, and he didn't even ask the way. I didn't think on that until now. How'd he do that?"

"A guide book? A map? Inquiring of someone he passed on the street?" Emma suggested, wishing the woman would keep her questions to herself, and praying that her grandmother would not think it wonderful to share whatever she had discovered about the man on her visit to Sir Edgar's bedchamber that afternoon.

Fanny tapped one slightly gnarled finger against her chin. "Possible. Possible. Oh, and he is not acquainted with the marquis. I already asked him that, and he said he did same as us, answering the newspaper advertisement." She smiled sweetly at Olive. "Someone read it to you, Mrs. Norbert?"

"I can read for myself," Mrs. Norbert said, raising two of her three chins in defiance. "I can also pick you up and toss you over my shoulder, old lady."

Emma stood up, putting herself between her grandmother and the irate seamstress. "Please, please, Mrs. Norbert, forgive my grandmother. She's, um, elderly?"

"She's mean as a snake, that's what," Mrs. Norbert said, sitting back in her chair and crossing her plump arms over her chest. "I know you don't want me here, think you're all so hoity-toity and better'n me. And I don't care. Long as I'm eating good."

"And Lord knows you're doing plenty of—" Fanny began, but Emma whirled on her and glared. "Sorry," she said quietly. "All right, all right, I'll put the gloves back on. It's this demned fog, that's what it is. Look at it, creeping in under the windowsills. We're all just stuck in here, cheek by jowl, and I'm tired of it. I have plans."

Hearing her grandmother mention that she had plans set Emma's teeth on edge. This couldn't be good....

"THIS FOG COULDN'T be worse," Morgan Drummond said, peering out the side window of his coach, trying to see past the minuscule yellow glow cast by the few gas lamps lining the street, to the buildings beyond. "I think we're close now, but I can't be sure. Wycliff? For God's sake, man, stop clutching the door as if a great fog monster was going to yank it open at any moment, pull you outside and bite off your head. I've given up my hopes of that a good hour ago. Ah—we're stopping."

Morgan drew the edges of his cloak over his knees and tied the laces at his throat, then reached for his curly-brimmed beaver on the seat beside him. "Heave to, Wycliff, we've arrived."

"How…how can you be sure, my lord? I don't see anything out there."

"True, neither do I. But as the nothing out there is highly preferable to the something in here, I'm willing to hazard the gamble." So saying, he opened the door on his side of the coach, kicked down the steps and then ignored them to hop onto the cobbles, nearly coming to grief as the slippery stones sent him momentarily off balance.

"We're here, your lordship," the coachman called down to him unnecessarily, even as servants riding in the second coach (normally following far behind the master's coach, but tonight, because of the fog, riding directly on its heels), bustled forward to assist the marquis. "We'll just drive around to the mews and unload the baggage and see to the horses."

"Do that, Briggs, and thank you. Make sure Sampson is taken care of, as well? Then take yourself to the kitchen, for something to eat."

"Yes, my lord," Briggs assured him, as assorted Westham servants and grooms got on about their business.

Wycliff pushed two of them out of the way in his haste to be the one who ushered Morgan up the rounded set of steps, to the double front doors, lit on either side by dying flambeaux.

"This way, my lord. Watch your step, my lord. I'll bang the knocker for you, my lord."

"Control yourself, Wycliff, before you do yourself an injury. I'm not in my dotage yet, I can knock at my own door," Morgan said, lifting the knocker.

Then he hesitated. "Strange. The knocker shouldn't be on the door, as I'm not in residence."

"Shoddiness, my lord," Wycliff said quickly. "It's the only answer. The master's gone and slack seeps in everywhere. I'll be sure to have a remonstrative word with the staff."

"Do, Wycliff, and I'll have a remonstrative word or two with you, understand? Thornley is my family's treasure, and is not to be read a lecture by a skinny shanks like you," Morgan said, giving the knocker three sharp hits against its brass base.

"But…but I should announce you, my lord. It's my duty…my pleasure…my—"

"I don't announce myself at my own door, either," Morgan said, putting a quick period to that argument. But he was maintaining his composure, albeit with a firm application of will. Wycliff did serve a purpose: proof that his master could control his once-volatile temper.

The door opened and Morgan was presented with a fairly well set up young footman, dressed in the Westham livery, wearing a powdered wig, as was the custom. And gnawing on a chicken leg, which was not.

Morgan looked at the lad, looked him up and down, and then stepped inside the mansion as the footman backed up three paces, his eyes wide, the chicken leg still stuck in his mouth.

"I'd hand over my hat and cloak, but I have a fondness for both, and wouldn't wish them clutched in your greasy paws. New, aren't you? What is your name, boy?"

"Ri-Riley, sir," the footman managed to choke out before looking at the chicken leg and quickly hiding it behind his back. This was the Quality standing before him, and Riley knew it. A very tall and broad and intimidatingly male bit of the Quality. "You…you'd be standing in the foyer, sir."

"Indeed, yes, how observant of you. But we'll soon correct that, won't we? Kindly rouse Mrs. Timon and tell her I wish refreshments in the drawing room in half an hour. She need not bother to cook anything. Cold meat and fruit will do. And a loaf, one with seeds, as I much prefer that."

"You…you're wanting…"

"Magnificent! So heavy, too. It could fall."

Morgan looked to Wycliff who, for all his fine promises that he was a valet of much experience and familiar with the workings of a great London house, serving an exalted master, was now standing, mouth agape after his exclamation, apprehensively staring up at the remarkable chandelier brought from France fifty years previously by an earlier Marquis of Westham.

"Here now, I can see the fog swirling up the stairs, Riley," Thornley called out as he looked over the curving banister. "Close the door, boy, and stuff those rugs against it again. Must I be everywhere at once? It isn't enough that young Mr. Clifford is—*my lord?*"

Thornley's heretofore unblemished record for being in the right place at precisely the correct time suffered a serious blow as, if he'd been in the right place at the correct time at this moment, he would be in deepest, darkest Africa, trying to hide himself from the marquis.

"Thornley," Morgan called out, smiling up at the man. "Good to see you again, my good fellow. Been a little slack at the post, have you?" he asked, gesturing to Riley, who was still trying to figure out what to do with the chicken leg.

"My lord, I—I—" Thornley all but stumbled down the stairs, stairs he would never otherwise employ, unless in the performance of his duties. "It's…it's so good to see you again, my lord."

"Good to see you as well, Thornley. I know it's late, nearly ten, isn't it? I would have been here much earlier, save for this cursed fog. And, by the look on your face, I see I also should have warned you of my arrival. But you've always run this pile with such efficiency, I didn't think it would matter. Beds aired and ready, I'll wager?"

Riley, now that the chicken leg was safely deposited in the sixteenth-century china vase that also held a few large umbrella sticks, had begun to pay attention. Slowly, and with increasing horror, the footman picked up all the bits and pieces of information that had been sent to his brain over the past few moments, and assembled them in something approaching order…to be immediately followed by sheer panic.

Wycliff had closed the door and kicked the rug back into place to keep out the fog, and was now gathering up his lordship's things, which left Riley with nothing more to do than hold out his hand, a move his terrified brain would not even entertain. No coin for his troubles, not tonight, and no place to put his head tomorrow night, either, unless it would be on moldy straw, in the local guardhouse.

He looked to Thornley in mute appeal.

Thornley was looking at Morgan.

And Morgan was beginning to think there might be something very wrong.

"Thornley? I'm tired, and would like to go to my rooms for a moment. I've already asked this boy here—what's your name again, boy? Riley, was it? I've asked him to have Mrs. Timon prepare something and have it ready in the drawing room once I've had myself a bit of a wash. I feel as if I've brought half the road dirt in here with me. So…?"

Morgan put out an arm, gesturing at the staircase, which Thornley still stood in front of, his long arms outstretched, one hand pressed against the wall, the other gripping the newel-post. "Thornley? I'd like to go upstairs."

Thornley blinked, something he hadn't done in more than a full minute, and looked to his right and left. "Forgive me, my lord," he said, dropping his arms to his sides. He should begin attending church again. God was punishing him for his sins of omission, that's what it was. And for thinking about Daphne Clifford's knees. "It's just that it has been so *long,* my lord. You…you resemble your late father more greatly now. In fact, you… you've given me quite a start."

"'Tis both a start and finish, I'd say," Riley muttered, backing against the wall in the hope his lordship would forget he was in the grand foyer at all.

Morgan started toward the staircase.

"If I may be so bold, my lord," Thornley said quickly, turning to climb the stairs just behind his lordship, "may I suggest that his lordship goes directly up to his rooms to rest and recover from his long journey. I will see that a bath is prepared in your dressing room, to ease the aches and indignities of travel, and personally bring you a repast of the best Mrs. Timon has in the kitchens."

Morgan hesitated at the head of the staircase, casting a look toward the closed doors leading to the main drawing room. "Got the place in dust sheets, do you, Thornley? All right, I understand. Nothing to worry about, I'm an understanding man. I wouldn't wish to discommode you or any of the staff this late in the evening."

He turned down the hallway and headed for the next flight of stairs, calling over his shoulder, "Just some warmed water and towels, Thornley, and that food. And a bottle. I'm so weary I could probably sleep where I am. As it is, I'll be asleep before my head hits the pillow, and I doubt even a pitched battle outside my windows would rouse me before noon tomorrow."

"Yes, my lord," Thornley said as he turned and headed for the servant stairs, to rouse Mrs. Timon and gather the rest of the meager staff, knowing that noon tomorrow would come soon enough, and that, unless he could conjure up a miracle, the pitched battle his lordship mentioned in jest would be taking place very much *inside* Westham mansion.

EMMA ESCAPED into the hallway to give herself a short respite from Mrs. Norbert's chewing, on the pretext of dashing upstairs for a shawl to ward off the chill, and an unwillingness to ring and bother Claramae, who was doubtless reluctant to brave the hallways at night for fear that Riley would try to steal yet another kiss.

Somehow, Emma was not quite sure precisely how it had transpired, Claramae had decided that Emma should be her confidante, and now bent her ear almost daily with stories about the wily Riley and his penchant for hiding himself around corners, in order to pounce on the maid, "all six arms and ten hands of him, miss, I swear it."

Not that Riley would ever be the man of Emma's maidenly dreams…but there were times she rather envied the housemaid, who at least knew what a man's kiss felt like. It had to be better than her mama had described it, and could not possibly be as wonderful as her grandmother claimed.

Emma had taken only a few steps when she heard footsteps behind her, and turned to see Thornley approaching, looking over his shoulder as if someone might be following him, then staring at the closed doors to the drawing room as if he might be contemplating finding boards and a hammer, so that he could nail those doors shut.

As a matter of fact, unknown to Emma, that was fairly close to what Thornley was thinking. Mostly, he had opted not to climb directly to the marquis's chamber via the servant stairs in order to check on his tenants, hoping they'd stay planted where he'd put them until he could figure out precisely where to stuff them next.

Emma smiled as she noticed the silver tray he carried, piled high with meat and cheese and fruit and a small, sliced loaf. "Oh, how lovely, Thornley," she said as he all but bumped into her. "For the gentlemen, I presume, as ladies are not supposed to care for such heavy food. Still, if you don't mind…" She reached out and snatched a shiny green apple from the arrangement.

Thornley smiled the sickly smile of the almost caught, but still with some life in him yet, if he could only muster a sufficient lie, and said, "You're very welcome, Miss Clifford. I was…I was just taking this upstairs, for Mr. Clifford. His stomach, he tells me, is at last sufficiently calm for thoughts of filling it. If you'll excuse me…?"

Emma stepped aside, only after snatching a rich, purple plum from the plate, as well as the bottle of wine. "I don't believe Mr. Clifford needs this, Thornley."

"No? Um, yes, Miss Clifford. You're correct, of course. What could I have been thinking? Lemonade, perhaps? I'll have Claramae fetch some at once."

"Oh, no, don't bother her, Thornley." She set the bottle on a nearby table, then put the fruit back on the plate and took the tray from the butler's nerveless fingers. "There you go. You fetch the lemonade, all right, and I'll take this tray up to Mr. Clifford. I wish to have a word or two with him in any case, especially now, while he's still suffering the pains of his foolishness."

"I…but…I wouldn't want you to…that is…"

Emma tipped her head to one side and blinked up at him through her long, dark lashes. "Yes, Thornley?"

The man smiled again, an even more sickly thing than his first effort, then gave up, thanked Emma, picked up the bottle he'd uncorked in the pantry and trudged back down the hallway. He was drinking from it, deeply, by the time he reached the servant stairs.

MORGAN EYED the large tester bed longingly. But he was still more hungry than he was tired, so he contented himself with watching Riley build up the fire in the grate as he propped himself against the side of a wingback chair and sipped from the wineglass the footman had produced along with two bottles of his lordship's finest wine.

It was good, being in the mansion again. It was even better that he'd dismissed Wycliff for the evening and could look forward to being blessedly alone.

"And there you go, m'lord," Riley said as he stood up, wiping one hand against the other. "Surely that should keep you warm and toasty all the night long."

Then he held out one rather grubby hand, palm up.

Morgan's left eyebrow climbed his forehead as he looked at the outstretched hand. "Yes?" he asked, transferring his cool stare to the footman's face. "I'm afraid I don't read palms, Riley. But if you were to go to Bartholomew Fair, I'm convinced you'll find any number of gypsies ready and willing to tell you that you'll be rich as Croesus, any day now. What I can tell you, my good man, is that I will not be the one who bestows such wealth upon you."

Riley snatched back his hand, putting both arms behind his back. "I'm that sorry, m'lord. It's only being that, that is, it just sort of…happened."

"Yes, I'm sure. Just as I'm convinced it won't…just sort of happen again. Not to me, and most certainly not to any of my guests when they call here. If your service is exemplary, and the guest so chooses, he or she may decide to reward you, but that will be their decision, not yours. You may go now."

Riley bowed and scraped and backed his way toward the door to the marquis's dressing room, which had no other exit. It did have Wycliff, who was busily unpacking his lordship's things, but even Morgan couldn't wish Wycliff on Riley at the moment.

"That way, Riley," Morgan corrected him, pointing toward the door to the hallway.

"Yes, m'lord, of course, m'lord. Sleep well, m'lord, and, well, um, welcome to London?"

"Thank you," Morgan said, watching the footman fumble with the latch, and finally throw open the door…only to just as quickly slam it shut once more.

"Forgot something, have you?" Morgan asked, intrigued both by Riley's action and the fact that the footman's ruddy Irish complexion had done a remarkably swift shift to a rather sickly white.

"No, m'lord," Riley said, opening the door once more, but a crack, and peeking out into the hallway. "It's only your food coming, m'lord. I'll…I'll just go fetch it."

"No, have Thornley come in, if you please. I want to apologize again for descending on him without notice."

Riley shot him a look that had Morgan shaking his head. Were those tears in the boy's eyes? "Oh, never mind," he said, putting down his wineglass and heading for the door. "I hadn't thought Thornley could inspire such fear in his staff. I'll do it myself."

As Riley looked on, his eyes so rounded they appeared capable of popping straight out of his head, Morgan threw open the door...to be presented with an empty hallway.

He stepped out and looked to his left, to his right, and saw a door closing at the very end of the hallway.

"My old rooms?" he asked himself, confused. "Has Thornley gotten past it at last? I haven't resided there since I was a child, too small for that large bed in here." He called Riley into the hallway. "Do you know why he's gone in there?"

"No, m'lord," Riley said, looking down at his toes where, the blessed saints be praised, inspiration appeared to be spending the evening. He'd wondered where it had been. He looked up again, grinning, and said, "Sometimes Mr. Thornley likes to take his ease in that bedchamber, m'lord, seein' as how there ain't nobody else to sleep there. It's...it's his back, m'lord. It sometimes pains him terrible, and he says the bedding in there is better than a mustard plaster."

"So he's gone to bed? Is that what you're saying?"

"Oh, no, m'lord, I'd not be saying that," Riley said, getting caught up in his lie. "It's gathering up his belongings he's doing, sure as check, ashamed as he'd be for you to know what he's been about. Sleepin' in the master's bed? Tch, tch."

Morgan considered this. "But…why would I have reason to go into those rooms?"

Riley rolled his eyes. "You know Mr. Thornley, m'lord. A real stickler he is, for what's proper."

"Proper, Riley, is that I get something to eat before my ribs start shaking hands with my backbone. Now, go get that tray."

"Yes, m'lord. I'll just be doing that, right now. You go sit yourself down, m'lord, rest your weary bones, and it's right back I'll be," Riley said.

He watched until Morgan closed the door behind him, then headed, lickety-split, for the servant stairs, where he met Thornley, who was ascending the stairs with a duplicate to the tray now residing in Cliff Clifford's bedchamber.

Crisis averted. Postponed. But not resolved.

"WE COULD TELL THEM there is a problem with the drains, and they'd die if they remained here," Thornley said as his small staff sat behind the closed and locked door of his private quarters, out of earshot from the Westham servants who had arrived with the marquis.

It had been a long and sleepless night. A worried one, too.

"Can we do that? I don't want to do that. Makes me look a poor housekeeper," Mrs. Timon said, worrying at a thumbnail with her teeth. A splendid cook, Hazel Timon was tall, reed thin, and with a spotty complexion that would make it easy to believe she herself subsisted on stale bread and ditch water…and nail clippings.

"Mrs. Timon, you're biting again," Thornley said, pointing a finger at her nasty habit.

"And *she's* snuffling again," Mrs. Timon shot back, folding her hands in her lap as she glared at Claramae, who had been intermittently crying into her apron the whole of the night long.

Riley leaned over to put a comforting arm around the young maid, allowing his hand to drift just a bit too low over her shoulder, which earned him a sharp slap from the girl just as his fingertips were beginning to find the foray interesting.

"No, no, no, we can't have this," Thornley said, clapping his hands to bring everyone back to attention. "Quarreling amongst ourselves aids nothing. Think, people. What else can we do?"

"I'd make up some breakfast," Mrs. Timon offered, "excepting for that Gassie fella took over my kitchens."

"Gas-*ton*, Mrs. Timon," Thornley said absently, staring at the list he'd made during the darkest and least imaginative portions of the night.

The plague. Discarded as too deadly. And where was one to find a plague cart when one needed one? Worse, who would volunteer to play corpse?

Measles? Too spotty by half and, besides, Thornley's memory had told him that his lordship had contracted the measles as a child, so covering Claramae in red spots wouldn't have the man haring back to Westham.

A fire in the kitchens? Mrs. Timon would have his liver and lights, and if it got out of hand, half of London could go up in flames. Their situation was desperate, but not dire enough to risk another Great Fire.

What was left?

Thornley's mind kept coming to the same conclusion.

"We...we could tell 'em the truth, give 'em their money back, and ask 'em very kindly to take themselves off," Claramae offered weakly, then blew her nose in her apron.

Just what Thornley had been thinking, which was a worriment, if the simple-headed Claramae thought it a good idea.

An expensive silence settled over the room.

Mrs. Timon thought about the locked box in the bottom of her closet. She was a year short of having enough to lease a small cottage by the sea, complete with hiring a local girl as servant of all work, and never cooking another thing for another person. She'd eat twigs before she'd stand over another stove in August.

Riley wondered where and how he'd come up with his share, as he hadn't saved so much as a bent penny, preferring to wager everything each year on such hopefully money-tripling pursuits as bearbaiting, cockfights, and the occasional dice game in his favorite pub.

Claramae, author of the idea, sat quietly and didn't

think at all, which was all right, because she really wasn't very good at it anyway.

Which left Thornley.

"I suppose we could. We were overly ambitious in the first place, I realize now. And, as it's nearly gone seven, and we have had no other idea, I suppose we'll have to resort to the truth. Come along," he said, getting to his feet. "The Clifford ladies and the rest will be rising shortly, as is their custom. We must speak to them before they ring for their morning chocolate and alert the other servants to their presence. We'll also begin with them simply because there are more of them."

"Yes, but the money...?" Mrs. Timon asked, shuffling her carpet-slippered feet as she followed Thornley.

"As this entire idea was mine, I will be responsible for all remunerations, Mrs. Timon," Thornley said gamely.

"Yes, but who will *pay* them?" Riley asked worriedly, trailing along behind, dragging Claramae with him.

EMMA HEARD THE KNOCKING on her bedchamber door, but chose to ignore it. She didn't want her morning chocolate. She didn't want morning, as she'd not slept well, a nagging feeling that something might be wrong in the mansion keeping her awake, alert for any sound.

The sound now, however—whispers mixed with whimpering—could not be ignored, so she kicked back the covers and padded to the door of the bedchamber and put her ear to the door.

"Claramae, I said knock and enter. As a man, obviously I can't go in there, not with Miss Clifford possibly still not dressed for the day."

"But I don't...I don't want to."

"Stand back, the lot of you. *I'll* do it."

"Riley, stifle yourself."

"Oh, for goodness' sakes, I'll do it."

Emma jumped back as the latch depressed, and barely missed having the tip of her nose nipped off as the door swung inward and Mrs. Timon stepped inside...followed by a widely grinning Riley, who took no more than two swaggering, arms-waving steps before a long, black-clad arm appeared, grabbed the footman by the collar of his livery and yanked him back out again.

"Miss Clifford?"

"Yes?" Emma said, stepping out from behind the door. "Is something wrong, Mrs. Timon?"

"Well, miss, you could maybe say that, miss...can I fetch your dressing gown?"

Emma frowned at the woman, then retreated to the chair beside her bed, snatched up her dressing gown and slipped into it. "Better, Mrs. Timon?" she asked, tying the sash tightly around her waist.

"Yes, miss, thank you, miss," Mrs. Timon said. "Your slippers?"

What on earth? Emma located her slippers and put them on.

"Thank you, miss. That should do it," the cook cum

housekeeper cum obscure visitor said, then opened the door once more.

In trooped Riley, still grinning (but no longer swaggering), followed by Thornley, who had his chin lifted so high his only view of the bedchamber could have been the painted ceiling, and Claramae, whose chin could not be lower as she, in turn, inspected the floor.

Emma sat down on the pink-and-white-striped slipper chair, tossed the long, fat single braid over her shoulder and folded her hands in her lap.

She'd been right. Something was wrong.

Her mother had tackled Thornley in the hallways and made a complete cake of herself.

Her grandmother had been caught out snooping in Sir Edgar's drawers.

Cliff had—well, Cliff could be guilty of most anything.

Miss Emma Clifford did not upset easily. With her family, a person who upset easily would be in her grave, white of hair, wrinkled of skin, and dead of old age at two and twenty, if she did not learn to control her feelings.

Her temper, however, was another thing, and although kept in check for the most part, when unleashed, as her mother would gladly tell anyone, it could be A Terrible Thing. Indeed, Emma was already working up a good scold for whoever had caused what she was sure to be the next very uncomfortable minutes.

The servants, however, having only witnessed the sweeter side of Miss Emma's nature in the week the Cliffords had been in residence, had no inkling that she would be anything but helpful in solving their dilemma. Understanding, even.

The three servants looked to Thornley, so Emma did, too. "Is there something I should know?" she asked.

ON THE FLOOR BELOW, Morgan turned over in his bed, half-awake after hearing what he thought was a rather loud, angry female voice in his dreams, and went back to sleep.

Moments later, he pulled a pillow over his head and made a mental note to instruct Thornley to keep all servants gagged until at least eleven o'clock of a morning.

Moments after that, his own heavy breathing was the only sound in the bedchamber...and he didn't hear that at all.

RILEY, HIS EARS STILL stinging from Miss Clifford's talking-through-her-clenched-teeth orders, knocked on Sir Edgar's door. He waited until he heard the key turn in the lock and then stepped inside...to be met by a man already dressed for the day, although his shirt cuffs had been turned back clear to the elbow. Sir Edgar had already retreated across the room, to stand with his back against the door to his small dressing room.

Riley thought the man looked rather odd. Like he'd been caught out at something.

"What do you want?" Sir Edgar asked, his hands covered by a towel.

"Smells funny in here, don't you know," Riley said, sniffing the air. "Smells like…like paint?"

"You'll smell out of the other end of your nose if you don't tell me why you've barged in here, my good man," Sir Edgar said, still carefully keeping his hands covered.

"Um…yes, Sir Edgar, your pardon, sir. It's…it's Miss Clifford, sir. She requests your presence downstairs, in the drawing room, in—well, *now*, sir."

Sir Edgar peeked under the towel to look at his fingers. He had at least ten minutes of scrubbing with strong soap in front of him. "She does, does she?"

"Yes, sir. Powerful clear she was on that, sir. *Now*, sir."

"Yes, I heard that part. Do you know why she wants to see me, boy?"

Riley shook his head furiously. "No, sir. It's not me knowing anything. Couldn't say that I do. I never know anything, you could ask anybody. But she wants everybody."

"Everybody, you say," Sir Edgar repeated, turning to the washstand and, with his back obscuring what he was about, reaching for the large bar of lye soap, first putting down the key he'd hidden in his hand. "Very well. Please deliver my compliments to Miss Clifford and tell her that I shall join everyone directly."

"Yes, sir, I'll tell her, sir. And it's thanking you I am,

and reminding you how I've been so very pleased to serve you, sir."

"Yes, yes," Sir Edgar said, keeping his back turned. "See me later for your penny. Now go away."

As he scrubbed, Sir Edgar could hear doors opening and closing along the hallway, and knew that he should hurry if he wished to not miss whatever was going to transpire in the drawing room. A wise man never missed anything.

Which explained just how wise Sir Edgar believed himself to be…and how wise he actually was…as he left the key to his small dressing closet sitting on the washstand instead of replacing it in his pocket as he headed downstairs.

EMMA STOOD with her arms crossed just beneath her bosom while Thornley explained to everyone else what he had explained to her just a short hour ago—it had taken Daphne a little while to complete even a cursory toilette, and Mrs. Norbert had refused to join the group until after she'd breakfasted on a thick slice of ham, a half-dozen coddled eggs and a lovely sugar bun.

"…and so, sorry as I am, I must ask you all to leave. Now, before the master awakes."

MORGAN SAT BOLT UPRIGHT in bed, his skin crawling, his nerves jangling as the echoes of a scream that could only have been produced by a considerable multitude of pigs simultaneously stuck in a grate shattered his peace.

"What in bloody hell—?"

He threw back the covers and headed for the door.

He came back before reaching it, still as naked as the day he'd been born, and slammed into his dressing room, to wake a sleeping Wycliff.

"Clothes, man. Get me clothes."

The valet who, Morgan was disgusted to learn, slept in a voluminous nightshirt, a large white nightcap with a point on it and displaying a tassel on the tip of it, and a violet-colored satin mask with no eyeholes in it, turned over on the narrow cot and continued to snore.

There was another female scream. Less bloodcurdling, but still with the power to reach his ears from a considerable distance.

"Testing me. That's what it is. The Fates are testing me, my resolve," Morgan grumbled, spying the pantaloons and shirt Wycliff must have laid out before going to bed last night.

Morgan looked at his hose and tossed them into a corner before pulling on his pantaloons over his bare bottom. He punched his arms into the sleeves of the freshly ironed white shirt and, without bothering to either button it or tuck it into his waistband, slammed out of the dressing room, through his bedroom, and out into the hallway.

By the time he got to the closed doors of the drawing room, five of the servants he'd brought with him from Westham were crowded around those doors, giggling and snickering and then quickly remembering that other duties called them when they saw their master descending on them like a devil just raised from Hell.

Morgan caught one of them by the sleeve as he tried to bolt. "What's going on, William?"

"Lady screaming, my lord," the under-footman said quickly. "Lots of talking."

"That's it? A lady, not one of the staff?" He hadn't been in town long enough to have offended a lady. "Wait a minute. How did this lady get in here?"

"Couldn't exactly say, sir. Can...can I go now?"

Morgan let go of the boy's sleeve and looked down at his own bare feet. A lady? Visiting at this time of the morning? And how did she know he had come to town? And why had she *screamed?*

He turned for the stairs, knowing he should finish dressing, but then he heard a very clear, well-modulated female voice say from the other side of the doors: "Mama, one more outburst like that and I shall be forced to send you to your rooms. *I* will handle the Marquis of Westham."

Mama? There were two ladies in his drawing room.

I will handle the Marquis of Westham.

The words danced around in Morgan's brain, their movement rudely pushing all his resolutions having to do with calm and coolness and self-control into a corner, and bringing a twinkle to his eye and a small smile to his lips. She would *handle* him, would she? Let her handle *this!*

He buttoned his shirt—most of it anyway—and turned back to the doors, took a deep breath, and pushed them open hard enough to bang against the walls inside.

Seven pairs of eyes, inside the heads that had immediately turned toward the door, gaped at this wild man, hair disheveled, barely clothed, who had burst into their midst.

He gaped back. He had expected to see two women, not a small army.

Nobody spoke until a small, thin lady who'd seen her share of summers said, "Well, now *that's* more like it! A *real* man."

"Mother Clifford!"

All right, Morgan knew that near shriek, the one coming from the younger woman, the plump one, dressed all in bilious green, currently sprawled on one of his couches and being fanned with a folded newspaper by a slick-looking young sprig who seemed to think red heels were still all the crack.

This lady was the screamer.

"My distinct pleasure, my lord," a man dressed as a gentleman, right down to his dove-gray gloves, said, advancing on him, right arm outstretched. "Sir Edgar Marmington, my lord, at your service, and may I say, my lord, you have a splendid residence. Simply splendid."

Morgan shook the hand, not even thinking about what he was doing, because he'd finally seen the girl standing in front of the fireplace.

A vision. An absolute vision.

But, as he'd never given her a tumble, never even met the girl, these people couldn't be here, three generations of them, to demand he make an honest woman of her.

"Go away," he said to the man, and stepped past him, moving deeper into the large room. He blinked. The vision in sprigged muslin was still there, as were the rest of his uninvited guests, unfortunately.

The dark-haired young beauty looked at him evenly, even accusingly, and suddenly Morgan was very aware of his bare feet and ankles.

Just as quickly, he was reminded that this was *his* house, and if he damned well wanted to trod through it barefoot, he damned well would.

"My lord," Thornley said, hurrying up from somewhere—frankly, after clapping eyes on the beauty, Morgan hadn't looked around any further. He *had* been sulking in the country for a long time. "I can explain, my lord."

"We ain't goin' nowhere, you hear me!"

Morgan attempted to look past Thornley's right shoulder, but that man stepped to his left, blocking his view. Morgan shifted to his left, and Thornley shifted to his right.

"Stop that," Morgan commanded, and the butler bowed and stepped all the way to his right, exposing a rather squat, wide woman of indeterminate years, but with her rough edges certainly showing, advancing toward him.

"You look here, m'lord," the woman said, wagging one short, plump finger at him. "I paid down good money for these lodgings, and I'm not budging no matter what this thieving bastard says, you hear me?"

Morgan turned to the thieving bas—er, Thornley. "You can explain this?"

"Sadly, yes, my lord," Thornley said, bowing yet again. "May I suggest we retire to your rooms and I might do that as you prepare for the day?"

"He means get some clothes on, sweetie, but don't bother on my account," the wizened little lady called out cheerily.

Morgan motioned for Thornley to move out into the hall. "Ladies, Sir Edgar," he then said, bowing, "I will be back directly. Feel free to ring for refreshments while I sort this out. I fear there is some misunderstanding, because, for whatever reason, you all must be in quite the wrong residence."

"The devil we are!" the coarse-looking woman said hotly. "And we were here *first!*"

WYCLIFF WAS UNCEREMONIOUSLY yanked from his bed, to go stumbling across the dressing room until he ran up against his lordship's dressing stand and held on with one hand while he removed the satin mask with the other.

"My lord?" he said, blinking furiously. "Oh, my lord, you tried to dress yourself?" He spread his hands and shook his head, as if to say *See? See what happens without my services?*

"Never mind that," Morgan said, stripping off his shirt, popping two buttons loose from their moorings in the process. "Ring for hot water, man, and find me some fresh clothes. I will be downstairs, shaved and suitably clad in fifteen minutes, or you will be sleeping in the gutter. And, in that getup, I'm convinced you'll have an interesting night of it."

Wycliff bolted from the room, whimpering, and Morgan turned to Thornley, who was in the act of picking up his lordship's discarded shirt. "And now—you."

"My lord," Thornley said, folding the shirt and holding it in front of him, almost as if to protect himself. "There is an explanation. You see…the mansion was empty."

The pantaloons were launched into a corner, and Morgan stood there, stark naked. "It damn well isn't now, man. And find my underclothes. It's drafty in here."

"Yes, my lord," Thornley said, doing his best to keep his voice even, because he was fairly certain he'd detected a slight quaver there the last time he spoke, and it wouldn't do to show the marquis any weakness. He knew the Drummonds, and showing any of them weakness, man or boy, would be like covering yourself with cow's blood and strolling into the lion's den crooning, "Here, kitty, kitty."

Wycliff reentered the room. Servants must be bustling

everywhere, for he already held a basin of warmed water at the ready.

Morgan sluiced water over his face and neck, cleaned his teeth, then submitted to Wycliff's mercies—that is, until he realized that baring his neck to a nervous man holding a razor might not be the most prudent thing to do. He grabbed the razor, staring more at Thornley than his own chin as he looked in the mirror attached to the top of the dressing table.

Although he did spare a moment to inspect his reflection, to notice that a small tic had begun to work in his left cheek. He was ready to explode, and he knew it, so he deliberately took a deep breath to calm himself.

"Go on," he said, twisting his mouth to the left. "Begin at the beginning. The mansion was empty?"

"Yes, my lord," Thornley said, trying to put a little more poker into his poker-straight spine. "You had fallen into that unfortunate duel with the Earl of Brentwood, and—"

"This is a recitation of your sins, Thornley, not mine," Morgan said as he grabbed a warmed towel from Wycliff and scrubbed his face with it. There. He was back under control. Marginally.

"Yes, my lord. So sorry, my lord. But you did say to begin at the beginning."

"I may have, not realizing that beginning, but now that I do, feel free to leap bravely ahead to the more relevant bits, if you please."

"Very well, sir. At first, having the mansion empty save for us few left behind was, well, my lord, it was as usual, as we are accustomed to the household being quite bare for several months a year. Your mother and father often were of a mind to visit again for the Little Season, but with your injuries, and your parting words—something to do with never setting foot in this Hell's Den again—we slowly began to realize that we were destined to…well, sir, to do nothing."

"And be bloody well paid for it," Morgan said, buttoning his pantaloons as Wycliff stood ready with his shirt and waistcoat.

"Yes, my lord, and we're that grateful, my lord. But, as two Seasons passed, and we were left with nothing to do but tend to a few aging carriage horses and keep the spiders from taking over the rest of the mansion, it occurred to me that you may have meant what you said, that you'd never return."

Morgan kept his chin high as Wycliff slipped a neck cloth over his head, then tied it himself, casually—his valet would have said sloppily. "And yet, here I am, Thornley. The world is chock-full of surprises, isn't it?"

"A stickpin, my lord?" Wycliff asked, holding out a velvet-lined box, the lid propped open to show a rather extensive collection of pins. "It might help."

"No, thank you. I prefer to go into battle without ornament, if you don't mind. You may go now, Wycliff. And for God's sake, man, burn that nightcap."

"My lord," the valet said, snapping his slippered heels together and retiring to a corner of the room, making himself as busy as possible while his ears positively quivered to hear what Thornley would say next.

Morgan turned toward the mirror one last time, pushed at a lock of hair that had a tendency to fall forward onto his brow, then, satisfied that he at least looked sane, returned his attention to his butler. "Where were we? Oh, yes, my empty mansion. *My* empty mansion, Thornley."

"For two years, my lord," Thornley repeated, making them sound like twenty. "At which time I thought, isn't this sad? Isn't this a waste? And doesn't our dear Lord detest waste? And then there were the other servants, my lord. They were becoming sadly out of practice, and needed to work or else grow lazy."

"Please, spare me these transports, Thornley, because I'm ahead of you. That horrible woman said she'd *paid*, didn't she? You rented out my mansion, didn't you? Turned the entire pile into a bloody hotel. I'm only surprised you haven't hung out a bloody sign. What do you call the place? The Absent Marquis? Good Lord, Thornley—are you mad?"

"I made up very strict rules, my lord," Thornley said, quickly grasping at any straw he could think of and then plunging into the rest of his sad story. "You—I—allowed our guests only small teas and intimate gatherings, and then only very rarely. No balls, no routs. In exchange for a modest rental fee, the tenants were allowed the permission to hint, always quietly, that they were in Grosvenor Square as the guests of the Marquis of Westham."

Morgan did a mental recalculation of the "guests" he'd seen in his drawing room, including the one that looked, and sounded, like a washerwoman. He'd never thought himself a proud man, or vain, but apparently he was both. "They go into Society, with my name attached to them?"

"Not all of them, my lord," Thornley said hastily. "Only the Cliffords, and Sir Edgar, although the fog of recent days has kept them at home, and they had no earlier invitations. They've only been in residence for less than a week, my lord. As for Mrs. Norbert, she seems content to stay inside, give orders, and eat her head off. Sir."

"Well, then that's all right, isn't it?" Morgan said, his voice dripping sarcasm. "Thornley—I'm going to have to kill you. You do know that."

"But we've been quite discreet, my lord. The first year there was only a very lovely widow with three daughters."

What he didn't mention was that, after chasing the youngest and the estimable Riley out of a few corners, Thornley had set up a few more rules, and taken over not only running the household but directing the tenants as well. He was not just their landlord, he was In Charge.

"Did they marry well?"

Thornley was brought back to attention. "Sir?"

"These three daughters. Did they marry well?"

"Oh, yes, my lord, very well."

"Did I provide dowries? I'm merely curious, you understand."

Thornley tried to laugh, but it came out as more of a strangled hiccup. "No, my lord. Would you care to hear about last year's tenants?"

Morgan took a cheroot from a box on the dressing table and Wycliff jumped forth with a lit candle, to light it. "If I am going to remain in London, and possibly encounter any of these previous tenants, I would say yes. Wouldn't you?"

"We, um, I overreached myself last Season, my lord, thanks to the success of our first foray into…into…"

"Into using your master's mansion and money to line your own pockets? Or am I wrong, Thornley, and you didn't feed these people with my money? Candles, green peas, feed for their cattle, and God knows what else. There are what, five floors and fourteen bedchambers in this pile? And you filled them all, didn't you? Even mine?"

"Oh, no, my lord. I would never rent out the master's chambers."

"How gratifying," Morgan said quietly…and then he exploded. He couldn't help it, and he doubted anyone would blame him for the outburst. "My God! You rented out my *home!* Wycliff, has the top of my head blown off yet? I feel as if it should have, or will, at any moment."

Wycliff, again, unable to recognize sarcasm, and never to be mistaken for a man overburdened with common sense, advanced with a brush in his hand and said, "Not blown off, my lord, but if I might suggest that I be allowed to brush at your hair? There is that one recalcitrant curl that—"

"I'll brush your damn skinny backside," Morgan said, growled, actually, turning toward Wycliff, and the valet scampered back to his corner.

Thornley wanted the rest of this over as quickly as possible, and was already mentally packing his bags, knowing he and those bags would be out on the flagway before luncheon. "I was overly ambitious, my lord, I agree. Which is why there are fewer tenants this year. And very carefully chosen, I assure you, although Mrs. Norbert may have been a mistake."

"If you mean that harridan who tried to attack me, then at last we agree on something, Thornley." Morgan looked at the man closely, remembering the beauty who was waiting for him in his drawing room. "Tell me about the remainder of these…guests."

Thornley nodded, more than happy to be of service. "As I may have mentioned, there is the Clifford family. Mrs. Clifford the elder, Mrs. Clifford the younger, her son, Mr. Clifford, and her daughter, Miss Emma Clifford."

Emma. So now he had a name to put with that face, those eyes. Emma Clifford.

"And the rest?"

"Sir Edgar Marmington, my lord, and the aforementioned Mrs. Norbert. Sir Edgar is very quiet, keeps to himself mostly, and Mrs. Norbert is a seamstress from here in London who recently came into some funds and wished a Season in Mayfair."

"Good for her. Everyone should have a Season in Mayfair. In fact, I'm sure anyone who knows me would say, yes, the marquis has often said that everyone should have a Season in Mayfair," Morgan said mildly. And just to prove that, indeed, the marquis had mastered his temper during his self-imposed exile, his voice raised only half an octave when he ended: *"Are you out of your mind?"*

"I'll…I'll gather the others and we'll be leaving, my lord," Thornley said, bowing stiffly. "I know what I've done is reprehensible as well as inexcusable, and I can only offer my heartfelt and most humble apologies."

"Right, right," Morgan said, his mind more fully occupied with a pair of penetrating gray eyes, and lips nearly the color of ripe cherries. All right, not quite ripe cherries, that was too fanciful, and would make her a devotee of paint pots, because nobody save heroines in marble-backed novels had lips as red as ripe cherries. Or eyes as gray as a stormy ocean in December.

Except perhaps Miss Emma Clifford.

He really needed her gone. He was becoming fanciful. Why, the girl was little more than a common housebreaker, even if she had paid her way through the doors.

"No," he said, coming to his senses. "Thornley, I'm not going to let you off so easily."

The butler squared his shoulders. "I shall gather the others and report to the nearest guardhouse, my lord? Only I think Claramae and Mrs. Timon would not survive being transported across the seas—Mrs. Timon's bunions, you understand, in particular—and Riley is probably already halfway to his sister's cottage just outside Wimbledon. So, if I may, sir, I will take the blame, and the punishment, firmly and entirely on my shoulders."

"Oh, cut line, Thornley," Morgan said, brushing past him, "I'm not an ogre. Nobody's going to the guardhouse. But, as I'm also not a saint, the four of you will be working here for the next year without wages. Now, for my first orders to you and your cohorts in iniquity, pack up these people and get them gone. I'm off downstairs, to inform them that they are no longer welcome in my house."

"WE'RE NOT LEAVING, you know," Emma Clifford announced with some heat as the doors to the drawing room opened and the Marquis of Westham strolled in. And it was a good thing she had gotten those words out before she really looked at him, because if he had been imposing half-dressed and sporting a morning beard, he was twice as intimidating now. Suddenly all the air went out of the huge room. "And…and you can't make us," she added less certainly.

Then she belatedly dropped into a curtsy.

"Where did everyone scamper off to, Miss Clifford?" Morgan asked, looking about the empty room. "Surely you are not here in the role of champion for all of them?"

She'd shooed everyone else away (or they had deserted her; she wasn't quite sure which), and after recovering the receipt Thornley had written out for them—and fixing her hair, making sure she looked her best—she had stationed herself here, to make very clear that she had every right to the use of this mansion until the King's Birthday in June.

Emma took a deep breath and began her prepared remarks…which had sounded far more declarative, and her voice less wobbly, when she'd practiced those remarks in her rooms. "I am here representing my family, my lord, and Sir Edgar and Mrs. Norbert as well. You can speak to me, although it will do you no good. As I have already stated, we are not leaving. We have *paid*."

"My goodness me," Morgan said, advancing across the room, not stopping until he was no more than three feet away from Emma. Beautiful she was, and no doubt, but she was also the most infuriating, contrary woman he'd ever met. "Please perceive me as veritably quavering in my boots, Miss Clifford, at the vehemence of what I fear you must, in your delusion, believe is your very reasonable argument. Now, that said, would you care to leave under your own power, Miss Clifford, or shall I simply toss you over my shoulder and carry you out?"

Emma backed up a pace, held up the receipt like a shield, and stumbled into her prepared speech, any eloquence she might have hoped for becoming lost somewhere in Morgan's angrily flashing blue eyes. "Here, look. We did, we paid. And Sir Edgar and Mrs. Norbert also have receipts. We *paid* to be here. Room *and* board, plus the use of the mansion's servants so that we didn't have to bring our own. See?"

Morgan grabbed the scrap of paper—bearing his crest, he noticed; Thornley had much to answer for—and read it. He chuckled ruefully. "For the four of you, you say? And this paltry sum is for the entire Season? Not just, oh, three hours spent nibbling cakes here in the drawing room and the chance to tell all your friends that you broke bread in the Marquis of Westham's domicile? Madam, you're standing in one of the grandest mansions in all of Mayfair. Do you have even the faintest notion of what it takes to maintain this pile? This amount is insulting."

"I agree that we all felt the price was rather a bargain," Emma said, grabbing the receipt back before he could toss it in the fire, which would be just like him, because he had to be the *nastiest* man she'd ever met. "But that's neither here nor there," she said, having gathered back some of her earlier courage, which had gone sadly missing as she realized how *big* the marquis was, how imposing. How very handsome…or he would be, if he'd stop scowling at her. "It is the amount we were asked to pay."

"And you never questioned it? You, your mother, your grandmother and your brother—four of you, for this miserly sum? How deeply have you all been buried in the country, Miss Clifford? A backward child would know this amount is ludicrous."

How she longed to box his ears. "There's no need to be insulting, my lord."

"You're right. My apologies, Miss Clifford. In truth, there's no need to be conversing with you at all. Where's your brother? I should be speaking with him."

"Cliff? Why, I sent him to his rooms, of course."

"*You* sent *him*—did you say Cliff?" Morgan grinned in real amusement. "That's his name? Cliff Clifford, Clifford Clifford?"

Emma bristled, because she might see how sorry a choice her brother's name had been, but she didn't need his so-supercilious lordship to point it out to her. "Yes, we call him Cliff, as that's his name. Is there something else we should call him, my lord?"

"James or Henry would be two suggestions," he said, then dismissed his words with a wave of his hand. "Well, never mind, that explains it. Cliff Clifford. Poor sot. Namby-pamby milksop ruled by three women. I almost pity him, and would," he ended, his smile fading, "except that he's in my house."

He leaned down, going nose-to-nose with Emma. She might be beautiful and spirited, but she was an interloper, and he would be out of his mind to think she could remain under his roof another moment. "And do you know something else, Miss Clifford? I don't want him in my house. I don't want any of you in my house. Because it is *my* house."

"There is no reason to shout, my lord," Emma told him with as much calm as she could muster. How he angered her. She had to ball her hands into fists, to keep from slapping his arrogant face.

"I'm not shouting!" Morgan said, then lowered his voice and repeated, "I'm not shouting."

"And if you could step back a few paces? You may think you are intimidating, but you are merely being unmannered and rude."

Morgan blinked. "Oh, that's above everything wonderful, Miss Clifford. You are illegally encamped in my house without my leave, and *I* am unmannered? And, I believe, insulting. Isn't that what you said?"

What an insufferable man! Did he think he was amusing? "Yes, I did say just that. And rude, definitely rude. I also said that, my lord. Although I congratulate you on realizing that you are also insulting. And now I will point out that you're still yelling, although not quite so loudly." She waved the back of her hand toward him. "Please?" she said and, wonder of wonders, if he didn't step back two paces.

"Satisfied now, Miss Clifford?"

"Marginally, yes." This wasn't so bad. All she needed was to be firm, and calm-headed. After all, she had Right on her side. Right, and Honor, and Justice. She tamped down a wince, knowing that she was now, horror of horrors, thinking like her mother.

Morgan gave her credit for bravery, but brave and beautiful, it didn't matter. His temper was roiling—*something* inside him was roiling—and he needed to regain his composure, that calm he had fought so long to achieve. He could not have survived Wycliff, only to fail when faced with this small, gray-eyed witch. He was stronger than that.

So he stepped forward again and leaned toward her once more. "You look a sensible puss, Miss Clifford. How can you stand here and tell me that I am in the wrong?"

"Because you are, my lord. Well, not really wrong, not…technically. But we are not at fault here, either. We are all unfortunate victims of a…a misunderstanding. Still, we have nowhere else to go, and you, a gentleman—and I employ that term charitably, my lord—cannot in good conscience insist that we leave," Emma said, pushing her face even closer to his. If she could stare down the village butcher when he was reluctant to advance them more credit until the end of the quarter, she could stare down this…this marquis.

Oh, Lord, he was a *marquis*. And who was she? She was a *nobody*. Was she out of her mind?

"What if I have no conscience, Miss Clifford?" he asked, standing his ground as a small part of him got lost in the depths of those unique gray eyes.

Emma forced herself to continue staring at him. If he was a marquis, why couldn't she use that fact against him! "I will remind you that you are a marquis, my lord. You have your honor to consider."

Morgan blinked first. He hated himself for it, but he blinked first.

"This is ridiculous. Of course I can make you leave. *Honorably.*" How would he do that? He might have threatened it, but he was a gentleman, damn it. He couldn't actually pick the dratted woman up by the waist and walk her out, toss her into the street. Maddening! "I could call the watch, have you bodily removed."

"Yes, do that, my lord," Emma said, because she'd had a good thirty minutes to prepare her arguments, although she'd dismissed most of them as unworkable. But now, she realized as she'd stared into this man's bluer-than-blue eyes, she had nothing to lose. If she did nothing but keep doggedly repeating that he couldn't make them leave, they would all be out on the pavement in mere minutes. She had to do more, even as she hated having to draw out what she'd considered those previously rejected big guns. So she took a deep breath and said, "But first, could you please direct me to Fleet Street?"

"Fleet—why would you go there? There's nothing there but print shops and newspaper offices and—" He narrowed those bluer-than-blue eyes. "You wouldn't dare."

"Yes, I would dare, my lord," Emma said, dipping her knees so that she could then turn and sneak past him, to sit down on one of the couches, carefully arranging her skirts about her. Her hands were trembling, but she clasped them together in her lap and smiled at him. She held the upper hand now, and she knew it. Playing fair had gotten her nowhere, so now she would play as her grandmother would, and not feel ashamed until later. Much later. "Your turn, my lord, I do believe."

Morgan attempted to push his rising temper down to where he'd found it possible for it to live, and for him to survive without doing anything too foolhardy. It sat uncomfortably, halfway down his throat, and he would worry that he might choke on it, except that he was otherwise occupied in not grabbing Miss Clifford by her throat and throttling her. "No. You wouldn't do that, Miss Clifford. Your mother and grandmother would never allow such a thing. Your reputation would sustain a larger blot than mine, I assure you."

"Perhaps. But I think not. After all, imagine the story as it would appear. Miss C-dash-dash-dash-etcetera was rudely and forcibly removed from the Marquis of W-dash-dash-dash-etcetera's Grosvenor Square mansion and tossed, homeless, into the gutter, along with her mother, brother and aged, infirm grandmother, because the marquis, having been thoroughly gulled by his staff during his absence from Mayfair, learned that this staff had been taking in boarders for the Season. At least, this is the story we are to believe. Could it be that the marquis is strapped for funds? It would go something like that, I believe. Yes, I could see where such a sad tale could hurt me. If anyone even knew who I am. *You*, on the other hand, my lord—?"

She smiled up at him and shrugged. There was something to be said for being daring, like her grandmother; doing whatever came into your head, and the devil take the hindmost. She was feeling stronger by the moment.

Good God, Morgan realized, the minx was right. He'd be thought a fool, or pockets-to-let, or both. Damn the woman!

"You can't stay here," he said once more, because he'd run out of new things to say.

Emma knew she had the advantage now and pressed on, knowing all she had left was one card.

But it was her trump card.

"You keep saying that, my lord. But where, oh where should we go after our stop in Fleet Street? Ah, wait a moment, I know. I suppose we could impose upon my mama's very good friend, and beg her to take us in."

The chit was smiling. He hated smiling women; they were always just about to drop a very heavy brick on your foot, one way or another. "Your mother's friend? She has a name?"

This was it, her last bit of ammunition, and if it missed its mark she would be defenseless. "Sally," Emma said, her grin widening. But this time she had him. She knew it. "My mama calls her Sally."

Damn. A very heavy brick. "And those who are not Sally's bosom *beaux?* What do they call her?"

He already knew the answer, and didn't even blink when Emma trilled, "Lady Sally Jersey."

Morgan dropped into the facing couch and let his chin fall into his cupped hands. "Silence," he grumbled. "They call her Silence, you know, because the dratted woman never shuts up."

"Dear lady. She has already deigned to visit us here, and asked after you, my lord, by the way. She also very kindly issued us vouchers to Almack's." Emma soldiered on, seeing her advantage and doing her best to drive it home. "That would be this evening, my lord, as the fog has at last dissipated. The opening Session. Would you care to escort us, as you have doubtless not had time to procure your own? The voucher includes an escort, and my brother has previously stated his aversion to coming within a mile of the place. Mama is, however, very much looking forward to the evening. As am I. I have a new gown, you understand."

Belatedly she shut her mouth, realizing she was in danger of becoming drunk with power.

Morgan almost gave in, gave up, accepted his fate. But then he looked at Emma, saw her smile, and hopped to his feet. "I don't care if you have five new gowns, madam, or if your mama regularly breaks bread with our new King."

"Well, as a matter of fact, my grandmother—but, no,

I won't say it." She wouldn't say it because she'd been listening to Fanny's fanciful tales all of her life, and had only believed half of them.

"I don't care if your grandmother will pine away, your mother will go into a sad decline, and your brother does back flips in his joy at not having to drag the lot of you to Almack's. You will *not* be leaving from here, and I will not be escorting you. You have one hour, madam, to get out of my house or suffer the consequences. Good day."

"And what would those consequences be this time, my lord?" Emma called after him, because now he *really* had made her angry, attacking her family that way.

He didn't answer, because he didn't have an answer, damn it. But he'd think of one. Just as soon as he returned to the privacy of his rooms and punched something.

FANNY OPENED DOORS in his lordship's dressing room and sniffed at the fresh linen smell. But there was nothing of interest behind any of those doors, or in any of those drawers, and she'd already inspected his lordship's jewelry cases, finding his selection to be limited but very fine.

She loved snooping. Not that she'd found anything of interest in Olive Norbert's rooms, but Sir Edgar's might be worth another visit if the man took the air again this afternoon.

Sipping from a glass she'd filled with wine she'd

poured from a decanter in the main chamber, Fanny returned there now and took up position in one of the wing chairs in front of the fireplace, the one with a clear view of the door to the hallway. Because her feet didn't quite touch the floor, she slid her bent legs up onto the cushion and tucked them under her gown, then sighed in real happiness.

She appreciated a fine chamber such as this. Spacious. Well-appointed. Lots of very good wood, and Chinese wallpapers lining the walls. Beany had a bedchamber very much like this one, in his mansion in Portland Place, as she recalled. Pity the man's idea of fun was to have her wear his Hessians and wield a riding crop. She'd had to give him up, finally, but by then she'd had Johnnie and, bless him, he'd been hung like a—

"…and make sure to count the silver before that Mrs. Norbert leaves," Morgan said, opening the door, then closing it behind him. "A madhouse, that's what this is," he told himself, heading for the drinks table. "I'm in Bedlam, with better furnishings."

"Talk to yourself, do you? My Geoffrey used to do that, quite often. Then again, he may have been talking to me, but I gave up listening after the first five years. Never liked him better than when we were going our own way, seeking our own pleasures. My lord? Would you care to bring your drink over here?"

Morgan was staring at the old woman. "My God, they're everywhere," he said, blinking.

"Don't just stand there, boy, sit, sit," Fanny commanded, waving her arm at him. "Don't worry, I'm not here to seduce you."

"There's a relief, madam," Morgan said, regaining his composure—it was becoming more difficult, but he'd had five years of practice, so he was fairly confident he wouldn't kill anyone for full minutes yet.

He took up his glass and headed for the chair, inspecting Fanny as he came. Short, which was probably where Miss Clifford got her small size, quite thin, and still rather handsome. Once a beauty, he was sure of that, and her eyes were still a vivid blue, but although he could see that her beauty had faded, obviously the woman looked into a friendly mirror. She was actually batting her eyelashes at him.

"Mrs. Clifford the senior, I presume. How did you get in here?" he asked after downing half his wine. "Or has Thornley decided to exercise some sort of insurrection, and take over the mansion for himself and his...tenants?"

"Nothing so dramatic, I'm afraid, my lord. I was forced to employ my own initiative, so I followed your valet up from the kitchens, tapped him over the head with a handy vase, trussed him up, and threw him out the window."

"Good," Morgan said, finishing off his wine. He couldn't be starting to *enjoy* himself, could he? "With any luck, he didn't bounce."

Fanny threw back her head and laughed, a most delightful, girlish laugh. "That's it, boy. Not easily ruffled, are you? Although I think you could be, seeing as how you're Harry's boy. Your mother didn't foist anyone else's brat off on him, either, for you're just like him, down to those truly magnificent blue eyes. Made me go weak in the knees, those eyes did, and I didn't go weak for many of them. I knew Mad Harry quite well. Quite well."

Morgan, despite himself, was intrigued. He'd never heard of this woman, but she spoke well, dressed well, and she'd known his father. "You've spent a lot of time in London, Mrs. Clifford?"

"Ages ago, yes. He was several years my junior, but we traveled in many of the same circles. You weren't even a glimmer in your father's eye then. Ah, the world you missed, son. We were young, we were free, we *lived*. None of this daren't-show-an-ankle sort of silliness that's going on now."

She leaned forward in her chair. "Do you know, I once rode up on the box with Johnnie Lade, before Letty got her claws in him. Paid the driver for an hour's use of the Mail Coach, and off we went. I threw my bonnet to some farmer standing on the side of the roadway, goggling at me, and let my hair fly free. I had black hair once," she ended wistfully. "Masses of it."

Morgan lifted one eyebrow but said nothing. He knew about Sir John Lade, and the man's wife, Lady Lade.

Crude, loud, but accepted everywhere, at least until their exploits became too much even for the more rough-and-tumble days of the last century. "Did he truly file down his front teeth so that he could whistle like a real coachie?"

"That was one of the talents it gave him," Fanny said, and damn if the woman didn't wink at him—and damn if Morgan didn't feel his cheeks growing hot with embarrassment. This was Miss Clifford's "infirm" grandmother? "But that's neither here nor there, boy. Have you given us all our *congé?*"

"Your notice to quit the premises? I have, yes. Thornley is supervising the packing up of your belongings even as we speak," Morgan said, putting up his guard, which he had lowered a fraction at the woman's outlandish bantering.

She held on to the arms of the chair as she stuck her legs out in front of her and looked at her own bare ankles, admired her own blue kid slippers like a well-pleased child. "We're not going, you know. Would you like to know why?"

"You have a receipt, you'd go to the gossip rags, your daughter-in-law is bosom chums with Sally Jersey. Yes, I know. But you're still going."

Fanny shook her head, sadly, as if she actually might pity him, poor deluded fool that he was.

"Good ammunition, I'll grant you, as I gave it to her, but the girl was outgunned by your perversity, I'm sure.

Still, I'll give her credit for trying. But now it's my turn, so batten down the hatches, my lord."

Morgan lifted his left eyebrow, amused in spite of himself. "You may fire when ready, madam."

"Oh, I'm ready, son. Loaded, primed, and flint at the ready. You know, of course, that we're here to pop her off. Beautiful girl, you'll have to agree, even with her pitifully paltry dowry. Spirited, which she got from me. Good name, too. The Cliffords go back to the Conquest, which is more than many can say. Daphne, that's my featherwitted daughter-in-law, and I are quite set on gaining her a first-rate match, for the gel, of course, but a good marriage would feather our own nest in the long run, and the few feathers we have now are sadly in need of company. Are you on the lookout for a wife, by any chance? You'd do, you know."

Morgan glared at her, his amusement gone, and said nothing. This was the frail old lady Emma Clifford had spoken of earlier? Ha! This woman was about as infirm as Alexander the Great in his prime.

"Yes, well, you don't have to answer now. We have the whole Season in front of us, don't we?"

"Not sharing this house, we don't," Morgan told her, aware that he was beginning to sound, of all things, desperate.

Fanny ignored this. He might as well be talking to the wall. "Cliff, the idiot, is here to see how much trouble he can get himself into—we think he became a man the other night, and about time, too. I'd begun to wonder about him, frankly. All that lace, and those red heels, you understand. In my time, the gentlemen wore satins with *élan*, but Cliff, for one, is too much the raw youth to carry it off."

Morgan looked up at the ceiling. Maybe this was all a dream, a nightmare. He couldn't really be awake, and this outrageous old woman couldn't really be saying all these things to him.

She was still talking. "Discussing Mrs. Norbert is a waste of breath, as I'm sure you've already deduced, as you at least look bright, but she goes nowhere, so that's all right, and you won't budge her, not without a nasty fight. Sir Edgar? Something's going on there. I don't know what, not yet, but I'll find out. Still, he's old, and relatively harmless. Not at all like me."

"You're not harmless?" Morgan asked, suppressing a grin in spite of himself. "I'm shocked, madam."

"Ha! As my late husband might say, ain't you the card. Didn't protest that I'm not dead old, did you. But the thing is, I'm the one what's going to snare a good match for Emma. Would you like to know how?"

Morgan stood up. "Madam, I could not imagine any subject about which I would care less. You have fifty minutes before you are thrown out of my house."

"I only need five," Fanny said, unruffled. "Have you heard about Harriette Wilson, my lord, stuck out in the country the way you've been?"

Harriette Wilson? He'd heard. Oh, yes, he'd heard. One of his mother's friends had written to her last year, to say that the famed courtesan was threatening to pen her memoirs, naming names, ruining reputations, although an offer of money would conveniently erase her memory of the individuals who paid for that lapse. His mother's friend had been convinced the late marquis's name would come up somewhere between the covers. His mother had retired to her bed for two weeks, until he could convince her that no communications had arrived bearing Miss Wilson's demands.

"Go on," he said, refilling his wineglass.

"You disappoint me, my lord. Do I really have to go explain this, as I would to a backward child? Oh, very well, if I must. Miss Wilson and her sister were common sorts even in their heyday, not at all upper drawer. But a lady of some quality—that would be me, son—who lets it be known to certain persons that she is anonymously penning *her* memoirs, also allowing it to be known that the application of a plea to not publish, followed by the promise of an introduction to grandsons, nephews, eligible, well-set-up young gentlemen in general, amends my memory quite nicely?"

"Blackmail? You're talking about blackmail."

"An interesting idea, yes? In fact, the letters, complete with small hints meant to refresh faded memories, are already winging their way across Mayfair. I believe there must be a dozen breakfast tables that have suddenly gone very quiet this morning. This should be a very busy place quite soon, my lord, with eager suitors underfoot."

"I still don't see what any of this has to do with me." Except he did.

"Yes, you do. Would you like to know how your papa first came by the name Mad Harry?"

All right, so he could no longer pretend he didn't know what Mrs. Clifford had in mind. He knew a threat when he heard one. Wellington may have been rumored to have told Mrs. Wilson to "publish and be damned," but Morgan would rather not go that route. He had his mother to consider.

"We stay for the Season," Fanny said after a long, tense silence.

"For the Season," Morgan agreed, feeling five long years of learning to control his temper shredding into tatters.

Fanny pushed herself out of the chair and stood up. "And you'll host a party or two for little Emma? Perhaps even a ball? Yes, I do think that a ball would be nice. Just the thing."

Regaining control, Morgan said coldly, "Oh, I seriously doubt that, madam."

"I don't. Did your mother—dear woman, how is she?—ever tell you about the time Harry and I rode our horses into a certain rural ballroom? It was a very *private* costume party, you understand, with only a few select guests, and I was Eleanor of Aquitaine. You remember? She rode with her husband, straight into battle. *Bare-breasted.* I imagine she thought it would rouse the troops. Ha! Bound to rouse something, right, boy? Anyway, and then Harry and I dismounted and—"

"Perhaps even a ball," Morgan said, knowing he had lost. He had to protect his mother. Digging up Mad Harry, or at least his rather lurid reputation, could not be considered a balm to an old woman's scabbed wounds, those inflicted by that same deceased husband.

"I think pink bunting in the ballroom, as well as perhaps a fountain? And only the best musicians."

He turned and glared at Fanny. "You are an evil woman, Mrs. Clifford."

Fanny shrugged. "Nonsense. I've only asked for your house for the Season. I didn't demand you court Emma, as you seem set against it. Now, if you'll excuse me, I'll go tell the servants to stop their packing. Luncheon will be served in two hours, my lord. Mrs. Norbert gets testy if she isn't put to the trough with regularity."

"The devil it is. I haven't yet had my breakfast."

Fanny smiled. "Yes, you have. And it wasn't easy to swallow it down, was it? Oh, and this conversation remains private, my lord. As far as my family is concerned, I will simply be entertaining many old acquaintances as they drop by to see me. If you want, I'll tell you what I would have written about each of them?"

"No, thank you," Morgan said. "It's bad enough I'll know why each of them is here."

"Ah, this younger generation. Too lily-livered by half for my tastes. Now, as I'm convinced you were not nice, go apologize to my granddaughter."

Morgan laughed, at last. "Never."

"Really? Then there was the time dearest Harry and I—"

He held up one hand, then opened the door for her. He followed her into the hallway, watching her move off toward the stairs and what had to be her chamber before he headed for the drawing room once more.

If he had any sense at all, he'd tell Wycliff to pack them up again and run, his tail between his legs, all the way back to Westham. But he'd be damned if he was going to let one reprehensible old lady and the rest of Thornley's gaggle of guests defeat him.

Besides, somebody was going to pay for his upsetment, his inconvenience, his dilemma born of his servants' ingenuity, and compounded by Mrs. Clifford and her memoirs.

And he knew just the person. It could only be hoped she was still in the drawing room.

SIR EDGAR UNLOCKED his door when Fanny Clifford knocked on it, then stood back to let her into the room—leaving the door open, as was proper. It was probably also safer, when the gentleman's guest was Fanny Clifford. He might not be a genius at understanding women, but he recognized a kindred spirit when he met one.

"Not yet packing, Sir Edgar? Good, because we aren't leaving, unless you really want to go. If you do, I'd consider it a kindness if you'd please take Mrs. Norbert with you."

"We aren't leaving?" Sir Edgar moved to stand in front of the closed door to his small dressing room as Fanny began circling the perimeter of the room, picking up a folded map of London on one table, sliding her gnarled fingertips over the surface of another. "How?"

"The marquis was made to see reason, of course, and was kindhearted enough not to throw us all out into the street," Fanny said, walking around the bed, to stand at its side, leaning back against the mattress. "You know, Sir Edgar, I understand why my family and I are here, and everyone knows why that Norbert person is here. But no one knows why *you* are here. Do you plan to go into Society?"

Sir Edgar wet his lips with the tip of his tongue. This woman was trouble, and about as subtle as a hammer falling on his head. "I *am* in Society, Mrs. Clifford. Perhaps not on the grand scale you wish for your granddaughter, but I have friends here."

Fanny was on the move again, now backing toward the small table holding the water pitcher and bowl. "Really? We're much of an age, Sir Edgar. We may have some of those friends in common." She stopped moving and glared at him. "Name some."

"I see no reason to—now what are you doing?"

Fanny had turned her back to him, and had lifted up the bar of lye soap. "So *that's* the smell I've been smelling. I know London can be dirty, Sir Edgar, but is such a harsh, smelly soap really necessary?"

She turned to face him, and the bar of soap clipped the handle of the pitcher.

"Watch out, you're going to—well, now look what you've done." Sir Edgar grabbed a towel from the top of the dresser and went to his knees, sopping up the water that had spilled when the pitcher toppled to the floor. "Madam, will you please *leave*."

"Certainly. No need to fly up into the boughs, Sir Edgar. It's only water." Fanny pocketed the small key she'd nipped from the table when the unwary man knelt down and, humming under her breath, left the room.

EMMA BLEW HER NOSE and stuffed her handkerchief back into the side pocket of her gown. She stared out the window once more, looking at the children walking with their nannies, the ladies taking the air, the gentlemen bounding onto the seats of their curricles as they were off somewhere. Bustling, bustling. The sun shone for the first time in an eternity, and London was coming to life.

Just as she was leaving it.

It wasn't fair, that's what it wasn't.

She had planned for so long, had even located an advertised set of rooms in Mount Street, when Grandmama Fanny had waved the small notice in the newspaper in front of her and they'd written to the address in Grosvenor Square.

The rental price was ridiculously low for an address in one of the most exclusive areas of Mayfair, and the marquis's crest on the letter they'd received back not a week later had served to make her grandmother do a fairly creditable jig in their small sitting room at Clifford Manor.

"I should have known something wasn't right," Emma told herself, seeking recourse to her handkerchief once more and dabbing at her tear-wet eyes. "But I was greedy, and I wanted a few more gowns. This is all my fault."

Where would they go? Home, she was afraid. Yes, she had threatened the marquis with Lady Jersey, but that had been an empty threat. And there was no money for another lease (she'd bought the gowns), and certainly very few, if any, acceptable addresses left in Mayfair at this time of the Season.

So they would go home. Back to Clifford Manor.

And all her dreams would die along the way.

"Oh, I *hate* him!" she said, stuffing the handkerchief away once more. "I hate him, hate him, *hate* him!"

"Now, why am I sure that the man actually responsible for this mess, the so-ambitious Thornley, is not the object of your vehemence, Miss Clifford? And, in that case, would you suggest I begin sleeping with a pistol under my pillow, as I understand Lord Byron did on occasion?"

Emma's eyes opened wide at the sound of the marquis's voice—and at the mocking tone she heard in it.

"Why are you always where I don't want you?" she asked, keeping her back to Morgan.

"I'm afraid I don't have any answer to that, Miss Clifford, other than to say that if you were not in my house, you wouldn't know where I was. Why aren't you upstairs, packing?"

Emma turned to face him. "I…I was simply taking a few moments to compose myself. You needn't dog my every step, my lord, your pocket watch open in your hand, to be sure we vacate in the allotted time."

"There could be another solution," Morgan said, crossing to the fireplace and standing beside the hearth, his hands clasped behind his back. He felt more in charge now, standing as master of his own house…and if he could find a way to lock the old lady in her rooms until the King's birthday, he'd feel ever better.

"Another…another solution?" Emma cocked her head to one side and looked at him. "And what would that be, my lord?"

He unclasped his hands and brought one forward, lifting it to his gaze, to pretend an inspection of his fingernails. "Some might offer you a liaison, in return for your lodgings."

His head bent, he lifted his eyes to peer at her from beneath his brows.

"You…I…you'd—you mean *me?*"

Ha! At last, a point to him. "You flatter yourself, Miss Clifford. I meant Mrs. Norbert, of course. I must confess that I find myself simply captivated by her myriad charms."

Emma's eyelids slitted. "Let me be the first to inform you that you're not amusing anyone save yourself, my lord."

Perhaps not, Morgan agreed silently, but she was right on one thing, he had amused himself. Besides, he certainly had Miss Clifford's full attention now, and had gotten them past the rather depressing "why" of his continuing to house this motley collection of people under his roof for the Season.

"This is how it will be, Miss Clifford," he pushed on, now that he felt he had the advantage. "As your residence here is already a known fact, and Thornley assures me that we'd be caught out if we poisoned the lot of you and buried your bodies in the cellars, we will be sharing this household. The division, however, will not be equal. My study will be, of course, out of bounds to all of you, as will be most of the house. You will have your rooms, use of this drawing room, and the dining room unless I need either, at which time you will take your meals in your chambers. At all times and in all ways you will be circumspect, as well as quiet and unobtrusive as the proverbial church mouse. Understood?"

What did the man think they were going to do? Hire a convenient traveling band of gypsies to dance on the tables? Emma wanted to slap the marquis's face for his insults (there were so many from which to choose), and storm out of the room. Still, much as she loathed the fellow, it would appear that something she'd said earlier had finally registered with him. But what? The threat of Lady Jersey, no doubt. Maybe she would speak to the woman after she'd married.

Regardless of how or why it had happened, she should be polite, because she had won, and a crowing victor is never appreciated.

"Will there be anything else, my lord?" Emma asked, taking up her former seat on one of the couches, because her knees were threatening to buckle beneath her.

"Anything else I can do to frustrate you, you mean? Oh, madam, allow me to list the ways."

Morgan made for the drinks table, intent on pouring himself a glass of wine, then decided against it. It was just going on noon, and he'd been drinking wine since, he felt, the crack of dawn.

So he stopped, turned and struck a pose. Like many of his contemporaries, he had studied Beau Brummell on his first visit to London, and he and Perry Shepherd had spent a rollicking hour one evening, deep in their cups, standing in front of a mirror, doing neat pirouettes and placing the heel of one foot against the instep of the other, dropping one hand against a hip, stroking the underside of their chins with the other as they composed their features into a look of pensiveness, or haughtiness or, as Perry had joked, acute dyspepsia.

Ah, youth. He hadn't thought of that evening in five long years. Maybe it was good, being back in London. It most certainly outstripped sitting at an early dinner table, listening to his mother describe her latest aches and pains.

"Your lordship? Is something wrong?" Emma asked.

"Wrong? No, of course not," Morgan said, dropping the pose, just in case Perry had been right about the acute dyspepsia. "I was merely collecting my thoughts."

Emma bit the insides of her cheeks, but as that had never worked before to silence her tongue, the exercise was doomed to failure now. "You wish me to beg a thimble from Mrs. Norbert, my lord? To collect them in, I mean."

All right, so maybe another glass of wine wouldn't come amiss. Morgan poured one for himself, not asking Miss Clifford if she wanted him to ring for lemonade or some other insipid drink. Did Thornley keep hemlock in the kitchens?

"I sense that it is time to sum up, before we actually come to blows, Miss Clifford. This is my house, my home. You and your family, to the world, are my invited guests, as your grandmother and my late father were acquainted in their youth and your grandmother applied to me to help introduce you to society."

Emma held up a hand. "What did my grandmother say to you? She said something to you, didn't she?"

Morgan looked her straight in the eye. "I have not yet had the pleasure of conversing with the woman. Now, please, Miss Clifford, pay attention, as this is our story. Being a generous, good-hearted fellow, I could not decline your grandmother's eloquent plea—not to mention your distasteful threats, and we won't. That said, you, all of you, are grateful to me, your kind benefactor, and will speak well of me in pubic. Glowingly, in fact. In private, you may tell me to go to the devil, just as I will wish you and your family on the far side of the moon. Is that clear?"

Emma nodded, keeping any other thoughts to herself, thoughts that ran along the lines of: He's lying in his teeth.

Later she would have a private word with her grandmother, for she wasn't such a widgeon that she believed the marquis had given in because of some sense of honor, or Lady Jersey, or any other farradiddle. She wasn't the heroine who had saved them all from an ignominious retreat back to the country. She hadn't gotten to him; her grandmother had gotten to him. How lowering. Ah, well, a victory was a victory.

"Miss Clifford?"

Emma blinked herself back to the matter at hand. "Yes, yes, my lord. We are to sing your praises to the skies, polish your reputation like a shiny red apple, and in return you will graciously allow us to remain here, with the use of some of the house, except when we are to lock ourselves in our rooms, because you will be entertaining friends. Do you have friends, my lord? And all because you don't know how to get rid of us. It's very clear. You're a vain man, not concerned a whit that we might have been left with nowhere to go, and it is only your reputation or well-being that means anything to you."

Morgan smiled. "Ah, you have been paying attention, Miss Clifford. Yes, I think that just about covers everything. You may notice that I'm ignoring that slap about the number of my friends. And it would be beneath me to point out that you are an ungrateful brat."

"Touché, my lord." Maybe there was still a victory left for her to claim as her own, and not her grandmother's— who Emma could not envision as ever putting herself out to help Olive Norbert. "But what about Sir Edgar? And the so estimable Mrs. Norbert? I must insist that they, too, be allowed to remain here."

"Thornley assures me that Mrs. Norbert never strays from the house."

"She barely strays from the table," Emma said quietly, for she really couldn't like Mrs. Norbert, no matter how diligently she tried. There was just something…something sinister about her. "And Sir Edgar?"

"Your mother's distant relation," Morgan said, having just decided on that explanation. "I have already learned—via the so-ambitious Thornley—that you and your family were not previously acquainted with the gentleman. However, as I do not consider it my duty to include him in any social events, if he is seen stumbling through the halls and remarked upon, that will be our story. Agreed?"

"It's not up to me to agree, it's up to Sir Edgar. He may have some objection."

"He also may object to finding himself on the street, Miss Clifford. I am being magnanimous, believe me. Now, as to your brother."

"Cliff? What about him? You haven't even met him."

"Oh, I've met him, or his like, several times, Miss Clifford. He will not go into Society with us, not until he loses that painfully green side of himself. As you say, I do consider my reputation. Keep him in the nursery, where he belongs."

"Cliff left the nursery ages ago. He's all of nineteen."

"My, quite aged. He probably enjoys only tame pursuits, like chess, and holding your mama's yarn while she rolls it, without a thought to complicating my life by being beaten into a jelly by cardsharps or running about the city, propping coffins at doors and the like."

"You speak from experience, my lord?" Emma asked, secretly believing that the safest place to keep Cliff would be in his rooms, one ankle firmly shackled to the bedpost.

"Just keep him away from me," Morgan said, looking into his wineglass, then depositing it on the table. "Now, about Almack's. I will graciously escort you ladies this evening, introduce you to the remainder of the patronesses, and even lead you into your first dance of the evening. This gesture, magnanimous in the extreme, will earn you no small measure of cachet."

He held out a hand to her, not that it appeared she was about to speak. "No, please, don't thank me, Miss Clifford. My indulgence knows no bounds. Kindly behave yourself, don't waltz until one of the patronesses has given permission, then please tumble madly into love with some half-pay officer and elope to Gretna Green by the end of the week, will you? That will be thanks enough, I assure you."

Well, that tore it! If he was going to be insulting, then she could goad him more about his seeming change of heart. "Why?" she asked, looking up at him. "Only a short while ago you were demanding that we leave. Why are you doing this? It can't all be your reputation, because I cannot believe you want us all running tame in your household for the next two months just to keep tongues from wagging. My grandmother, for one, will want an explanation."

"Startling as this may be to you, Miss Clifford, I really don't care what you think. And I've already spoken to your grandmother, and she has by now informed everyone that I am allowing you to remain here, in residence."

Emma sat back, bit her lips between her teeth. Men. They were *so* easy to manipulate. He probably didn't even realize what he'd just admitted. "So you have spoken to my grandmother."

"That's what I said, yes," Morgan said, avoiding her eyes.

"But just a minute ago, you said you hadn't spoken with her."

Morgan gave himself a mental slap. He hadn't realized it would be so difficult to keep his lies straight while half his mind was recording the curve of Miss Clifford's lovely cheek, the disconcerting way she had of looking up at him through those long, dark lashes. He attempted to regroup. "I meant not at any length, Miss Clifford. I have not spoken with your grandmother at any length."

"No, you doubtless didn't speak with her at any length, my lord. She spoke to *you*." Emma folded her arms across her midsection, letting him know without words that she would not be fobbed off; she would hear it *all*. "What did she say?"

Morgan felt an insane urge to bolt from the room. The grandmother wasn't the only formidable woman in the Clifford menagerie. "As I told you, I spoke with her and—"

"No. No, no, no. Please listen, my lord. I didn't ask what you said to her. I asked what she said to you. She threatened you, didn't she? With that horrible story about writing her memoirs. You said I should say she knew your father, and it was she who put that idea into your head, along with her threat."

She jumped to her feet, not feeling triumphant at all,

but thoroughly ashamed. "That pernicious old woman! Oh, I'm *so* sorry, my lord. We'll leave at once."

"Miss Clifford, wait," Morgan said as Emma headed for the hallway. "You *know* what your grandmother is planning?"

Emma stopped, turned around. "I found the stack of letters she wanted Riley to send out yesterday," she told him. "For a penny, he let me have them for a few minutes and…and I opened one of them."

"I see," Morgan said, but he didn't really see at all. "So, you know what she's about, and you condone it?"

"I most certainly do not!"

"Then you burned the letters?"

Emma looked at the floor. Oh, why had she started this? Why hadn't she just left well enough alone? "No. I gave them back to Riley."

"Because you're here to find a husband, and you don't mind if your grandmother blackmails someone into handing one over to you? That's not very attractive of you, Miss Clifford."

Emma attempted to defend herself, knowing it was a losing battle. "I would only have been delaying the inevitable, my lord, as my grandmother would have merely penned new notes. Or worse, she might have confronted the poor gentlemen in public."

"No. Those are good reasons, but they aren't the real reason. Are they?"

Emma lifted her gaze and glared straight at him, remembering her grandmother saying, more than once over the years: "May as well be hanged for a sheep as a lamb."

"I'm nearly one and twenty, my lord. I have a dowry that would fit in that thimble, leaving room for all your *thoughts*. My father left us near to penniless and my brother wants me to buy him a set of colors in the army. Did I really have a choice? But…but now that I see the power Grandmama has, enough to bring even such a mighty peer as you to your knees, my lord…I…well, yes, I'm ashamed."

"As well you should be, Miss Clifford," Morgan said, but his heart wasn't really in the rebuke. "Does your mother know? Your brother?"

"Goodness, no. Mama would have a fit of the vapors. And Clifford? I wouldn't care to think what he might do with any such dangerous knowledge. Nothing good, I'm sure. As I said, my lord, we'll be leaving. Do not concern yourself that my grandmother will say one word about your father, not to anyone."

Not even if I have to sit on her for the next six months, Emma added to herself.

"Very well," Morgan said, seeing his chance to be free of the Cliffords and the other two uninvited guests. All he had to do was to pick up his cane and hat, his cape if it was still cool, take himself off for a few hours, and he would return to blessed peace, tranquility, and no houseguests.

No lovely gray eyes.

Emma dropped into a curtsy. "Thank you, my lord."

"Although," he heard himself saying, "as long as we both know that I am no longer constrained to be your host. In that case, I can just be magnanimous, can't I? I admit to liking that much better than being blackmailed by a little old lady who has lived, by her report, a much fuller life than I could ever hope to do."

"I…I don't understand. You want us to stay?"

"I admit that I do not understand, either, but, yes, I rather think I do want you to stay, Miss Clifford. But," he added as a small bit of sanity bit him in the brainbox, "only as long as you can convince Mrs. Norbert to take her meals in her rooms."

"Do you really want to make my grandmother *that* happy, my lord? I think not." Emma grinned, curtsied again and ran from the room before he could change his mind.

"SO WHAT IS IT you'll be doing now that you're tossed out on your ear, Mr. Clifford?" Riley asked as he walked alongside the young man, on their way to Piccadilly.

No two sadder young men were to be seen. One a well-dressed lad with a handsome face marred by a profound sulk, the other a liveried footman with bowed legs, his powdered wig stuck half into his coat pocket.

"I'm not going home, if that's what you mean," Cliff told him after a few moments, kicking at a loose cobblestone in his path.

Riley shuffled along, hands dug deep into his pockets. "No, sir. It's not going back I'm thinking about, neither. Mr. Thornley had a *face* on him."

"You only say that because you didn't see my sister," Cliff said, rolling his eyes. "I'll bet she can make Thornley run to pull the covers over his head. But it was nothing like the look on the marquis's face back there in the drawing room. He came bursting in searching for someone to kill."

Riley nodded. "Nope. Not going back there, just to be told to take myself off again."

"At least Thornley's a man. How'd you like to be led around by a gaggle of women? Cliff, do this. Cliff, don't do that. What did you do with the half crown I gave you last month, Cliff?"

Riley pulled a pilfered plum from his pocket, and bit into it. "A bleedin' pity, ain't it. Mrs. Timon boxed m'ears last week, she did, just for slicing m'self a bit of ham. Women are the very devil in petticoats, that's what they are. I'd be haring off to m'sister's, excepting she'll just want to know what I did wrong, what briar I'd landed m'self in now, and similar. Women always think we men did something wrong, don't you know."

"You know what we need to do, don't you?" Cliff said, jingling the few coins in his pocket. "We need to find a way to get ourselves rich. Then we wouldn't have to answer to anybody. Not Thornley, not the marquis, and most certainly not any women. Here we are, in London.

Got to be thousands of ways to make money in London. We just need to think of one."

They walked along in silence again for a while, two young men bonded by their mutual misery, before Riley said, "I saw a hanged man the once, I did. Highwayman. He might have lived good, but he died with his neck stretched. Then they dipped him in tar or something and hanged him up for everyone to see. Crows were pecking at him when my mam took me to see him."

"I didn't say we'd become highwaymen. But there must be something we can do that wouldn't get us hanged."

Riley chewed on this for a while, along with the plum. Finally he said, "Well, I do know this fella…"

THE KNOCKER BEGAN going at one. Morgan was in the drawing room at the time. He ended up passing insipid remarks about the weather and the King's latest expensive bit of ridiculousness meant to tip the entire empire into bankruptcy before Fanny Clifford came to join them and Morgan could escape, to wonder what on earth Lord Boswick could have done to be worried about the woman's threat.

At eighty, because the man was that if he was a day, you'd think he'd be happy to have it known he was once a rutting dog, or whatever it was he had been before his gout had him walking with two canes, and unnerving white hair had begun sprouting out of both his ears.

Morgan made it only as far as the landing before Sir

Willard climbed the stairs, the ever-patient Thornley pushing him from behind, and he was forced to spend another quarter hour waxing poetic over the weather that hadn't changed since Lord Boswick had first mentioned it. Worse, Sir Willard had been grinning at Mrs. Clifford the whole time, leering actually, and Morgan had been caught between wanting to flee the room screaming, his hands clapped over his eyes, and believing he should stay, and act as chaperon.

He'd actually made good his escape to the upper floor when the knocker went again, and he peered over the railing to see Thornley accepting a hat and cane from— good lord, the new head of the Admiralty!

"They've begun to arrive? All the penitents?"

Morgan jumped, and would have toppled over the railing if he hadn't been holding on with both hands. He turned to Emma. "Do *not* do that again, Miss Clifford," he said, tight-lipped.

"I'm sorry, my lord," Emma said, stepping past him to take a peek of her own. "My, distinguished looking, isn't he? Who is he?"

Morgan told her.

"Oh. Him." Emma felt herself coloring. "He should have come bearing buckets of gold coins, or at least three strapping grandsons."

"Why? What did he—no, don't tell me. I see you're dressed for an outing, Miss Clifford. May I ask where you're going?"

Emma tied her bonnet strings, as she had left them hanging when she'd spied out Morgan leaning over the banister like a child on Christmas morning. "Nowhere, my lord. I just wish to take the fine air in the Square for an hour. Mama would have joined me, but she's still lying down, recovering from her exertion of the morning."

"Yes, screaming at the top of one's lungs probably does take a lot out of a person."

Emma glared at him. "My mother is very delicate."

"Browbeaten would be a better explanation, I'd think, stuck between you and your grandmother."

"This is a very large mansion. I'd rather you'd ignored us, my lord," Emma said, peeking over the banister once more, straight down to the foyer. "I think it's safe for me to sneak out now. Excuse me, my lord."

"Wait, I'll go with you."

"It's only the Square, my lord. I don't require a chaperon."

"I was thinking more of making my own escape, Miss Clifford, and I am not beneath using you as my excuse. Come on."

He grabbed her elbow, she shook off his hand, and they fairly raced down the stairs to the first floor…just as the knocker went on the ground floor and the front doors were opened yet again.

Morgan peered over the railing. "Good grief. Quick, come here," he said, grabbing Emma's elbow again and unceremoniously pulling her around the corner and into a shallow alcove where they now shared space with a statue of Venus. As a matter of fact, Morgan would probably wear the bruises for a week, where his back had slammed into the goddess's unclad front.

Emma found herself smack up against Morgan, chest to hip, as he put his arms around her and warned her to be quiet.

She put her palms on his chest, to try to keep her balance. Goodness, but he was solid. "Why? Who is it?"

"The bloody King," Morgan said, knowing he sounded in awe. Not in awe that the King had come to call, but in awe of a little old woman and the power she held over the most exalted personage in the land. "Please tell me you don't know anything about him."

Emma shook her head. "I don't think so. Grandmama said she knew him well, and I did see his name on one of the messages, but I never thought— It's really His Royal Highness down there?"

"And coming up here, so be quiet," Morgan whispered, pulling her deeper into the alcove.

"Why? I don't understand. I've practiced my curtsy for months. I'd really enjoy meeting him."

"And I don't want him to think I know why he's here, damn it," Morgan said. "Listen, I can hear him on the stairs. Shut up."

She tried to push herself free. "Shut up, is it? You are as rude as I said you were, my lord. I will not shut up. I'd much rather peek around the corner and see—"

Would the cursed woman for the love of heaven *shut up!*

He took one hand off her hip and clapped it over her mouth, which seemed to serve to open her gray eyes wide enough that there was the distinct possibility they might just pop straight out of her head.

"Mmm…mmmph…*mmmmmph!*"

He moved his face within inches of hers. "Quiet," he warned yet again, then, while still holding her close with his other hand, sort of sidestepped the two of them to the edge of the alcove.

Those wide eyes looked left, and Morgan looked along with them, to see the new King, dressed in the finest clothes he couldn't pay for, composing himself outside the closed doors to the drawing room. An ounce more lace on the man's cravat or at his cuffs, and he'd look like a wave, crashing against the shore.

"Mmmph?"

"No," Morgan whispered, now cheek to cheek with Emma. "Not yet."

"Mmmph!"

Thornley opened the doors to the drawing room and His Royal Highness waited until he was announced, then dragged his well-corseted bulk out of sight.

At which time, Emma brought the heel of her soft slipper down on Morgan's instep, which didn't really hurt him. Still, he took his hand off her mouth. "You— you *madman!* Unhand me at once."

Morgan found himself reluctant to do so. This was

nice. She smelled good, she felt good, and he was mightily tempted.

But then sanity caught up with him. "Of course, Miss Clifford," he said, stepping back and bowing to her. "That was a close-run thing, wasn't it. Shall we go now?"

"I'm going, my lord," Emma said, stepping past him. "However, if you attempt to follow me, I shall stand here and scream *fire* at the top of my lungs, right before you are forced to introduce me to His Royal Highness."

She would, too; Morgan could sense that this was no empty threat. "Have a pleasant stroll in the Square, Miss Clifford," he said, bowing again, then went off to relive the past few minutes—mostly those having to do with how close he had come to silencing her with his mouth, rather than his hand.

"FLORIZEL!" Fanny exclaimed, hopping up from her position on the couch (one lordship to the left of her, another to the right of her), and dropping into a deep curtsy (which she was then helped out of by the lordship on her left and the lordship on her right). "Your Majesty, it has been an age. Don't you look splendid!"

"Fanny, my dearest." The new King maneuvered his overdressed bulk in her direction and bowed over her hand, turning it at the last moment, to press a wet kiss in her palm.

Good old Florizel. He'd never clapped eyes on an older woman he didn't like, although he usually liked them more "cushioned."

Fanny's laughter trilled through the room as the gentlemen performed their bows, none of the three of them actually meeting the Prince Regent's eyes.

"How many more, Fanny?" His Royal Majesty asked as Thornley, proud but never flustered (at least, not after the events of this morning, after which he might never be flustered again), returned with another tray of refreshments, having sent a footman running to the kitchens directly from the foyer.

"How many more what, Your Majesty?" Fanny asked, sitting herself beside the prince, which left two of the lordships to wander about the room, looking for somewhere else to settle themselves, as Sir Willard rivaled the prince for bulk, and adding another body to the facing couch could prove perilous.

"Naughty men in London, of course," the prince said, winking at her.

"Never you, Your Majesty," Fanny said, winking right back at the grand Florizel—who, rather than being a mere shadow of himself as he moved on in years, had seemed to have expanded in every direction. "Have I ever hinted otherwise?"

"No, my dear lady, you have not, and I thank you for your kind invitation to come see all those who were naughty. And I'll want details, now won't I? Oh, not while you're here, gentlemen, so gasping in outrage will gain you nothing. Be proud—you were *real* men! Yes, even you, Boswick, mind-boggling as that is."

The other three men in the room muttered unintelligible sounds and slowly sank deeper into their seats, which made Fanny laugh again.

Bless dear Florizel. She knew she could count on him. Because now they knew, now they all would know. Nothing traveled through Mayfair with more speed than the whispered words, "Don't dare breathe a word of this to anybody, but…"

Cross her, refuse to fall into line with what Fanny Clifford wanted, and she would run to the new King to tattle, and it would be all the worse for them.

"Tea, Your Royal Highness?" Fanny asked, and the head of the Admiralty raced to play mother.

Ah, she thought, settling back against the cushions, one gnarled hand on the King's plump knee, being back in Society was *such* fun!

DAPHNE CLIFFORD, recovered from her earlier upset, just happened to be dressed in a new gown, and just happened to be walking down the hallway (actually, she'd been lurking behind a potted plant, but who's quibbling?) when Thornley appeared at the opposite end of the corridor, having moments earlier left the drawing room.

"Madam," Thornley said when he spied her and realized he had no avenue of escape handy. "May I be of assistance to you in any way?"

Daphne spent a flustered few seconds mentally listing the ways, and then said, "No, no, Thornley. I just wanted to see you, and tell you that I harbor no ill feelings toward you for…well, for what happened. We seem to have come right, in any case, and I am entirely sure you are blameless in the matter."

Thornley bowed. "Thank you, madam, but I fear that I am *entirely* to blame. His lordship, however, has proved most forgiving, for which I am eternally in his debt. That you might also forgive me would remove the remainder of the sting I feel at my truly unforgivable transgression."

In truth, Daphne had pretty much lost the thread of that sentence around the word "eternally." She'd been much too busy wondering if Thornley's lovely mix of silver and black hair would be soft, or stiff, to the touch.

"Is there anything else I might get for you, madam?" Thornley asked when he realized that Daphne wasn't going to speak.

But she was thinking. What could he get for her? A book of poetry, perhaps, that he would read to her in the seclusion of the music room? Perhaps a single flower, that she could delicately sniff as he read? That would make for a wondrously romantic scene, just like something she'd read in one of Fanny's marble-backed novels.

"Madam?" Thornley inquired again, realizing that Mrs. Clifford's faded gray eyes had become somewhat unfocused as she looked up at him. He felt so protective of her he could barely stand it!

"Um…? Oh. Oh, no." Daphne smiled quickly, revealing her dimples, and then frowned. "There is nothing, alas, that you can do for me, Thornley. Excuse me."

He watched as she picked up her skirts, turned on her heels and ran back down the hallway.

Thornley tipped his head to one side and hoped for a glimpse of dimpled ankle as she ran.

SIR EDGAR, still wearing the remnants of the worried expression that had put a crease between his eyes the moment he'd realized he'd misplaced the key to his dressing room, stopped just inside the tavern and waited until his eyes adjusted to the dimness.

As for the rest of it, all that had transpired at the mansion in Grosvenor Square earlier today, he was quite unconcerned. Things always had a way of coming right, or going terribly wrong. That was Luck, and Sir Edgar was intimately acquainted with Luck, mostly of the unfortunate sort. That he'd had a bit of a "win" this morning, concerning his lodgings, could only be considered a welcome omen of better luck to come.

If John Hatcher had actually shown up, that is.

"Hoo! Over here, Sir Edgar!"

Sir Edgar winced, not wishing his name to be called out, or remembered, and hastened to the corner where John Hatcher sat, two empty bottles already lined up on the table and pouring from a third.

"Been reading about them alchemist monks of yours,"

Hatcher said even before Sir Edgar could sit down. "All dead, you know. Whacking great lot that says about how smart they were, what?"

Smiling indulgently, Sir Edgar slipped into his chair and said, "Ah, but good sir, perhaps they merely transported themselves to another plane."

Hatcher chewed on this possibility for a few moments. "You mean they could have taken themselves off somewhere? Plains, huh? I would have thought a mountaintop. You know, perched there naked under their robes, long white beards, spouting words of wisdom nobody understands. That sort of thing."

Sir Edgar opened his mouth to explain but quickly thought better of it. The ignorance of others had always been his staunchest ally. So he signaled for a bottle and glass, and remained silent.

After a few moments, probably spent contemplating how cold one would be, perched on a mountaintop sans one's drawers, Thatcher leaned close and whispered, his breath sweet with wine, "Did you bring it?"

Sir Edgar looked around the room a few times and noticed a rather plainly rigged out man sitting alone at a table in the dimness of the opposite corner of the common room, apparently watching them. The man looked away when Sir Edgar raised an eyebrow to him, and he dismissed the fellow as being of no consequence.

The man looked nothing more than a fairly well-dressed clerk, and Sir Edgar knew clerks. Dull, uninspired men, usually younger sons with no prospects, showing a penchant for dressing in muddy browns, and having to turn the cuffs and collars of their shirts, to hide the fraying as they attempted to hold on to some semblance of being a part of the Quality. He had nothing to fear from a clerk.

Sir Edgar reached into his pocket and pulled out a small, purple velvet bag. "I have it right here," he said unnecessarily, as Hatcher was already staring at the bag, bug-eyed.

"Give it over."

"Now, good sir, you must understand that this is *all* that I have, and it took years—years, sir—to achieve even this small success. And I have promised no miracles."

"Yes, yes, I remember. Years. Miracles. You already told me all that. Give it over," Hatcher said, reaching for the bag.

Sir Edgar deftly kept the bag out of the man's reach. "You've told no one?"

"Me? I'm the one should be asking that. This is you and me, right?"

Sir Edgar nodded. "I feel very badly about this. I mean, his lordship has been financing me for a long time."

"But he's not here, and I am. I'll not weep buckets for that stick Claypole, I tell you. I've a draft for one thousand pounds in my pocket, man. Do you want it or not?"

"One thousand pounds is a start, Mr. Hatcher. It is not

the finish. I would not wish for you to think that it is. Although the reward? The ability to turn any base metal into gold?" Sir Edgar shrugged, in the Gallic manner, he thought, doing his best to appear merely the nervous inventor, rather than so excited he could barely restrain himself from tossing Hatcher to the floor, then digging in his pockets for the draft. One thousand pounds! If he called it quits tomorrow, he'd be set for years! "You have to be certain you wish to do this."

Hatcher made another unsuccessful stab at nabbing the velvet bag. "Damn and blast, man, let me see it. I don't care what it costs."

"Are you quite certain? I would not think of taking your money, Mr. Hatcher. Not without showing you definite proof of all I've told you."

"Right. Thousand pounds, ten thousand pounds, what does it matter? You'll have it all, all you need. Now give it over," Hatcher said, making yet another grab for the velvet bag.

Ten thousand pounds? Suddenly one thousand pounds sounded paltry to Sir Edgar. Visions of ten thousand pounds, twenty thousand pounds—more, if he could find other simpletons with money, and he was already convinced he could. He had been thinking too small, wanting one investor; why, he could have a dozen! Luck was on his side, and for once, it was Good Luck. Why, there was no limit to the money he could relieve them of, was there?

This time, Sir Edgar let Hatcher succeed in grabbing the velvet bag, not because the man was, God bless him, as thick as a post, but because the bag actually did contain real gold.

As Sir Edgar knew: nothing and no one has ever been caught with an empty hook.

Hatcher hunched over the table, turned away from any prying eyes in the room and tipped the contents of the bag into his palm.

Sir Edgar watched as Hatcher's jaw dropped and his eyes grew wide. He could already feel the crackle of the bank draft as he slipped it into his own pocket.

Hatcher hefted the small, heavy lump in his hand and grinned. "Heavy, ain't it? What was it before?"

Sir Edgar looked straight into Hatcher's eyes and said solemnly, "My shoe buckles, sir."

EMMA WAS WAITING for the marquis to join her, and she wasn't disappointed. Only moments after the King's coach and outriders moved off, he appeared in the doorway, hat in hand, to stand there, looking for her. He did not appear to be a happy man which, in turn, improved her own mood immensely.

She waved from her seat on one of the benches neatly tucked into an oasis of greenery in the Square.

"I've been expecting you, my lord. Gentleman that you are at heart, you've come to apologize for your assault on my person," she said as he sat down beside her.

"Madam, if I ever wished to assault your person, I would first have to lose complete control over my wits. I was merely keeping the two of us hidden, and for very good reason. I for one don't intend to spend the remainder of this Season ducking out of the way of the King in order to spare both his and my own blushes."

Emma could have pushed the point, but the marquis had a good deal on his plate already, and she had grown up fully believing that gentlemen—when not fighting wars or otherwise amusing themselves as they supposedly dealt with matters of great import—were fairly dim-witted, easily confused creatures. "Please, don't go on so, as I know this must be quite embarrassing for you. I shall simply accept your apology, my lord, and we'll speak no more about it."

Morgan sniffed, and shook his head. "You Cliffords are all mad as hatters."

"I imagine you are referring once more to my grandmother, and the fact that all those desperate men have dragged themselves to your door, hat in hand? And to think, my lord, there were a dozen letters sent out only yesterday. She may be many things, my grandmother, but mad is not one of them. Crafty, perhaps? Yes, she'd like to be considered crafty. Oh, look, here comes another one."

Morgan shot a quick glance at the ancient landau that had just pulled up, one of his own recently transplanted footmen running to the horse's heads. "I don't recognize that crest on the door," he said as a gentleman wearing a very unbecoming bottle-green coat and faded yellow buckskins was helped to the flagway. He would never admit it aloud, but these arrivals were proving to interest him very much.

"I'm going to put a stop to it, you know. Writing her memoirs, that is." Emma shook her head. "As if she really would."

"You're right, she won't do it," Morgan said, to soothe himself as well as agree with her, as he was the one with Mad Harry hanging from the family tree. "But only because the threat seems to be working nicely. Buck up, Miss Clifford. Any time now a vehicle will approach carrying something other than an octogenarian, and you can rush over there and pounce on him."

Emma lowered her parasol and turned to glare at him. "Make light of it, my lord, but gaining the correct introductions is invaluable to a woman seeking marriage."

"The correct introductions? Oh, that's rich. What you Cliffords are doing is indulging in a form of blackmail, pure and simple."

"Grandmama would say you're splitting hairs, my lord. Split them far enough, and you could even say this is just another form of an arranged marriage, which is done all the time in the *ton*. But, in this case, no one is demanding a marriage, merely that I should be put in a position to meet eligible gentlemen. I'm actually becoming comfortable with the idea. Marginally," Emma ended, putting up her parasol once more and unfurling it with a snap.

"Naturally you are, Miss Clifford. Women are always able to bend the worst possible scenarios to suit themselves and their sensibilities. You, by the by, should fit into Society quite well, as you appear to have the sensibilities of a cardsharp."

Mention of cardsharps brought Emma back to a worry she'd been fretting over while awaiting the earl's appearance. "I can't seem to locate Cliff, my lord, nor can Mama find her pin money. He may have gone off to sulk, which means he has yet to learn that we have not been evicted. If he doesn't return soon, my lord, where should I look for him?"

Morgan pinched the bridge of his nose with his thumb and forefinger. The boy was going to be trouble, he'd known that the minute he'd clapped eyes on him. Barely a bit of peach fuzz on his face, and rigged out like a mummer in those red heels, his cravat dripping lace. If the idiot had money in his pocket, it wouldn't be there for long.

"You will not look for him anywhere, Miss Clifford," Morgan told her, realizing that, damn it all, he was rapidly taking on all the less wonderful traits of a guardian. Or a keeper. With Fanny and the unfortunately named Clifford Clifford, at least, his job would be more of keeper. Was it too late to have Thornley transported?

Emma dropped her attempt at sophisticated disdain and turned on the bench to say, "Oh, but I must find him. He's only a boy. There's no knowing the trouble he could land himself in out there, with Riley."

"Riley?" Morgan frowned. That name was familiar. "Oh, my most ambitious footman. I remember now. Well, then, Miss Clifford, as he's not alone, I should imagine he'll be fine."

"Then you'd imagine incorrectly, my lord." Emma's chin dropped and she spoke into the neckline of her pelisse. "The other…the other night we think Riley took Cliff to a…a domicile of not quite a healthy reputation."

Morgan's mouth lifted on one side as he translated those last few words in his mind. "A house of ill repute, perhaps?"

"I didn't want to say the words, thank you so much for saying them for me," Emma said, wanting nothing more than to close her parasol, then bang it, repeatedly, around the marquis's head and shoulders. "Cliff could be taken advantage of, that's all I meant to say. He's an innocent."

"Not anymore he's not, if your assumptions are correct," Morgan told her, not bothering to hide his delight in shocking her. "Leave him be, Miss Clifford. Either he'll wander back here, his tail between his legs and minus your mother's pin money, or Riley will get word to us from the local guardhouse as to the nature of the boy's crimes."

"Oh!" Emma blinked back quick tears. "The guard-house? Do you really think…?"

"Miss Clifford, unless a raw country youth has been dragged off to the guardhouse at least once, his education in town life will remain sadly lacking. Give your brother his head, he'll find his way home."

"Did you? Find your way home, that is? Or were you locked in the guardhouse?"

Morgan had a quick flash of Perry Shepherd and himself, both at least three-quarters in their cups, being prodded in the spine with a watchman's truncheon as they stood on the minuscule portico of the Lord High Mayor of London's domicile, propping a coffin holding a fully dressed straw corpse against the door…and just preparing to bang on the knocker. It would have been the guardhouse for the pair of them, had Morgan not had a heavy purse with him, a purse made much lighter once the watchman had pocketed several coins.

"Naturally not," Morgan said, wishing that particular piece of his misspent youth to remain his own secret. "I was merely stating what I've often heard said about young gentlemen and their follies. Now, if we might return to the subject of your grandmother?"

Emma shrugged. "There is nothing more to say, my lord. She has done what she has done, and I have condoned it because I am a terrible person who is desperately assuaging her conscience with the promise that Grandmama's memoirs will never be written, let alone published. I know you cannot like any of us, my lord, but you have promised to house us for the Season, so I will promise that we will be no trouble to you."

"Do not promise what you cannot possibly deliver, Miss Clifford. You and your family are already a world of trouble to me. God's teeth, woman, I've got a gaggle of old men cluttering up my drawing room, begging for their youthful transgressions to be forgotten if they offer up a grandson or nephew to you on a silver platter, apples stuck in their mouths. Do you really think none of them has noticed where they are? They are in *my* house, madam, which makes me either woefully ignorant of what goes on there, or a part of the conspiracy."

Emma swallowed down the word "oops" and averted her eyes. She hadn't thought about it exactly that way, that her grandmother's scheme could stain the marquis's escutcheon. "I'm sorry, my lord," she said at last, truly meaning every word. "I didn't realize."

"Neither did I, Miss Clifford, until a few minutes ago, or I would have never bowed to your grandmother's threats. Better Mad Harry be dug up for another airing than that the Westham name be damned forever."

Emma recovered herself from her momentary bout of conscience. "Damned forever? Oh, cut line, my lord, it isn't anything quite so dramatic. It's only twelve old men, eleven, if we don't count the King, and none of them will be racing about Mayfair, cursing your name. Why, they probably think you are yet another one of

Grandmama's victims, which you are in a way, and you are not only offering us shelter for the Season in return for Grandmama's silence, but you are one of my suitors. My first, and quite eager, as you also are escorting us to Almack's this evening."

She looked up at him, as he had fairly leaped from the bench. "My lord? Are you all right? You're looking pale. Where are you going?"

He took three steps away from her, then remembered himself enough to turn and bow. "Where am I going? Why, Miss Clifford, I'm off to murder my butler. I thought that would be obvious."

SIX. SEVEN, with Florizel, but he'd only been there to frighten the boys.

All in all, a successful day, if Fanny didn't linger overmuch on the particulars of the thing. Unfortunately, she couldn't seem to shut off her brainbox, which insisted on digging at her. Her conscience had departed for the south of France decades ago, was much calmer for being at a distance from her, and wasn't expected to return any time soon.

She sat back and rested her head against the cushions, looking up at the stuccoed ceiling of the drawing room. Ah, the memories. Although Bosey Boswick had been much more appealing with all his teeth, and poor Willie would never see the sunny side of seventy again.

How had they all gotten so old? *She* wasn't old. Not

in her mind, she wasn't. In her mind, she was still a young girl; beautiful, adventurous, eager for any flight of fancy. Although the years after Geoffrey died had seemed like two very boring lifetimes, stuck as she was in the country and forced to be responsible; raising Samuel, marrying Samuel off, attempting to feed everyone on her very limited allowance while her son gambled the rest away once he'd reached his majority.

Almost forty years she'd been gone from Society, locked in the back of beyond, where the successful passage of any day could be claimed by the person who got through it without setting fire to her shoes simply out of boredom.

Had she really hoped that London would not have changed in her absence? That the men she had danced with, laughed with, tarried with, would not age?

She'd kept up-to-date with the goings-on in Society through newspaper accounts and by milking the rare traveler for all she was worth, but nothing could have prepared her for the sight of her once daring, darling young beaux.

Why, Freddie and Bosey had spent half their time today comparing the separate, and quite depressing, states of their health. Aching joints, spotty livers, gout—the men seemed to be holding a small contest as to which of them was falling apart faster.

And Willie? She'd secretly marveled at the notion that Willie could keep from drowning in his tub, let alone ever have been Minister of the Admiralty, never imagining the laughing young randy who'd lured her onto the Dark Walk for some slap and tickle (and a lot more!) would one day turn so dull, and pompous, and so distinctly without humor.

By the time the last of them had limped off, Fanny had believed herself well rid of them, even Dickie Harper, who she'd once seriously considered running off with, leaving Geoffrey and an infant Samuel to fend for themselves.

Now Dickie had misplaced his hair and found a very unnecessary expanse of belly, and had squinted at her over his spectacles to say, "The years haven't been kind to you, Fanny, have they?"

Ha! Had he looked at himself?

Old. They were all dead old. In fact, one of her letters had gone to a widow, as the hopeful target had turned up his toes only last week, having, so Florizel had told her, suffered some sort of apoplexy while attempting to climb onto the seat of his curricle. The Widow Carstairs. Now there was a woman in for a nasty shock as she read through the notes of condolence delivered to her door this day. She'd probably be wishing she'd buried old Georgie upside down.

"Uh-oh, you're smiling," Emma said, entering the drawing room. "That doesn't bode well for the gentlemen."

Fanny grinned at her granddaughter and patted the cushion beside her. "Sit, sit. I have good news."

"We're soon to have a second parade? This one a few

years younger, I should hope. Were they very upset at your threat?"

Fanny's smile disappeared. "You know? How do you—my letters. Gel, did you read my letters?"

"Nonsense, Grandmama," Emma told her, pleating the skirt of her gown with her fingers. "I had Mama read the tea leaves this morning, and she saw your entire terrible scheme there."

"Your mama wouldn't see a purple pachyderm in her dressing room," Fanny said, sniffing. "I should have known I wouldn't be able to fob you off with some farradiddle about having asked my old beaux to drop by and then they offered to help ease my dear granddaughter's way into Society."

"You might have, as I'm convinced your spelling is not up to writing more than those letters. Memoirs would be totally beyond you."

"True enough, although a good child wouldn't be so rude. Are you going to cry rope to your mama on me? Let me know, please, as I wish to be on the other side of the sea when she starts screaming."

"I won't tell her, I promise," Emma said soothingly. "I even approve, except for threatening the marquis. You shouldn't have done that. I already had him half agreeing to allow us to stay here."

Fanny looked at her granddaughter and grinned. "You think so, do you? Why? What did you say that had him half agreeing?"

"Oh, I mentioned how I could apply to the newspapers and tell our tale of woe. You'd mentioned that as a good threat, remember? And, well, I mentioned Lady Jersey. I really didn't like doing that, as I can't find it in myself to like the woman. So, you see, the marquis was very close to seeing the advantage in allowing us to remain under his roof."

"Close, my dear, but not there. I am the one who pushed him past the brink. And I did it with a passel of crammers that I couldn't believe the man would swallow, but he did. Riding bare breasted with his father, pretending I was Eleanor of Aquitaine? I may have had my fun, but I never made a spectacle of myself."

"So his father didn't do anything so terrible?"

"Mad Harry? The man invented outrageous behavior. Wenching, dueling, drinking himself into a stupor. And his temper was legendary. It was dueling that finally got him. Straight through the heart, I believe. His lordship, the one here now, I mean, couldn't have been more than a babe when it happened. Youngest marquis ever I heard of, I think."

"Oh." Emma found herself feeling very sorry for the Marquis of Westham. But not sorry enough to have them all pack up their belongings and take themselves home. She was softhearted, not softheaded. "I told him you wouldn't say anything about his father, or write your memoirs. He seemed mollified, although he is still very angry with Thornley."

"Couldn't blame the man. So, it sounds as if you've been speaking with the marquis at some length. What do you think of him? I say he's a well set up young man, if a bit starchy. Seems to be reining himself in, you know, in a way Mad Harry never attempted, let me tell you. But I see hints of some life in those wicked blue eyes of his, and none of the meanness Mad Harry had in spades. You could do worse."

Emma felt her cheeks growing hot, and turned her face away from her grandmother. "I would not consider the marquis, Grandmama. He is quite above my touch and, even if he wasn't, he loathes us, individually and collectively. He's made that abundantly clear. Repeatedly."

Fanny shrugged. "Very well. Not the marquis. I already have three very eligible young gentlemen prepared to meet you this evening, and they will be only the beginning. Especially when it's learned that the Marquis of Westham is your guardian."

"My…my *guardian*. Nonsense!"

"Really? We're under his roof, ain't we? If you aren't going to set your cap for him, all the better. It will give you more to choose from and, believe me, gel, once word gets out that Westham's your guardian, along with the ones I've scared up, we'll be knee-deep in suitors before the week is out. You'll have your pick of this year's litter of eligible bachelors."

Emma sat there for several moments, trying to digest

everything her grandmother had said. "But…why would I become more eligible if the *ton* thinks the marquis is my guardian?"

"Later, dear," Fanny said, hopping to her feet. "I think I just saw Sir Edgar heading up the stairs. I want to assure him again that we're as welcome as the posies in May, so that he can thank the marquis next he sees him."

"But—" Emma sat back against the cushions and watched her grandmother trot out of the room, her gray head at least a foot ahead of her toes, as if she was in a powerful hurry to get where she was going. "I don't understand," she muttered to herself. "Although I'm fairly certain the marquis does, and that he doesn't like it, not one bit."

MORGAN SAT in his private study on the ground floor of the mansion, his fingers steepled in front of his nose. Anyone peeking in the doorway might have said *sulked* rather than *sat,* but probably not to his lordship's face.

So he sat, and he thought, and he marveled.

Less than a day in London, and he'd acquired a menagerie.

And, he would admit only to himself, a new interest in life. Some excitement, which had been sadly lacking these past five years.

Fanny Clifford was amusing, in her own way, rather like an aged, slightly demented wood sprite. He was tempted to confer with her again about Mad Harry, a man he couldn't even remember. His mother refused to speak of her dead husband, and the older servants only whispered when they thought their young master wasn't listening. Morgan knew he wanted to learn more about his father; surely there had been more to him than a roving eye and a nasty temper.

Daphne Clifford and her son he dismissed as being of no importance, although he was convinced he'd be hauling the boy out of one briar after another for the next month or more.

Which brought him to Miss Emma Clifford, who would be extremely grateful for any assistance in riding herd on the boy. If he were out to ring up points with the young lady, that would be important to him, even an avenue to pursue.

He recalled those moments in the alcove. He should have kissed her, rather than silencing her with his hand. He deserved a kiss, because he was the most generous of men not to have tossed them all out on their ears this morning.

Her eyes had gone so huge. Her body had been so soft against his.

He really needed to think about a visit to Covent Garden, where he could find himself a convenience to assuage these feelings that had begun to surface the first moment he'd glimpsed those haunting gray eyes.

But first, he had to get through this evening. Dinner with the menagerie, which unfortunately included that

Norbert woman, and then his return to Almack's. He'd
been there only the once five years ago, and had found
the assembly rooms overwarm, the refreshments insipid,
and the company depressing in the extreme. All those
giggling debutantes; all those turbaned dowagers.

If the patronesses could have greeted him at the door
with a sign to tack on his back, stating his name, social
rank and annual income, he wouldn't have felt more like
a piece of meat being offered up for sale.

What had Perry said? Oh, yes: "Give me a penny,
Morgan, no more, and I'll strip to the buff right here.
That ought to help the ladies make up their minds."

They had avoided Almack's after that, not because
Perry had actually stripped, but because Morgan had
been sorely tempted to hand over that penny.

And now he was going back. Not just because he'd
been blackmailed into it, but because he'd already listed
Almack's among the tortures he would be forced to en-
dure in order to seek out his bride, the mother of the next
generation of Drummonds.

When he found her, she would be the opposite of
Miss Emma Clifford. She would have an unexceptional
family, not a harum-scarum collection of idiots and
blackmailers. She might not raise him to great passion,
but she would also not ignite his temper. His mother
would approve, he'd retire to the country once more, and
he would enjoy the even tenor of his days.

"God, I need a drink," Morgan said to the empty

room, pushing himself up out of his chair to head upstairs to the drawing room, because there was only brandy in his study, and he thought it better to stay with wine if he wanted his head clear for the evening.

He opened the door to the hallway just in time to hear a short maidenly squeak, followed by a giggle, followed by a slap…and immediately followed by the sight of a young housemaid racing toward him, her head turned to look behind her, her more-than-ample bosom bouncing as she ran.

He watched that amazing bosom for a full second, before realizing he was about to be run down.

Morgan grabbed at her arms, which brought her up short, and peered past her, down the hallway, to see the footman named Riley stepping out into the hallway from what might have been a closet, his grin wide as he used both hands to adjust the powdered wig on his head.

"Oh, laws," the girl in his arms said, and Morgan let go of her. She dropped into a quick curtsy and then began to cry.

"Did he hurt you?" Morgan asked, glaring at Riley, who was no longer smiling. The thought sprang into his head that here was a chance to punch someone, and his head seemed to like the idea.

"Oh, no sir, he was just…we was just…"

"Never mind," Morgan said. "What's your name, girl?"

"Clara…Claramae, my lord," the blond housemaid said, dropping into another quick curtsy. Dear Lord, but the chit was blessed with a fine bosom. Perhaps even overblessed.

"Ah. And you would be co-conspirator with Riley here?"

"Oh, no sir, m'mother said I weren't never to do that, not lessen I was wed first. It was just a kiss he was stealing, my lord. I'm a good girl, I am."

Morgan bit the insides of his cheeks, then said, "Very well, you may go now. Not you," he added, as Riley turned to head off in the opposite direction.

"M'lord?" Riley said, pulling down at his livery jacket. "Would there be something you'd be wanting?"

"Yes, but as it would probably get me hanged, I'll forgo the pleasure. Are you prepared to wed that girl?"

Riley blinked, then swallowed down hard. "Wed her, my lord?"

"Yes, not bed her, wed her. A simple change of one small letter, but a shift in your life that would appear to be something you have yet to contemplate. Well?"

Riley frowned. He was smart enough to know that being stupid was often his best asset. "Well what, sir?"

"Never mind. Tell me, is young Clifford returned from his travels?"

Riley relaxed slightly, because now at least he had an answer. "Been home this hour and more, m'lord, all right and tight. And may I make so bold as to say that it's pleased and chock-full of thanks I am for your kindness, m'lord, to our guests, and to us belowstairs most especial. To the guardhouse, that's where I thought we'd be going."

"And in return for my kindness, Riley?"

"Sir," the footman said, drawing himself up to his full height. "My pleasure is to serve you, m'lord, and similar."

"How above everything wonderful. I shall sleep so much more peacefully for that," Morgan drawled. "Not just a servant, but my own loyal slave. Good. And here is what you will do for me, Riley. You will stick to young Clifford like a barnacle on a hull. You will keep him out of trouble, if you have to tackle him as he attempts to climb the stairs of a gaming hell or any other den of iniquity—any bad place, Riley," he added when the footman frowned. "He goes nowhere without you, and you report to me upon your return every thing he has done. Agreed?"

"You'll be wanting me to cry rope on Mr. Clifford, m'lord? That don't seem sporting."

Morgan sighed, and dug into his pocket to pull out his purse. "How about now? Your worries assuaged now?" he asked, after two gold coins had changed owners.

"Sleeping like a babe in arms, my worries is, m'lord."

"Good. And keep your hands off that girl, and any other servants under my roof. Otherwise, you will be walking crooked for a week. Do you understand that?"

Riley's complexion began to resemble his powdered wig. "Yes, m'lord," he said, then bowed, and walked away with such alacrity that one could believe he was being prodded from behind by a sharp sword.

FANNY WAS STANDING just behind the slightly ajar door to her bedchamber when Sir Edgar mounted the stairs and came down the hallway, humming as he walked… and barely limped. Wasn't that nice, that he was such a happy man?

She'd soon fix that.

She waited until he'd opened his door, then scampered across the hallway and slipped inside his room just as he was about to close the door.

"Good afternoon, Sir Edgar," she said, closing the door for him. Before he could more than open his mouth to protest, she slipped her right hand from behind her back and held up a key. "Misplace something?"

"I TELL YOU, I can't find it," Daphne lamented, wringing her hands as Emma sat at her dressing table, Claramae (who had quite a talent for it) twisting her mistress's long black hair into ropes threaded through with faux pearls.

"Yes, so you've said, Mama. Several times." She waved Claramae away and turned to look at her mother. "Now, if you would tell me precisely what it is you can't find, perhaps I might be able to help?"

"The voucher, of course," Daphne said, plopping herself down on the bench at the bottom of Emma's bed and fanning herself with the ribbons on her gown. "The voucher for Almack's. We need to present it to gain admittance. I'm sure of that."

Emma relaxed. "Mama, I've already tucked it into my reticule. See? Nothing to fret about. And you look wonderful tonight, although are you quite sure about the turban?"

"Your grandmother swears it is expected of a widow escorting her daughter. She read it somewhere."

"Did Grandmama say it had to be purple?" Emma asked, privately thinking her mother, with her round face and flushed cheeks, greatly resembled a confectionery treat with plum sauce. "Your gown, after all, is green."

"I know, I know, but it's the only turban I have, and it's older than you, as it was once my mama's and she's been dead these thirty years. And it itches."

"Claramae?" Emma prompted, pointing to her mother. "Could you possibly perform one of your miracles on my mother's hair? Really, Mama, you're years too young for a turban. But we must hurry. His lordship was adamant about having us ready to leave by nine."

Emma stood up from the dressing table and walked over to the window as her mother sat down and Claramae began unpinning the offensive turban.

His lordship had said to be ready by nine. He had said many things at the dinner table this evening, most of them having to do with other strictures his imaginative mind had conjured up for all of them.

Sir Edgar was never to be a part of their party in Society, and would make himself scarce in the event the Grosvenor Square mansion was opened for any activities.

Emma had expected Sir Edgar to protest, but the man had looked nearly oppressed when he'd come late to the dining room, and had only nodded his agreement with the marquis's plan. In fact, that nod was the only animation Sir Edgar had shown. He'd pretty much just sat there and stared at his plate, and barely nibbled at his food.

Her grandmother, on the other hand, had been particularly vivacious as she sat at Sir Edgar's right. Talking nineteen to the dozen about this and that, regaling everyone with a fine imitation of Lord Boswick's lamentations about the sad state of his liver.

She'd had a sparkle in her eyes and a spring to her step as the ladies had retired to the drawing room, and then suddenly cried off from going along to Almack's because she had the headache. It certainly had come on suddenly, perhaps caused by Olive Norbert, who had been quiet through their meal (except for the volume she raised with her chewing, which was considerable).

Once out of earshot of the marquis, Olive had seemed to feel the need to empty her budget of several complaints.

"He says I can't come to the table no more," she'd spit angrily. "Who is he to say such a thing to me? Me, what's paid down good money to be here. Just because I don't have no hoity-toity ways about me."

Emma had reminded the woman that the marquis had promised to return her entire lease payment, and still allow her to remain in residence, which had calmed Olive somewhat, until she'd said, "And I can't go to no parties if you have them!" And then, shocking everyone greatly, she had run from the drawing room in tears.

"Mama?" Emma said now, remembering Olive's tearful flight. "Do you think I should speak to the marquis about Mrs. Norbert? She seemed quite overset to hear she won't be included in any small parties we might have here during the Season."

"Yes, that was odd, wasn't it?" Daphne frowned into the mirror as Claramae brushed her hair into a topknot. "Perhaps she wished to move in Society more than she let on?"

Emma came to a decision. "I'll talk to him. Sir Edgar, on the other hand, didn't seem to mind at all, although I longed to question the marquis, as Sir Edgar is, after all, a peer. But he's an odd sort, isn't he? Either out and about, or locked in his rooms."

Fanny, who had been reclining on a slipper chair in Emma's bedchamber, a cool cloth to her forehead (and faintly moaning every now and then), said, "Nothing wrong with Sir Edgar, gel. Leave him be. I like the man. We're going for a drive together tomorrow as a matter of fact. Shame we have to use that hulk of a coach. Do you think you could get his lordship to give us use of his curricle, Emma?"

"I highly doubt that, Grandmama," Emma said, knowing she would rather champion Mrs. Norbert than plead use of a gentleman's curricle and horseflesh. Especially since Cliff had asked that same favor at dinner and had his head nearly bitten off. "I don't think his lordship's magnanimity stretches that far."

"Then the coach it is. Probably better for what I have in mind anyway."

Emma's eyebrows lifted as she turned to look at Fanny. "Why? What are you planning, and do I really want to know?"

"I don't," Daphne said, patting at her hair as she peered into the mirror. "Thank you, Claramae. I feel much more the thing. I do hope it's proper. I know, I'll go find Thornley and beg his opinion."

"There she goes," Fanny said, lifting the cloth from her eyes as her daughter-in-law all but skipped out of the room. "Any day now she's going to tackle the poor fellow, and the next thing we know there'll be a clutch of little bastard butlers running around Clifford Manor, amusing themselves in polishing the silver." She shrugged, replaced the cloth. "Maybe I should sic one of the old roués on her instead of offering up a grandson to you. Would you mind one the less?"

Emma picked up her fine wool shawl and draped it around her shoulders, taking time to inspect her reflection in the pier glass. She looked tolerably well in white, although she longed for more color than debutantes were allowed. Still, the overall effect wasn't unpleasing. "Ten rather than eleven, as I'm already convinced that the King is rather above my touch? I think I should be able to sustain the loss."

"Don't be too generous, pet. Willie never married, so he's little use to us, and Dickie Harper had only daughters who produced more females. Florizel whispered to me that Bosey is all but under the hatches, and his whole family with him. We don't need to fall into another debt-ridden household."

"But I thought you said we'd be knee-deep in suitors, Grandmama."

Fanny readjusted the cloth over her eyes. "I did. But it may take some time. There's still some who haven't come crawling over here yet. And I've got other irons in the fire."

Emma walked over to the slipper chair and lifted the cloth, to stare into her grandmother's face. "Do I want to know about them? These other irons?"

Fanny grabbed the cloth and replaced it, then folded her arms on her stomach. "No, you do not. Now go away."

Emma tried again. "The marquis was not best pleased to see that parade of your victims today, Grandmama, so he'll be delighted when I tell him your plan hasn't been all that successful. As am I, I have to say. Will either of us like your new plan?"

Fanny didn't answer.

"Grandmama," Emma said, jamming her hands down on her hips. "I would consider it a kindness if, whatever grand idea you've taken into your head now, you discard it, along with your never-to-be-written memoirs. You could have some faith in me, you know. I'd like to think I might actually attract an eligible gentleman on my own."

"Ha! You'd need a whacking great dowry for that, gel, no matter how beautiful you might be. What dowry we have for you isn't enough to interest a second son." She lifted the cloth once more. "But you do look top of the trees tonight. Much like me in my grasstime, although my blue eyes were more the rage. Admirers you'll get on your own, but you need either my threatened memoirs or a whopping great dowry to get any of them to the altar."

Emma bit her bottom lip, knowing her grandmother was right. True love was for fanciful novels; in the *ton* marriages were more convenient than hot-blooded. "And you have irons in the fire about—about what? Another way to bring eligible admirers to the sticking point, or a way to gain me a dowry? Tell me, Grandmama. Tell me now, or I will leave the marquis and Mama both downstairs to cool their heels, because I will *not* go to Almack's, or anywhere else. I don't trust you."

"Smartest thing you ever said," Fanny told her, sitting up and swinging her feet down to the floor. "Go, and stop fretting. I said I have irons in the fire, not that we'll all be clapped in irons. And smile at the marquis. It wouldn't hurt your consequence any to have him drooling over you for the whole world to see."

"I...*drooling!* I would never...how could you? Isn't it enough that we're living under his roof? Poor man. I do have some conscience, you know. Oh, I'm leaving. But I warn you, Grandmama, do anything horrid and I will never forgive you."

"And I thought your mama was the dramatic one," Fanny said, rolling her eyes. "Now, go, go. I never held with this business of keeping a gentleman waiting."

An Evening at Almack's

Now for drinks, now for some dancing
with a good beat.
—Horace

IF ONE SALLIED forth into London, specifically searching for the most mundane, colorless, uninspired building in which to hold a weekly dance Assembly, ending up at Almack's would be considered a major triumph of discovery.

For anyone hoping for more than overheated, banal surroundings, aged musicians definitely past their prime, and refreshments seemingly designed to tempt the tastes of no one—well, then, welcome to Almack's.

But there was an *air* inside Almack's, variously perceived by those who entered through the hallowed portal. To the ladies, both hopeful mamas and nervous debutantes, it was the heady smell of the hunt, and the scent of Eligible Man. To the gentlemen, it was the tense atmosphere of the hunted, and if they trod carefully, their gazes ever vigilant, it was because of stories they'd heard about others of the hunted, and their ignominious captures.

Many a young miss could be heard to say that Almack's was a pitiful place, a crushing bore with rules that were Positively Medieval, and that those who attended were Desperate In The Extreme. These would be the young misses denied vouchers, who on Wednesday evenings during the Season spent their time cooling their heels at tame parties and gnashing their teeth, a lot.

Young men attended because their mamas insisted, or their papas rendered sage advice on the lines of, "You have to get yourself an heir, boy, so you may as well get it over with and get on with your life."

In any event, Almack's was the Marriage Mart, and both the females and males of the species approached it in full armor, alert and poised to pounce or retreat.

The Patronesses, and self-appointed Doyennes of Social Arbitration, wielded their power with the subtlety of peacocks on the strut. They decided who was eligible. They decided who was deserving. They decided who should be left out in the cold, to weep bitter tears of rejection.

They even decided when a debutante would be allowed to waltz, not only within the walls of Almack's, but anywhere in Society.

In short, in long, they were a starchy gaggle of self-important bullies who had somehow convinced the Polite World that they deserved to rule it. If nothing else, Morgan admired them for that, because setting yourself up for greatness only works if there are lesser minds who agree to worship at the altar you have constructed.

Daphne, who had listened to all of this from Morgan

as his crested coach inched along King Street, slowly approaching this dignified den of iniquity, nodding at all the appropriate and not so appropriate times, said at last, "How low do we curtsy to a Patroness, please?"

Emma, who was still smarting over the fact that the Marquis of Westham hadn't so much as blinked when she slowly descended the stairs in her finery—and she *did* look fine, she knew it—said, "We don't curtsy, Mama. We kneel, then kiss the hems of their garments."

"Even Sally?" Daphne asked, aghast. "Surely, as old chums from school, she wouldn't make me—oh!" She sat back against the velvet squabs and glared out the off-window. "That was exceedingly cruel of you, Emma."

"I'm sorry, Mama," Emma said, patting the woman's pudgy, gloved forearm. "I believe I must be out of sorts, and I aimed my barb at entirely the wrong target."

Morgan lifted one eyebrow and looked across the dimness of the coach. "Pardon me, ladies. Did someone call my name?"

Emma's palms itched to slap his supercilious face. "You could at least *pretend* that you see something even marginally laudable in the evening ahead, my lord. As it is, I suddenly feel not only moneygrubbing, but somehow grubby."

"Nonsense, Miss Clifford," Morgan said, picking a bit of nonexistent lint from his sleeve. "Grubby? I should say not. You look passably fine. You carry a reticule, not a net to cast over the first unwary male you see. We approach a jungle, surely, but you will hunt with your smile, your fluttering fan, your delightful repartee, your graceful step as you go down the dance. The money-grubbing, however, I would leave stand."

She looked down at her gown, covered as it was by her cloak, knowing that this was her third best gown, and if not of the first stare, at least fashionable in cut and color. Passably fair? How dare he! She was much more than passably fair.

Emma decided she would not respond to the marquis's obvious baiting of her, and merely shifted the subject to himself, and others of his ilk. If her voice dripped venom as she spoke, well, she couldn't help that, could she? "And which are you, my lord? A man avoiding matrimony, or one on the lookout for a fitting broodmare to give you sons, along with a large dowry?"

"Emma…dearest…" Daphne said, looking from her daughter to Morgan. "You are not being gracious."

"No, Mama, I'm not. But if he can attack me, I should be able to attack him back," Emma said, then winced when she realized how very juvenile that excuse sounded. "Moneygrubbing. It's insulting."

Morgan, noticing that the coach had stopped for what seemed like the last time, leaned over and opened the door, then kicked down the steps. "Sheath your claws, Miss Clifford, for we have arrived."

"Oh, yes," she said, rolling her eyes. "We will be in public in a few moments, won't we? Where we Cliffords are to sing your praises to the sky, and all of that drivel. I must have been out of my mind to agree to this charade."

"I'd agree, Miss Clifford, save that I would be agreeing to my own guilt in a truly mad scheme. But, as we are committed to this farce, please put a brave face on it and tackle the first eligible man you spy. Get yourself bracketed within the month, Miss Clifford, and I'll go so far as to buy you a lovely present. Something Wedgwood?"

"Go to the devil," Emma said as a liveried footman inserted his hand into the coach, to assist her down to the flagway.

Morgan assisted Daphne in descending, smiling as he realized that holding one's temper, at least for the moment, was giving him much more pleasure than did those minutes spent in his rooms earlier, where he had tossed not one, but two, vases at the wall. His temper, and his mood, improved with every spark that shot from Miss Clifford's lovely eyes, each insult that sprang from her lips.

Yes, he was enjoying watching her lose her temper, much more than he had ever enjoyed losing his own.

"Now, now, don't lose the reins on your temper, Sir Edgar, for it will do you no good, and may even prove injurious to your spleen, or so I've heard. Besides, I have been ranted and raved at by the best, and anger neither frightens me nor moves me. Now, I ask again, why should your brilliant scheme line only your pockets? Especially when it's already obvious that, between the two of us, mine is the superior brain."

"How so?" Sir Edgar asked, jumping up from his chair and beginning to pace.

Fanny smiled and began ticking off her reasons on her fingers. "One, I took one look at you that first day and knew you were up to something shifty and shady. Two, I found the key you so clumsily left lying about for me to find. Three, I saw what's in those chests. Four, after looking into those same chests, I deduced exactly what you are planning. Five—"

"Women! I detest women!" Sir Edgar said, which caused Fanny Clifford to sit back even more at her ease, her smile broad and satisfied, rather like a cat with canary feathers sticking out of the corner of her mouth. "But to demand to be my partner? You can't mean that."

"Yes, I can mean that, Sir Edgar. I *do* mean that."

Sir Edgar walked from one side of his bedchamber to the other and halfway back again, stopped in front of Fanny, held up one finger as he opened his mouth to say something, then shook his head and retreated to his bed, leaning back against the side of the mattress. "I can't believe this is happening. To *me*."

"I see no reason for you to fly up into the boughs, Sir Edgar, and hysterics are so fatiguing. All I'm suggesting is a simple partnership. I do not interfere with your aims. On the contrary, I will be bringing you new prospects. *Rich* prospects. You would prefer them rich, I imagine. And brick-stupid. I cannot begin to tell you the most prodigious length and breadth of my acquaintance with rich, brick-stupid men."

Sir Edgar, who had been feeling so very lucky after his afternoon with John Hatcher, knew himself to have been cast into doldrums of despair such as he hadn't known since that terrible day during the victory celebrations after Waterloo, when he had barely escaped being clapped in irons for attempting to sell Hyde Park to two very accommodatingly naive and thoroughly bosky visitors from Russia.

"I work alone," he said at last, but fatalistically, as he already knew further protest would do him no good. Fanny Clifford was a sort he recognized, almost a kindred spirit, and once she got the bit between her teeth, there was no stopping her.

"So do I, Sir Edgar, for the most part. And quite successfully, if I must say so myself. However, there can never be any such thing as too much success. That said, how much do you think we can make, from Hatcher and the others I will bring to you, chickens ready to be plucked?"

"Hatcher? How do you know about—oh, never mind. I mentioned him, didn't I? Do you ever miss a trick, Mrs. Clifford?"

"No, and you may call me Fanny, as long as we're

going to be cohorts in crime. *Edgar.*" She hoisted her slim body upright, ignoring the way her bony knees creaked, and refilled her glass from the bottle she'd carried with her to Sir Edgar's room after everyone had departed for Almack's. She held up the bottle. "Are you quite sure you don't want any? And there's more in the drawing room, should we still feel dry. The marquis keeps a tolerable cellar. There's not a bottle down there less than five years old."

"WHAT HAS IT BEEN, Westham? Five years? Sulking in the country, that's what I heard."

Morgan opened his mouth to say something, what, he wasn't quite sure, but he should have known better. Sally Jersey didn't really ask questions, not really, and if she did, she then answered them herself.

"Yes, that's it. Five years. After that duel with the dear Earl of Brentwood. Ah, Perry. I haven't seen him here in many a year. Do something about that, will you, Westham? I seem to remember that you two ran tame together. Until you pinked him. Quite a dashing scar. Where's yours?"

Morgan ignored that question, about the only one Sally Jersey couldn't answer for herself, thank God. "I'm here this evening, Lady Jersey, to—"

"Find yourself a bride," she finished for him, winking broadly, which served to make him grit his teeth. "About time, too. I imagine your poor mama has been nattering you to death, to find a wife and populate her nursery. Wants grandkiddies, I suppose. Most women do. But not me. What on earth would I do, being a grand-mother? I can't see it, can you? No, I can't see it. So. Don't you have anything to say for yourself?"

"I—" Morgan closed his mouth, shook his head and inclined his head to the countess. "Are you quite done, madam? I wouldn't wish to interrupt."

Lady Jersey slapped his arm playfully with her furled fan. "Impertinent pup. I'm never quite done, didn't you know that? Why, I haven't even begun to question you about the Cliffords. Dragged them here with you tonight, didn't you? Of course you did. I was friends with Daphne once, aeons ago. Childhood friends, you understand. Al-though she's older. She has to be older, I'm sure of that. I know I don't look that old. Do I look that old? No, of course not."

Morgan was getting the headache. "Lady Jersey," he said firmly, "I have approached you this evening to ask you to step over to speak with Miss Clifford for a few moments, lend her your great consequence, and give her permission to dance. If you would be so kind."

"Kind has nothing to do with it, Westham," Lady Jer-sey said, already heading across the uneven wooden dance floor in full sail, Morgan following in her wake. "This is what I do, and I have to do more of it, we all have to do more of it, or Almack's will go the way of so many wonderful things that were once here, and now are gone. But she's pretty enough, don't you think? And with you as her guardian, she should have no trouble bracketing herself in her first Season. You're not a stingy sort, so I'm going to presume that the dowry is more than sufficient?"

And there it was. He hadn't been inside Almack's above ten minutes, and his main worry of the day had been voiced by none other than a woman whose tongue fair ran on wheels.

If he said he was not actually Miss Clifford's guardian, it would be all over Mayfair by breakfast time tomorrow that his interest in the girl was not quite above-board.

If he said he was acting as her guardian but was not providing a dowry, he would be considered closefisted and mean, and still considered as fodder for any gossip that would have him cast as hardened seducer of innocent maidens.

If he said he was a totally avuncular friend, acting as her guardian, giving her a ball, and gifting her with a substantial dowry...well, any way he looked at the thing, there was no way he was going to win, was he?

"Miss Clifford!" Lady Jersey said, coming to rest in front of Emma, who had immediately dropped into a well-executed curtsy. "La, aren't we looking splendid this evening? Of course we are. Daffy?"

"Lady Jersey," Daphne said, dropping into a curtsy fit for royalty, the move ruined only when she hesitated at the bottom of it and began to drift to one side, so that Emma had to quickly reach down and steady her until she could regain her balance. "It is such an esteemed honor, a true condescension, a most rare treat and a greatly appreciated—"

"Oh, cut line, Daffy," Lady Jersey said, and Daphne obediently shut up. "Where's your turban? You're on the shelf, Daffy, you do know that, don't you? Of course, you do. It's the chit here we're to pop off, not you, you silly widgeon. And if not a turban, feathers, at the very least, don't you think? Of course, you do. Why, I have feathers in my hair, and I'm *years* your junior. Now, Lord Westham? Is there something you want to ask me? Of course, you—"

"Lady Jersey," Morgan interrupted hastily. "It is my greatest hope that you will graciously offer Miss Clifford here permission to dance."

Sally Jersey turned to look up at him, smiling. "A waltz is next, my lord. Do you wish permission for that, as well? You don't think that's a little fast? Of course, you do. But I don't. I love the waltz, just adore it. Miss Clifford?" she asked, turning back to Emma. "Do you waltz? Or has that lovely dance not yet made it to the hinterlands? Lord knows our fashions haven't quite made the trip, have they? Not that you don't look just fine but, between the two of us," she said, leaning close to Emma, "your mother's ensemble needs some updating. No turban? For shame."

"Thank you so very much, my lady," Morgan said quickly, as he watched Emma's eyelids narrowing even as her jaw seemed to set itself in a line that all but screamed: "Everybody down! The battle is about to commence!" He took Emma's hand in his. "Shall we dance, Miss Clifford?"

"Bring her back when you're done, my lord," Lady Jersey called after him. "I'll have eligible gentlemen all lined up to scribble their names on her dance card. It's what I do, you know. Of course, you do."

"WHAT AN INSUFFERABLE, arrogant, *mean* person."

"And redundant," Morgan added, stopping once he'd gained the dance floor. "Is she redundant? Of course, she is."

"Don't try to brighten my mood," Emma said as she walked into Morgan's light embrace, as waltzing did much resemble an embrace, even if the space between their bodies was kept to a prudent two feet. "I didn't like her the first moment she opened her mouth, and my opinion of her has not risen one small inch. How dare she insult my mother that way? No turban. Is *she* wearing a turban?"

"Of course she's not."

Emma glared up at him. "Please resist this urge you seem to have to attempt to be amusing. No, she doesn't wear a turban. And she's the older, you know. Mama is three years her junior, but she promised not to say anything because her ladyship says she has her consequence to consider, while Mama has no consequence at all. Why, if I were a man—"

"I would look dashed silly, out here on the dance floor with you," Morgan said, sweeping her into another turn.

She moved with a fluid grace, even as she glowered at him. "I suppose you will persist in thinking that you're hilarious, or that you're diverting me from what I really wish to do, which is to go back over there and—"

"Your steps are fine, Miss Clifford, and you bend to my lead quite graciously, but if you do not soon lose that scowl and begin to pretend you are enjoying yourself, I shall leave you here to die of embarrassment."

"You wouldn't dare. And it's not as if you're enjoying yourself. You're dancing with me out of protest, you know it, as do I, so don't pretend, or ask me to pretend with you. I see no reason to—"

"The entire roomful of inquiring eyes are on us, Miss Clifford."

"And don't interrupt me again. Sally Jersey is a vile, vicious—what did you say?"

"Ah, ah, don't stumble now, Miss Clifford. You were doing so well. Remember, your behavior reflects on me, your guardian."

All thoughts of Sally Jersey and turbans flew straight out of her head. He was saying again just what her grandmother had said. "My guardian? Never."

"I beg to disagree. Sally Jersey is even now racing through the assembled guests, spreading that very news."

"Well, I won't have it."

"I don't want it, either, Miss Clifford, but there you are. Now, stop scowling."

This was good, arguing with him. Arguing with him kept her mind away from thoughts of holding his hand, of having his hand pressed against the back of her waist, of laughing with him, for he really was rather funny, once he unbent himself enough to smile. But his smile unnerved her, cut into her resolve. As long as she argued with him, she could refuse herself permission to think about him at all. For full seconds at a time.

Emma kept her feet moving, how, she didn't know. "People actually are being told that I am your ward?"

"It would be their natural conclusion, yes. Do you know, Miss Clifford, after my initial horror, I began thinking about that part. You, as my ward. You, subject to my approval. Why, your suitors will have to apply to me before they can hope to court you. One of them will actually be asking me for your hand in marriage."

He swept her into one last turn, then kept hold of her hand as the music faded away. It was a good thing the dance was done, because Emma was fairly sure her feet had just gone numb. "You…you will be *in charge* of me?"

"In charge? Yes, I like the sound of that. And you really should call me *my lord* more often. Respect, you understand. Indeed, it would behoove you, Miss Clifford, to be very nice to me. In private as well as in public. You see, when you get right down to it, I have your life right here, in the palm of my hand."

He held out his hand, and she glared at it, then winced involuntarily as he slowly and deliberately closed that hand into a fist.

"I didn't see Thornley as we left, my lord," she said as he guided her back to her mother. "Have you killed him yet?"

Morgan looked sideways at her, slightly confused by this shift in topic. "No, I haven't. Why?"

"Because then I shall have the pleasure, that's why," she said, tugging her hand free and sitting down next to her mother.

"You forgot to curtsy," Morgan told her as he bowed. "Appearances. My reputation. Be nice, Miss Clifford."

And then he walked away, a new spring to his step, a smile on his face. He felt good. Vindicated, although he didn't know why that particular term had crept into his mind.

He just knew he was enjoying himself, watching Miss Emma Clifford with her hackles up, clearly not enjoying herself half as much as she must have supposed when the voucher first arrived at the mansion.

His smile lasted until he'd found himself a convenient post to lean against, at which point he turned, cast his gaze in the general direction of where he had left Miss Clifford, only to realize that he couldn't see her.

He couldn't see her because there had to be at least a dozen young fools surrounding her, vying for her attention, clamoring to scribble their names on her dance card. Why, one gentleman—his shirt points ridiculously high—was actually holding that dance card over his head, and other idiots were jumping up, to grab at it.

Disgusting.

This undue attention was thanks to her conniving grandmother, no doubt. That could be one reason. Or Sally Jersey had gotten out the word that the Marquis of Westham was sponsoring Miss Clifford for the Season, complete with a fat dowry.

Or it could be that the rest of London's gentlemen were not blind, and they all had realized that Miss Emma Clifford was one of the most beautiful, fascinating women to have ever set foot in Society.

Suddenly Morgan's evening wasn't feeling quite the success it had earlier.

"HE'S FINE ENOUGH, I suppose, but we'll never be much of a success with only the one," Cliff said, hanging a small but vicious looking set of spurs from his bedpost.

He wasn't quite sure how it had happened. One moment he was contemplating his bleak future, and the next he was carrying home a cage with a gamecock in it, all his mama's pin money gone for the bird and a cage and a bag of feed. And these spurs. They truly were fine spurs. Sharp, too.

Cliff sucked at his fingertip, the one he'd cut on one of the spurs when he'd tested its point.

Riley, who had finally succeeded in shoving the angry gamecock back into its wooden cage, stripped off his heavy gloves and sat back on his haunches. "And I'll be telling you again, Cliffie, Leaky Ben said as how this one here is his best cock. If we lose with him, he'll not be trusting us with the rest, he won't. He wouldn't be selling us any of them, exceptin' that his missus says she'd done with him unless he finds himself another line of work, as it were. Now don't you go leaving him out of his cage again, all right?"

Cliff, looking slightly abashed, and still with his finger in his mouth, said, "I just wanted to pet him. I named him Harry."

"Saints alive, you don't name a fine fighting cock Harry. Killer. That'd be more the like. But you don't name him nothing. You poke him with a stick, if you do anything. How's he gonna fight, if he thinks he's a part of your bloomin' family? Named him Harry? You're a looby, Cliffie."

It did not occur to Cliff Clifford that this servant was treating him as an inferior. It did not occur to him because Cliff Clifford was young and inexperienced, and Riley had impressed him all hollow when he'd dragged him along twisted alleyways, to Leaky Ben's tumbledown hovel.

To Cliff, Riley was a man of the world. Even better,

together, they would become rich. Rich, followed by independent, followed by not having to take orders from a gaggle of females who still thought he should be in leading strings. Ha! He'd show them!

"It smelled pretty rank inside Leaky Ben's," Cliff said now, "so I couldn't stay too long. Not long enough to count all the cages. How many cocks does he have?"

Riley stood up and grinned. "I always been wanting to say one, but then I've always thought it amusin' that a man could go round braggin' that he had twenty cocks. One's all a good man needs, if you take my meaning."

Cliff giggled, because he was of an age and inclination that found such coarse nonsense amusing. Besides, he had gotten himself laid down and taken care of a few nights ago by Stutterin' Betty, and if it had only taken five minutes and one pound six-pence of his allowance, it still had made a man of him.

Riley pointed to the wine decanter Cliff had ordered up to his room, and the younger man nodded his permission.

Riley was enjoying himself, he was. Hobnobbing with the gentry, calling Mr. Clifford Cliffie, just like they were great chums, drinking wine instead of penny-a-pint gin from his favorite pub in Piccadilly. It was a bloody portent, that's what it was, a portent of great things to come. A better life. Cock of the Walk, that's what he'd be soon.

Or had it never occurred to the young looby over there that he'd be going back to the country at the end of the Season, forced there by his mama, while Riley would be left behind, with his cockfighting business bringing in money hand over fist?

"Twenty-five, he's got. Two dozen even, plus Harry here," Riley said when Cliff repeated his question. "But we start with the one, and when Leaky Ben sees how well we do, he'll let us have the rest. We fight 'em, giving Leaky Ben half our winnings until we pay him the blunt he wants. From then on, Cliffie, we're swimming in the deep end of the gravy boat, all by ourselves." He lifted his wineglass in a salute. "Ah, 'tis a great day this, boyo."

Cliff picked up the cage by its handle and placed it in his small dressing room, closing the door on the beginnings of his fortune. "And you're sure Claramae won't cry rope on us when she comes to take care of my room?"

"I'll handle Claramae," Riley said with a wink. "Got the girl fair eating out of my hand, I do. Now, first contest for us is tomorrow night, down off Threadneedle Street, in the cellars of the Cock and Woolpack."

Cliff nodded. "Um…what exactly do we do?"

Riley rolled his eyes. "All right, listen up. You brings Harry in, see, whilst I come in separate, and see you, and make a big to-do about what a fine cock you got there. I say I want to wager some blunt on him, and you take the bet. Don't be letting anyone else take the bet, because between us we don't got the blunt for it, and if Harry here gets kilt, we'll be in big trouble."

"Gets killed?" Cliff stole a look toward the closed door to his dressing room. "But…he'll be wearing spurs. He won't get killed."

"Right," Riley said, rolling his eyes once more. Heaven preserve him from idiots. "But the cock he fights will have his own spurs, don't you know. They ain't being thrown into the pit to dance with each other, Cliffie. This is a dangerous business, this is."

"Oh. Right," Cliff said, knowing it was too late to re-think his commitment to going into business for himself. "I understand that. And, after Harry wins, what do we do next?"

"Why, we fight him again. And this time, others will be bettin' on him as well. Harry wins, we start getting rich. We gets the rest of Leaky Ben's cocks, and we get richer."

Cliff nodded. "Where…where are we going to keep the rest of the cocks?"

Riley grinned, spread his arms. "It's a hulking great pile, this is. There's lots of rooms nobody even thinks to use."

EMMA STOOD with her back to the outside wall as she hid on the balcony, longing for a respite from smiling, and chatting inanely about the weather, and having her toes trod on by gentlemen who obviously found it beyond their scope of achievements to both dance and converse at the same time.

She'd been introduced to, and danced with, Lord Boswick's brother's second son, a rather spotty faced grandnephew of Sir John's, Lord Beattie's grandson (doing her best to keep her expression blank when he'd introduced himself as "Beany's off-shoot," as it had been Lord Beattie's note from her grandmother that she had read before Riley had taken it back again).

That these "swains" were dancing attendance on her on orders from their elders did nothing to encourage Emma that she was making any splash of her own, on her own.

But then there were the rest of them. Seven, by her last count, who seemed to owe nothing to her grandmother's machinations.

That had been lovely, except that two of them had been almost embarrassingly pointed with their questions about the marquis, and the fact that he was her guardian. She had at first wondered if the odious man had actually picked out the worst of the worst in the ballroom and sicced them all on her, but it hadn't taken her long to realize that there was another truth—one that was even worse.

These men had been fortune hunters. She knew that, because within breaths of gushing at how above all things wonderful were her lively gray eyes, her flawless complexion, the exquisite tilt of her head…they all had found a way to bring the conversation around to the size of her dowry.

That's when Emma had pleaded fatigue to her last partner, sent him off to fetch her some lemonade, and then escaped to the balcony the moment the man's back was turned.

How could she not have realized sooner? If the wealthy Marquis of Westham had taken it into his head to be her guardian for the Season, then naturally he would have gifted her with a dowry. A considerable dowry, as he had his own reputation to uphold.

No wonder he was so unhappy with her. Not only had he discounted her rental fees as an insulting pittance, he now had to house them all, feed them all and, horror of horrors, actually *pay* to get himself shed of her.

Why hadn't she realized all of this sooner? She'd certainly had enough hints, from her grandmother, from the marquis himself.

The moneygrubbing, however, I would leave stand.

"Oh, how did this happen?" she asked herself, hugging her arms around her waist. "And what do I do now?"

"If I might be so bold," came a male voice from the shadows, "we could begin with finding another hidey-hole, one not quite so public."

Emma swallowed down hard and peered into the darkness. "Who's there?"

A well-dressed gentlemen stepped out of the shadows, then performed a most elegant leg before rising once more to say, "Jarrett Rolin at your service, Miss Clifford. Oh, yes, I have discovered your name. How, you might ask? It was simple. I simply inquired of the first peach-fuzzed idiot I encountered that he give me the name of the most beautiful woman in the ballroom. Your name instantly sprang from his lips."

Emma inspected the man as he spoke, beginning with his voice, which was rather deep, and faintly sinister. Oh, not really sinister. Mysterious. Yes, that would be a better word.

And he was handsome, if her second glance also told her he was older than she had first supposed. Forty, at the least, which she would have considered ancient, especially with the snow-white wings at his temples that contrasted so with his very black hair, except that he didn't seem ancient in the least.

His eyes were green, a most bewitching color, and they seemed to twinkle in the moonlight.

"Mr. Rolin," Emma said, racing into speech and into a curtsy, both of which she suddenly realized she had sadly neglected as she felt herself dazzled by this exotic, mysterious creature. "I'm afraid I cannot take you up on your kind offer to find another hidey-hole, or else my mother will commence making the rounds of the ballroom, calling out my name in her agitation. That could prove embarrassing."

Mr. Rolin smiled, exposing two rows of very white, straight teeth. "Yes, mothers can always be depended upon to be embarrassing. Mine, rest her soul, once called me *Precious* in front of three of my school chums I'd brought home with me from Eton." He sighed theatrically. "I had to thoroughly trounce all three of them before they'd desist in addressing me as *Precious* at every opportunity."

Emma giggled, because the story was funny, and because she could not imagine anyone as imposing as Mr. Rolin being called *Precious*. "My mother used to call me Emmie-baby, which wasn't too terrible, and my grandmother still refers to me as that *pernicious brat* when the spirit moves her. Families, even loving ones, can be a trial."

"As can be evenings at Almack's, Miss Clifford, or have I misunderstood your reason for being out here on your own? Which you shouldn't be, by the way. And I shouldn't be speaking with you, as we have not yet been formally introduced."

"Oh," Emma said, realizing Mr. Rolin was correct. "Forgive me. I'm more used to country dances, where everyone knows everyone else, and manners are much more free. I suppose Lady Jersey, if she were to see us together, would be justified in withdrawing my voucher. And I also wonder," she said, smiling, "why that doesn't upset me as it should."

"Perhaps because you are so clearly a cut above the majority of the insipid ladies inside, and find the blatant matchmaking abhorrent to your finer sensibilities?"

"Oh, my, that sounds so very flattering to me, Mr. Rolin," Emma said honestly. "But, unfortunately, that *is* why I am here this evening, and why I have traveled to London. Surely it does not come as a shock that a miss of marriageable age has come to town in hopes of finding herself a husband?"

"Ah, candor. How refreshing, Miss Clifford. Although it is not every man that appreciates such honesty. Please, may I escort you back inside before your dear mama mounts a search? But only if you promise to drive out with me tomorrow at five."

Emma took his offered arm. "It would be my pleasure, Mr. Rolin. Um…do you know if anyone in your family is acquainted with my grandmother? Fanny Clifford?"

Mr. Rolin shook his head. "No, I can't say that the name is familiar, and my parents are dead these many years, so I cannot, I'm afraid, apply to them. Does it matter? Will I be turned away if your grandmother does not know me?"

"On the contrary, Mr. Rolin," Emma told him, smiling up into his face. "I would say that not knowing my grandmother makes you eminently welcome to call. Oh, do you know where we are staying?"

"Dear me. I fear I forgot to ask a most important question," he said, walking with her down the line of chairs, to where Daphne sat, looking flustered as she cast her gaze around the ballroom, obviously on the lookout for her chick. "Where would that be?"

"The Marquis of Westham's mansion in Grosvenor Square, Mr. Rolin. Do you know it?"

"I know his lordship," Mr. Rolin said, inclining his head to the left. "As a matter of fact, I do believe he's that gentleman approaching now, with the rather fierce scowl on his face."

He withdrew his arm from Emma and bowed toward the marquis. "Westham, your servant, and all that rot."

"Rolin," Morgan bit out shortly. "I did not realize you and my ward had been introduced. I was just looking for her. Thank you for returning her to her mother."

"How remiss of you, Westham, to lose your hold on the reins. But it was my pleasure, as always, to take them up in your stead. It has been a long time, hasn't it?"

"Not long enough," Morgan bit out, and Emma had to control a gasp at his words, at his tone. "Now, if you'll excuse us, I wish to have a word with my ward."

Mr. Rolin bowed low over Emma's hand as he gifted her with another look at his, at the moment, amused-looking green eyes. "Until tomorrow, Miss Clifford. I shall count the hours." And then he turned to the marquis and bowed yet again. "Always a delight, Westham," he said, then melted away into the crowd.

The tension that had filled the air when Westham approached did not go with him.

"Excuse me, please," Emma said just as she was certain Morgan was going to speak to her, undoubtedly to say something cutting, "but I see Mr. Leverton approaching. I had promised him this next set, I believe." She opened the card tied to her wrist. "Yes. Yes, indeed, my lord. Mr. Leverton. You do approve of Mr. Leverton? His great-uncle was great friends with my grandmother."

Morgan sneered, and it didn't improve the scowl that was already marring his handsome face. "A blackmailed swain. And that doesn't bother you, Miss Clifford?"

"On the contrary, my lord. You know that old saying, the more the merrier. It would appear that my grandmother has been very merry in her time, and I am reaping the benefits."

She stepped forward, waving to Mr. Leverton, a rather rotund redhead who would probably do himself a great service to give in and have himself fitted for spectacles. "Yoo-hoo, Mr. Leverton. Over here."

"We'll talk later," Morgan whispered to her. "And there will be no drive tomorrow with Jarrett Rolin."

"We won't, my lord, and there most definitely will," Emma said, then all but ran to intercept Mr. Leverton, who was about to trip over a potted palm.

"I WILL SAY AGAIN, Fanny, I see no reason for the two of us to drive out together tomorrow," Sir Edgar said as he and his newly acquired Adventuress sat at their ease in the drawing room, having graduated from his lordship's wine to warmed snifters of his lordship's brandy.

"And I will say again, Edgar, that we have to establish which of my acquaintances would appear to be the easiest pigeons to pluck. You have already secured Mr. Hatcher, and I commend you for that, but you are thinking entirely too conservatively. One pigeon, when there is an entire flock of idiots out there?"

"It never pays to be too greedy, Fanny," Edgar said, remembering how quickly he had expanded his thoughts to greater profits when gulling John Hatcher had proved so simple. "And, if you know these gentlemen so well, I cannot see why you would wish my opinion."

"I don't require it, not really," Fanny said honestly as she stuck out her legs and rested her small feet on the low table between the couches. "But, as I do know these gentlemen, they'll want to see proof, for one thing, and they won't believe that I have discovered the alchemists' formula for turning base metals into gold. Would you?"

Sir Edgar looked at her, sitting low on her spine and very much at her ease, her bony ankles exposed, and crossed one over the other, her snifter of brandy balancing on her concave belly. "I suppose not."

"Good man, Edgar. I knew you'd see the sense of my argument. Now, show me again."

He rolled his eyes. "You've already seen it three times, Fanny. It hasn't changed." But he reached into his pocket and extracted the small bag, then tossed it to her.

"Curious how heavy it is," Fanny said, holding on to her snifter with one hand, and dumping the misshapen golden lump into her lap. "I know you swore it's real gold, but I have to tell you, Edgar, if it weren't, it would still convince me. Must be worth a good five hundred pounds or more. Where did you get it?"

"Let me just say that several of the ladies I befriended over the years were generous with presents. I melted a few of them down. In either form, watch fob, ring or lump of gold, I have not lost a bent penny."

"Oh, you bugger, you," Fanny said, then laughed, a faintly evil sounding cackle. "Edgar, my man, we're going to have us some fun."

"Fun I've had aplenty, Fanny," he told her solemnly. "It's money I'm looking for now."

Fanny hefted the heavy nugget. "We're all looking for something, Edgar. We're all looking for something."

PERRY SHEPHERD, Earl of Brentwood, had made his entrance only moments before eleven, a time after which no one was admitted to Almack's.

He'd been to his club, several of his clubs, with no success. He couldn't quite believe his luck when he'd chanced to look out his carriage window and espied the Westham crest on a coach parked around the corner from King Street, and he certainly had trouble believing that he'd find Morgan propping up a pillar at Almack's. But he was on the hunt, and could not overlook any possibility.

The Patronesses hopefully sent him a voucher every year, and every year he tossed it into the fire, but he'd had no worries that he would be turned away because he hadn't carried one of the silly things with him when he'd mounted the steps to the hallowed portal. He was, after all, eminently qualified Marriageable Material.

Thank goodness he had worn breeches, because of an earlier commitment he'd deserted as soon as possible without insulting his hostess, for no gentlemen, no matter how eligible, entered Almack's in pantaloons. Perhaps the very thought gave the Patronesses the vapors, or perhaps they merely liked putting out hoops, and then watching the gentlemen of the *ton* leap through them.

Paying little attention to the stir his arrival had made among the mamas set to pop off their daughters to the best title, estates, and fortune they could find, Perry halted three steps inside the ballroom, put his quizzing glass to his eye—just because he liked to do that—and allowed his always-alert yet languid-appearing gaze to skim over the assembled guests.

What a crushing bore. Indeed, more and more, life was a crushing bore. No wars left to fight. No worlds left to conquer. A clutch of acquaintances, but no real friends, not since Morgan Drummond had fled to the country and taken to his bed, or whatever it was tortured idiots did these days.

"Aha!" Perry exclaimed as he spied out his old friend standing halfway down the dance floor, leaning against a pillar and scowling at anyone who dared to look at him. Perry thought, if he looked hard enough, he might actually be able to discern the dark cloud hanging over the man's head.

Allowing his quizzing glass to drop to his waist, supported as it was by a thin black riband, the Earl of Brentwood leisurely sauntered down the floor and presented himself to Morgan, bowing low, then saying, "I see you've elevated that horrid scowl of yours to even greater heights than when last we met, good friend. What's sticking in your craw tonight, may I ask?"

Morgan didn't react at once, because he had long since trained himself not to react to most things—another reason he was so very put out by Miss Emma Clifford.

Instead, he slowly raked his eyes up and down and up again, taking in Perry Shepherd's appearance. Same thick, faintly unruly blond hair, same amused green eyes, same square, chiseled jaw that kept him from being too pretty. Same tall, graceful frame, with his broad shoulders and long straight legs. Same flair for flattering his tailor.

Five-inch-long, crescent-shaped scar on his left cheek, just above that chiseled chin.

That was new, only five years old.

"What next, Perry?" Morgan said, pushing himself away from the pillar, to bow to his old friend. "You pull out a glove from somewhere in that ragtag rig-out some tradesman talked you into, and slap my face, challenge me to a duel?"

"A duel?" Perry smiled, and the scar pulled slightly at his cheek, which did nothing to mar his handsomeness, but only made him look rather rakish. "Good God, man, why on earth would I do that?" He spread his arms. "And I'm hardly dressed for it, although my tailor might take umbrage with your description of my ensemble and challenge you to darning needles at dawn."

"It's a nasty scar, Perry," Morgan said, knowing he had two nasty scars of his own, but not so visible.

"On the contrary, my good fellow, I'll have you know that this little beauty mark has been the making of me. The ladies adore it, you understand. In point of fact, I also believe myself to be quite dashing. But, then, I always have thought that," he said, leaning closer to Morgan. "Now, stop scowling, man, and greet your old friend with more than an insult."

Morgan relaxed, but only slightly. "I've missed your idiocy," he admitted. His smile faded. "But the fact of the matter, Perry, is that I damn near killed you, and you damn near killed me."

"Oh, hardly *killed*, Morgan. We neither of us had the aim for killing. But I've been meaning to ask you something about that argument we had. A question that's been niggling at me for years."

"Ask me what? Why I left London? I would think that would be perfectly clear. I was not fit to be with civilized people, not with my violent temper. Not when that temper had almost cost another man his life, and had cost me a friendship I'd treasured."

Perry looked at Morgan for a full minute, then began to laugh. He laughed so hard, and so long, that several heads turned in their direction, only to look away again as they encountered Morgan's expression.

"That's it? *That's* why you left? Always said you were a hotheaded skipbrain," Perry said at last. "Blister me, Morgan, we were both so drunk we were reeling. Your temper be damned, tempers had nothing to do with our duel. We were idiots, more than three sheets to the wind, and we did a stupid thing. As I think I've already said, we couldn't have killed each other, not the way we were reeling and blinking and—was that you or me?—casting up our accounts all over the grass as the seconds conferred. Hell, man, we were so deep in our cups we were lucky to have pinked each other at all. Which leads me to my question, if you're done being a jackass. I mean, you should be. You've had five years."

Morgan felt the weight of his guilt sliding from his shoulders, and only then realized how heavy that guilt had been. "You're mad, do you know that? You should hate me. I swung so wildly, I could have taken your eye."

"And I swung so wildly after *you* swung so wildly and ended with your back to me, that I'm willing to wager you had to travel home to Westham on your belly. It was your backside I got, wasn't it?"

Morgan grinned. "I sat on pillows for a month, damn your hide. I only admit to the shoulder wound, thank you, even if it was self-inflicted, as I fell on my blade."

"A pair of bloody fools," Perry said, polishing his quizzing glass with the lace on his cuff.

"Very bloody, as I recall it. Your cheek was laid open

to the bone. Now, what did you want to ask me? I think we've covered all the most embarrassing details."

"Save one, my friend. What *was* that girl's name?"

"You don't remember, either?" Morgan asked, chuckling.

Perry laughed, then sobered. "All I remember, Morgan, is Jarrett Rolin, who acted as your second. He and Freddie were supposed to be the cool heads that talked us out of that stupid duel. Freddie told me later that Rolin refused to discuss a calmer settlement. He was laughing at us, old friend, and prodding us on to fight, just so that we could amuse him more. If we had died, either or both of us, I imagine he would not have been able to control his mirth. Sadly, I didn't figure that out until I was sober once more, nursing my wound, and you were gone, but that's what Rolin did."

"Yes, I know. I also came to that conclusion. Our good friend, our mentor in the ways of the world, I believe he called himself back then. There would have been no duel if I hadn't listened to him. Although I blame myself, because I *did* listen."

"We were so raw, so gullible, so ready for his praise and guidance, the bastard. He's still here, you know, welcomed everywhere, and still playing his nasty little games. I think he sees all of Society as his puppets, and he holds the strings. Personally, I cut a wide berth around him, hoping one day he'll meet someone who pulls *his* strings. I want to be there to watch, see how he reacts when he becomes the butt of the joke."

"Well, don't look for him around me. I've already encountered him this evening, and made it clear that I want nothing to do with him."

"Not good, Morgan, not good, although, having played with you, with me, he probably won't come back to play again," Perry said, shaking his head. "The man has looks and a powerful family name, and he has found life to bore him in the extreme. He got the pair of us easily enough, fuzzy-cheeked fools that we were, and when he became bored with us, probably because we were too easy to be a challenge, he set us against each other, just to watch what would happen. Mostly, I've decided, he only wants what he cannot have. Unfortunately, as far as I can see, he has yet to find anything, or anyone, he cannot have."

Morgan looked across the dance floor to see Miss Clifford going down the dance floor with a safe enough looking young gentleman. He wondered if she would become Rolin's next quarry—because of her beauty, because of her "connection" to him—and decided that would never, never ever happen. He would not allow it, even if she was hell-bent on destroying herself.

He took Perry's arm. "What do you say we find ourselves a corner and two glasses. Then you can tell me why on earth you're here. You can't be on the lookout for a wife. Not you. I remember your sentiments on that subject."

"Too true. Bracketing myself is the last thing on my

mind, now or ever. I came here to find you," Perry said as he lifted two glasses of inferior wine from a servant's tray and walked alongside Morgan.

"I beg your pardon? I'm only back in town for a single day. How did you know that I—oh, God." Morgan closed his eyes for a moment, then opened them again. "Sir Willard Humphrey, former Minister of the Admiralty. He's your uncle, isn't he?"

"Always the sharp one, Morgan. Yes, Uncle Willard summoned me this afternoon, all atwitter. He told me all about this blackmailing old biddy, and then set me out to romance the granddaughter, mentioning that the chit was residing under your roof, of all places, that you were back in town. Hang Uncle Willard's indiscretions, I thought, and hang the chit. I need to find my friend."

"I'm glad you did. So, you're to be your uncle's sacrificial lamb, Perry? Would it help to say that none of this is my fault, that you are looking at a truly innocent as well as oppressed victim? Oh, and if you remember Thornley, I should probably tell you that if he turns up missing, I will be the one responsible."

Perry handed one glass to Morgan, then pounded his friend on the back. "I'm supposing this is going to be a long story, and one I can't wait to hear. Then you can point me out to the Clifford girl, and I can prostrate myself at her feet, as per my orders. What's wrong with her, by the by? Horse teeth? A squint? Spots?"

Morgan sort of sucked on his lips as he pointed out

onto the dance floor. "See the dark-haired one? Pearls in her hair?"

Perry lifted his quizzing glass to his eye just as Miss Clifford gracefully tripped past, smiling broadly at her companion in a rousing Scottish reel. "Good God, what a sweet morsel! Bless you, Uncle Willard, bless you. I see I shall soon have to desert you, Morgan. To gallantly sacrifice myself for mine uncle, you understand."

Morgan, so happy to have encountered his friend again, so happy that they were friends again, had to fight back a sudden urge to plant a facer square on that friend's grinning mouth.

THORNLEY WALKED through the halls of the mansion, doing his nightly inspection of the premises. He made mental notes that the maids were to pay particular attention to his lordship's bedchamber tomorrow, as well as redistribute the remainder of their guests to the third and fourth floors, away from the marquis, who couldn't possibly wish to encounter them with any regularity.

That would take Sir Edgar and Mrs. Fanny Clifford up one flight, along with Mr. Clifford, putting all of his tenants where he could count their noses without having to chase all over the mansion to find them.

Although Mrs. Fanny Clifford, spry as she was, might have some difficulty with all those stairs, which would keep her downstairs, on the first floor and in the draw-ing room most of the day. Thornley mentally wiped the slate in his mind, keeping Fanny in her current room.

As long as she would remain on that floor, he might as well leave Sir Edgar there as well. Only Mr. Clifford would be moved, first thing tomorrow morning.

Miss Clifford and her dear mother were already on the third floor, which was very proper, as they were both un-married ladies, and should not be sleeping just down the hallway from his lordship. Not that his lordship would be interested in the two older ladies, and he didn't seem at all attracted to Miss Clifford.

Yes, that would work. Having mentally rearranged and then rearranged his guests again, Thornley felt safe in heading downstairs and inviting Mrs. Timon to join him in his small parlor for a glass of sherry. The dear woman was delighted to be back in harness, as it were, released from the confines of the kitchen and given a full staff to bully and direct, as well as menus to plan, sheets to order washed, and silver dragged out to be polished—all by somebody other than her.

Thornley was slightly concerned for Claramae, who was not best pleased with the idea of sharing her attic room with another maid, but he had settled that by sug-gesting that, as she was acting as lady's maid in any event, she could sleep on the cot in the dressing room Miss Emma and her mother shared.

It had been a long day. A distressing day, but everything seemed to be in order now. Except for one small problem—and there he was now.

"Riley, stop right there."

The footman did as he was told, for Thornley's voice brooked no argument, and turned to see the butler advancing on him down the hallway. "Top o' the evening to you, Mr. Thornley. You'd be wanting something?"

Thornley stopped two feet from Riley, tucked his hands behind his back and looked down on the smaller, younger man. "What's that smell? You smell like a barnyard, Riley."

Riley bobbed his head, his quick Irish mind working nineteen to the dozen. "Yes, Mr. Thornley, and I was just going off to wash myself up of the stink. Plucking chickens in the kitchens I was, to help Claramae." He winked at Thornley. "Kind of sweet on her, Mr. Thornley."

Well now, there was a bald-faced lie, because Claramae had been released from all duties save some light cleaning and serving the Clifford ladies. Riley, tripping about town at Mr. Clifford's heels, couldn't know that. But Thornley did. His expression did not change, although he began rocking back and forth on his heels as he gazed penetratingly at the footman, who was smiling at him as if he believed himself to be the most amenable, most open and honest creature in the world.

"At midnight, Riley? You were plucking chickens at midnight? In your full livery?"

All right, so it wasn't easy to gull Mr. Thornley, but

Riley was willing to give it another shot. "It's late for such work, I know, Mr. Thornley, but I was that busy, trailing after Mr. Clifford just like his lordship told me to do. I'm to stick to him like mustard plaster, sir, so says his lordship. Leaves me precious time for cozying up to Claramae, but I do the best I can. Sir."

"We're fully staffed now, Riley," Thornley reminded the footman. "I could let you go and not notice the loss. I could have let you go two weeks ago, and not noticed the loss."

"And don't I know it, sir. Thank you for keeping my miserable self, sir," Riley said, inwardly stringing up Thornley by his toes, over a pit of vipers. "Sends money home to my sister every quarter, I do, and she and the kiddies depends on that something fierce. Keep you in their prayers, they do, every night. You'd tear up, sir, to hear the bitty ones, praising your name."

"Really? I might remind you that I do not appreciate being lied to, Riley, and you cannot play on my heart-strings with that piece of nonsense in any event. Now, where did Mr. Clifford go to this evening?"

"Like I'll tell his lordship, it was very tame tonight, what with me riding herd on the boy, keeping his toes on the straight and narrow and such. Just a few bottles cracked at the Oxford Arms, down in Warwick Lane. Interesting spot, the Arms, Mr. Thornley. They've got themselves a hearse there, willing to carry a body anywhere in England. We're thinking they must pack it with ice from their own kitchens, don't you think, Mr. Thornley? Stables are right up against the London Wall, snuggled in there all right and tight. Mr. Clifford inspected the hearse up close, saying something about how his grandmother would fit in there right and tight. Amusing sort, Mr. Clifford."

"I see. And did his lordship tell you why you're to report Mr. Clifford's activities to him?"

"No, sir. Just that I was to keep the young mister outta trouble. That's me, I can do that."

"Yes, thank you, Riley. His lordship has set the fox to watch the pigeons," Thornley said, then turned on his heels and went seeking Mrs. Timon, who had th the chest containing the headache powders.

EMMA WAS CERTAIN her cheeks were going to wither and fall off if she had to smile one more time, her toes were going to run away in protest if they were stepped on by another dancing partner, and her stomach had declared that the meager refreshments served at Almack's were first swept up from the street before they were put on plates and offered to the unwary.

She stifled a yawn and wondered at the hour as she sat beside her mama, inspecting her dance card. It must have gone midnight an hour ago. Only two sets left, and she could go home, let down her hair—one of the pins Claramae had stuck in her coiffure was digging into her skull. She could take off this gown, kick off her dancing slippers and collapse into her bed, not rising until Friday, at the earliest.

"Who will be partnering you in the next set?" her mama asked her, peering at Emma's dance card. "You're quite the Sensation of the Evening, my dear. I always knew it, but to see it? Well, I am So Very Happy for you."

"Thank you, Mama," Emma said, fully aware that her rather stunning popularity arose from two sources: her grandmother's blackmailing scheme, and word of the supposed dowry bestowed on her by the marquis.

Neither piece of knowledge did much for her wish of coming to town and making a brilliant match. In fact, she was hard-pressed at the moment to remember why she thought being married would solve all her problems, all the problems of her family.

It was as her grandmother had said: never forget for a moment that marriage includes being shackled to a man. And if tonight's assortment of gentlemen was representative of the rest of London's gentlemen, she'd rather remain a spinster until she died, surrounded by her coterie of cats and small pug dogs.

"As a matter of fact, Mama, I have no partner for this dance. I deliberately kept it open, so that Mr. Rolin could ask me, but it would seem he is gone."

Daphne pursed her lips disapprovingly.

"What's wrong?" Her mama so seldom disapproved of anything.

"Well, dear, it's not for me to say…"

"You're my mama, Mama. If it's not for you to say, who should say?"

Daphne shuddered. "Your grandmother, for one. I can hear her now, my dear. She'd say good, pick him, he's already got one leg dangling over the grave."

"Oh, Mama, Mr. Rolin isn't that old."

"Perhaps it's different for gentlemen. Yes, I'm sure it is. He was in Society when I was first Out, you know, not that he remembers me. At his age, I'd have been nearly two score years into my caps if I hadn't married your father. But gentlemen? Ha, they're still out and about, and eligible. That doesn't seem quite fair, but that's neither here or there, Emma. I won't have you bracketed to a man who is nearly as old as your father would be, were he alive, rest his soul."

"I don't remember Mr. Rolin asking for my hand, Mama, just to take me on a drive tomorrow. Goodness, you and the marquis should put your heads together, you seem to have so much in common."

"The marquis thinks Mr. Rolin too old, as well?"

"He thinks something," Emma said, looking across the ballroom to see his lordship walking toward her. He was not alone. A gentleman of about his same height and age was with him. A very handsome blond gentleman, with a faintly wicked smile. "Here he comes now, Mama. Perhaps he wishes for us to leave, as there are only two dances remaining. Please don't say no, because I am more than ready to be shed of this place."

"You don't like it here? Oh dear. Please don't tell Sally, she'd be that upset. She confided in me that attendance has begun falling off these past two years, and she would not only consider you ungrateful, but as adding to her budget of woes. She fair dotes on being a Patroness, you understand."

"Sally Jersey fair dotes on being Sally Jersey, Mama," Emma said, then stood up before dropping into a curtsy. "Your lordship," she said, raising her gaze to his face…and she nearly gasped.

He had changed. How on earth had he managed that? He seemed younger somehow, his blue eyes clearer, his entire posture more relaxed, less ready to spring. Why, he was actually smiling at her.

"Mrs. Clifford," Morgan said, inclining his head to her. "Miss Clifford. Please allow me to introduce to you my very good friend, Perry Shepherd, Earl of Brentwood, and a rascal of the first water. Your lordship, Mrs. Samuel Clifford and her daughter, Miss Emma Clifford."

Then he stood back, to watch. If Miss Clifford was husband-hunting, Perry must appear as if a gift from the gods. Imagine her chagrin when she found out he was here on orders from his uncle.

Daphne had scrambled to her feet and both she and Emma curtsied to the earl. "A pleasure to make your acquaintance, my lord," Emma said as her mother mumbled something indistinguishable.

"The honor, I assure you, Miss Clifford, is entirely mine," Perry said, bowing over the hand she quickly yet belatedly held out to him, as she was still cudgeling her brain, trying to scare up a reason why his lordship looked so happy, so very nearly *smug*. "I will be forever in the marquis's debt for gifting me with this introduction. Shall we name our second son after him, Miss Clifford, do you think? The first will be Perry, quite naturally, as I am a vain man."

Emma regained her hand—she'd had to tug at Perry's grip twice, before he released her. An imp of mischief knocked on her brain. She let it in. "I'm convinced his lordship would be very pleased, my lord. Do you think we could marry before the end of the week? The marquis requested that boon of me, most particularly, as the sooner he is shed of his unwanted ward, the better."

"Emma!" Daphne exclaimed, sinking back into her chair. "Oh My Stars."

Brentwood turned to the marquis, his quizzing glass somehow already stuck to his eye. "Stap me, Westham, have you misplaced your brains somewhere in the country in the years you've been gone? I would have thought you'd want this beautiful young lady for yourself, and here I find out you are pushing to be rid of her. Very well, if you must be so obtuse, allow me to take Miss Clifford off your hands."

"I thought we'd decided that before you dragged me over here to introduce you," Morgan said. But he was still smiling. "Before posting the banns, however, you might want to acquaint her with your dearest relative?"

"You've a mean streak, my friend. I'd never noticed that until now. Now, excuse us, as we'll be off." Perry allowed the quizzing glass to drop as he returned his attention to Emma. "For this next dance, Miss Clifford. After that, who knows? I may surprise myself and make my old friend happy."

"Don't believe him, Miss Clifford," the marquis said as Brentwood held out his arm. "I just heard it from his own mouth, not an hour ago, that he plans never to marry."

"Oh, unkind, unkind! And, unfortunately, quite true, although you already knew that, didn't you, Miss Clifford? I am a wastrel, and his lordship here is a fool. Come, instead of fatiguing ourselves in the dance, where we could not hope to converse below a bellow, shall we stroll on the balcony, take the air, and dissect the good marquis?"

"I'd be delighted, my lord," Emma said, glaring at the marquis over her shoulder as she walked away on the earl's arm. Once out of earshot, she said, "And you can tell me about this relative his lordship is so keen for me to know, as I am already fairly sure I have at least already heard his name. And then, my lord, we can abandon this entire farce, before the marquis becomes so doubled over with mirth that he makes a spectacle of himself."

FANNY AND SIR EDGAR were just abandoning the drawing room, neither of them walking too straight nor too steadily, when a footman opened the door to the marquis and the ladies Clifford.

"Oops, best take ourselves off, before they see us," Fanny whispered. Or it would have been a whisper, if she'd had less brandy. In truth, her words came out as more of a shout, and Sir Edgar winced as he grabbed her arm and raced her toward the stairs.

"Mother Clifford? Mother Clifford, wait!" Daphne called up from the foyer, and Fanny stopped to wait for her daughter-in-law to join them on the landing.

"Something's up," Fanny said to Sir Edgar. "Fool woman completely forgot to simper to Thornley before racing for the stairs."

Daphne fairly ran up the curving staircase, huffing and puffing as she reached the top. "Oh, I'm So Very Glad you're still awake, Mother Clifford. Hello, Sir Edgar."

"Madam," Sir Edgar said, inclining his head to the woman, but not too far, because he felt himself beginning to lose control of his lower limbs. "If you ladies will excuse me?" He grabbed on to the stair rail with both hands and proceeded to pull himself up the stairs.

"Can't hold his spirits," Fanny said, shaking her head as she looked after her cohort in crime, then grabbed at the newel-post, as the action had sent her head spinning. What a queer feeling, drinking to excess, and such a rare one—it had been decades since she'd felt so...so *free*. "So, how was your evening, Daphne? Better, how was Emma's evening? Knee-deep in eager suitors, I'll wager."

"Oh, it was terrible, Mother Clifford. Simply Terrible! The ungrateful girl has taken the marquis In Umbrage."

Fanny, eyebrows raised, toddled over to the staircase leading down to the foyer, and leaned against the banister. "Still breathing, the both of them. And there they go, straight into his lordship's private study, and without a chaperon. What's the problem? Are we going to have to listen to another threat to throw us out of here on our rumps?"

"I don't know," Daphne said, wringing her hands. "I just know that they didn't speak two words to each other all the way here in the coach. But their eyes? Oh, Mother Clifford, their eyes were saying the most Terrible Things. Mother Clifford? Where are you going? We Must Talk."

"I don't think so, Daphne, not unless you wish to converse while I have my head over the chamber pot," Fanny said, and disappeared up the stairs with more haste than it would be thought someone of her age could muster.

"Sherry?" Morgan asked, lifting the decanter and displaying it for Emma, who was already sitting on one of the pair of burgundy leather chairs placed on either side of the fireplace.

"Thank you, no," she said, stripping off her gloves with a calm she didn't feel, and laying them in her lap.

"Very well," Morgan said, eyeing the decanter of wine and then dismissing it to walk over and sit down in the facing chair. "We'll do this dry, as it were."

Emma saw the grin on his face, the unholy gleam in his eye, and could take it no longer. "You did that deliberately."

Touching a hand to his chest, Morgan furrowed his brow, doing his best to look confused. "Did what deliberately, Miss Clifford? I've done so very much since arriving in London last evening."

"Introduced the earl to me, of course, knowing full well he'd been sent to Almack's on orders from his uncle. And he's your friend, which makes it all the worse. The pair of you obviously set out to make a May Game out of me. How the both of you must have been laughing at my expense."

"You held your own, as I recall," Morgan said, steepling his fingers beneath his chin, attempting to look like the older, more sober one. The more responsible one. Did he look imposing? He hoped he looked imposing. After all, he was a marquis. Not that his title had yet seemed to impress this contrary female. "However droll you were, I feel it my duty to warn you to be careful with what you say, Miss Clifford, or else you'll soon be considered fast."

"I don't care what I'm considered, my lord," she said angrily. "I'm already thought to be the offshoot of a blackmailing old biddy by some, and as a target for those of your gender who believe marrying the dowry you're supposedly posting around the *ton* like some sort of reward for taking us all off your hands would be a fine thing. Being thought fast could only be *considered* an improvement."

"My gender, Miss Clifford? You are looking to marry a deep pocketbook, I do believe," Morgan said, pointing out the obvious, which must have rankled, for her complexion immediately went an attractive pink. "Tell me, why is it that what is so proper for the goose is so reprehensible for the gander?"

Emma looked at him, her eyes wide. "I...I don't know. It just is, that's all."

"Ah, the female mind, always a wonderment. And, if I might make a comment, it would appear that my friend the earl, rather than being put off by your grandmother's blackmailing ways, has found you to be quite appealing. You should be honored, Miss Clifford. Perry is known far and wide as never having been smitten by anyone. Save himself, of course."

If anyone was keeping score, and Emma was, Morgan was winning their verbal battle quite handily. She decided to go on the attack. "His lordship told me about your duel, my lord. How you were the one who scarred his face, and all over some ridiculous argument neither of you remembers. No wonder you went off to hide your shame in the country. Five years was scarcely sufficient. A drunken duel, my lord? And you dare to cut up stiff at my grandmother? She's only having herself a bit of fun. You could have killed your best friend."

Morgan opened his mouth to point out that Perry had been as much a part of their "drunken duel" as he, and that Perry's foil had found its mark as well, skewering him square in the—no, he wasn't going to say that. He wouldn't say that if Emma tied him down and poured hot pitch all over him. And he did look like the more guilty party, damn it, because he had retreated to Westham, while Perry had continued to move in London Society.

"I see you have nothing to say to that, my lord," Emma said, satisfied. "At least you have some sense."

"No, I don't, Miss Clifford," Morgan told her. "If I had any sense at all, I would have had you and the rest of the ragtag assemblance that has commandeered my home thrown out of here this morning."

"We—"

"Paid. Yes, I know," Morgan said, watching as two small rounds of hot color appeared on Emma's cheeks. Interesting. Her entire face seemed to react to embarrassment, but only these two small spots showed her temper. "I'll ring for Thornley, Miss Clifford, and he can bring you a small platter of ham and cheese, at which point I do believe I can begin toting up what you owe me over and above what you have *paid*."

"It wasn't that much of a pittance, my lord," Emma said, those flags of color still flying high in her cheeks. "I could have run our home for a full year on that amount."

"I'm sure you could, Miss Clifford. And you're mightily fatigued doing it, which is why you're here, to snatch up a wealthy husband who will put a period to your days of pinching every penny that happens to drop into your paws."

"We've fairly beaten this subject to death today, my lord, and I'm heartily weary of it," Emma said, getting to her feet, so that he had to rise as well. "What I wish to discuss now is this ridiculous idea of you providing me with a dowry. I won't have it."

"No, you won't. Your hapless groom will have it, and I am giving serious consideration to doubling the figure that originally entered my mind. The poor fellow will doubtless earn every penny, leg-shackled to you."

Emma gifted him with a long, dispassionate stare, the sort of look that would have had her brother, for one, ducking under the nearest table, his arms wrapped protectively about his head. "Say what you will, my lord, poke fun as you may, I will *not* be a party to this ludicrous dowry business, and will so inform anyone who assumes otherwise."

"Really? Perceive me, if you will, as wonderfully impressed. You can see inside minds now, Miss Clifford? Deduce that a person is looking at you but seeing my money? Amazing."

"I don't have to see inside anyone's head, my lord," Emma said, her palms itching to slap that supercilious smirk off his face. "They tell me, straight out, when they ask what they believe are clever questions about my *guardian*, about how *generous* he is to be sponsoring me in Society. Why, they all but pull out scraps of paper and ask me to write down the figure so that they might then place it beneath their pillows and dream of it at night."

It took some doing, but Morgan withheld his smile. "Take advantage of your good fortune, Miss Clifford, not umbrage. I can well afford most any amount, to be rid of you."

"No." As she'd jammed her fists against her waist while she bit out the word, it could only be a mistake to think she was saying one thing yet meaning another.

Morgan, no longer with any inclination to smile, glared at her. "Now you're being ridiculous. By tomorrow morning all of Mayfair will know that you are my ward, and that I have offered a dowry. Sally Jersey, all by herself, will have told two hundred people or more, and even plucked an amount out of the air before repeating it as gospel. You cannot contradict what is already a fact, not without considerable embarrassment."

"To you, my lord. To you."

"Damn—yes, Miss Clifford, to me. And to you. Think. If I have you under my roof, I am your guardian. There is no other male to gift you with that *honor*, if I can call it such and, believe me, if I could think of another word that wouldn't blister your feminine ears, I would employ it. If I have you under my roof and I am not your guardian, then I must have ulterior motives, luring your gullible grandmother and mother under false pretenses and planning a great seduction of your admittedly beautiful self."

"That's ridiculous. Nobody would think that." She would not lower herself to engaging in an argument as to whether or not she was beautiful, because she was too modest to protest what she knew to be the truth. But she would not cringe at fighting him, tooth and nail, on this silly business of guardianship.

Morgan arched one expressive eyebrow. "Ah, the innocence of youth. Dare I say stupidity? No, I am not so cruel."

"Then don't be so condescending, either, my lord," Emma told him, slapping her gloves against her palm. "I like you little enough as it is."

"At last, something we have in common, as I am not enamored of you, Miss Clifford, no more so than I would be of any thorn sticking in my side. But, that said, you cannot contradict the existence of a dowry."

"I do contradict it. I want to be shed of the sort of fools I encountered this evening, my lord. Between the ones that were dancing attention on me because of my grandmother's ridiculous scheme, and those who were out to snag what they believe will be a small fortune from you, I had a most uncomfortable evening, one I do not wish to repeat. It was only Mr. Rolin who spoke to me as if I were a person in my own right."

How he hated hearing that name on her lips. He felt a tic beginning in his cheek. "As I believe I said earlier, Miss Clifford, you are not to encourage Mr. Rolin. I, as your guardian, will pen a note and have it sent round to him in the morning, crying off from your drive."

"I will allow no such interference from you, my lord. You are not my guardian, I am not your ward, and I will do what I wish. I will tell anyone and everyone that you are not my guardian, but only housing us for the Season, and that there *is* no dowry. And I will go driving with whom I wish, and I wish to go driving with Mr. Rolin."

She didn't end with "So there!" but the words hung in the air anyway.

"I'll speak to your mother," Morgan said, then added, after conjuring up a mental picture of Daphne Clifford, "or perhaps your grandmother. One of them should see the sense in listening to me."

Emma stepped quickly to the door and pressed her back against it, her arms outstretched, to bar him from leaving. "You will do no such thing. You will talk to me."

"I've *been* talking to you, Miss Clifford, and found the exercise about as productive as beating my own head against a rock. Step out of my way."

Emma couldn't believe it. Couldn't believe what she was thinking, feeling. In the midst of her anger, how could she be thinking about his lordship's bluer-than-blue eyes? About the way his skin creased at the outside edges of those eyes, as if he spent considerable time squinting into the sun. Something inside her went very cold, then very warm.

He was standing close, too close. All at once she recalled the lateness of the hour, how alone the two of them were here, in his private study. Wasn't that just like her, acting, and then only later, thinking. And it was all his fault, because he was the one who had roused her temper to a point where any thoughts of self-preservation had flown out the window. Why, she had barely been able to contain herself until they could return to Grosvenor Square, where she could be alone with him.

Alone with him. Why had her mama allowed such a thing? One answer would be that her mama already believed that the marquis was her daughter's guardian. But, then, her mama could be talked round to believing the sky was green, if the argument sounded reasonable. Unless her mama, a sweet but rather featherwitted woman who admittedly had once had a Season, understood something she did not. And *that* was a difficult pill to swallow.

"Do…do you really believe Society would think that I was here, under your roof as you say, because you wish to…to ruin me? If I remain here, and there's no dowry, no talk of you being my guardian?"

Morgan pushed the fingers of both hands through his hair. "Ruin you? You really do wish to speak with the gloves off, don't you? Good Lord. *Yes,* Miss Clifford, that is exactly what Society would think. Society loves nothing better than a delicious scandal, real or made up out of whole cloth. Under my roof—although clearly the expression annoys you—with only two dotty females and an idiot boy to guard your reputation? If my mother were your hostess, she would be here. She is not."

Emma thought about this for a moment, then said, "She could be too ill to travel and have prevailed upon you to stand in her stead."

"True. Which would make me your guardian," Morgan gritted out from between clenched teeth. "My God, we're going in circles here. Apply to your grandmother, Miss Clifford, for I'll say no more on the matter. Except," he said, looking at her, seeing an innocent yet spirited morsel who would be so easily crushed in Jarrett Rolin's opportunistic hands, "for the one more thing, one more turn around the obvious, if you please. You will *not* see Mr. Rolin. I won't have it."

"You won't have it?" Emma said, realizing that she was still standing with her back to the door, still stupidly holding her arms out at her sides, her gloves gripped tightly in her right hand. "*You* won't have it?" she repeated with more force…which would have been about the time her brother would have scampered out from beneath the table and run for the nearest exit, to save himself. "Do you wish to learn, my lord, how very uninterested I am in what you will or will not have?"

"Oh, the devil with it," Morgan said, talking to himself. "I should have done this the first time."

So saying, he reached out, which wasn't too great a stretch, for he'd been inching closer and closer to Emma, in order to impress his consequence on her (or impress himself against her; he wasn't quite sure), and brought his mouth down on hers.

To shut her up. That's all. To shut her up.

Emma's eyes popped open wide and she looked at him, seeing a bit of his nose, one closed eye, the lock of darkest black hair that persisted in falling onto his smooth forehead.

She felt his body against hers, hard and unyielding, became aware that his leg had somehow insinuated itself between her thighs.

She tasted him. She smelled him.

And then she began pummeling him on the back with both fists as she struggled to be free of him.

Morgan felt Emma's fists against his back, as ineffectual as feathers beating on London Wall, and smiled slightly as he drew her even more firmly into his embrace—leaving her just enough "fighting space" so that he could feel her softness moving against him.

He was vindicated, he deserved this. She had humiliated him, and now it was his turn. His turn to do what? Humiliate himself? No. He'd sort that out later.

Lifting his lips just slightly, he slanted his mouth and took hers again, this time insinuating his tongue, for she had taken that slight opportunity to open her mouth, most probably to tell him something outrageously female like: "Unhand me this minute, you rotter!"

And that's when it happened. That was when he realized that, blast him for a fool, he *liked* this impossible woman, *desired* this willful, stubborn woman. That was when the smile, both the inward and the outward ones, faded from Morgan, to be replaced by an emotion that had nothing to do with humor, or anger, or even some juvenile attempt to get some of his own back.

Emma's fists still pounded against him. Then her open hands. Then she stilled, her fingers spread against his back, so that she could concentrate on what he was doing to her mouth, with her mouth.

She held on tight, her anger forgotten, *experiencing*. Melting against him, only to stiffen when she felt his hand cup her breast, then going fluid once more.

Angry. They had been so angry with each other, their tempers running hot.

But this was another sort of heat. Morgan felt it. Emma felt it.

Her knees buckled, and she felt herself sliding toward the floor, Morgan with her, still holding on to each other, their mouths still locked together, their hands roving, until they were both on their knees, their bodies fused together, melted together in this new, unexpected and overwhelming heat.

Morgan dragged his mouth from hers and buried his face against the side of her neck. "You drive me insane."

Lifting her head, so that she could feel his kisses against her skin, savor the small bites he teased against that same skin, Emma whispered, "I really, really dislike you."

"I know." He shut her up again, taking her mouth even as he slid his arms around her back and, with more haste than finesse, lowered her to the floor.

He felt her arms as she wrapped them around his neck, pulling him closer, and the heat burst into flame— just before the Real World, using the voice of Thornley, came through the door, dousing those flames with the force of a bucket of cold water poured over his head.

"Ohmigod," Emma said, her eyes wide as she looked up at Morgan as if she'd just realized what she'd been doing…what they'd been doing…what they'd been about to do. "My lord," she whispered, blinking. "If you…if you would desist in pawing me and help me to my feet?"

Morgan was just as shocked, coming back to himself with a sudden shame at his ungentlemanly actions. He'd been…he'd been about to…*was he out of his mind?*

"Certainly, Miss Clifford," he said with what he believed to be remarkable sangfroid, taking her hands and helping her to her feet.

She began straightening her gown, which was sadly askew and badly wrinkled, even as he picked up the end of the strand of faux pearls and tried, without much success, to jam it back into her hair.

"My lord? I had thought you wished refreshments," Thornley said from the foyer.

"Not…not really, no," Morgan said, casting a quick look down at himself, then just as quickly turning his back to Emma and walking over to stand with his front against his desk. Damn revealing breeches. "Thank you anyway, Thornley."

"You're welcome, my lord. It's gone two, my lord. I imagine the young lady is ready for her bed. And may I say that you, too, my lord, have had a very long day."

Morgan translated that bit of information in his head, and it came out: *You're a rutting boar, my lord, and should be ashamed of yourself, but it's not to worry for I, Thornley, am here to save Miss Clifford from your brutish behavior.*

He turned as he heard Emma walking toward the door, probably to open it and assure Thornley that she was just fine, thank you, and he quickly raced after her, grabbed her arm while he put a finger to his lips, warning her to silence.

"Miss Clifford is upstairs this past twenty minutes or more, Thornley. You're losing your touch if you didn't see her go."

There was a silence on the other side of the door that had Morgan feeling twelve again, and caught out trying to light one of his mother's guests' cheroots he'd found half-burnt in a dish.

"Yes, my lord," Thornley said at last. "Forgive me, my lord. I understand completely."

"And he does, too," Morgan said once he was sure Thornley had withdrawn his ear from its place, pressed against the wooden door. "He'll give you time to escape to your rooms, to save your embarrassment."

"Why didn't you let me open the door? He sounded worried, dear man."

In answer, Morgan took her hand and pulled her over to the gilt-edged mirror hanging between two bookcases. He laid his hands on her shoulders and turned her to the glass. "Does this answer your question, Miss Clifford? I wished to spare Thornley his blushes."

She looked, and then goggled. Where was the proper and composed young miss in her virginal white gown and pretty faux pearls woven into her hair? She certainly wasn't looking back at her from this mirror!

Why, she looked…she looked positively *abandoned*. Her hair tumbling, her neckline crooked, her lips swollen. There was even a slight redness on her chin, which she suddenly realized must have come from his lordship's slight growth of beard rubbing against her tender skin.

"Oh, my stars," she said quietly, just before she saw his smug, satisfied smile, reflected above her, and turned in his arms, to slap him sharply on his cheek. It was, she was sure, the proper thing to do, although she was employing the exercise a good ten minutes too late.

Morgan released her, to press one hand against his cheek. "What was that in aid of, Miss Clifford? Your sin, or mine? A kiss may be dismissed, but what we have very nearly done cannot be so easily forgotten, nor forgiven. You do know you've just been compromised, don't you? Perhaps we will name our second son Perry?"

"Surely you're not serious. There is no reason for any such thing. No one knows what happened here, unless you tell them. I most certainly am not going to run through the streets, ringing a bell and announcing it to the world."

Morgan felt a wash of relief, followed quickly by a niggle of doubt. Shame for his reprehensible behavior would come later, he knew, but for now, he found himself rather stung. Had she been totally unimpressed by his lovemaking? No, he wouldn't believe that.

She'd responded like a wildcat in his arms. She was an untutored but definitely sensual young woman who had reacted when he'd acted.

And yet, simply put, the girl flat out simply didn't like him. She'd just been given the chance to gain any debutante's wildest dream—a title, unlimited wealth—and she had turned both it and him—mostly him, he knew—down without a blink. It was insulting, that's what it was. An insulting, lucky escape. So why didn't he feel lucky?

"Are you saying, Miss Clifford, that you wish this interlude to be erased from our minds?"

"Good God, yes!"

"Very well, it is erased, and never to be repeated. Are you happy now? Lord knows I, for one, am ecstatic. Miss Clifford?"

She didn't answer him. She couldn't answer him. So she picked up her skirts and fled, running straight past Riley, who grinned at her in the most humiliating way. She didn't stop running until she was in her bedchamber, where she stopped, gathered her breath and then tip-toed over to close the door to the dressing room, so as not to wake Claramae.

Morning would be time and enough to pack, and leave this madhouse.

Mayfair Madness

> It is sweet to let the
> mind unbend on occasion.
> —Horace

"I'M MIGHTILY SURPRISED, Miss Clifford, if I might be so bold as to say so, that your guardian allowed us this excursion," Jarrett Rolin said as he expertly tooled his pair so that the curricle was neatly blended into the line of equipages making the round of Rotten Row in Hyde Park.

Emma simply smiled, then went back to examining her surroundings. She kept quiet, because she longed to agree with Mr. Rolin, just as she longed to inquire as to why the marquis had taken the man in such dislike.

But, as she had passed beyond her initial urge to flee London and never return, she had also been reassured by the note Claramae had passed to her along with her morning chocolate: *Miss Clifford. I fear I have taken a nasty knock to the head by some unknown hand, and cannot now recall anything that transpired as of early last evening. If I might request an interview with you this evening in my private study, at eight of the clock, perhaps we can, with luck, reconstruct those events, putting them in their proper order. Your servant, Westham.*

What that note meant, she'd been sure, was that the

marquis was willing to lie if pressed for details of whatever it was that had transpired between the two of them last night, and thought it best that they got those lies straight. It seemed a sane and workable solution, and if his note both pleased and saddened her, she wouldn't think about that at all.

"You know, Miss Clifford," Rolin said after a few moments spent wondering if the chit had somehow bitten off her tongue since their fairly witty repartee of the previous evening, "I have been longing for this moment all day. Indeed, the clock refused to move at times, so eager was I to speak with you again."

There. Perfect. That ought to get her talking.

"Ah, Mr. Rolin," Emma said, turning to look at him. "That statement puts me much in mind of a dancing bear. You wish me to perform for you?" Her smile softened her words, but she already had deduced that this was a man who said what he thought, and thought very much about what he said.

Rolin grinned at her, then bit back a curse as some cow-handed creature attempted to cut his ridiculously oversize high-perch phaeton in front of him in line, employing a generous use of the whip to direct his horseflesh. "Ignorant puppy," he said, turning back to Emma. "Not you, Miss Clifford. That idiot in front of us. If he had succeeded in scraping the wheels of my curricle I should have had to desert you to beat him soundly about the head and shoulders."

"Would you? I mean, would you really do something like that?" Emma asked, watching as the youth's showy and unruly team, undoubtedly weary of the sawing on their reins as well as the constant use of the whip, got the bits between their teeth, and the phaeton took off across the grass. "Oh, my stars! There are people walking on the grass. He could kill someone. Mr. Rolin, do something!"

Rolin watched the phaeton as it gained speed, even as the ridiculous young dandy toppled from the seat, onto the grass. "Alas, I cannot leave you, Miss Clifford, nor expose you to danger by attempting to chase down those horses in my curricle. The marquis would have my liver and lights if anything untoward happened to his ward, I'm sure. And, alas again, this sort of thing happens more often than you might suppose, as young pups are handed the reins long before they know how to employ them."

"But—but somebody should do something," Emma swallowed down hard as the phaeton seemed to pick up speed.

"And someone most probably will," Rolin said wearily, bored by the entire exercise, because he had not instigated it. "Just not me. It is left to us to sit back and enjoy the show. Do you think he cracked his head, Miss Clifford? Danger and possible bloodshed to one side, there is nothing like a diversion to liven up the hour."

"That's not amusing, Mr. Rolin," Emma said as she turned on the seat, looking about to see if someone, anyone, would come to the rescue before the phaeton came to grief.

There were shrieks of alarm. Women and nattily dressed gentlemen ran for the cover of sheltering trees. Horses unnerved by the shouts, the excitement, began to rear in their traces. Even Rolin, a known whipster, had all he could do to keep his blacks from bolting.

The scene had all the makings of an out-and-out disaster.

Emma felt anger at Mr. Rolin, who was reining in his horses rather than employing them in an attempt at rescue. She felt impotence, as she knew there was nothing she could do to prevent a possible carnage.

And then she felt joy, because suddenly, appearing as if from nowhere, came the Marquis of Westham astride a magnificent bay stallion, riding with his body pressed low over the horse's head as he raced across the wide expanse of grass, the stallion's hooves throwing up huge clumps of the perfectly manicured turf as it moved in a full gallop toward the runaway phaeton.

"Oh, bless us, if it isn't the marquis to the rescue," Rolin said in disgust. "How depressingly expected of the man."

Emma barely heard him. She was much too busy watching the marquis, watching how he directed his horse toward the phaeton from an angle, cutting the distance almost by halves with each long, powerful stride of his mount.

"My God, he's going to jump onto one of the horses, isn't he? He can't do that. He'll be killed."

His own horses now back under his control, Rolin looked toward the scene unfolding within one hundred yards of the Serpentine. *Bloody show-off,* he thought, but said, "Westham the hero. How very splendid. Don't look, Miss Clifford, for you're correct. This could end badly."

Emma, unceremoniously and without thought to what she was doing, rudely pushed Rolin back, as he had leaned forward, to block her view. "No, he's not going to jump. I thought he was going to try to jump onto one of the horses. They're heading straight for the Serpentine now. He's *herding* them there, into the water. Brilliant, Westham! Brilliant!"

In a moment, the chit would be standing in the curricle, giving his horses fits with the movement, waving her arms wildly and shouting "Huzza! Huzza!" Rolin's upper lip curled. "Indeed," he drawled, setting the brake on his curricle, wrapping the reins about the stick, and then folding his arms across his chest, bored with the entire affair.

Holding her breath, Emma watched as the team charged straight into the water, slowed, and then stopped when the phaeton's wheels sank into the mud, even as the stallion was neatly turned at the last moment, not so much as stepping one hoof into the water.

She watched as the marquis masterfully controlled his horse, the stallion dancing in circles, still with so much energy to dissipate. Then, satisfied that the worst had been averted, he turned his mount and headed back across the grass at a canter, the stallion's head held up almost smugly, its tail high and waving like a flag.

He stopped the horse and dismounted near the dandy, who was just then nearing Rotten Row, walking a little unsteadily while bemoaning the grass stains on his pantaloons.

Emma leaned forward even more, straining to hear what the marquis said.

"Damned nags," the dandy grumbled, looking up at the marquis. "Need more of the whip, that's what. And let me tell you, sir, if one of them is injured, I'll see to you for payment."

"Ah," Rolin said, once again interested, and knowing full well of Westham's temper. He had, after all, used it to serve his own amusement in the past. "This, I believe, Miss Clifford, would be the moment the good marquis delivers a whipping himself, to that young idiot."

Emma bit her bottom lip. What Rolin said was not unreasonable. She certainly would relish the opportunity to take her riding crop to the ungrateful whelp.

"Your name," she heard Morgan say, his voice low and controlled. Why, he even smiled at the ungrateful whelp, who idiotically drew himself up, jutted out his chin, and said, "I am the Viscount Felstead. And who, my good man, are you?"

"Oh, you're right, Mr. Rolin. What a foolish young man. The marquis has every right to beat him into flinders."

Then her mouth dropped open as Morgan inclined his head, only slightly. Then he smiled. "My lord. As it would appear that you have five thumbs on each hand, as well as half the wits of a puling infant and less concern for your fellow man than a doorstop, I will tell you that I am the gentleman who is relieving you of the dilemma presented to you by your horses and equipage being stuck in the Serpentine. For the price of one pound, which you will gratefully accept, the team and phaeton are now mine."

"The devil they are! Didn't you hear me, man? I'm the Viscount Felstead. Who are you, to talk to me in such a manner?"

"The Marquis of Westham, at your service," Morgan said, inclining his head once more.

"Well, I don't care," the viscount said, seeing the pound note that had appeared in Morgan's hand and grabbing it, ripping it in two and letting the pieces flutter to the ground.

"Oh dear," Emma said as Morgan bent down and picked up the destroyed note.

"Not a pound, my lord?" Morgan said, shrugging. "Very well then, a half pound." He tucked one half of the pound note behind the top button of the viscount's flashy waistcoat, leaning in close to whisper something in the youth's ear.

Even from this distance, Emma could see the viscount's eyes widen, before he said, "Thank you, my lord Westham. Yes, indeed, thank you very much."

A groom in Westham livery rode up as the viscount was still bowing and thanking the marquis, and Morgan directed him to the equipage still stuck in the mud.

Pedestrians who had gathered, hoping to see something more spectacular than what had played out, drifted away even as Morgan mounted the stallion and followed the groom to the banks of the Serpentine. The line of carriages and curricles, landaus and phaetons was set into motion once more.

"Well, that's that, Miss Clifford," Rolin said, releasing the brake and lightly flicking the reins to give his team the office to start. "By the time you arrive at your third social event of the evening, it will have been a team of four, not two, Westham's horse will have been snorting real fire out its nostrils, and the good marquis will have leaned half out of the saddle to swoop up three hapless infants and their nanny, removing them from harm's way in just the nick of time."

"But that's not what happened."

Rolin smile at her kindly. "By tomorrow morning, someone will be saying Parliament should be petitioned to erect a statue of Westham, just over there, beside the Serpentine, and by next week, no one will remember anything of the incident at all. Welcome, my dear Miss Clifford, to London."

THE AGED COACH, badly sprung and still smelling vaguely of the cowshed where their neighbor had kept it stowed until Emma bartered for its use, rolled along Brook Street, on the way back to Grosvenor Square.

Fanny Clifford, who had taken the forward-facing seat as no more than her due, looked across the coach to Sir Edgar and smiled.

"A successful afternoon's work by and large, wouldn't you say, Edgar?"

"I'm not sure, Fanny," he told her, then grinned, for he was a happy man at the moment. "I mean, both men invested, there is that. But I don't believe I've ever before seen an earl bite on a piece of gold to be sure it's real."

"I told you. Not got the brains they were born with, Beany or Johnnie. And I wasn't even in the room when you reluctantly agreed to take their money. That's the beauty of it, Edgar. Even when it all comes to nothing, they'll see me as no more than another victim, just a dotty old woman who believed an adventurer who pretended to love her. Not that they'll talk about it, to anyone. Nobody likes looking the fool."

"I don't know why you had to say that about the two of us, Fanny. And holding on to my arm all the time? Gave me the creeps, no insult intended."

"None taken. Put any fears to rest, Edgar, that I'll soon be chasing you around any tables, hoping to launch myself on top of your old bones," Fanny said, then rubbed her palms together. "So, how much did we get?"

"I haven't looked," Edgar said truthfully, reaching into his pocket to pull out two packets of folded banknotes. He hadn't looked, counted, because that would have been a shabby thing to do in front of his investors; but he did know the amounts. He handed one packet to Fanny, and began counting the other one himself.

"Three thousand pounds," Fanny said after a moment. She had licked her finger and shuffled through the notes with the dexterity of a cardsharp. "Not all that much to be brought in as partner to the group that will create gold out of chamber pots. What did you get?"

"Only half that amount, but I didn't wish to press, or be thought suspicious," Edgar said, quickly sliding the notes he'd been counting back into the packet and then reaching out a hand to take back the rest of it, mingle the two piles together. "And by the time they think to ask for more proof, I'll be halfway to Paris. Always wanted to see Paris."

"And I'll be weeping into my handkerchief, bemoaning the fact that my beau lied to me, used me horribly, and then ran off with all my jewelry. You cad, Edgar."

"I am that, Fanny," Edgar said cheerfully, depositing the six thousand pounds back in his pocket, grateful she hadn't asked to count all the money. He didn't feel guilty, either, for hadn't the scheme been his idea in the first place? "How many more?"

Fanny shrugged. "Two? Three? No. Just the one. Willie. He's got more money than God."

"Willie?" Edgar nearly choked on the hard candy he'd popped into his mouth (having earlier popped it into his pocket, at Lord Boswick's). "That would be Sir Willard Humphrey, former Minister of the Admiralty? Oh, Fanny, I don't think so."

"Why not? Show me a man in government with half a brain, Edgar. That's how they get into government, you know. Someone asks all the ignoramuses in the realm to raise their hands, and half the ones that do are then given all the important posts in the kingdom. The rest are hired out as village idiots. Willie could have gone either way."

Besides, Fanny had already decided, Willie had turned so old, so dour. Why, when he'd visited her in Grosvenor Square he'd actually had the nerve to remind her that one day she'd face her God, and what would she say then about blackmailing old friends? This was the same man who had made love to her in the gardens of Carleton House? Pitiful, that's what it was. The man deserved to lose some of his money into her pocket, if for nothing more than the way her panniers had been bent all out of shape when he'd pressed her down against the grass.

"All right, but he will be the last one. Four is a very good number. I've always heard that."

"And if we could only lure three, you'd declare three a very good number, wouldn't you, Edgar? But I've one more for you to consider. Five, Edgar, one for every finger on this greedy little hand of mine. Not as much profit involved, I'm sure, but why not take advantage of every opportunity."

"Who else do you have in mind? And if you say our new King, Fanny Clifford, I want you to know I'll think you're Bedlam bait and wash my hands of you."

"No, no, not Florizel. He doesn't have the ready, for one thing. No, I thought closer to home." She pulled on her gloves as the footman opened the door of the coach, then looked slyly at Sir Edgar. "Olive Norbert."

Sir Edgar sat very still for a moment, considering this. Olive Norbert, seamstress. Olive Norbert, spending some of her inherited blunt on pretending she was a real Mayfair lady. Olive Norbert, who didn't seem too bright, but did seem to enjoy money. This could work. Indeed, he was mildly surprised he hadn't thought of it himself.

"How will we approach her?" he asked as he and Fanny climbed the few stairs to the front door of the mansion.

"Why, Edgar, I would have thought that was obvious. You're to romance her, of course."

Sir Edgar's step faltered, and he nearly fell. "Ro-romance her? Olive Norbert?"

"I have every faith in you, Edgar," Fanny said, slipping her arm through his as Thornley stood at the open door, to welcome them home.

MORGAN FELT about as welcome in his own house as a rat catcher showing up with his sack at the front door, all bright and cheerful and ready to work, just as the King was alighting from his carriage for a dinner party.

Fanny Clifford, thankfully gone all afternoon, had, however, trapped him this morning, in the music room, intent on setting a date for the ball he'd been blackmailed into hosting for Emma. And she'd gotten one, for Friday next, damn his own weakness.

And Wycliff wouldn't stop nagging at him until he'd told him what he wished to wear this evening, so that the valet could have it All Prepared for him, then went off to sulk when Morgan had chosen the midnight-blue over the bottle-green.

Thornley was always dogging his heels, as if ready to steer him away from any rooms where one of the "lodgers" might be taking their ease.

And, as it seemed that where Thornley could be found, Daphne Clifford also could be found there within moments, Morgan had retreated to his private study for most of the day, until he had ordered Sampson saddled so that he could follow after Emma and Rolin, like some sort of overly protective chaperon.

He was skulking around his own house, to hide from everyone. He was skulking around Hyde Park, to spy on Emma Clifford. He had gone so far as to take his evening meal in his bedchamber, because otherwise Miss Clifford would be sure to mention this afternoon's events, and everyone at the table (save Miss Clifford, whose grandmother would doubtless soon correct that lapse) would know he'd only been at the park to spy on her.

How had he been brought so low?

Now, here he sat—skulked, sulked, something-ed—waiting for Miss Clifford to keep their appointment, before all of them would head out, *en masse,* to the evening's entertainments. Oh joy, oh happiness abounds.

Morgan poured himself another drink, splashing wine onto the tabletop when there was a quick, solid rap on the door. "You may enter," he called, snatching up a square of white cloth and covering the spill with it before turning to face Miss Clifford. "Good evening—Thornley?"

The butler bowed from the waist. "Miss Clifford sends her regrets, my lord, but she is otherwise occupied at the moment and will be unavoidably detained for some minutes yet."

What a mouthful of clever evasion, Morgan thought, taking a sip of his wine. "What's going on this time, Thornley?"

"I...I'd rather not say, my lord. It is a matter of some confidence."

"I hear that Newgate accepts prisoners at all hours of the day and night, Thornley. Shall we see if this is true?"

The butler stood up very straight. "Pardon me, but that would be blackmail, my lord."

"Yes," Morgan said, smiling. "There seems to be a lot of that making the rounds. Now, what's happening under my roof? It's a relatively new phenomenon for me, knowing what's going on in my own house, but we'll both strive to get used to it, yes, Thornley?"

"It's Mr. Clifford, my lord," Thornley said on a sigh. "He and that rapscallion Riley seem to have disappeared, gone missing without telling anyone their plans."

"Clifford didn't pin a note to his pillow, beg permission, perhaps leave a trail of bread crumbs? By God, Thornley, I'm shocked, I tell you. Astounded. What is the world coming to when a man of a bare nineteen summers has the audacity to untie his sister's apron strings?" He narrowed his eyes. "Miss Clifford, Thornley. Have her here in ten minutes, or I shall go find her myself."

"Excuse me, sir, but do you really want to do that? We are speaking of Miss Clifford, are we not? Miss Emma Clifford?"

Morgan stared into his glass. She'd balk, he'd yell, she'd yell louder, and he'd be kissing her again. Damn. "All right, a half hour." He glared at the butler. "And not a moment longer."

"Yes, my lord," Thornley said, and bowed his way out of the room.

THEY'D BEEN WALKING for nearly a half hour, in streets Cliff Clifford decided were little more than mud, paved over with offal and two broken cobblestones. "That was a near-run thing, you know, getting Harry moved to my new chamber without Thornley being the wiser."

"Ha! I have Mr. Thornley wrapped right around this little finger. This little finger right here," Riley said happily, as he had broken their walk with a few quick pop-ins at local pubs for a penny glass of gin, and was feeling quite mellow with the entire world at the moment. "They all kowtow to me, you know, being as how his lordship has picked me out for his special favor. Fair dotes on me, his lordship does."

"Why?" Cliff asked, stepping around a particularly vile looking pile of garbage…that turned out to have arms and legs and a toothless grin, something he didn't want to think about just then. "What makes you so special, Riley?"

"Never you mind, I just am, that's all," the valet answered quickly, because it wouldn't do for young Clifford to know his new friend was also his keeper. "And this would be it, the Cock and Woolpack. Ain't it grand?" he said, smiling up at the tall, narrow building.

"That's it?" Cliff was disappointed, to say the least. The dimly lit tavern seemed an insignificant site for the birth of his fortune. "It's rather small, isn't it? Are you quite sure?"

"Sure as I can be, Cliffie. Now, come on," Riley said, hefting the cage with Harry inside, a hood over his head.

Cliff followed, fairly having to squeeze himself down the length of the narrow room lined with a few tables on one side, a long bar on the other, and what seemed to be a thousand dirty, sweaty bodies everywhere else.

Through a doorway they went, once a burly man guarding it said "Fightin' or sellin'?" and Riley responded, "Fighting and winning, boyo. Pay the man, Cliffie. Halfpence each."

Once through the doorway, however, Riley handed Harry over to Cliff, saying, "I'll go down first and you follow in a minute or two. We're not together, remember?"

"Yes, but that man back there...he saw us."

"And he don't go down the stairs, Cliffie boy. He minds 'em. Now, remember what I told you. First cock hits the pit, you hold up Harry and call out, 'This one's mine. Who's to be bettin'?' Simple enough, right, and then I'll be taking it from there and you just keep yer yammer shut, doing your best to look country stupid."

"And Harry? When do I let him out of his cage? He's been in there all day."

"Hooded, trapped, and madder than a devil neck-deep in holy water, you're right about that. Look, when they're calling you out, saying they're ready, you put the cage down in the pit and wait for the man to tell you to open it. Then get that cage and yourself out of there fast as you can. The rest, Cliffie boy, is up to Harry."

Cliff nodded as he squeezed a hand around the handle of the cage. "I'm sorry, Harry, but I have to do this. And then I'll get you something nice from the kitchens, when we get back, all right? That's a good Harry."

"Oh, for the love of heaven, next you'll be kissing the blessed thing, and knittin' him little booties."

"Will not," Cliff said, stung.

He watched Riley trip off down the rickety stairs, then stood aside as a vile-smelling man carried three cages past him. Finally, after counting to one hundred, he squared his shoulders and headed down the stairs.

"THORNLEY, WOULD IT BE possible for you to have some refreshments sent up to the drawing room?" Emma asked, locating the butler hovering in the foyer as she descended the stairs, the man looking torn between knocking on his lordship's study door and bolting out into the street. Poor Thornley, he'd been under a considerable strain since his lordship had come to town.

"Oh, Miss Clifford, and with two minutes to spare," Thornley said, coming very close to smiling at her. "Certainly, I'd be happy to. Refreshments? For the ladies?"

"Mrs. Norbert and my mother, yes. We've decided to remain at home this evening, and I'm afraid my grandmother has already taken to her bed, pleading the fatigue of a long day. She and Sir Edgar were gone for most of the afternoon, you know."

They'd been gone for three hours and twenty-six minutes, to be exact, but Thornley didn't share that information with Emma. "Mrs. Clifford, your mother, that is, is she well? Claramae has already told me that all evening plans have been canceled."

Had he sounded inquiring, rather than worried? Concerned, rather than half-willing to seek out Daphne Clifford and tell her never to worry, never to fear, for Thornley, her dearest love, was near. He was so ashamed of himself.

Emma bit her bottom lip, for Thornley's ears had gone red, and she wondered just how long it would be before her mother, her sweet mama, created the Scandal of the Season by running off to Gretna Green with a butler. And then she wondered, only briefly, why this didn't pitch her, the loving daughter, into an absolute panic. Maybe it was because her mother seemed so happy when Thornley was near.

Then Emma recalled her mother's earlier distress when she'd told her about the fortune hunters after the marquis's money. She couldn't tell the woman about Fanny's blackmailing scheme, but she had to give some explanation for her own unwillingness to go back into Society just yet. Could she say as much to Thornley? No, best to leave it alone, leave it all alone, and let these two silly people sort themselves out without her interference. Fanny's interference would be more than enough!

"Mama's fine, thank you, Thornley. She and Mrs. Norbert are selecting threads for a piece of embroidery, as a matter of fact, an activity Mama much enjoys."

"Very well, Miss Clifford," Thornley said, edging toward the door to the study, one hand already outstretched to the knob, as the tall clock in the corner of the foyer had just struck the half hour. "I'll see to refreshments at once."

"Thank you, Thornley," Emma said, and motioned for him to knock on the door. "We mustn't keep the marquis waiting, must we?"

So Thornley knocked, and Morgan bellowed "Enter!" and Emma, one hand in her gown pocket, wrapped around her sharpest hatpin, stepped inside the study. "Good evening, my lord. Excuse my tardiness, but we seem to have misplaced Clifford, and my mother was much concerned."

Morgan looked at her from his stance in front of the fireplace, one arm resting negligently on the mantel. He'd tried out sitting behind his desk, then had taken up a more relaxed pose on the window seat for a few moments.

He'd tried standing in the middle of the room, his hands clasped behind his back, but had finally settled on the post of Master of the House at the mantelpiece—right after he'd slammed his palm against his forehead and warned himself that he was verging on becoming a thorough idiot. Never in his life had he been so unsure of himself. He was even unsure as to why he was unsure of himself, although he was certain that Miss Clifford was to blame.

"And has your brother been located, Miss Clifford? I should not sleep tonight, were he to be believed out there alone, with only Riley to protect him, babe in arms that he is. Why, I was no older than your brother when I was fighting in Spain, although that could not possibly have been more dangerous than cutting up a lark in Mayfair."

Emma rolled her eyes, even as she spread the skirts of her palest yellow gown and sat down in the same chair she'd occupied the previous evening. "Oh, cut line, my lord, you've more than proved your point. We are naught but silly women. And you could care less if Cliff has been knocked on the head and tossed onto a ship bound for New South Wales. In fact, I would think you'd be hard-pressed not to break out into a jig, if it were true."

"It would make one the less housebreaker underfoot, I'll agree to that," he said, crossing the room to seat himself in the facing chair. He felt more comfortable in the chair, because the chair was closer to her, and he liked being close to her.

"Before we move on to other subjects, my lord, I want to say that you were quite magnificent today in the park. Very much the hero."

Morgan kept his expression on the shady side of disinterest, but not without effort. "I only did what had to be done, Miss Clifford."

"Yes, but you were the only one who seemed to understand what must be done." She had to say it, give the man some credit, because credit was due him, and just hope he wouldn't gloat to the point where she'd long to box his ears.

Morgan caught the disapproving tone in her voice and liked it very much. "You're speaking of Mr. Rolin now?"

"I am, yes. It may please you no end, my lord, but there's no hope for it but to tell you that I don't much care for Mr. Rolin."

He allowed himself a small smile, only a small smile.

Inside, he was doing that jig she'd spoken of earlier. "I did warn you to stay away from him, Miss Clifford," he said, doing his best to sound properly guardianlike.

"No, my lord, you *ordered* me to stay away from him. And I will, henceforth, but now it is *my* decision," she said. "But tell me, what did you say to that young idiot that had him so suddenly happy to have lost his phaeton and team?"

"Nothing too terrible, Miss Clifford. I merely told him that he was two short seconds from having both his legs broken, and his nose fed to him, unless he thanked me kindly and disappeared. Sometimes, Miss Clifford, a whisper is far more productive than a shout."

"Oh, that's famous!" Emma exclaimed, then shifted her weight slightly. Her eyes went wide at the sharp stab of pain, she let out a most unladylike howl and leaped to her feet.

Morgan was on his own feet in an instant. "What? My God, Emma, what's wrong?"

Emma stood very still, her lips clamped between her teeth, and reached into her pocket. She located the hat pin and gave it a tug, pulling its tip free of her thigh, then sighed. "Oh, that's better."

"What's better?" Morgan asked. "What happened? What—what's *that?*"

Emma felt her cheeks warming as she held up the hat pin, bent sideways about a half inch from its tip. She resisted the urge to rub at her thigh but not without supreme effort. "I'm fine. It only penetrated a little."

Morgan looked at the pin and blinked. "You put a hatpin in your pocket and forgot about it?"

Emma considered this explanation for a moment, then shot him a very bright smile. "Yes, that's exactly what I must have done. Shame on me."

She placed the pin on the table beside her and sat down once more, folded her hands in her lap and, looking at him inquiringly, said, "Your note said that we were to come up with matching answers if anyone should ask what we were discussing last night after our return from Almack's?"

But Morgan was still just standing there and staring at the bent hatpin. "That was meant for me, wasn't it? If I was to pounce on you again."

"Nonsense," Emma said, much too quickly.

He raked his fingers through his hair, an action that would have reduced Wycliff to racking sobs had he seen the result, and glared at her. "You're afraid of me, aren't you, Miss Clifford? Oh, you put on a brave face, and a smart mouth, but you're afraid of me."

"I'm afraid of at least one of us, my lord," Emma said, concentrating on her own fingers, noticing with just a small part of her mind how her knuckles had turned white.

Morgan sat down again with a bit of a thump, feeling completely deflated. "Miss Clifford...I apologize. I would apologize a thousand times, if I thought that would help."

Emma brought up her chin, and he could see anger flashing in her eyes. God, he couldn't find his feet with this woman; she was constantly rocking him back on his heels, keeping him off his balance.

"And you should apologize, my lord," Emma told him. "You all but ravaged me last night." She held up her hand as he was about to speak, and added, "But that does not absolve me from what I did. Or, should I say, what I did not do. I did not scream, my lord. I did not go tattling to my family to tell them what happened. I said nothing. I said nothing, did nothing," she repeated hollowly, and blinked back sudden tears. "What does that make *me*, my lord?"

"I...I hadn't thought about that," Morgan said honestly. "You did rather...participate, didn't you? Even enjoy yourself?"

"Oh, my stars, look at him. The man's proud of himself!" Emma's tears dried before they could run down her cheeks. "You take unfair advantage of a...of a young lady, and you have the audacity to be *proud* of yourself?"

Morgan found he was liking this conversation. A lot. He was liking how her eyes flashed, how those twin spots of color appeared high on her cheeks, how her bosom heaved in her agitation. God, he was a bastard.

"You enjoyed it, didn't you, Miss Clifford? Come on, own up to the truth. You enjoyed it."

"I slapped you," Emma reminded him, wishing she'd never spoken, never met the marquis, never come to London at all.

"Yes, you did. But, as I recall, that came fairly late in the game, didn't it? Until Thornley's rude or opportune interruption—how do you see that, Miss Clifford, I wonder?—I think things were progressing quite nicely between us."

"Ooh!" Emma sprang to her feet once more. "I loathe and detest you!" Then she winced. Now she sounded like one of those insipid heroines in a Pennypress novel.

Morgan also got to his feet, because he was a gentleman (although he might not fit that description at this precise moment), and because if Emma was going to bolt for the door he wanted to be ready to stop her.

He deliberately slipped a hurt expression onto his face. "Then you did not enjoy yourself?"

"I...no gentleman would ask such a...you *attacked* me, took me off guard, and...oh, never mind. I'm a terrible person, that's all," she said, and sat down once more.

Feeling much like a jack-in-the-box, a favored toy in his nursery days, Morgan sat down again as well. "Let's discuss what happened last night, Miss Clifford. Calmly, rationally. I was angry with you, yes? And you were angry with me. Also yes? Yes. Our blood was running high. We mistook our tempers for something else. Why, looking back on it, I imagine what happened was inevitable, given our mutual agitation. But," he added as she blinked at him, "I believe what happened to be an isolated reaction, one that would not strike at us so deeply had we not been angry with each other."

"And our blood running high," Emma said, nodding, eager to latch on to this interpretation, because it involved both of them, with equal amounts of blame. "Yes, perhaps that's it. It's certainly a more reassuring explanation than that I'm—" She shut her mouth and stared at her fingers once more.

"Fast, Miss Clifford?" Morgan asked, because he couldn't help himself.

She nodded, keeping her head down. Why was she still here, listening to him, discussing such an irrational act so rationally? Why wasn't she running away? Because she liked being here, no matter how embarrassing the situation, that's why, she told her naughty self. Naughty, naughty, naughty. There would appear to be more of her grandmama Clifford in her than she had previously suspected.

"There is a way to put this matter to rest, you know, if it was our tempers that were to blame." Oh, he was evil, Morgan told himself silently. Not that the thought hadn't just hit him, rather like an inspiration; but although he hadn't planned for this, he was evil just the same. And enjoying himself.

She looked up at him, searching his expression, and finding nothing there but that same handsome face that had haunted her dreams last night. He looked, why, he actually looked *innocent*. "You aren't…you couldn't be suggesting that we…"

"Kiss?" Morgan stood up, took her hand and eased

her to her feet, not moving too quickly, because that might frighten her, but not lagging, either, because—well, because happy circumstance was about to get him what he wanted, wasn't it?

"Yes," Emma said, liking the way her hand fit in his larger one. "That."

"*That*, Miss Clifford, is precisely what I am suggesting. Think about it, if you will. One kiss, and then we'll know, won't we? For I will admit to being curious, and still rather shocked at my own behavior of last evening. My reaction had to be an isolated one, never to be repeated. Circumstances, Miss Clifford—we became victims of circumstances, the stress and strain of an exceedingly difficult day."

"But now, now that we've settled everything, and another day has gone by, and cooler heads have seen that we can all coexist here for the Season—well, now those circumstances have ceased to be a problem? Yes, I can see that," Emma said, then took a deep, steadying breath. "All right, my lord. I'm willing to try, if you are."

And then she put her hands behind her, closed her eyes, lifted her head and pursed those nearly cherry-red lips.

Morgan grinned down at her for a moment, like a child finding his favorite present on Christmas morning, then realized that a moment was all he had. Putting his arms firmly behind his back, a sop to any bit of conscience he might have left, he leaned forward and lightly touched his lips to hers.

It was a kiss, just a kiss, and a mighty tame one at that. He might as well be kissing his mother good-night.

The devil it was! He wanted her, wanted her here, now, on the floor, any way he could get her, and he was going to hell for it. And he didn't care.

But he did care. So he had to control himself.

"There," he said, standing straight once more, forcing a smile to his face. "See? Nothing. Nothing at all. Circumstances, temper. We're cured, Miss Clifford."

She opened her eyes and looked up at him. Then she smiled. "Oh, thank you, my lord. I can't tell you how very relieved I am." She curtsied, picked up the bent hatpin and tossed it into the fire, then left the room before pausing in the foyer and touching her fingers to her lips.

He'd felt nothing? Her heart was still in her throat, and he'd felt nothing? She'd longed, crazily, to all but throw her arms around his neck, use them to pull herself up and wrap her legs around him and kiss him until the end of Time, and he'd felt nothing? *Nothing?*

Emma looked at the footman lingering in the foyer, and the footman looked at his toes, and Emma turned, reentered the study and closed the door behind her.

"Nothing? You felt nothing?"

Morgan, who had been seriously contemplating getting himself well and truly drunk for the first time in over five years, turned from the drinks table to see Emma crossing the carpet toward him.

"And this is also nothing?" she asked, and before he knew it she had raised herself on tiptoe, clapped his face between her hands and pressed her mouth to his with more force than expertise.

Unleashing the demons of hell on an unwary populace could not have been met with more shock than Morgan felt as Emma ground her lips against his. But Morgan was made of stauncher self than a silly populace, and he recovered within an instant.

"No, pet," he said, pulling slightly away from her. "Like this."

He cupped his hands over hers and slid his mouth against hers once more, insinuating his tongue as he lightly stroked the backs of her hands. "And like this," he breathed, biting her bottom lip gently, flicking his tongue across that pouty lip until her soft moan had him releasing her hands so that he could gather her close.

She allowed his kiss. She allowed his hands. She allowed the sensations that were still not familiar, but that pleased her in a way her senses had never been pleased before.

"Like this?" she asked on a sigh, then dipped her own tongue into his mouth, scraping it against his gums, dueling with his tongue before capturing it, sucking on it, because something inside her told her that what she felt was pleasurable, but this might please her even more.

It did.

He broke the kiss at last, burying his head against her

shoulder even as his hands cupped her buttocks and she felt herself pressed against his hardness, a hardness that unleashed a whole new flurry of sensations she did not understand and longed to investigate.

So she pushed him away, stepped back and tried to control her own breathing as he held his arms out, looking at her. He looked so adorable. The cad.

"I…I think we've just ruled out circumstances, my lord," she said, then turned and ran from the room.

"Ah, Mrs. Norbert, just the person I'd hoped to see," Sir Edgar said, allowing a footman to pull out a chair for him at the otherwise deserted breakfast table.

Olive Norbert, her mouth half-full of kippers, mumbled, "Me? What for would you want to see me?" She jammed a heaping spoonful of porridge in alongside the kippers, so that she could not say more, even if she wanted to, and just stared at Sir Edgar expectantly as she chewed, openmouthed.

The woman was a veritable eating machine, and her bulk had measurably increased since her arrival in Grosvenor Square. A few more good meals and she might have to step sideways through doorways. One more week, and she would be in danger of having the already strained seams of her gowns explode around her. No one close to her could possibly escape injury when all that flaccid flesh was released.

Still Sir Edgar smiled. He'd been smiling and lying

for decades, and he could do it again this morning, even if he had to go have a lie-down afterward. "Why, it should be obvious, Mrs. Norbert. It is a fine spring day, and I thought to myself, I thought, why not share it with dear Mrs. Norbert? You would like to take a ride in the park, wouldn't you, Mrs. Norbert? Smell some fine, fresh air?"

He didn't say that the fine, fresh air would improve her appetite, because, for Mrs. Norbert, blinking could increase her appetite.

"A ride in the park? Me?"

"Yes, indeed. Mrs. Clifford has kindly allowed me use of her coach in the mornings, before she might need it to visit friends, or whatever."

Olive was having some trouble digesting this, the only problem she'd had with digestion since she'd mistakenly swallowed down a bite of wax fruit the other day in the music room.

"You want *me* to go driving with *you?* Blimey. I never rode in a coach, you know, not ever. Just hackneys, and they always stink, and the straw's piss-wet on the floor, and—me?" She began chewing again, her mouth still open, and stared at Sir Edgar. He was fairly certain he could hear small gears turning in her head. "Why me?"

This was proving even more difficult than he'd thought, but he pressed on, keeping the smile on his face.

"Ah, Mrs. Norbert, please, spare my blushes. Is it so

astonishing that a man like me would be in your company, day in, day out, and not wish to be alone with you for some moments?"

"Har! If that don't beat the Dutch. Me?" Then she blushed. Dear God, the woman blushed. "Really?" she asked, clearly dumbfounded.

"Really," Sir Edgar answered, not dumbfounded, but not feeling too well, either.

Olive stood up so quickly her chair tipped over. "Well? Let's be off then. I'm too old to waste time, Edgar dearie. Could we ride by my old shop, d'ya think? Stop mayhap, and go in there, stepping outta that fine coach, me hanging on your arm all wispylike and fragile? That would suit me to a cow's thumb, it would."

"Anything you desire, Mrs. Norbert," Sir Edgar said, trying to picture Olive wispylike and fragile, an effort akin to balancing a mountain atop a pea; it simply couldn't be done.

Casting one longing look at the plate of coddled eggs, he then followed after Olive, who had hesitated only long enough to pluck a blueberry muffin from the sideboard and stuff it, whole, into her mouth.

DAPHNE STOOD at a window in the drawing room, the curtain drawn back, to watch as Sir Edgar and Mrs. Norbert rode off in the Clifford coach.

"I didn't believe you when you told me, Mother Clifford," she said, returning to the couch, "but you were right. Sir Edgar is actually smitten?"

"Smitten, bitten, sat on, whatever," Fanny Clifford said, shrugging. "No accounting for tastes."

"No, of course not, Mother Clifford." Daphne folded her hands in her lap. "Ah, isn't this lovely? Mrs. Norbert gone, Emma off for another of her dreadfully long airings in the Square with Claramae. We two can have a Lovely Coze."

Fanny wished for a lovely coze with Daphne as much as she wished for a throbbing toothache. Besides, she had things to do.

She twisted her pinched lips from side to side, cudgeling her brain for a way out of the room. She decided to toss her daughter-in-law a bone; the idiot woman caught so few of them. "I cannot believe Sir Edgar could have developed a tendre for…for that woman. I had so hoped…never mind. It's not as if I'll pine away."

She then slapped her knees and got to her feet, holding her chin at a defiant yet tragic angle. "Excuse me, Daphne. I think I must go lie down for a space."

Daphne just blinked as Fanny's heavy-handed hint sailed *pfthfft*, straight over her head. "But…but it's just gone ten. You only awoke an hour ago. I thought we could take this time to have a Lovely Coze, as we seem to be Ships Passing In The Night, Mother Clifford, and have not had a chance to talk at any length since Emma and I went to Almack's. There's so much I wish to tell you."

Sad, so sad. Daphne Clifford wouldn't recognize A True Symptom Of Unrequited Love if it penned her a note, with diagrams, and tossed it through her window, tied around a rock.

"How nice of you to watch over me, Daphne," Fanny said, then added, "Now stop it. As for Emma and Almack's, she was a sensation, because I wouldn't have had it any other way. So why don't you go chase down Thornley and drive that poor man insane with your daft mooning and sighing, and leave me be. And Sir Edgar doesn't mean a thing to me," she added, giving it one last shot, this time tossing away the rock and employing a sledgehammer, "so don't think I'm going off to pine over the ungrateful man, because I'm not."

Fanny stomped, quite sprightly, out of the drawing room, then hid herself behind one of the doors and waited. And waited.

And waited.

Finally she heard Daphne say in some surprise: "Oh, I see it all now. Poor Mother Clifford. Disappointed In Love. She's off for a good cry, I suppose."

"Finally! At least now she won't come looking for me. Lord, what a looby," Fanny said, and took herself off upstairs.

In the drawing room, Daphne's mind quickly loosed its grasp on her mother-in-law's troubles. After all, she had her own troubles. She picked up her embroidery and wondered if she could manage to down even one more cup of tea without sloshing when she walked if she were to ring and ask Thornley to fetch it for her.

She was a Terrible Person, she knew that, but the highlight of her day had become watching from behind as the Dear Man bent over to put down the tea tray.

ANDERSON WATCHED as John Hatcher, nightcap askew over one bloodshot eye, thumbed at the wax seal and unfolded the note his man of business had just delivered to him in his bedchamber.

"Came by messenger, you say? Just now?"

"Just now, yes, sir. A messenger," Anderson said, hoping he had sanded the ink enough before folding the thing and using a plain seal to press the wax.

"Says here it's from—well, never you mind who it's from. Let me see… 'My dear Mr. Hatcher, I take pen in hand with some reluctance and write to you…' etcetera, etcetera, etcetera '…experiment…new success…procure additional im…imp…' What the devil?"

Implements, you idiot, Anderson screamed inside his head. *I knew I should have gone with tools.*

"Oh, wait…got it now." Hatcher squinted as he read the remainder of the note, then ripped it into small pieces he dumped in his hot chocolate. "Anderson, fetch me my box."

"Yes, sir. Immediately, sir," Anderson said, already on his way to the clothespress, and the small, locked box that rested just behind his employer's dancing shoes. "Here you are, sir."

Pulling a chain free from the neck of his nightgown, Hatcher fitted the attached key into the lock and twisted it.

Anderson stood quietly, itchy palms carefully behind his back, and waited while Hatcher counted out five thousand pounds in crisp banknotes.

"The messenger is waiting below?" he asked, closing and locking the box once more.

"Yes, sir. If I may say so, sir, I think it may be time for you to confide in me. I am, after all, your man of business."

"And this is no blasted business of yours, boy," Hatcher said, holding out the banknotes. "You think I don't know what I'm doing? Now, put this in something and then hand it over to the messenger."

Not ten minutes later, for his bags were already packed, a smiling Anderson was on his way down the servant stairs, heading for the kitchen door and blessed freedom.

His calculations had told him he needed another ten years of inching five hundred pounds a year out of his employer's books and into his pocket before he had enough to take himself off to Paris, and a new life. That had been ten years too long.

But this was perfect. The damn fool was shoveling money at that natty little gentleman in the pub who'd spun him a tale of alchemists. Why not shovel that money to him, instead?

He could have just taken the box, of course, but then an alarm would be raised, and he'd be hunted down as a thief. But this…ah, this was a gift from the gods…and John Hatcher's truly marvelous stupidity.

FANNY LOOKED UP and down the hallway, assured herself that she was alone, and then inserted a key into Sir Edgar's bedchamber door and slipped inside, locking the door behind her. Fool man, didn't he know what she'd discovered—that one key unlocked all the bedchamber doors?

Not that she was about to tell him that; she'd just be here, waiting for him with a full decanter of wine, when he returned from his drive with the seamstress. Poor man, two decanters might not be enough.

Quickly, but careful not to disturb anything, Fanny rifled through Sir Edgar's clothing, his drawers, and even beneath his mattress. She finally located the packet of money jammed behind a particularly ugly painting, and fanned her way through the notes, toting them up in her head.

"Aha, just as I'd supposed. Magically, four thousand five hundred pounds has become six thousand pounds. Well, then, Edgar, that makes us about even, considering how Johnnie sent over another two thousand pounds this morning you'll know nothing about."

She took a moment to admire her reflection in a small mirror standing on the dresser top, patting at her hair as she gave herself a wink. "Ah, Fanny, you'd enjoy men more if you were young again, when they were young and randy and stupid. At this age, they're merely stupid."

She tucked the packet back where she'd found it, then used the key he had left on the washstand to open the door to Sir Edgar's small dressing room. She took a pillow from the bed and tossed it onto the floor. Smiling as she looked inside the closet, she pulled on a pair of thick gloves she'd "borrowed" from one of the gardeners and lowered herself creakily to her knees on the pillow.

She opened the smallest of the trunks and pulled out the pot of gilt and a brush, depositing them on a cloth on the floor. Next, she opened one of the four larger trunks and took out three red bricks, hefting them one at a time in her gloved hands.

One entire box of the bricks were gilt now, as she and Sir Edgar had worked most of the night on them, painting them, lining them up to dry.

She began humming to herself as she reached for another brick.

DAPHNE DROPPED her spoon, then bit her bottom lip between her teeth and watched as Thornley bent to retrieve it. "Oh, I'm just So Horribly Clumsy, Thornley. Please forgive me."

"That's quite all right, madam," Thornley said, taking another spoon from his pocket, for this was the third time this week Mrs. Clifford had managed to drop her spoon. He had knives in the other pocket, for she seemed to lose her grip on those, as well. "Accidents do happen. Now, if there's nothing else?"

"Actually, Thornley, there is something else." Daphne, who had prepared for this for a good hour (preparations that had included a quick trip to the water closet in her chamber) before daring to ring for him, reached for her embroidery bag and pulled out a fistful of different threads, threads she had carefully tangled beforehand. "I need some small assistance with my embroidery, you see."

"I will admit that I've taken the liberty of looking at your embroidery, Mrs. Clifford, and I must tell you that I doubt I could be of much assistance, as every stitch you place is perfect, a true work of art."

Daphne squeezed the threads in her cupped hands as Heavenly Music began playing inside her head. "Oh, thank you, Thornley, that was…Poetical."

He bowed. "Nothing more than the truth, Mrs. Clifford." Actually, the truth was more like Thornley sneaking into the drawing room after everyone else was abed and stroking a piece of half-done embroidery before lifting it to his face, to smell the faint, lingering perfume that was Mrs. Clifford herself. Not that he'd mention that, not unless he was prepared to go to the kitchens, take up Gaston's sharpest knife and then slit his own throat.

"But…but there is a problem. I wish to start a new color, but Mother Clifford is gone, Mrs. Norbert is gone, and Miss Emma is No Use At All with such matters. I was hoping," she continued, sparing only a moment to furiously bat her eyelashes—because Samuel, Rest His Soul, had once, just the once, told her that her eyes were her most pleasing feature— "Well, I was wondering if you would be so kind as to offer your opinion on colors for my embroidery."

"Something in your eye, Mrs. Clifford?" asked Thornley, who had never been flirted with in his life and was unschooled in the nuances of that particular mating call.

Daphne blinked again, a small part of her fearful she just might be Making A Cake Of Herself, but then another part of her, the more desperate part, realized that Opportunity had just come to call.

"Oh, yes, yes. Something—" she raised one hand to her eye, careful to extend her little finger, as was proper "— something seems to be there…right there. Can you see it?"

Oh, Thornley could see it. He could see all of it, now that he was really looking. But the thing was…well, the thing was, he didn't care. He had spent too many nights alone in his quarters, dreaming up fantastical ways to get himself closer to Mrs. Clifford, and now that one had come knocking on his door with all the subtlety of a red brick (the Grosvenor Square mansion was chock-full of red bricks, it seemed), he was not about to spend *this* night cursing himself for a fool that didn't go answer the door.

He skirted the table and sat himself down right next to Daphne, taking her chin in his hand to turn her to face him. He brought his own face close to hers, pretending a great interest in locating the offending object in her eye while his real interest lay somewhere else on the dear woman's anatomy.

Using a corner of her serviette, he dabbed, oh, so carefully, at the outside corner of her eye, then sat back and folded his hands in his lap so they wouldn't misbehave. "Blink for me, Mrs. Clifford," he said. "That may help."

She blinked, then blinked again, and then she smiled. "Why...I think it's gone. Oh, Thornley, you're A Genius. I don't know how I can Thank You Enough."

"That I was able to be of assistance is thanks enough, Mrs. Clifford," he told her, and he just knew his ears were red, because they felt hot, and they even began ringing as he watched those lovely dimples appear in her cheeks.

He felt an angel on his right shoulder, whispering into his ear that if he was not a gentlemen, precisely, he was a man of impeccable morals, entrusted with the care of this woman, and he should even now be getting his so-proper backside up off this couch cushion and racing to the pantry to slap some cold water on his face.

"I...I should go now," he heard himself say, as the devil he'd belatedly noticed perched on his left shoulder quite indelicately blew raspberries into his ear. "Unless you still wish for me to look at the colors?"

"Yes, oh yes, would you?" Daphne asked, grabbing at the threads with both hands and tangling a few more of them. "Oh, drat, what a mess. Look what I've done."

"Here," Thornley said, placing his hands on hers. "Allow me to assist you."

Their hands now touching, Daphne raised her head and looked into Thornley's eyes.

He looked into her eyes.

The world got so much smaller.

And while the angel on Thornley's right shoulder prudently hid its face behind its hands, the devil on Thornley's left shoulder sat back, crossed its legs and lit its pipe, content to watch.

MORGAN PULLED OUT a chair before the servant could help him and straddled it, the better to watch his friend Perry attack either his very late breakfast or his very early dinner.

"You want some?" Perry asked, pointing a forkful of eggs at his friend. "Fairweather? Fetch his lordship a plate, if you please."

"Never mind, Fairweather, thank you," Morgan said, waving the butler away.

Perry arched one brow as he looked at his friend and said, "And take yourself off, Fairweather, there's a good man." Once the two of them were alone in the morning room of the Portland Square mansion, he said, "I've seen you looking better, old fellow. Am I about to hear something interesting? Perhaps even scandalous?"

Morgan frowned. "You'd like that, wouldn't you?"

Patting his lips with his serviette, Perry said, "Oh, good. Scandalous. Quickly, quickly, I'm all agog."

"Oh, cut line, Perry, it's just the two of us. Nobody here to impress with your insistence on being thought of as a total fool."

Perry shrugged. "Ah, but life is so much easier for fools, you understand. Nobody asks us to speak in Parliament or have opinions on the Irish Question, or even comment on the weather—which I always declare to be beastly or splendid, in case you might be wondering. Why, all I have to do with my life, save enjoy it, is to evade parson's mousetrap, and since I do nothing else, I've learned to do both of those very well. Yes, I do enjoy my life. Do you enjoy your life, old friend? I don't suppose so."

"Finished now?" Morgan asked, reaching out a hand to snatch an already buttered scone from a small plate. "Because I've come to ask you a question."

"Oh dear. A question? And you'll probably be tiresome enough to demand an answer as well," Perry said, pushing away from the table and signaling for Morgan to follow him down the hallway, to the smaller drawing room. "Wine?" he asked, walking to the drinks table.

"All right," Morgan said, subsiding into a chair. "I've been briefly considering becoming a dedicated drunk, as a matter of fact."

His back turned to his friend, Perry smiled. It was just as he had hoped when he'd heard Morgan had come back to town; he was about to be entertained.

"Here you are, drink up," Perry said, handing Morgan a glass and then carefully splitting his coattails before he, too, took up his seat. "Now, give me a few moments to guess, if you will. I have often fancied myself as having special powers of deduction, you understand. Almost magical."

Morgan took a sip of wine. "Very well, go on, amuse yourself at my expense."

"How well you know me. I have every intention of doing just that. Let's see, where to begin my deducing? Ah! Shall we begin with your houseguests? Yes, of course. Tell me, have you renamed your mansion, perhaps? I do believe Drummond Arms suggests a certain panache."

Morgan, who was already feeling better thanks to Perry's foolishness, glared at his friend, because that was what he was expected to do, and he did not wish to disappoint that friend. "Does it upset you at all that I would dearly love to punch something and you're looking remarkably like a target at the moment?"

Perry pretended a wince. "Very well, I'll do this quickly. Just nod, all right?"

Morgan nodded.

"Your foul mood has to do with the so-ambitious Thornley's paying customers?"

Morgan nodded.

"Again, the need for deduction. Shall we begin with the current bane of mine uncle's existence, Mrs. Fanny Clifford?"

Morgan considered this for a moment, then nodded.

"Mine uncle, by the by, is quite pleased with me for having rained attendance on the Clifford chit, as per his express orders. I now bask in the soft glow of his gratitude. Why, he only declared me a worthless, posturing idiot the once, last I saw him."

Morgan chuckled and shook his head. "So your uncle Willard is satisfied?"

"Well enough, yes," Perry said, looking into the bottom of his wineglass. "And you know, that baffles me. I mean, he was all hot to have me chasing Miss Clifford's skirts and now he's given me permission to withdraw from the lists of her doting admirers. He sent round a note to that effect just this morning. Is there something I should know?"

Morgan hesitated, then said, "I should have an answer to that question, shouldn't I? But I've been rather involved in my own affairs..."

Perry clapped his hands, then waved them, as if erasing his response. "No, no, let's not go there, not quite yet, as I always believe in saving the tastiest morsel for last. Now, why do you suppose Uncle Willard feels it no longer necessary that I be one of Miss Clifford's suitors?"

"Why ask me?" Morgan said, draining his wineglass. "You're the one spouting off on how splendid you are at deducing. Deduce."

"Very well, I shall," Perry said, taking Morgan's glass

from him and sauntering over to the drinks table. "One—" He turned to Morgan. "I so love order, you know. Very well, I'll begin again. One. Uncle Willard needed an eligible male to fire at Miss Clifford in order to keep the Widow Clifford from penning horrid tales of him in her memoirs. Two. He no longer requires my services. Three. He's still as nervous as a long-tailed cat around a rocking chair, to quote one of the tortured nannies of my checkered youth, but even more excited than nervous. I questioned him on it, but he'd say nothing more than that a recent investment was to soon bear fruit. As a matter of fact, his banker was announced just then, and he whisked me out of his house to meet with him. Anyone would think Uncle Willard was about to come into a fortune. Now, don't you find that odd?"

"I suppose so, but it has nothing to do with the Widow Clifford. She calls him Willie, you know," Morgan said, taking the newly filled glass.

Perry sat down with a theatrical thump. "Willie? Uncle Willie? E-gad, man, I'd never dare. It might be worth my while to visit Widow Clifford and ask her about mine uncle's lurid past. Uncle Willie. The mind boggles."

"And it isn't just your uncle she went after, Perry. I told you about the others at Almack's, but there have been two more come to call since then. They walk in, all angry and strutting, and crawl out, broken men. And she's doing all of this while living under my roof. I can scarcely look anyone in the eye when I'm walking down the street, I swear it."

"No, Morgan. No, no, no. Don't avoid them, single them out. Smile at them. Wink, if you dare."

"But I don't know anything. I don't *want* to know anything. Isn't it bad enough that I'm also being blackmailed, because of Mad Harry?"

"Which brings us to number three," Perry said smugly. "Three. You allowed this, Morgan, old friend. You could have thrown the bunch of them out on their heads, had them all locked up, and Thornley with them. But you didn't. Because of Mad Harry?"

"Because my mother is still above ground, and I would not wish for her husband's old scandals to be dug up for another airing."

"What a good and devoted son." Perry shook his head. "Before meeting Miss Emma Clifford, I might even have accepted that rather self-serving excuse. She certainly is a fetching piece, and intelligent with it all, which you will admit is a rarity among our fair debutantes. The family must be a drawback, but then, families almost always are, and you cannot allow that to weigh with you. So, if you've come to tell me you're about to declare yourself, allow me to offer you my felicitations, and my condolences."

"I'd have to be out of my mind to ask Miss Clifford to marry me," Morgan said, trying very hard to mean what he said. "But…but I have to admit to a few…complications that might make it necessary to do just that."

"Complications? What? She has developed a tendre for someone else? Or does she merely loathe you on general principles? No, wait. Silly me. That's not at all the sort of complications you're talking about, is it? My God, man, what have you done? You have done something, haven't you? Will I find myself moved to clap you on the back and be proud of you? And speak slowly, I don't wish to miss a word."

"Damn you, Perry, you're hopeless. You've been acting the fool so long, you've begun to believe yourself in the role."

"Insulting me now? Oh, dear man, say no more. You must be in love."

SIR EDGAR DIDN'T LIMP as he pulled himself up the stairs to his bedchamber, for the pain in his head so outstripped the discomfort of the pebble in his shoe that he quite forgot.

His ears still rung with Mrs. Norbert's exclamation to Mrs. Daphne Clifford as she raced to join that lady in the drawing room, words to the effect that Olive and her "dearest Ed-gie" had spent a splendid few hours getting to know each other.

If she asked Thornley to call in a minister to arrange announcing the banns, he wouldn't be shocked at all.

For there was, he knew now, such a thing as too much success. He'd hoped to impress Mrs. Norbert with his attentions, flatter her all hollow, and then tell her about his grand discovery of the alchemist's secret, take the money she handed over to him, report half that amount to Fanny, and be done with it.

What he'd forgot, what Fanny had forgot, was that Olive Norbert was no lady. She didn't know how to simper, or behave coyly; nor did she harbor a shred of modesty in that corpulent form of hers.

Instead of being flattered, and blushing, and careful not to show more than a genteel interest at this early stage of the pursuit, Olive had all but jumped on him upon their return to the coach after their stop at her former place of employment, where she had introduced him as "Sir Edgar Marmington, my very own Ed-gie."

In fact, when she'd grabbed his head and pushed his face into her bosom, he'd feared for his life, sure he would be smothered.

Worse, when he became desperate to change the subject from how well the two of them suited— "Always knowed you had an itch for me, Ed-gie, and now we can scratch it" —and had dared to bring up the subject of his great discovery, she had laughed in his face, even as a sharp jab in his ribs had sent him flying up against the far end of the coach.

"Har! That's a good un, Ed-gie," she'd told him. "And I regular spin gold from straw, m'self." Why, she'd even pulled up her skirt and extended one tree trunk of an ankle, saying, "Here, tug on this one, it's got bells on. I'm not such a flat, to believe such a farradiddle, Ed-gie."

He couldn't believe it. He'd fooled Hatcher. He'd fooled peers of the realm. He'd even gulled the former Minister of the Admiralty. But this…this *woman,* was telling him she didn't believe him? A *woman?* Not even one woman, but two, remembering Fanny Clifford.

Oh no, he wasn't going to stand for that!

"Here, look," he'd said, pulling the pouch from his pocket and dumping the nugget into Olive's fat hand (once he'd removed that hand from his…well, he'd have nightmares about that for weeks, he would).

Edgar winced as he remembered how Olive had reacted to the nugget. First, she'd hefted it, then she'd sniffed it, and then she'd tried to take a bite out of it.

"Real, ain't it?" she'd asked, narrowing those already beady little eyes, momentarily distracted from mauling him, thank a most benevolent God. "All right, maybe you do have something here, Ed-gie. Tell your Olive all about it."

So he had, and she'd believed him. Or she hadn't believed him, but thought herself in love with him, and pretended to believe him. That was the real beauty of women, in Edgar's estimation. When they thought love had walked in the front door, sweet reason already had its hat on and was running out the back.

No matter what the reason, she'd promised him two thousand pounds after he'd told her about the four trunks of gold bars in his dressing room. As the daft besom carried all her money with her, fearful the Westham servants might steal it, he already had the two thousand pounds tucked into his pocket.

That had been the good part. The bad part had been when, after handing over the money, Olive had dropped the nugget down the neckline of her gown, then winked and told him to go fetch it.

Edgar had never spent a more miserable afternoon.

He'd just climbed the last step and turned to go down the hallway, find Fanny, and thank her very much for ruining what had once been his rather pleasant life, when his lordship's housekeeper stepped out from a small alcove holding a potted plant, saying, "Psst! Sir Edgar, sir? Over here, if you please."

"Mrs. Timon?" he asked, following the tall, thin woman as she beckoned him to step into the alcove with her. "Is there a problem?"

She touched the keys at her waist, and Edgar tried not to wince as he took in her badly bitten nails, which kept him from realizing the significance of all those keys.

"Been up here doing my rounds, sir, to check on Claramae, you understand. Misses the corners, she does, except when she's hiding in them, playing slap and tickle with that rascally Riley."

"Indeed. However, I fear I don't understand what that has to do with—" Edgar's gaze dropped to the keys once more, then shot to Mrs. Timon's face. "You were in my chamber? My dressing room?"

Hazel shook her head. "Don't go into places guests

lock up. Not their personal sort of locked-up things. I'm not so nosy."

"Really," Edgar said, backing up a step as the house-keeper edged closer. "Where…where do you go? I mean, I am quite sure I locked the door to my chamber, and you went in there."

"I had to check on Claramae. I told you that," Hazel said, her explanation reasonable, he supposed. She jangled the keys at her waist. "And then I had to put away your clean laundry, because that's Claramae's work, and I'm always doing Claramae's work."

"Go on," he said, experiencing that sort of sinking feeling he got in his stomach when someone he passed on the street stopped, pointed and called out, "Hey! You! Aren't you the one what sold me fifty shares in that diamond mine in Bristol two years ago?"

"Well, sir, I was hoping sort of that you'd do that. Go on, that is. Explain to me those three big bars of gold sitting right here, in the bottom of your dressing closet."

"You…you saw…three bars, you said?"

Mrs. Timon nodded furiously. "That I did, sir. Big bars of gold. Three of them, just sitting there for anybody to see. Shame on you, sir."

"Yes, well, I, that is, um—" Fanny must have gone to his chamber, to gilt a few more bricks, then left them out to dry. This was it, the only explanation.

The jig was up, and he'd been found out by a simple

housekeeper. Women! They were fast becoming the bane of his existence. She'd tell his lordship, his lordship would call in the Watch, and he'd be spending his declining years lowering a string and basket through the bars at Newgate, begging passersby for farthings. A fine end, that, to all his ambitions.

"It's real, isn't it?" Mrs. Timon asked, pulling him further into the alcove. "I was waiting for you, meaning to tell you that you'd best be more careful with that rascally Riley in the house, not that I'd say anything about what I seen, no, not me, not Hazel Timon. No one will hear a word from me. Why, I just took a quick peek, and lickety-split locked the door again. Not my gold, you understand. And it looked so shiny and new. Didn't so much as touch anything, because I'm an honest woman, I am."

"As the day is long, Mrs. Timon, I'm sure," Edgar said, wondering just where this conversation was going, because it no longer appeared headed for Newgate.

He smiled at her. She smiled at him. They smiled at each other.

"So," she said at last, "where'd you get it? All that new-looking gold? You know, I'd like to get me some of that. Not that I'm asking for any favors, you understand, but I did want to warn you. About Riley, that is."

Edgar relaxed completely. He nearly slid to the floor, he was so relaxed. He'd always known Mrs. Timon was thin, but now she appeared to be almost transparent. He could see right through her friendly warning to hide his gold from Riley. She'd had entirely another reason to stake herself here, in this alcove, to wait for him. He smiled, just as Good Luck smiled on him. This woman was not going to get the upper hand on him, or his name wasn't Edgar Marmon...er, Sir Edgar Marmington. "Are you interested in gold, Mrs. Timon? Of obtaining un-limited supplies of gold?"

She nodded furiously. "Won't be no more coming from such as you, and his lordship says no pay for a year, for what we done, you understand. All I got is my sav-ings what I put by. I was just about to take myself off to the seaside, rent me a small cottage, and now I can't. I surely would like me some gold like that, yes, sir."

"Have some money set aside, do you?" Edgar asked, smiling up at the woman, who towered over him by a good half foot. He reached a hand into his pocket, clos-ing his fingers around the velvet pouch. He could do this, he would do this, and without a word to Fanny, so that every penny gained would be his own. "Odd you should mention that..."

WYCLIFF HELD OUT the velvet case. "The gold or the sil-ver, my lord?"

Morgan, who had been staring at his reflection with-out really seeing it, slid his eyes left, examined the dia-mond stickpins arrayed in the small box, and said, "The gold, I suppose," saw his valet's wince and amended, "The silver."

"Oh dear," Wycliff said, snapping the lid shut.

"Oh dear, what?" Morgan asked, dragging his thoughts away from the evening ahead of him, an evening begun at the theater, with the remainder of it passed at Lady Oxford's ball, a dreary expanse of time doubtless to be spent dancing the first dance with Emma, then watching her being drooled over the remainder of the night by every Johnny Raw, fortune hunter and, God help him, eligible bachelor in the *ton*.

"Nothing, my lord," Wycliff said in an aggrieved tone, one he had elevated to nearly an art form. "It's just that…well, I admit that showing you only this selection was in the way of a small test, my lord."

All right, so now the valet had his full attention. "To what end, Wycliff?"

"Well, sir, you're wearing stark black, sir."

"Yes, although admitting to be rather occupied with other thoughts, I had noticed," Morgan said, looking down at his, to him, quite unexceptional rig-out, one that had been perfected by Brummell not that many years past, and was still considered quite correct evening attire for a gentleman. "What should I have chosen?"

"Red, my lord. Rubies. Or sapphires. Emeralds, my lord?" he said, proffering a second velvet box. "Color, sir. As is my duty, I have been alert to all changes in fashion, and a small splash of color is just what is sorely needed here. As am I, obviously, my lord, else you would go into Society ill-prepared."

"Was I about to terminate your services, Wycliff?" Morgan asked.

Wycliff giggled, another example of the man's unerring ability to laugh at precisely the wrong time. "In truth, sir, you have on occasion voiced a certain…unhappiness with my services."

"Really. And when was that, Wycliff?" Morgan asked as the valet selected an emerald pin and carefully inserted it just above a fold in his lordship's cravat.

"When you ordered me out of your chamber during the course of your bath this evening, my lord, when I went to wash you."

Morgan looked at the man levelly. "Wycliff, I allowed you to scrub my back, yes?"

"You did, sir," the valet said, now employing a sadly injured tone. "But then—"

"But then you forgot that *I* wash anything below the level of the water, Wycliff."

"I was merely…that is…did you have to throw the soap at my back, my lord?" he ended on a near sob.

Morgan smiled. This was why he had hired Wycliff, to test him on his temper. Clearly he had failed that test earlier. Or perhaps not, because the irritating moron still could stand upright. Either that, or he had mellowed, at last conquered his anger? Possibly. More possibly, he had found an emotion he enjoyed more.

"A thousand apologies, Wycliff," he said, giving the man a reassuring pat on his nearly nonexistent shoulder.

"And just to show you how deep is my sorrow at having upset you, you may have the remainder of the evening for yourself."

"But who, sir, shall undress you?"

"Don't push me too far, Wycliff. I'm being magnanimous, enjoy it," Morgan said, heading for the door leading back into his bedchamber. "Now go find a pub littered with likewise abused valets and sob in your ale as you tell them all how sorely you are used by your employer. It will do you a world of good, I'm sure. Empty your budget of whining, so that you have none left to spend on me."

"I'm quite sure I don't *whine,* my lord," Wycliff said. And, in this instance, he was correct. That last statement had come out as more of a whimper.

One Morgan manfully ignored. "Oh, and here, enjoy yourself," he said, fishing a coin from the small purse in his waistcoat pocket and tossing it to the man (who missed it, because Wycliff could barely catch the sniffles, let alone a coin, and it bounced off his bony chest). "Nincompoop," Morgan muttered under his breath, but only because it seemed the thing to say, and escaped the bedchamber, only to come face-to-face with Cliff Clifford.

"Mr. Clifford," he said, with a nearly imperceptible inclination of his head. "Have you lost your way? I believe you have been moved upstairs."

"Yes, my lord, I have," Cliff said quickly, and just as

quickly hid his hands and the small burlap sack in them behind his back. "I was just…that is, I cannot locate a book I had been reading, and thought I'd search for it in my former chamber?" His words were more in the form of a question, as if he were asking himself if his reason seemed…reasonable.

"You read? Astounding. What are you reading?"

"Um…well, I…something Byron, my lord?"

Morgan would have pursued the subject, for clearly the young idiot was lying in his teeth, but he did not have the time or, frankly, the inclination. He was much too eager to get himself downstairs, to see Emma. "Very good. Byron. We English have done the man a great injustice. Very well, carry on."

"Yes, my lord," Cliff said brightly, and took himself off down the hallway, nearly at a run, his hands now hidden in front of him.

Morgan watched after the youth for a moment, then turned his steps for the staircase, so that he would be lounging in the drawing room before Emma arrived.

It was only when he reached the drawing room, poured himself a glass of wine and, taking up his seat on one of the couches, one foot balanced on his opposite knee, that he noticed something stuck to the sole of his dancing shoe.

"Grain?" he asked of the empty room as he rolled one of the small golden kernels between his fingertips. And then he tossed it to the floor and got to his feet as he heard Emma's voice in the hallway, inordinately pleased by that voice, and not caring that he seemed, even to himself, the besotted fool.

When he also heard Jarrett Rolin's affected baritone, he nearly broke into a run.

JARRETT ROLIN DID NOT bother to suppress his smile of delight as he saw Morgan burst from the drawing room, but merely inclined his head and said, "How delightful to be here once more, in this most grand establishment. Thornley, bless him, remembered how I was once used to running tame in these beautiful surroundings, and did no more than bow as I told him I'd show myself up, and just in time to see this vision of loveliness descending toward me. I know, I know, there was no invitation to call, but I simply couldn't stay away, Miss Clifford. You will have pity on a desperate man, won't you?"

Thornley, who had only just reached the head of the staircase, looked to his master and frowned. He'd done the wrong thing? Mr. Rolin had all but lived here five years ago, so how had he done the wrong thing? But clearly he had. He had been more than willing for Mr. Rolin to announce himself, for then he could go back to concentrating on the third line of the ode he was composing to the glory of his dearest Daphne's dimples.

Remembering that he still had the paper in his hand, Thornley quickly retreated back down the stairs, away from his employer's angry expression, and already renewing his search for a word that rhymed with dimples. Crimples? Simples? Pimples? No. None of those…

"Thornley!"

The butler halted in mid-thought and mid-step and hastened back up the stairs at the sound of Morgan's bellow. "My lord?"

"Mr. Rolin was just leaving," Morgan said even as he advanced three paces, to place his left arm protectively about Emma's waist and draw her close. The way the bastard had been looking at her! The way he was still looking at her! Morgan was about to lose his temper in a way that made any angry outburst that had come before it resemble no more than a stroll through Hyde Park with the Archbishop of Canterbury by his side. He spoke through clenched teeth. "Weren't you, Mr. Rolin?"

"Of course," Rolin said, bowing deeply. "Thornley, you may show me out, as I appear to be *persona non grata* this evening for some reason."

"My lord?" Thornley, his mind still partially engaged in finding the correct word, which he was certain was just at the edge of his mind, looked to Morgan in question.

"You're right, Thornley," Morgan said, stepping away from Emma, who had been standing stock-still, riveted in place by the scéne unfolding in front of her—why, she could nearly see the sparks flying between the two gentlemen. "I'll escort him out myself. Rolin? Feetfirst or headfirst, it makes no never-mind to me."

"Mr. Rolin, sir, if I might escort you?" Thornley said

quickly, even as Jarrett Rolin took a single step toward Morgan. "Please, sir."

Rolin smiled. "So, it sits like that, does it, Westham? Still the crude, unmannered puppy who once trailed at my heels, eager for either a pat or a kick."

"No, my lord," Emma said, grabbing onto Morgan's sleeve as, growling low in his throat, he lunged toward Rolin. "I'll not have you two fighting over me."

"Over you, Miss Clifford?" Rolin, who had prudently retreated to the head of the stairs, shook his head. "Why, I do believe you're correct. My, how delightful. Almost wonderful." Then he bowed once more and allowed Thornley to show him down the stairs, and out.

Which left Emma with Morgan, and suddenly realizing that she was still holding his arm in both of her hands. "You weren't really going to push him down the stairs, were you?"

Morgan blinked, looked down at her hands on his sleeve and shook them off. "I wouldn't have given him that satisfaction. Be ready to leave for the theater in five minutes, Miss Clifford, or stay home," he said, then turned on his heels and headed for the staircase to his rooms—just like any naughty boy who'd been sent to his bed.

Which left Emma to think over Rolin's parting words, and to realize that whatever animosity there was between Morgan and the man may have predated her arrival in London but had been exacerbated by that arrival.

Which left Morgan to pace his bedchamber, counting to ten once, twice, a third time, in an effort to tamp down his temper, which still ran a distant second to a new concern for Emma Clifford, thanks to, yes, Rolin's parting words.

Which left Jarrett Rolin standing on the portico outside the Grosvenor Square mansion, also rehashing every word that had been spoken inside, his devious mind already plotting a way to destroy his one-time adoring pupil, who had dared to learn too much. These titled idiots, how he loathed them. Brentwood was a fool, barely worth his time five years ago or now, but Westham needed another lesson in humility. And, thanks to Miss Clifford, he had just the lesson in mind.

Which left Thornley, formerly the Compleat Butler, who once knew everything, saw everything and managed everything, standing in the foyer, his finger in his mouth as he struggled simply to *find* a thought, muttering, "Wimples? Skin white as wimples? No, that's not it...."

OLIVE NORBERT, just returning from a quick walk to locate a meat-pie seller—for no matter how lovely the victuals in Grosvenor Square, she could not quite tamp down her love for the greasy treat—spied Mr. Jarrett Rolin standing on the front steps of the mansion.

She knew him, of course. She knew most of the *ton*, at least by sight, as she always made it a point to sit and sew by her window, which overlooked the front of the dress shop. Mr. Hatcher, Mr. Rolin, so many of them, bringing their bits o' muslin by for fittings.

But Mr. Rolin, he sort of stood out, because Olive had more than once had to bring her tape and measure one of his mistresses, and they'd had, to the last of them, bruises on their bodies that could only have come from the man now paying to cover those same bodies.

No, not a nice man, Mr. Rolin. But his pockets had been deep.

"Mr. Rolin, sir, how good to see you again," Olive trilled, dropping into an awkward curtsy, then heading for the front door. How she enjoyed entering the mansion this way, not shuttled around to the servant's entrance. Why, she entered and left at least three times a day, just for the joy of being bowed back into the mansion. "You don't have to use the knocker, sir, you can just nip inside with me."

Jarrett Rolin looked down at the squat, and fairly enormous woman, not recognizing her, but certainly recognizing what she was, no more than a servant. "I beg your pardon? You reside here?"

Olive grinned, exposing the last bite of meat pie as her lips and chin gleamed greasily in the light from the flambeaux on either side of the door. "I do. Mrs. Olive Norbert, that's who I am. Guest of his lordship. So? Mayhap you're leaving, not coming?"

Rolin attempted to understand what he was seeing and hearing. He smiled. "Departing, actually, my good—

that is, Mrs. Norbert. I have just been visiting with Miss Clifford. Delightful young woman, don't you think?"

"Young Emma? Ah! You sweet on her?"

"Yes. Yes, indeed, I am. However, his lordship seems to want her all for himself, and has just now depressed my pretensions."

"Huh?"

Rolin tried again. "The marquis would keep us apart, Mrs. Norbert. Miss Clifford and myself. He's not a nice man."

"Oh, he's not so bad. He even let me back at the table, but that's because Miss Clifford must have asked him to. Little high in the instep, the marquis. But he likes me fine," she added quickly. "I live here, as a guest. His lordship's guest."

"Yes, so you said," Rolin said, taking the woman's arm and leading her back down to the flagway. He didn't really care why she was here, he was much more interested in what he could do with her because she was here. "You'll have to tell me all about that, and yourself. But first, Mrs. Norbert, have you a fondness for true love?"

Olive grinned again. She was being walked by a toff, a real toff. If the bitches back at the shop could see her now! "True love? Oh yes, sir, I do. Why, me and Ed-gie, we're gonna be bracketed, soon as he asks me. That'd be Sir Edgar Marmington, Mr. Rolin. He lives here, too."

Rolin ignored that as well, for he had formulated a plan, and it already consumed him. "My felicitations,

Mrs. Norbert, on your coming nuptials. Alas, I have no such hopes for Miss Clifford and myself, now that the marquis has banned me from her presence. I…I don't know what I shall do, truly I don't. If only there were some kind person who would be able to arrange for me to see her…even from afar."

Whether it was the thought of True Love, or the fact that she couldn't help but see that Mr. Rolin had taken a fat purse from his waistcoat pocket and was now holding it to his heart, Olive heard herself saying, "Well, now, there's to be a ball here Friday next, you know. Lots of people about, so that one person wouldn't even be noticed, if you was to catch my meaning? That's what Miss Clifford said, that I could come to the ball, because his lordship wouldn't notice one body more. He wouldn't notice you neither, stands to reason. Iffen somebody was to, say, open the right door from the mews, and let you pop inside?"

Rolin stopped, took the woman's greasy paws in his hands, and, when he let go, his purse had changed possession. "You would do that for me? I had quite lost hope, only moments ago, but now my crushed heart beats again. Do not tell her, Mrs. Norbert, I beg of you. It will be our secret. An elopement. How romantic, don't you agree? And I know just the door. In the morning room. You could possibly leave it unlocked for me, the evening of the ball? You'd do this for my dearest Emma and me, Mrs. Norbert? In the name of True Love?"

Olive stuffed the purse down the bosom of her gown. "What? Oh, sure, sure, for that, too."

"AND I'M TELLING YOU, Harry has to come down here with the rest of them," Riley said as he and Cliff Clifford closed the door to the hallway leading to a large storage space directly behind the card room that adjoined the Westham ballroom. In that storage room were twenty-four cages, all holding hooded gamecocks.

"But Harry's the best of them. He deserves his own quarters," Cliff said, still unconvinced. "It wasn't as if his lordship caught me out."

"I don't care, Cliffie boy. You was lucky, that's what you was, but we don't want to be using up all our luck just hiding Harry, now do we?"

"No, I suppose not. All right, we'll bring him down here with the rest of them. Are you sure they'll be safe here?"

"Safe as houses," Riley told him confidently. "All the chairs and such as are stored there are already in the ballroom, for the big to-do next week. Nobody will come nosin' in here until after the ball, and then we'll just move 'em all right and tight into them closets back there for a space. It's perfect, I tell you. Now nip on up the servant stairs one more time to fetch Harry, and then I'll be bringing you and me some hot water for a wash and brush up. We smell like gamecocks, we do."

"All right, Riley," Cliff said, wondering if being independent was worth all this fuss. Except for the thrill of putting them to the fight, gamecocks seemed to be all feeding them and then scraping the bottoms of the cages with a knife he'd pilfered from the kitchens.

"MOLTING, RILEY?" Thornley asked a few minutes later, as he picked a brown feather from the footman's livery and held it up for the boy to see.

Riley grinned, that grin rather resembling a rictus, as his nerves were stretching near the breaking point. He was beginning to feel the pressure of this entrepreneurship thingamajig he'd thought he'd wanted so much.

"Yes, Mr. Thornley, sir. That's what it is," he said, then snatched a bit of blue embroidery thread from the butler's sleeve and held it up beside the feather. "And how is Mrs. Daphne Clifford going on this evening, sir?"

Thornley took a step backward. "Carry on, Riley. I believe you were taking hot water upstairs?"

"That I am, Mr. Thornley," Riley said. "Things are turnin' hot all over this lovely place, and no mistake."

Once Riley had gone, Thornley patted the small book of poetry he'd liberated from the library and slipped into his pocket, gave himself a small shake and headed back into the morning room, where Daphne, dear Daphne, awaited him.

He did give a moment to worrying about his lordship, and another to sighing about that rascally Riley, but neither thought stuck in his once orderly and precise mind. For his lordship and Miss Clifford were at the theater, Mrs. Clifford the elder was closeted with Sir Edgar—and both much past the age of requiring a chaperon—Mrs. Norbert was wherever she was and could stay there for all he cared. Daphne's dimples awaited....

THE EARL OF BRENTWOOD lifted his quizzing glass to his eye as he struck a pose and waited for Morgan and Emma's approach as they weaved their way through the throng. "Ah, such a delight to see you both. Truly the high point of an otherwise dismal evening. I've half a mind to nip downstairs into the pit and purchase a few oranges to aim at the stage if that horrid woman dares to sing again after the intermission."

"Oh, but my lord, I thought she was wonderful," Emma said, dropping into her curtsy even as Perry bowed over her hand, placing a kiss just a breath above her kid glove.

Perry stepped closer to whisper, "As did I, Miss Clifford, as did I, but as I proclaim never to attend the theater for anything other than showing off my always-impeccable ensembles, I wouldn't wish anyone to know I was near moved to tears by that last aria."

"Still acting the fool, Perry?" Morgan said, shaking his head.

"At least I acknowledge who I am and what I want, dear man," Perry drawled, winking at Emma, who obviously had absolutely no idea what the man had meant.

"Yes, I'm sure you do," Morgan drawled right back at his friend. Damn Perry for being here, when the only reason he had invited Emma to the theater was the hope of being alone with her. "And how is Uncle Willie this evening? I did see him sharing your box, did I not?"

"In point of fact, I am sharing his, as I do not have mine own. I much prefer to flit from box to box, imposing on all my friends. May I join you after intermission? I fear Uncle Willie has begun to snore, and unless I wish to pass the remainder of the evening dabbing drool from his chin, I would be elsewhere until the last curtain falls."

"Yes, please do," Emma said quickly, as she had spent a most uncomfortable hour sitting alongside Morgan, who seemed to radiate anger this evening. Claramae, her nominal chaperon, insisted on sitting at the back of the box, well into the shadows, gnawing on a taffy-coated apple she had procured somewhere. Between the silent anger and the occasional noisy *slurp*, she knew herself ready to scream.

"Actually, Perry, we were about to return to our box, gather Miss Clifford's belongings and depart for Grosvenor Square, as Miss Clifford has just now complained of the headache," Morgan said in a tone that dared Emma to contradict him. "So, if you don't mind, we'll be off now. Consider use of my box this evening as my gift to you."

Perry bowed. "And you may consider my apparent gullibility in swallowing that obvious crammer my gift to you, old friend. Miss Clifford, a pleasure, as always. Do be kind to his lordship. I believe he is in considerable pain."

As Morgan glared at his friend's back, Emma said, "How cryptic. Was I supposed to understand any of that, my lord? Or anything that has happened this evening? In all, I should say we had no need of attending the theater this evening, as I do believe I am already caught up in the midst of some play. I only wish I had a program."

"Forgive me, Miss Clifford," Morgan said, leading her back to his box, to gather up the maid. "I should have begged off earlier, as I am not in any fit mood for company tonight."

"Only tonight, my lord? I vow I hadn't noticed anything out of the ordinary in your disposition," Emma said, snatching up her shawl and settling it over her shoulders. "Claramae?"

"Yeth, mith?" the maid said, pulling on the stick holding her treat, trying to disengage the taffy apple from her top teeth.

Emma sighed. "Come along, dear. And don't touch anything, please, for I fear you'd adhere to it."

"No, NO, IT'S TRUE, I swear it," Fanny Clifford said as Sir Edgar looked askance at her when her story was done. "It's one of the dozen or more reasons we all called him

Mad Harry. Bit poor Jamie's nose half-off before their seconds could pull them apart."

"Because Sir James deloped? I should think the marquis would have been grateful," Sir Edgar said, sitting down beside Fanny as he returned to the couch, two refilled glasses of port in his hands.

"You would. I would. But not Harry. He saw it as just another insult. His son is nothing like him, thank God, or we'd be having this conversation in the guardhouse." She took a deep drink and crossed her ankles, which were already resting on the table top. "Ah, Edgar, this is the life, isn't it? You, me, all that lovely money. We're a fine pair, aren't we?"

"If you promise never to make me go within fifty feet of that horrid Olive Norbert again, yes, I suppose so. I still marvel that I allowed you to talk me round to the idea in the first place."

"Poor oppressed darling," Fanny said, reaching over to plant a loud, smacking kiss on his cheek, because she knew he'd dislike such a gesture. "Ah, Edgar, I'll say it again. We're a fine pair, a fine pair."

"And soon to be very rich," Edgar said, allowing her to rest her head against his shoulder because she was, after all, a fine woman. Very nearly a match for him.

"Yes," Fanny said, sighing. "You know, you were right about those trunks of yours. I'm beginning to become quite attached to all that sparkly looking gold upstairs. Nothing quite so satisfying as making it yourself, is there?"

Olive Norbert put a hand to her mouth, which happened to be full of the cold pork chop she'd just filched from the kitchens, and ran back from whence she'd come, the servant stairs. She descended the narrow, steep flights with some effort, some heavy breathing, and while fighting the stinging behind her eyes.

What to do? What to do? She hated them, how she hated them! Hated Fanny Clifford. She could not quite bring herself to hate Sir Edgar, because he probably had not meant what she'd heard him say up there. Her Edgie was merely a man, and fickle, as men were wont to be. He would pay court to both she and Fanny, until such time as he realized that a soft pillow was years better than a paltry chicken breast of a bosom.

And, if he didn't, she could show him the way, couldn't she? When he had only one to choose from, he could do nothing else but choose her. Yes, she'd have to do that.

But first…first she would see about the trunks in Edgie's rooms, because it had sounded as if he might be hiding something from her. If that were the case, he would also feel her wrath.

With tears in her eyes and anger in her heart (and the pork chop in her pocket), Olive Norbert plucked the large key labeled Bedchambers from the board she'd seen in the hallway outside the knife room, and headed back toward the servant stairs.

EMMA HANDED HER WRAP and gloves to Riley (who had all but given up seeing another penny from any of the Cliffords), then headed for the stairs, intent on putting as much distance between herself and his lordship as she could before he said something terrible like: "Would you care for a small sherry in my study, Miss Clifford?"

Not that he'd said above two words to her all evening. Not a word about what had happened in his study last night, or that first night. Not a word about what had passed between him and Jarrett Rolin.

But the heat? That was still there, emanating from his eyes, from the way he walked, even from the way he kept silent. She could feel that heat, and because it drew her she would run away. She should have run away the first time she saw him. The first time he'd looked at her with such intensity. The first time her heart had fluttered.

"Miss Clifford, would you care for some sherry? I have some downstairs here, in my study."

Emma shook her head, her back still turned to him. "I very nearly had that word-for-word," she said, then put her hand on the newel-post. "No, thank you, my lord. We've been nattering on so all evening, I fear we've run out of conversation."

"Riley? Don't you have somewhere else to be?"

"Yes, my lord, and that I do," the footman said, and all but skipped from the foyer, to pass beyond the baize door to the servant's section of the mansion.

"I fear I must insist, Miss Clifford," Morgan said,

even as Emma climbed to the third step, refusing to break into a run, because then she would appear afraid of him. And she wasn't. She was afraid of herself…and that heat.

"Oh, very well," she said, turning on the step and descending again, all but slamming her slippered feet against the marble floor. "But only if you promise to tell me about Mr. Rolin. I would be delicate and say I sensed a certain coolness between you, but I am not that subtle. And, once you are done, you can then explain why it is all *my* fault."

"Your fault?" Morgan shook his head, even as he put out his arm and escorted her into his study…or his den of iniquity, as he had begun to think about the room.

"Of course," Emma said, settling herself into what she had begun to think of as her chair. "You and Mr. Rolin may have differences in your past, you may dislike the theater on general principles, why, you may even have that headache you ascribed to me, but when we dig deeply enough to reach the bottom of the thing, if I hadn't answered the advertisement and been camping out in your mansion, none of this would have happened."

Morgan, his back turned as he poured her sherry, and himself a snifter of brandy, smiled as he said, "And Thornley is innocent? I fear you have not gotten entirely to the bottom, unless we also see there my once-trusted butler."

Emma accepted the glass, then shrugged. "Oh, don't

blame Thornley, my lord. He is, after all, a valued family retainer. It is much easier to blame me."

"Fair enough. You *can* be annoying," he said as he sat down in the facing chair, then smiled, because she had the audacity to look shocked at his words. And, yes, there they were, those two flags of hot color rising in her cheeks.

"*I* am annoying? I am *annoying?* If that is not the pot terming the kettle black, my lord, I truly don't know what is. Or am I to suppose that I am the one who assaulted you, right here, in this study? Twice."

"Once," he corrected. "Twice for me, once for you. I have been keeping track, you know."

"Oh! You're impossible. I agreed to come in here to learn about Mr. Rolin, not discuss…other things. You're no gentleman, my lord."

"Not lately, no," he said, smiling ruefully. "I was, once. Right up until the moment I awoke in my own bed, to hear your dear mother screaming to bring down the ceiling on my head."

Emma placed her glass on the table beside her chair. "No, my lord. We will not go there again."

"It's not a journey I wish to take, no," he agreed, then sobered. "You want to know about Jarrett Rolin."

"Wouldn't you, having witnessed what I did earlier this evening?"

Morgan sat back at his ease. "You know, Miss Clifford, young ladies are not supposed to be quite so direct."

"Young ladies are not supposed to be alone in a

gentleman's study, most especially after what has already transpired between the two of us in this same room. Now. Mr. Rolin?"

"Is not a very nice man," Morgan said, wondering where to begin, and likewise wondering if there were some way he, himself, might come off better in the telling. And, since there was no way to accomplish that bit of magic, he decided on the truth. "The Earl of Brentwood and I met Rolin five years ago, during our first Season. My only Season."

"Yes, I had already deduced as much. It wasn't a pleasant encounter?"

"The meeting was pleasant enough," Morgan said, smiling slightly. "It was the parting that wasn't quite as enjoyable. You see, Perry—Lord Brentwood—and I were young, and green, and sadly gullible. Rolin was older, quite popular, and when he deigned to take us up, make us a part of his entourage as it were, we were ignorant enough, and flattered enough, to believe the man might actually enjoy our company."

"He didn't?"

Morgan took a sip of brandy. "There are in this world, Miss Clifford, people who insert themselves in the middle of a friendship just to have the best vantage point from which to watch when their machinations start a war."

"I...I don't understand." But that was a lie, because she did. "Are you saying that Mr. Rollin offered his friendship, just so that he could turn you and the earl against each other—then stand back and watch what happened next? For his own amusement?"

"So you do understand. And I nearly killed my best friend, only to *amuse* Rolin, who would have been very much at home in the Coliseum, turning thumbs down on the gladiators. For my sins, I didn't realize this at once. It took several months of reflection for me, licking my wounds in the country, to see the genius of what he'd done. Act the friend to both, flatter both, and then begin whispering to both. According to the earl, he's still at it."

"I liked him, at first."

"And saw him for what he is much more quickly than either Perry or myself, for which I commend you."

Emma was silent for some moments, then said, "Why did he come here this evening? Surely it could not have been to apologize."

"Why he came here, Miss Clifford, might never be understood by either of us. But I do know how he departed, believing that you are important to me. That's why I wished to speak with you. I've given what I'm about to say serious consideration all evening. I cannot allow you to walk in the Square again, Miss Clifford, not without me. I cannot, in fact, allow you to go anywhere without me."

"He'd…he'd want to hurt me?"

"No, Miss Clifford, he'd want to hurt me, and he believes he has found the perfect way to do so. Now do you understand?"

Emma looked down at her hands, as if examining them for flaws. "And am I? What you said a few moments ago, that is—am I important to you?"

"It doesn't matter what I think, just what Rolin believes. And he won't give up. Not Rolin."

Emma lifted her chin and looked at him levelly. "Then there's nothing else for it, I shall have to leave London and return home, as I shall not become a millstone around your neck, my lord."

"Too late for that, Miss Clifford," Morgan said, then smiled. "Would it be so terrible, being in my company?"

"I really do hate when you decide to be amusing," Emma said, and got to her feet. "Now, if you'll excuse me, my lord?"

Morgan had also gotten to his feet, knowing he couldn't shout "No, don't go!"

He had to find another way, one that would keep her temper high enough that she might not realize that he was all but on his knees before her, begging her to stay. "Off to pack, Miss Clifford? Ah, but you've forgotten the ball in your honor Friday next, haven't you? The invitations have been delivered, the flowers and food ordered, the musicians already tuning their violins. I have, in short, gone to great expense for your benefit. Are you prepared to recompense me?"

"Don't be ridiculous!"

He might not yet know the way to her heart, but he had to commend himself as being unerringly astute at locating her temper. "Yes, I thought not. Therefore, Miss Clifford, you have no choice but to remain here, in London, stuck tightly to my side, until I can be assured that Rolin has been rendered harmless."

Emma's eyes grew wide. "You…you wouldn't challenge him to a *duel?*"

"I try to pride myself on not making the same mistake twice, Miss Clifford. Duels solve nothing, even between enemies. No, I will find another way. Or not," he added, stepping closer to her.

"Or not?" Emma repeated, stepping back a pace, because Morgan was looking at her *that* way again, the way that made her knees go all wobbly as she remembered being held tight in his arms, and what his mouth and hands had done to her.

"He would move on to greener pastures, once he realizes that I intend to make you my countess. Even Rolin would not dare his mischief then, for he's not a fool, and wishes to continue to move in Society."

"I…I see no need for anything quite so…so desperate, my lord," Emma said, or at least she thought she'd said the words; it was difficult to know, with her heart pounding so loudly in her ears.

Morgan placed his hands on her shoulders. "No?"

She wet her lips with the tip of her tongue. "No? Um…I mean *no*."

For five long years Morgan had fought to kill his temper, and in doing so, he had tamped down all his emotions, something he hadn't realized until this maddening woman had come into his life, arousing not his temper, but a whole new awareness. A never-before-experienced *joy*. He was alive again, for the first time in those five long years.

He wouldn't let her go.

"I can think of several reasons for doing something…desperate, Miss Clifford," he said, then lowered his mouth within a breath of hers. "Your delectable lips…" he said, kissing her, before moving on, kissing each part as he said it "…your magnificent eyes…the perfect shell that is your ear…this one…um, yes, this one, too. Your enticing throat…the intriguing shadow, just here, between your sweet breasts…"

Somehow, Emma found herself lying on the carpet in front of the fireplace. How she'd gotten down there she had no idea, but here she was, and if she had been going to protest, she had certainly left it too late. Besides, one would need to feel a reason to protest, and all she could feel was Morgan's mouth on her, his hands on her…his body pressed against her…

A small part of Morgan knew that what he was doing was wrong. Another small part of him remembered that he had dismissed Wycliff for the evening, and that his bed was much more comfortable than the floor, no matter how soft the carpet or warm the glow from the fireplace.

But the rest of him, the majority of him, wouldn't have stopped what he was doing, feeling what he was feeling, not for what was right, not for a fine feather bed, not for the promise of immortality.

Because all there was now was the *now*. The feel of Emma, the taste of her, the mad rush of blood that sang in his head, rushed into his loins, filled his heart almost to bursting.

And when her arms went around him, when she sighed into his mouth, when she moved her lower body in a way that told him she wanted more, more, he shut down his mind and let his senses lead him where they may.

He ripped a seam in his jacket in his struggle to be rid of the formfitting thing, and nearly strangled himself in his effort to be rid of his neck cloth.

Moments later, spangles from Emma's gown littered the carpet like small, twinkling stars sparkling in the firelight, but the soft pink glow that fire cast on her bare breasts held all of Morgan's attention. He stripped off his shirt, eager to feel his flesh against hers, eager to cover her before maidenly embarrassment broke through the sensual fog he could see in her bewitching gray eyes.

They kissed, deeply, then kissed again, and Emma's hands roved over his back, her fingertips digging into his skin as he lifted himself slightly, to push her gown down, down, over the flare of her hips.

"My God," he breathed into her ear as, shed of his

breeches, he sank against her once more, careful not to put his full weight on her, but unwilling to ask her if he should stop, because she might say yes.

"I…I don't know what to do," Emma told him breathlessly. "But…but I must do *something*."

"Just let me love you," he told her, capturing one breast in his hand and trailing kisses down her throat, across her silky-smooth flesh, until he could capture one sweet, rosy nipple in his mouth.

Again she moved against him, lifted herself to him. And when he tried to raise his head, she grabbed at his ears and pulled him back to her.

Laughing softly in his throat, he ministered to her again, for she might not know what to do, but clearly had already learned what she liked, and was not shy in asking for it.

He moved his attention to her other breast, then dragged his mouth down her smooth belly as she raised up to meet him. He kissed her hip, tongued her navel, pressed kisses on the insides of her thighs…

"Morgan, I—" She sounded suddenly panicked.

"I know, sweetness, I know," he said, moving back up her again, to kiss her ears, her hair. "It's too soon for that. But we've got forever. I don't want to hurt you."

"Shut up," she breathed into his ear, her tone a caress, even if her words came from someplace inside her that must owe much of its existence to her paternal grandmother, who had been, if anything, too tepid in her description of the joys of lovemaking.

Because she *wanted*. She wanted *so much*. So when Morgan insinuated a leg between her thighs, then lifted himself, positioned himself, she smiled against his chest, feeling no fear, no apprehension. Just anticipation.

There was pain, but it was fleeting, and then he was moving inside her, and she was moving with him, climbing toward an unknown something that lay just out of reach…then closer…then closer…then…

Morgan caught her startled exclamation with his mouth as he pushed himself deep inside, held her tightly, and gratefully surrendered himself to the inevitable.

DAPHNE HEARD THE SCREAM that was so suddenly cut off, and raced from the drawing room, where she had been patiently waiting for Emma and dreaming sweet daydreams about her dearest Aloysius.

"Mother Clifford!" she shouted, as doors opened and footsteps could be heard running from everywhere, including a swollen-mouthed Claramae and a clearly frustrated Riley, who seemed to appear from the alcove holding the statue of Venus.

But that wasn't important. What was important was that her mother-in-law was lying on her stomach halfway down the staircase, her head positioned toward the first floor, her skirts over that head, exposing two skinny legs and a rump pointed toward the second-floor landing.

"In the name of all the saints!" Riley said, and raced to assist Fanny.

Daphne also ran to her, pulled up the disheveled skirts, then thanked the good Lord that the old woman was already beginning to moan. "Oh, I thought you were dead. Gone To Your Heavenly Reward."

Fanny looked up at her even as she struggled to right herself and sit on one of the steps. "Don't be in such a rush, you twit, for I plan to haunt you. *Ooh*, every bone in my body is broken. Bloody marble steps." She grabbed Daphne's arm. "Did you see him? Did he get past me?"

"See who, Mother Clifford? I didn't see anybody. Riley? Did you see anyone?"

"Yes, did you see anybody, boy?" Fanny, climbing Riley as one would a tree, hand-over-hand, got to her feet at last, and descended the few remaining stairs to the first floor, wincing as she went.

"No, ma'am, and that I didn't. Here, let me help you into the drawing room. Claramae, fetch Mr. Thornley."

"Don't fuss, I'm fine," Fanny said, but she moaned as she lowered herself onto one of the couches, and allowed Daphne to raise her legs onto the cushions, even cover her with her shawl. "I just want to know who pushed me."

Daphne sat down, right on the low table between the two couches. "Push...*pushed* you?"

"That's what I said, yes," Fanny said, trying to reposition herself on the cushions, because her hindquarters were beginning to pain her, as she'd managed to catch hold of the rail at first, and had bumped down half the flight on her haunches before that last inelegant pitch forward. "Why else would I tumble down the stairs?"

Daphne took a deep breath, which served to bring the smell of strong spirits to her nose. "Mother Clifford, You've Been Drinking!"

"So what? I can drink two sailors under the table, and always could. I was pushed, I tell you, so stop looking at me as if I'm some dotty old fool who doesn't know when she's been pushed."

And then she shut up, because she suddenly realized who could have pushed her. Edgar. Edgar, who would have all the money if she didn't need her half because she was interred in the family mausoleum. Edgar, who had seemed so friendly, so—if not overjoyed, at least tolerant of her inclusion in their little game.

"Mother Clifford, are you sure you're all right? You…you look… Rather Strange."

"What? Oh. Oh, no, I'm fine," Fanny said quietly. "Where is Sir Edgar?"

"I'm here, Fanny," he said, and she looked up to see him standing behind the couch, his complexion pale. He put out a trembling hand and she raised hers, allowed him to squeeze her fingers. "Please tell me you're all right."

Fanny smiled. No, it wasn't Edgar. She knew her men, and the old fool was genuinely upset. Possibly because she may have cracked her head, become delirious and begun mumbling all about painting bricks gilt…but he *was* genuinely upset. "I fell, Edgar."

"Yes, my dear lady, I know. You rest now. Thornley has sent someone for the doctor."

"Indeed, Mother Clifford. Aloysius will See To Everything."

"Aloysius? Who the blazes is that?" Fanny asked, then closed her eyes. "Maybe I am a little...muddled."

Everyone was in the drawing room now. Everyone excepting Morgan and Emma, who had tiptoed across the foyer, passed through the baize door and then raced up the servant stairs to change into their nightclothes before descending the main staircase as if risen from their (separate) slumber.

Also missing was Olive Norbert, who had locked herself in her rooms, ink stains on her lips and tongue as she nibbled on her pen, squinting at her spelling of *Hattchure* and patiently waiting for someone to come tell her that Fanny Clifford was dead.

Not that Olive still wanted Sir Edgar, once her dearest Ed-gie, but now the man who had broken her maidenly heart. Not once he'd shown himself for a two-timing rotter and, worse, teasing her with one small lump of gold when he had trunks full of the shiny stuff in his dressing room.

And then, just to make matters worse, she'd seen the list on his dresser, the list of names, with hers and even Mrs. Timon's on it. The only other name she recognized was that of John Hatcher.

Edgar was taking all their money, using it to make

gold with his great discovery of that alchemist-trical business, and planning on keeping it for himself and that man-stealing Clifford woman.

Olive's anger was all directed at Edgar, now.

Pushing a drink-clumsy Fanny down the stairs had been simply getting some of her own back, that's all. Justice.

Carrying away all that lovely gold she'd seen in Edgie's dressing room was also justice, Olive knew, even if she needed a man to do the toting, and therefore had to share her fortune with John Hatcher. But she knew she could trust him. He was, after all, a toff.

At The Ball...

Let a play have five acts,
neither more nor less.
—Horace

"COME ON, DARLIN'. I know just the place where we can be all alone and by ourselves."

"Riley, no, I daresn't," Claramae said, rebuttoning her gown. "Me mum said never to give away what you should by rights pay for."

"Money? It's money you'd be wanting? Oh, *aingeal*, it's money I've got. I've got me fistfuls of money."

"Not money, Sean Riley," Claramae said, trying to push past him, out of the alcove. "A weddin' ring, that's what you have to pay for."

"A wedding ring, is it? Me? I'm no more than eight and twenty. Little more'n a boy. You'd put a collar on a baby, *aingeal*?"

Claramae didn't answer him. She was much too occupied in blinking wide eyes at the Marquis of Westham, who had taken up position on the opposite side of the hallway, leaning one shoulder against the wall, his arms crossed as he watched. And listened. "Oh, Lawks," she said, then lifted her skirts and ran for it.

"Claramae! Blimey," Riley said to himself. "It was so close I was this time, too."

"Not really, Riley," the Marquis of Westham said evenly.

"My lord!" Riley spun about to face Morgan, his complexion pale enough for Morgan, if he so desired—and he didn't—to be able to count every freckle on the footman's cheeks.

"I thought I told you to stay away from the maids, Riley."

"And that you did, my lord. It's just Claramae, you understand. All that lovely bosom…"

"There is that," Morgan said, allowing the ghost of a smile to soften his features. "Very well, consider yourself the recipient of a pithy lecture on gentlemanly behavior, and we'll move on to other matters."

"Yes, my lord, thank you, my lord. Other matters? And by that you'd be meaning Mr. Clifford, sir?"

"Oh, yes, definitely Mr. Clifford. But first, I'd like you to explain this business about fistfuls of money, if you don't mind."

Riley coughed into his fist, for he had nearly swallowed his tongue. "Oh. That."

"Yes, Riley. Oh. That. It was my understanding from Thornley that you have managed to spend every bit of your ill-gotten gains, those being your gains, Riley, at my expense these past three years."

Riley looked down at his toes. No inspiration there. So he looked up to the ceiling. No, none there, either.

"Has Mr. Clifford been paying you to accompany him about town, Riley?"

Ah! Lord bless the man for helping him. Riley arranged his features in an expression of shame. "I tried to naysay him, my lord, and that's a fact, but he would insist."

"I should have guessed as much, I suppose. You've been entirely too eager to be of service and, as I refused to line your pockets, you found another way. What amazes me is that Mr. Clifford has the blunt to spare, considering the fact that you've been bringing me stories of the two of you touring the Tower, and several libraries, where the boy purchases a multitude of books. Mostly sermons, I believe you said."

"Well, my lord, that might have been just a small bit of a fib," Riley said, sticking his hands in his pockets. "It's really more like Mr. Clifford had himself a good run of luck at a dice toss I happened to lead him to, begging your kind indulgence, my lord."

"All right, Riley, I don't think I wish to hear anything more. Just keep close to Mr. Clifford, and keep yourself as far from Claramae as possible. Do you understand?"

"Yes, my lord, that I do."

Morgan watched the footman scurry off down the hallway, and sighed. How had he gotten himself involved with a footman? Oh, yes, he remembered now. He'd done it to reassure Emma, who would otherwise worry herself sick about her feckless brother.

He pulled out his pocket watch and checked the time. Not quite half past eleven. With a clearly insulted Wycliff banished to a room on the top floor this past week, the arrangement had been that Emma joined him in his bed-chamber at midnight each night, to return to her own chambers just before dawn.

It was a shabby arrangement, and he'd be ashamed of himself if he wasn't so thoroughly enjoying that same self.

They did attend some parties, but mostly during the day, and then only making an appearance at two evening gatherings each night, before heading back to Grosvenor Square.

In public, his cold stare had managed to depress the pretensions of the fortune hunters, the half-pay officers and the dozen or so very acceptable and eligible bachelors who seemed besotted with her...until they met that cold stare.

He was certain Perry had been laughing at him each time they happened to meet, but he didn't care.

Fanny Clifford didn't seem to be alarmed by his attentions to her granddaughter. She'd had to take to her bed for several days after her fall, for one thing, but was now getting around again, slowly, and walking with a stick. Mostly she spent her days closeted with Sir Edgar, either in his chamber or hers. Either that, or they were in the main drawing room, sending dagger glances at anyone who might attempt to take their own ease in that room.

The drawing room? Yes, Morgan decided. That's where he'd left his copy of *Paradise Found;* either there or the morning room. There was a particular passage he wanted to read to Emma.

He walked over to the closed doors, and opened them just in time to hear Fanny Clifford's cackle. "Ha! Stap me and my broken and bruised backside if that's not ten million pounds you owe me now, Edgar. Here—deal."

"I think I liked you better feeble, and leaning on me for support," Sir Edgar said, picking up the cards with both hands, then noticing Morgan, and looking at him with all the joy of a man who has just spied a moth hole in his best coat. "Oh, good evening, my lord. Is there something you require?"

Yes. He required his mansion back! Not that he'd say that, not when Fanny Clifford had been winking at him each time he saw her, almost as if she knew exactly what was going on every night after midnight. She seemed delighted by the notion, in fact, naughty old woman.

"I was just searching for my book, Sir Edgar," Morgan said after a cursory look around the room.

"Reading? Didn't think you had the time, boy," Fanny said, and winked.

Morgan bowed, to be polite, and to hide the sure shock that showed on his face, and took himself off to the morning room to continue his search.

Once more he had to open a door closed to him in his own house, and once more he found the room to be occupied, this time by Mrs. Daphne Clifford and—good God. Thornley? Thornley, sitting close beside Daphne Clifford, holding both her hands in his? Thornley, with his lips pressed to Daphne Clifford's lips?

Morgan quietly shut the door.

No wonder nobody cared what he and Emma were doing. They were *all* doing it!

EMMA KNEW she was late. She had purposely remained in her rooms until half past the hour, pacing the floor, not wanting to linger, but not wanting to seem too predictable, either.

After all, it had been nearly a week.

Yes, Morgan had spoken of marriage. Eventual marriage. He'd spoken of plans to announce their engagement at the ball tomorrow—just at midnight, which he seemed to consider romantic.

But not a word of love had passed between. Not one.

There was passion, definitely. There was even laughter along with the kisses.

But not a word of love.

She could hear Claramae in the dressing room, fumbling about as she prepared for bed, and at last decided that she could wait no longer. Morgan might take it into his head to come find her, and she doubted Claramae's sensibilities could survive the shock.

With one last look in her mirror, Emma exited into the hallway and tiptoed down the servant stairs to the second floor, peeking around the corner to be sure the hallway was clear before racing to Morgan's door and quickly entering his chambers.

"Where were you?"

She hadn't even gotten the door shut, and already he was at her. Good. She wanted to be angry anyway.

She turned and leaned her back against the door, trying not to melt as she caught sight of him in his dressing gown, his hair disheveled as if he'd been running his fingers through it in distraction.

"I didn't think I was to appear at any precise time, my lord, as if on command. I could have fallen asleep, or even decided not to visit you tonight. I could do that, you know."

Morgan held up his hands. "You're right, and I'm an idiot. I'm sorry, Emma. But...but, my God, woman, I think I'm running a brothel!"

Emma blinked. "I beg your pardon," she said coldly. "Or did I mishear you when you said, repeatedly, that you will be announcing our engagement tomorrow evening, and that the only reason you have not already done so was because Society would see any earlier announcement to be extremely rushed? Although ten days' acquaintance certainly will never have you charged with dragging out our courtship to interminable lengths."

"No, no, you don't understand me, Emma," Morgan said, taking her hands in his and leading her over to the bed. "It's not *us*. We've anticipated our marriage, I grant you, but we *know* what we are doing."

"Do we?" Emma asked, deserting the bed, and him, to sit in one of the chairs on either side of the fireplace. "At times, my lord, I question exactly what it is we are doing. Tiptoeing down the servant stairs at midnight? It's almost shoddy. No, it *is* shoddy."

Morgan knew she was right. He hated what they were doing, what he'd talked her into doing, but he had his reasons. He didn't want Jarrett Rolin close to her until their engagement was announced, but he couldn't live without her once he'd been with her, touched her, loved her. He was a selfish bastard, trying to cloak himself in reasonable excuses, and he was ashamed of himself.

Not enough to spend a night without her by his side....

"Tomorrow night, Emma," Morgan said, taking up the facing chair. "Tomorrow night, and everyone will know that you will be my wife. I've already written to my mother, so that she doesn't hear about our engagement from anyone else. Monday, we will leave for Westham, to post our banns."

"Really," Emma said, rather impressed but not willing to let him know that. "You seem to have taken care of everything, haven't you, Morgan?"

"Not everything," he said, smiling at her. "I've yet to kiss you today."

"Only because you were so very busy railing at me for having the audacity to keep you waiting."

"I know, I know, I'm a terrible person, and I cannot ask you to forgive me, although I will. It's...it's just that..."

"This mansion has been turned into a brothel, I believe you said. Now, if you were not referring to us, what precisely do you mean?"

Once, Morgan had decided, he'd not been in control of his temper. Now he seemed to have conquered his temper, but all the rest of his life had turned upside down.

He rubbed at his forehead. "Where do I begin? Riley, pawing Claramae in every corner? Your grandmother, constantly closeted with Sir Edgar, when she's not acting the madam and winking at me—because she knows what we're doing, Emma. The woman doesn't miss a trick."

"I know," Emma said, lowering her head to hide her blush. "She pressed some money at me this afternoon, telling me to go to Bond Street and find nightwear more suitable for a man's eyes."

Morgan smiled in spite of himself. "Then she must be beyond it, Emma, for all her stories of her lurid past. I prefer you in no nightwear at all."

"You're incorrigible," Emma said, laughing, for any maidenly modesty she might have brought with her from the country had packed up and traveled back there without her since the first time Morgan had made love to her. "And proud of yourself."

"Yes, I am, rather. But to get back to what I was saying. I was searching for my volume of *Paradise Found* tonight, and first stumbled over Riley and Claramae, then interrupted your grandmother and Sir Edgar. Finally, in the morning room, I nearly disturbed your mother and Thornley, although the way the two of them were kissing, I doubt they'd have noticed if I'd marched in there, beating a drum."

Emma got up and walked toward the bed, untying the ribbons at the neckline of her dressing gown and letting it slide to the floor before slipping beneath the covers. "She knows it's not proper, but she can't help herself, and neither, I suppose, can Thornley. But, as she is happier than I've ever seen her, I think it highly wonderful and romantic."

Morgan stripped off his dressing gown and walked around the bed, to lift the covers and prop himself against the headboard beside Emma. "That, my sweet, is because you have not considered what I am considering."

Emma turned on her side and began unbuttoning Morgan's shirt, for he had remained in his evening shirt and breeches, although his hose and shoes were gone. "And what are you considering, Morgan?"

"Thornley as my father-in-law," Morgan said with a wince. "I can already hear a delighted Perry making jokes."

Emma turned her face into his chest to smother a giggle. "Will he call you *son*, do you think? And you can call him Papa Thornley."

"How gratified I am that you find this all so amusing," Morgan said, reaching over to lift her chin, so that he could look into her eyes. "Emma…that's not all. Mrs.

Norbert is skulking about, avoiding everyone, not that I mind her absence from the dinner table this past week, but it is odd, considering how very much she once wished to be a part of all activities."

"I believe she is uncomfortable at table, sensing that she doesn't quite fit in, poor thing, although I do happen to know that she's very much looking forward to attending the ball tomorrow night. I did not, of course, also tell her that you said one more ill-mannered person wouldn't matter in a ballroom undoubtedly crammed to the rafters with them. Now, is that it?" Emma asked, for he had begun sliding the strap of her nightgown off her shoulder and then stopped, as if he'd forgotten what he was doing. "Or is there more?"

"There's more. Mrs. Timon is whistling, and even smiling. A good woman, Mrs. Timon, I've known her since I was in short coats, but she's one who has rarely been known to smile. And never known to whistle."

"Sounds ominous," Emma said, picking up Morgan's hand and moving it to her breast. She might as well not have bothered. "Oh, for goodness' sake, Morgan, just tell me everything. Riley, Claramae, Grandmama and Sir Edgar, Mama and Thornley, Mrs. Norbert and even Mrs. Timon. All you've missed is Clifford, and I'm already convinced he must be doing *something* you don't like."

Morgan sighed. "All right, but I wasn't going to say it on my own. Your brother…your brother *smells*."

Emma sat up quickly, leaving Morgan's hand holding nothing…which was when he realized it had been holding something, and now missed that something.

"How dare you! He *smells?*"

"Not all the time," Morgan hastened to clarify his words. "But…but sometimes, yes."

"What does he smell like?" Emma asked, pulling her strap back up on her shoulder, no longer in the mood for lovemaking.

"What does he smell like?" Morgan considered this for a moment. "I'm not quite sure. A barnyard? A stable? No, wait a moment. He…he smells like *Riley.*"

Emma plumped up some pillows behind her and lay back against them, looking up at the burgundy canopy above her head. "You do know that you're making absolutely no sense, don't you?"

Having heard the words as he spoke them, all of them—emptying his budget of his every concern and complaint—he felt ashamed but no more enlightened. "Emma," he said, turning on his side and beginning to inch down that same strap for a second time. "Do you ever feel there are things going on here that we know nothing about?"

"To be honest, Morgan, I suppose there are. But, as I, for one, wouldn't want anyone asking too many questions about what's going on *here,* do we really want to know?"

Morgan smiled. "No, I suppose not. Now come let me kiss you, sweetness. You've talked my ear off long enough."

"I've talked *your—oh!*" Emma reached behind her and pulled one of the pillows free so that she could pummel Morgan with it as he halfheartedly attempted to hold her off.

Laughter died as he managed to get her over on her back and straddled her, his questing hands having at last located *both* straps of her nightgown and pulled them down, to reveal her breasts. "See here, look what I've found."

Emma felt herself blushing. "Get off me, you great oaf," she said, but she didn't mean it. He knew that by the way she reached up her hands to stroke his chest. "I vow I don't know why I put up with you, Morgan. Mauling me, without a word of love."

Morgan frowned. He might be no more than a confused man suddenly in the mood for some lovemaking, but she had meant that last bit. "I haven't?"

"No, Morgan, you haven't," Emma said, pushing at him, and he obliged by rolling off her. "You love my eyes, you love my mouth, you love my—well, never mind. But have you ever said that you love *me?* No, my lord, you have not."

Morgan stabbed his fingers through his hair. "I could have sworn…I've *never…?*"

"Oh, for pity's sake, Morgan, *no.* And you're not saying it now. I'm beginning to believe you are marrying me only to have some of your own back on Jarrett Rolin, if I still believe he's as dangerous as you say he is."

"If he could get his hands on you, he'd ruin you, just to spite me."

"Yes, so you've ruined me first. Was it to spite him?"

"Now you're being ridiculous."

"I know that," Emma said, blinking back quick tears. "And, if you say you love me now, how will I believe you? I should never have said anything. I should have gone to Grandmama. She would have known what to do."

"Oh, yes, I'm quite convinced of that. The woman is a veritable fount of knowledge," Morgan said, pinching thumb and finger on the bridge of his nose. "Is that why you were late tonight? You weren't planning on coming to me at all, were you?"

Emma plopped a pillow on her belly and clasped her hands together on it. "I gave it some thought, yes."

"But you're here," he said, covering her hands with one of his own.

"Oh, don't be so smug, Morgan, it doesn't become me."

He threw back his head and laughed at her words. "I do love you, Emma. Madly. Feel free not to believe me, for then I'd have to convince you."

Emma bit back a smile. She was so silly, just like a female. She liked hearing the words, but she hadn't needed them, not really. "In that case, my lord, convince me."

The pillow went flying. All the pillows went flying, as did their clothing a few moments later.

But this would be no mad rush into lovemaking. Morgan would take his time, prove his love as he worshiped her body, brought her pleasure.

This time when he dared to kiss the insides of her thighs she did not call to him to stop, nor did she push him away.

He found her with his hands, his mouth. Found her center, claimed it as his own.

Emma bit her bottom lip in an ineffectual hope of holding back her soft moans of pleasure. She lifted her legs around his back, reached for him as she raised herself, almost blindly groping for him. But her muscles wouldn't allow it; they had gone fluid, completely yielding, with all her mind, all her senses contracted to one intense ecstasy that was half pain, half glory.

So she lay back on the bed and surrendered herself completely to his mouth and tongue.

And then it was all glory. Wide and wild, with colors bursting behind her closed eyelids, with her breath caught hard in her throat until at last, at last, she arched her back and let herself go, rising almost out of herself, not floating back down until Morgan's arms enfolded her.

Emma clung to him, pulling him closer, closer, until he was buried deep inside her, and he was kissing her hair, her throat, saying over and over again, "I love you...I love you..."

"I DID SO SAY IT," Emma whispered as she and Morgan took their places at the head of the curving staircase that led up and into the ballroom at the rear of the mansion.

"No, that was the echo of *me* saying it," Morgan teased, squeezing her gloved hand in his. "In any case, say it again."

"I love you," Emma whispered out of the corner of her mouth, for she could see a small group of their guests approaching, herded along by Thornley. "Now behave yourself. And where's Grandmama? Shouldn't she be here, with Mama and Cliff?"

"I'd trade Cliff's presence for hers, yes," Morgan said, earning himself the pressure of Emma's dancing slipper on his instep. "Ah, Sir Willard," he then said brightly, grinning at Perry. "Forced to drag your reprehensible nephew with you, I see. Please, allow me the pleasure of introducing to you…"

"WOULD YOU STOP that fussing! I hear carriages arriving," Fanny Clifford said, tapping her toe against the carpet as Hazel Timon, her tongue stuck against her cheek, did her best to pin a shockingly purple turban with three peacock feathers on the old woman's head.

"'Tis not that I ever do this, ma'am. Claramae is helping out downstairs, useless girl. I run the household, I am not a lady's maid," Mrs. Timon protested, hands fumbling as she worked. She was about to be a very rich woman…so what was she doing here, playing servant to this cranky old besom? "There!" she said at last, stepping back to admire her handiwork. "Only a little crooked."

"Good enough, as I'm a little crooked myself these days," Fanny said, frowning into the glass over the dressing table. "I still can't believe I was so bosky I fell down the stairs. All right, now all I need is to—damn and blast! My glove has ripped at the seam. Quickly, Mrs. Timon, fetch me another pair."

Everything happens for a reason, God blesses the pure of heart, and foul deeds will Out. Ask Hazel Timon and she'll tell you, for she had lived with those beliefs all of her life—that last one never more so than when she returned from the bureau with another pair of kid gloves to see Mrs. Fanny Clifford stripping off her ruined gloves to expose gold-tipped fingers.

"Damn fool gilt paint. I told Edgar that…" Fanny mumbled, then lifted her head, sensing something wrong. Her gaze collided with Mrs. Timon's shocked expression. Shocked, then angry, to be followed hard on the heels by *incensed*.

"Now, Mrs. Timon…" Fanny began, then frowned. "Wait a moment. *You're* not one of the investors, are you?"

"That *thief!*" Mrs. Timon screeched, throwing down the gloves and stomping from the room.

"Shame on you, Edgar. You men, you're all the same," Fanny said, using the curved end of her cane to neatly corral and then fetch up the gloves. "Never happy unless you're deceiving some poor helpless woman like me. Well," she ended, knowing her well-hidden purse was full to bursting, "maybe not me."

"DO YOU TRULY LOVE ME, Sean?" Claramae asked as she
rather boldly backed Riley into the butler's pantry. "Honestly and truly?"

Riley, once over his shock, lowered his eyes to the sin-
fully fetching low neckline of Claramae's best uniform,
to look at what his own father would have called a prime
apple dumpling shop. "Honestly and truly, Claramae,"
he said, then reluctantly stepped away from heaven, and
sweet temptation. "Mr. Thornley expects me back in the
ballroom in another minute. Tomorrow, Claramae," he
promised her. "Everyone will be tired and lazing about,
and we can meet tomorrow."

"Oh, but I thought…"

"You thought *tonight?*" Riley tried and failed to with-
hold a whimper. "All these months you've been tortur-
ing me, and you'd be picking *tonight?*"

Claramae shrugged, which did magnificent things for
Riley's view of her incredibly lush bosom. "I thought…
well, I thought I was looking fine tonight, Sean," she
said, smiling up at him.

"And that you do, Claramae, no lie. But—" He looked
over his shoulder, sure he'd be seeing Mr. Thornley bearing down at him at any moment. He took Claramae's
hands in his own. "Later, dumplin'. Here, see this?" He
pulled his brand-new cheap pocket watch from his livery and pressed it into her hands. "Do you know what
half past eleven of the clock looks like?"

Claramae nodded furiously.

"Good. And it's my sweet dumpling, you are, and no mistake. At half past eleven of the clock, you bring your serving tray into the card room, and I'll meet you there.'

Her eyes went wide. "In the card room! You want us to do it in the card room? Won't all the gentlemen be there?"

"No, no, not in the card room. But there's a storage room at the back, and alongside that is a closet. Big, lovely closet, full of table linens and such. A nice, cozy closet, Claramae, if you catch my meaning. Put down your tray somewheres and sneak inside to wait for me if I'm not already there, all right?"

"Will...will it be dark?"

"I'll have a small lamp burning," Riley said, his ardor nearly buried beneath his growing exasperation. "Just be there, all right? Because you are my sweet dumpling, aren't you?"

WYCLIFF CLOSED his portmanteau with a snap, and sat down on the edge of his narrow bed. Valet to a marquis, and shunted off to live in an attic. It was an insult, that's what it was.

But tonight, ah, tonight had been the worst. Black. His lordship had dared to toss the robin's-egg-blue satin to one side and *insist* on the black.

Why was he here, if his lordship wouldn't heed him? What was he doing, if he was only tolerated and not respected?

Horatio had warned him about the Quality. And his

brother should know, seeing as how he'd been tossed out of three fine houses in the past decade.

Better to listen to Horatio, and join him in the Midlands, where a valet was treasured, respected. Nothing like an upstart mill owner with money so new it sparkled to trust his valet with his clothing, his choice of accessories, every inch of his appearance and behavior.

Wycliff needed respect. He needed peace and stability. The Westham mansion was a madhouse! Old ladies drinking deep and singing bawdy songs in the hallways at all hours. Nothing but a trumped-up seamstress sitting at the table and walking, bold as brass, into a ballroom. That obnoxious, jumped-up little footman parading and preening because *he* was valued, *he* had been made companion to Mr. Clifford.

Well, enough, and more than enough! Let his lordship fend for himself; he certainly seemed to believe himself capable. For tonight Wycliff was leaving Grosvenor Square. He would walk to the White Horse Cellar in Piccadilly, pass the remainder of the night in the public taproom, and then board the early coach headed to the Midlands.

But, first, he probably should nip downstairs and lay out his lordship's dressing gown....

MRS. TIMON GOT UP from her knees, holding on to the one small chest that hadn't required a key to open it and then inspect its contents.

A tin of gilt, some gold-stained rags and brushes. All

the proof she needed to brand Sir Edgar a low, conniving criminal. She relocked the dressing-room door with her set of keys, then the bedchamber door, and raced down the servant stairs to hide the chest in her small sitting room just off the kitchens.

"Mrs. Timon!"

"Mr. Thornley," she said, turning to face the butler, attempting to pretend she wasn't holding the small chest.

But it didn't matter. Thornley was much too harried and preoccupied to notice. "I'm afraid I can't find Claramae anywhere, and these trays must be passed among the guests. "Would you mind?"

Go into the ballroom? Sir Edgar was in the ballroom.

"No, sir, not at all. I'll just go put on a fresh apron?"

"Thank you, Mrs. Timon," Thornley said, then headed back toward the ballroom, because his Daphne was there, looking so very beautiful in her garnets and feathers, and he couldn't bear her out of his sight.

In her sitting room, Mrs. Timon used the tip of her uncomfortable shoes to push the small chest—her proof of Sir Edgar's perfidy—under a couch, then nipped into the kitchens to take up her favorite rolling pin. With a tray of delicacies in one hand, and her other hidden under her apron, clutching the rolling pin, she headed toward the ballroom.

"YOU ARE BEGINNING to feel like my shadow, Morgan," Emma said, pulling her elbow free of his grip. "Honestly, what could happen to me here? Or did you invite Mr. Rolin?"

"I'm sorry, Emma. I just want our engagement announced. Rolin is no gentleman, but he does know when to cut his losses and move on to greener pastures."

"I'm withering here? Turning dry and brown?" Emma asked, glancing around the ballroom, smiling at their guests. "Oh, thank you so much."

"Maybe I should fetch you some lemonade," Morgan said, knowing he'd been acting the possessive fool.

"Perhaps you should," Emma agreed. She counted to ten once he'd gone, then took herself off to hide at the opposite end of the ballroom. She loved the man, loved him dearly, but she was safe as houses in this multitude of people, didn't he know that? Besides, it was nearly eleven, and she still hadn't seen her brother.

ELEVEN O'CLOCK.

Olive Norbert wended her way through the crowds at the sides of the ballroom, crowds that seemed to part with her approach—she'd think about that later—and made her way to the head of the stairs.

Busy, busy, busy. She'd already unlatched the French doors in the morning room for Mr. Rolin, and now it was time to meet with the next person in her plans.

"Evenin' to you, Mr. Hatcher, sir," she said, tugging at the bodice of her bright red gown that she had let out as far as possible, but which still pinched her dreadfully.

"Mrs. Norbert?" John Hatcher said, squinting at her. "No, still don't recall you. But that's no never-mind. Is everything ready?"

"Just as I said in my last note to you, yes, sir," Olive said, holding out her hand for Hatcher to bow over, kiss. When he just looked at her quizzically, she sighed, lifted her skirts and tramped down the small flight to the first floor of the mansion. "Just you come with me, all right?"

"You said you'd arrange transport," Hatcher said, following her up the servant stairs. "Can't trust my own coachman. Can't trust anyone, not with my man Anderson taking off the way he did, without giving notice. Took my silver inkwell with him, if you can believe that, after penning me a note that said he had to visit his sick mother. Didn't even know he had a mother. Well, I won't be seeing him again, that's for certain, not now that he nipped off with that inkwell. Servants! Feckless, the lot of them."

"Don't worry your head none, Mr. Hatcher, I've got everything arranged all right and tight," Olive told him, using her own room key to open Sir Edgar's door, then employing a pilfered key to unlock the dressing closet. "Betts, what I worked with, sent her boy Young Tommy around to hitch up the horses and have Sir Edgar's coach ready in the mews."

It wasn't Sir Edgar's coach, it was the Cliffords' rickety, borrowed traveling coach, but she saw no need to complicate things with too many facts. It was enough that Betts's boy could be trusted to deliver Mr. Hatcher to the stable Olive had rented, and then lock both the man and the gold inside until she could get there. After that? Well, after that, Mr. Hatcher might just have to have himself a small but very final accident.

"Here we go, Mr. Hatcher, sir," she said, opening the second door and pulling out yet another key. "He doesn't even know it's gone missing, so arsy varsy he is over that ancient Clifford woman," she ended, dropping to her knees and opening one chest after another.

And there it was. Gold, gold, lovely gold. Stacks of it. Four trunks chock-full of beautiful gold.

"There you are, sir, just like I wrote you. And Sir Edgar was going to keep it all for himself and some doxy."

Hatcher nearly knocked Olive over as he hurriedly reached down to heft one of the bricks…er, *bars*. "Heavy," he said, hefting it. "I can't carry this all at one go."

"No, sir," Olive said, getting to her feet. "I'd've done it m'self, but nobody here much likes me. You're a guest of the ball, sir, and no one will question you if they was to see you, not even if you was to tote off his lordship's favorite chair. Now, I must get back to the ballroom. There's still something that needs doing there, soon as I find her, and then I'll be meeting up with you later to divvy up the booty."

"AH, WELL MET, Brentwood! Look at you, standing there, not dancing. Still being the dedicated waste you've always been? Of course you are."

Perry bowed deeply from the waist, kissing the air just above her ladyship's outstretched hand. "If I am predictable, dear lady, it is only to please you."

"Brentwood," Lady Jersey said, "you delight me, as always."

"And you terrify me, my lady, as always. I am constantly awaiting the moment when you pop a spotty debutante from behind your skirts and sic her on my hapless self, in the way of a bulldog clamping its jaws about my ankle."

Sally Jersey smacked him on the arm with her fan and toddled off to find someone else to harass, knowing she'd never get the earl to take to the dance floor on her command, and Perry went back to watching the world as it passed by him.

"Lose something, Morgan, old friend?" Perry asked a few minutes later, pushing himself away from the pillar he'd been dedicatedly holding up this past hour or more. Raising his quizzing glass to his eye, he made a great business out of inspecting the interior of the ballroom. "Or, to be more precise, *someone?*"

Morgan took in Perry's tone and sighed. "Not now, Perry. Have you seen her?"

"Her? Oh, yes. *Her.* I might have, earlier, but I don't think she wishes to be seen. Now why is that?"

Morgan looked at the now-warm glass of lemonade still in his hand and stuck it in a nearby potted plant. "Because I've been dogging her footsteps this past week or more, allowing her no privacy, no fun, no—why would she pick tonight to decide she's had enough?"

Perry shook his head. "I probably should be understanding this, shouldn't I? But I'm not."

"All right," Morgan said, knowing his friend would give him no peace until he knew everything. "It's Rolin. I have good reason to believe he thinks Emma is important to me."

"Old chap, a blind man would have reason to see that you're considerably more than fond of the girl. I myself had begun to believe you two have been joined at the hip these past days. Oh, wait. Rolin is the reason behind your behavior?"

"He knows I'm in love with her, Perry."

"Old chap, a blind—no, never mind. I can see you haven't the time to be amused, or even indignant with my silliness. What do you think Rolin might do?"

"Abduct her, ruin her, then tell the world she'd made a dead set at him. Just for the spite of it, Perry. He tried romancing her, but Emma saw straight through him. So now he'll content himself with ruining her, to punish her, but mostly to destroy me."

"Yes, that does sound like our old friend. Quite nearly Machiavellian, our dear Rolin. And, like Machiavelli, he only knows how to obtain power, but has never quite known how to use what he's gained. So he keeps reaching, reaching for more. But surely he isn't here."

"No," Morgan said, looking around the ballroom once

more. "And once he hears that I announced our engagement tonight he'll go away, probably to pull the wings off butterflies until he discovers someone else to amuse him."

"True. And I would have to say you're correct on all counts. If the fresh-from-the-country Miss Clifford fell to him, it would be a giggle to most everyone. But if he were to accost the future Countess Westham? He'd be more ruined than your dear Emma. He'd have to leave Society, where he is not in such good odor at any rate. You know, I hear he's up to his eyes in tradesmen's and gambling debts. Remember how you and I always seemed to be the ones dipping into our pockets when we went about with him?"

"Another time, Perry," Morgan said, barely listening. "Excuse me. I've got to find her before midnight. Damned silly I'd look making my announcement while she's flirting in the supper room or something."

"When you locate her, you might want to put a bell around her neck," Perry suggested, then smiled as he leaned against the pillar once more, to watch the throng. It was either that or join Uncle Willie, who kept insisting that he had yet another "great favor" to ask of his only heir.

And, as the man had hinted on the way to the ball that once more the favor had to do with a woman, Perry would continue to avoid his uncle for some weeks yet, just as that natty-looking little gentleman seemed to be rather nervously avoiding the female servant who appeared to be actually *chasing* after him with a tray of delicacies.

No. Never dull with Morgan in town. Perry sighed, then abandoned his pillar to stroll the ballroom, on the lookout for someone who should not be there....

HATCHER STOPPED on the landing, huffing and puffing, put down the heavy cloth sack and wondered if he should be seeing those little dancing fairy lights in front of his eyes.

He'd been carrying down the single sack the Norbert woman had provided, unloading the gold into the coach, climbing the several steep flights once more, lugging down the empty chests he'd cleared out in the closet, arranging the gold back into each chest, climbing the stairs, loading the sack and lugging it down again, then back up, then back down....

"Excuse me, sir," Wycliff said, standing on the top step but unable to move past Hatcher on the narrow landing to turn and climb to the next floor. His lordship's dressing gown and slippers laid out, he was now free to climb to the attics one last time, gather up his portmanteau and quit this horrible place. "Sir? Are you all right?"

Hatcher blinked, and some of the fairy lights winked out. He peered at the man in front of him: tall, rail thin, looking very proper yet unintelligent, and homely as his sister Myrtle into the bargain. But, Hatcher realized, not in the least surprised to see him standing there. Not about to send up an alarm, nothing. It was true. An invited guest can go anywhere, as long as he's well-dressed and... well, affable. He could be affable.

"I say," Hatcher said, smiling at Wycliff. "Valet, aren't you? Dressed like a valet. His lordship's man?"

Wycliff drew himself up to his full height. "I was, sir, but I am in the process of leaving the marquis's employ. He...he does not appreciate me, sir."

"Well, damme, if that ain't rude of the man. Yes, yes, even shabby. Tell you what, help me down with this bag his lordship gave me, and a few others, and I'd appreciate you all hollow. Be my assistant. You'd like that? I'm John Hatcher, by the way, and I'll double anything the marquis was paying you."

Wycliff and his rather sad lack of imagination considered this. He did not exactly have a position waiting for him in the Midlands, just his brother's words. As a matter of fact, he was already feeling a little uneasy about his decision to leave Grosvenor Square. Such a fine address. "Double, you said, sir?"

Hatcher reached down and hefted up the sack with both hands. "That I did. Here you go. Now hop to. I'm...I'm in sort of a rush."

THE MUSICIANS PLAYED. The throng in the ballroom talked and danced. Combined, the two carried the noise level in the large, high-ceilinged room to near earsplitting levels.

Nobody heard Sir Willard call out, "I say ten on the one with the split tail feathers. He looks a bruiser."

Nobody outside the card room heard him, that is, except for Cliff, who quickly closed the door to the ballroom behind him and goggled at the sight in front of him.

There were the card tables, turned on their sides, and with their tops used to form a circle in the center of the room. There were a good thirty of his lordship's male guests, viscounts and earls and various other lordships, even a duke, all gathered around the outside of those tables. There were the gamecocks, unhooded in their stacked cages, scratching and puffing up their tails, eager for a good fight.

And there was Riley, standing in the middle of the circle, resplendent in his fancy, formal silver Westham livery, his powdered wig on his head, and holding up Harry, Cliff's own dear Harry.

"Cliffie boy!" Riley called out, spying his business partner standing slack jawed at the door. "Be a good lad and hold the stakes, will you?"

Cliff approached the crowd around the makeshift ring. He looked into it and saw sand spread on the floor. "How…where…?"

"Hush, Cliffie," Riley said, stuffing a multitude of pound notes into his hands. "It was fair bored to flinders they was all looking, and too quiet in here by half for what I've got planned. So I said to myself, I said, why not give the gentlemen something to do?"

Cliff looked back toward the door. "God, man, if my sister…if his lordship were to find out!"

Riley winked. "And are you going to be running off to tell him? He's so arsy varsy over your sister he's deaf and dumb to anything else, and that's a fact. Ah, and here comes my other business now. Take over, Cliffie boy, and we'll both be rich before this night is over."

Cliff stood there and watched as Riley removed the tray of drinks from a giggling Claramae's grip, took her hand and then threaded the both of them through the oblivious gentlemen, disappearing into the hallway leading to the storage room.

"We going to fight these cocks, or what?" somebody called out, snapping Cliff back to attention. "Fifty pounds says the split-tailed brown will take your champion."

Take Harry? Oh, Cliff didn't think so. And fifty pounds? They'd been fighting Harry at the Cock and Woolpack for two, and often less.

"Fifty?" Someone else called out. "Always were cheeseparing, Billy. One hundred—on the brown!"

"I'll match that!"

"And me, on the red!"

"Cursed lot of you are nothing but old women—I say a monkey on the brown!"

A monkey? That was five hundred pounds, wasn't it? And to lay all that on the brown, *against* his magnificent Harry! Casting his fears aside, Cliff took a deep breath and called out, "Anyone else? Gentlemen, come, come, place your wagers!"

HAZEL TIMON TUCKED the rolling pin into her apron pocket and slapped away the reaching hand of a rather imperious looking lady (if not for the beak that resembled that of a chicken possessing an inordinate supply of Attitude), and pushed on through the throng with her tray. She wasn't about to stop, just to let some chicken-beak peck at her tray.

Because she had sighted Sir Edgar again, and she was not about to give up on the chase now.

Another gloved hand reached out to the tray, and Mrs. Timon turned on the pesky person, only to see Mrs. Daphne Clifford standing there, bottom lip between her teeth as her hand hovered over the tray, moving back and forth between the adorable tiny shrimp impaled with sticks and something that looked rather like it had already been chewed, then spread on a bit of toasted bread. Pitiful. That Gaston called himself a cook?

"Oh dear, oh dear, I can't seem to decide."

Sir Edgar was making his way toward the stairs, obviously weary of avoiding Mrs. Timon, or so Hazel thought, and about to nip away with all her gold (it was all hers now, in her mind).

"Here," she said, shoving the tray at Daphne. "Have what you want, then pass the rest around," and took off after the no-good, thieving little gent.

"Oh, but—" Daphne said, frowning at the silver tray she now held. Surely this couldn't be right. She never passed trays, not even in her own home. But this *was* London, so perhaps things were done differently here.

Daphne, munching on a shrimp—she'd always liked pink—moved toward a small group of ladies at the edge of the dance floor and said, "Sally? Would you care for some shrimp or some…would you care for some lovely shrimp?"

"Daffy?" Lady Jersey goggled at the woman, simply goggled. "I…I—"

"Excuse us, Lady Jersey," Thornley said, taking the tray from Daphne even as he grabbed her elbow and led her away from the for-once-speechless Silence. "Daphne, dearest, what are you doing?"

She bit back a sob. "Not what I should be, obviously. Oh, Aloysius, I'm So Sorry. Oh dear, I do believe I'm Going To Cry."

Stopping only to deposit the offending tray on a small table beside the open French doors, Thornley steered Daphne out onto the long balcony that ran the length of the ballroom and pulled her out of sight. "Here, here," he said, dabbing at her moist cheeks with the handkerchief he pulled from his pocket. "Nobody saw."

"Just…just Sally, and all her Horrid Friends," Daphne said, sniffling. "I don't like London anymore, Aloysius, I really don't."

"Then we'll leave, and never come back," Thornley said, tipping up her chin and dropping a soft kiss on her forehead. "Not that his lordship would let me return, in any case."

"Yes, Aloysius, thank you. Oh—they're playing a waltz. How dearly I'd love to waltz with you, Aloysius."

He had not been born a gentleman, but he prided himself on being a gentle man. He also saw the end of his tenure here in Grosvenor Square and, although he would miss it, there were some things more important than being a butler. Stepping back from Daphne, he bowed deeply and said, "Mrs. Clifford, you would make me the happiest of men if you were to share this waltz with me."

Daphne looked around, toward the ballroom, out over the dark, deserted gardens lit only by a few widely scattered flambeaux. "Here?"

"Sadly, yes. I am not so brave as to suggest we hazard the dance floor inside."

"No, of course not. How silly of me. Sally is still in there." Daphne dropped into a curtsy, even as she held out her hand. "I should be Delighted, Mr. Thornley."

It began to drizzle, but neither of them noticed.

FANNY SMILED at Archie, the earl now, although he'd been nothing more than a second son before old age had taken his father and older, childless brother, then frowned as she looked past his shoulder and saw her addlepated daughter-in-law whirling about at the far end of the balcony. With Thornley.

How bizarre. How inappropriate. How…very wonderful.

"Yes, yes, Archie, I do remember that," Fanny said quickly, as the man laughed at his own telling of an incident in which Fanny, Archie, and a hot-air balloon had figured prominently. "But I'm so dry, Archie, so warm. Why, this drizzle even feels wonderful. Be a dear and fetch me a shawl and a glass?"

"Lemonade, Fanny?" he said, but winked as he asked.

"Only if you wish me to do you an injury. Wine, you old poot. Now hurry. My tongue is sticking to the top of my mouth. Go on…go on." She turned him about, aimed him at the ballroom and gave him a small push.

Looking down the length of the balcony once more, she walked over to a place where that same balcony curved out into a roomy half circle, meant to be employed to gaze out over the gardens.

She propped her cane against the balustrade, placed her elbows on the cool stone and smiled at the romantic couple, then turned up her face to feel the cool mist of drizzle against her heated skin. If only she'd gone for happiness rather than convention, she would have run off with Georgie, the knife boy, and none of these past fifty or more years would have happened.

"Ha! First time for money and position, I say, and second time for love," she muttered. "My Geoffrey was no prize, and neither was Samuel. So you do it, Daphne, you just go on and do it."

A sound to her right, far in the distance, caught Fanny's attention. Was that a coach, back there in the mews? Yes, she could hear horses stamping, milling about. Certainly none of her guests would be so shabby as to clog the narrow mews path that way, and certainly no tradesmen called this late at night. Strange.

Wait…there was another coach, just behind the first one. Fanny leaned forward, squinting through the darkness. Who would be going out at this late hour, and with the ball still in progress? Was someone stealing coaches?

And then she felt a push at her back, and she was holding on to the balustrade for dear life as somebody worked to lift her, push her over the edge and down onto the flagstones below.

"Steal my Ed-gie would you? And m'gold!"

Fanny wasn't as young as she used to be, nor as nimble, but she was no die-away old weakling, either. She'd had brothers, and had wrestled with them. She'd wrestled with a few men, too, not to put too fine a point on it.

She gave a mighty push, then reached for her cane, managing to bring it up and back in a wide arc, where it collided quite soundly with Olive Norbert's head.

Without a sound, other than some heavy breathing and one or two moans, a macabre dance began, in sharp contrast with the graceful one at the other end of the balcony.

IT WAS DARK inside the closet that smelled of fresh linens and candlewax and, sadly, just a bit like burnt cloth, for

Claramae's last-moment attempt at maidenly reluctance had backed her up over the candle Riley had placed on the floor, and he'd spent a full minute stomping out the stubborn flames.

But now she was thoroughly kissed, and remarkably eager, bless her.

Riley's satin jacket was on the floor, and his breeches hung around his ankles.

Claramae had been reduced to her underslip, her pantaloons already gone the way of Riley's jacket.

He'd saved the best for last, even cracking the door open slightly so that he could see her in the light from the hallway.

He kissed her one last time, his palms itching for the feel of her warm flesh.

"Oh, Riley…" Claramae said on a sigh, as he skimmed those palms across her shoulders.

She turned around, putting her back to him, and he breathed heavily, blinking away the darkness, and watched as she slipped one arm, then the other, free of her the final barrier to his personal heaven.

Then she turned, chin high, and stood there, proudly naked to the waist, her magnificent apple dumpling shop free at last.

"Oh, Claramae…"

SIR EDGAR, hiding behind a rather low and ineffectual shrubbery in the gardens, having lost Mrs. Timon and her rolling pin some minutes earlier, stood up, looked toward the balcony and said, "Oh, my God, Fanny! *Fanny!*" And he began to run.

"OH, ALOYSIUS, that was wonderful," Daphne said, sighing as he brought her hand to his lips for a kiss before finally releasing her. The waltz had ended but, to Daphne, she still heard the chorus of angelic music.

Hmm…perhaps not quite so angelic. And not music, either.

Thornley put his hands on her shoulders and moved her aside.

"What is it? Aloysius? I believe I heard someone calling Mother Clifford's name."

"It's…it's Mrs. Norbert, and she's—*oh, my God.* Stay here, Daphne. Stay here. Don't look!"

But she grabbed him, held him when he attempted to break into a run. "But what is it? I can't see that far, Aloysius. What's the matter?"

"Not now, Daphne, or I'll be too late." And he was off, running down the length of the balcony.

A QUARTER TILL MIDNIGHT?

Emma quickly stood up and smoothed down her gown.

She'd enjoyed evading Morgan for a few minutes, teasing him by hiding herself amid their guests, but then she'd realized that Morgan was going to make the announcement of their marriage, and she could either sneak off to her chambers and try to compose herself before that most important moment, or she could burst into silly tears as he spoke to those same assembled guests.

Maidenly nerves. How utterly surprising, considering how she hadn't discovered any such thing lurking in her mind as she'd nightly tripped down the stairs and into Morgan's bed.

So she'd escaped to her chambers, to compose herself, sip on a glass of lemonade, and—why, she didn't know— run over the proper forms of address for viscounts, earls and the like, and their wives and offspring, as well.

She wanted Morgan to be proud of her, pleased with her, and it was only as she had looked at the mantel clock and seen the time that she realized she'd been gone for over an hour. Not only was she being silly, but Morgan would be less than "pleased" with her if she didn't return to the ballroom at once.

Holding up her skirts, she tripped down one flight of stairs, then two, gaining the first floor, then turned to head for the rear of the mansion and the small flight leading up to the ballroom. She was faintly out of breath by the time she reached the bottom of the flight leading to the ballroom, and paused for a moment to compose herself.

"Good evening, Miss Clifford."

Emma froze in place, looking toward the stairs, realizing that no footmen lingered there, as they were all busy serving the guests. She was quite alone, not even sure anyone would hear her if she were to call out. Scream. No. She would not scream. She would not give the man that satisfaction.

"Mr. Rolin," she said, not turning toward his voice. "I do not believe you were issued an invitation."

"Yes, how shabby of his lordship to overlook me."

"And how shabby of you to show up in any case," Emma said, putting a foot on the bottom stair. "I'll see that you are escorted out."

"No need, Miss Clifford," he said, and his voice was directly behind her now. "You can show me out. After all, we're leaving together."

She whirled to face him. "Stop it," she said, stamping her foot. "Just *stop it*. I'm not afraid of you."

"Really? You should be, Miss Clifford. I'm not a nice man."

Emma felt her cheeks going pale. "Morgan!" she shouted, right into Rolin's face, then picked up her skirts, already turning back to the stairs. *"Morgan!"*

Then something black was dropped over her head, she was lifted up, up, and over Rolin's shoulder, and he was running—running in the direction of the morning room.

MORGAN STOPPED, lifting his head, as he actually thought he'd heard Emma, calling for him.

Ridiculous. Music was playing, people were speaking to each other at near shouts. And he'd thought he'd heard Emma calling him? Did all men in love turn into fools?

Still, he looked toward the entrance to the ballroom and began to walk that way.

Behind him there was a loud crash, like that of doors being slammed back against walls, followed by a few of the ladies screaming, and he turned to see Fanny Clifford and Olive Norbert. They were locked together, and rolling across the dance floor as guests jumped back to give them space.

Morgan just stood there, trying to comprehend what he was seeing.

Fanny was on the bottom, and Mrs. Norbert, her horrible red gown ripped in several places, was about to punch the old woman square in the face.

But, before he could react, Fanny's cane seemed to appear out of nowhere, and Mrs. Norbert was holding on to her head with both hands as Fanny scrambled out from beneath her, then jumped on the larger woman's back.

"My kudos, old friend," Perry said close to Morgan's ear, trying to be heard above the shrieks and shouts. "You certainly are an entertaining host. Five pounds on the Widow Clifford. You game?"

"Shut up, Perry," Morgan ordered, "and help me break this up, for God's sake."

"If I must," Perry said, and the two of them waded in, neither of them in a very large hurry to grab hold of any part of either woman's anatomy, some of which was showing and which should have been hidden.

Morgan did manage to wrest away the cane before Fanny, still straddling Mrs. Norbert's back, could bring it down on the woman's generous hindquarters, rather like a riding crop.

The crowd around the fighting pair, their blood among the bluest in England, and dressed in their silks and satins, began to loudly hoot their disapproval of his interference.

"FIGHT! FIGHT! Ladies, fighting!"

Thirty previously occupied gentlemen turned as one at this information, shouted at them from the doorway of the card room, then ran to be the first to see this titillating spectacle.

Elbows slammed into ribs, heels trod down on toes...and cages, rickety bits of wood at best, were knocked over, breaking apart.

The gentlemen burst into the ballroom. One by one, the gamecocks, rather angry after being so unceremoniously dumped onto the floor, began to follow after them.

"Harry, stop! Wait! Not you, too. *Harry!*"

Cliff Clifford, with pound notes sticking out of every pocket, looked around him, at the overturned tables, the sand on the floor, the smashed and empty cages.

He had a moment's insight, probably the first of his

young life: He probably shouldn't be here when someone came into this room.

But where to go? Where to go? He needed a place to hide.

JOHN HATCHER HANDED the empty sack back to Wycliff who, on orders from his new employer, delivered each sack and then stood back, out of sight of the coach door, as Hatcher carefully arranged each new load in one of the trunks.

Hatcher still had to climb the stairs, to load the sack each time, but at least he didn't have to carry the heavy gold himself.

"Should be one more trip for us and we're done, boy. Damned rain. We'd best hurry," Hatcher said, his dancing slippers squishing in the puddles caused by what had become a downpour. The two of them, Wycliff holding the empty sack, made for the door to the kitchens one last time.

"ONE MORE KICK and I swear, madam, I will not hesitate to punch you into insensibility," Rolin said, cutting through the deserted gardens, Emma still dangling over his shoulder, but far from a willing captive.

And then he stopped, peering through the darkness, through the pouring rain. "Damn! Damn and blast!"

There were two coaches in the mews, his being the

second, and unable to go forward or turn around unless the first was moved.

As Emma beat on his back with her fists, yelling "Morgan! Morgan!" Jarrett Rolin adjusted his plan.

"ANYBODY BETTING?" Sir Willard asked, skidding to a halt at the front of the crowd ringed around Fanny and Mrs. Norbert.

"I've got ten on the fat one."

Fanny picked up her head—she had been biting Mrs. Norbert on the shoulder—and yelled, "I heard that, Archie!" just before Morgan bent down and lifted her clear of the seamstress, arms and legs still flailing.

"Much as I value your friendship, dear boy," Perry said, planting a foot on Olive Norbert's ample belly, "this is as far as I go." He spread his arms and appealed to the crowd. "Some assistance, if you please? Gentlemen, come, come now, you would not ask me to float a barge on mine own, would you?"

"She tried to kill me!" Fanny shrieked. *"Twice!"*

Morgan would have asked her what she meant, but just then there were more female screams, a multitude of them, coming from the rear of the crowd ringing them.

He looked up, to see befeathered women swooning into gentlemanly arms. A veritable *ripple* of movement seemed to be running through the crowd, lifting them, one after another, off their feet.

And then he saw Harry....

CLIFF PACED IN CIRCLES, wringing his hands, listening to the shrieks and shouts from the ballroom, and made up his mind.

He bolted for the hallway behind the card room, heading for the storage room. But there was another door in the hallway, already partially open, and one hidey-hole was as good as another, at least until he was forgiven…which could possibly happen before he starved in here.

He yanked open the door.

He saw the most magnificent set of…

Claramae screamed.

Riley moaned.

Claramae bent and snatched up her underpinnings, pressed them to her bosom and all but knocked Cliff down as she burst from the closet, screaming at the top of her quite generous lungs.

"Riley?"

The footman took a quick step and fell flat on his face, as his breeches were still around his ankles.

"Did you…?"

"No, thanks to you and damn your eyes, I didn't!" Riley said, pulling up his breeches and getting to his feet. "Which way did she go?"

"Toward…toward the ballroom. Oh, Lord, *toward the ballroom!*"

Riley cursed again and set off after her, leaving Cliff to step inside the closet and softly close the door. But then, realizing that his beloved Harry could come to grief, he manfully opened that door again and joined the fray.

WOMEN, CRYING HYSTERICALLY or swooning. Gentlemen, chasing after gamecocks, except for the one old gent who was standing on a chair, swinging his stick at a rather large red bird that seemed to be on the attack below him. Noise, everywhere. Mayhem, everywhere. Gamecocks, everywhere.

And no Emma.

"Thornley," Morgan said, grabbing the butler's sleeve as that man did his best to support a swooning Daphne. "Have you seen Miss Clifford?"

"No, my lord. We were out on the balcony and—"

The balcony! He hadn't looked on the balcony!

Morgan bounded through the doorway out into the dark, now rainy night, just in time to hear loud masculine cheers rise from several hundred male throats, and too late to see Claramae, sobbing, her uniform only half covering her front, and nothing at all covering her shapely derriere, race through the ballroom, a half-dressed, still bewigged Riley running after her, holding his coat in both hands. All eyes, and much applause, followed them both.

Morgan skidded to a halt at the balustrade and looked both ways. Nothing. Emma wasn't out here. The entire world had exploded inside the ballroom, and she wasn't there, either.

Something was wrong. He winced at the thought. Hell and damnation, *everything* was wrong. But the worst was that he couldn't find Emma.

Morgan looked to his right again and saw carriage lamps in the mews. Carriage lamps? There was no reason for anyone to call out his carriage.

He ran toward the end of the balcony, rain streaming down his face, and all but leaped down the steps leading into the gardens.

WHILE BEDLAM REIGNED in the ballroom, it was also becoming rather confusing in the mews.

"Move that damn coach!" Rolin said, glaring up at Young Tommy, who was a hulking lad with little regard for the Quality. "I *demand* that you move this coach!"

"Up your arse," Young Tommy said, his foot firmly against the brake.

"Stap me, what's going on here? You—get away from my coach. *Rolin?*"

Rolin turned. *"Hatcher?"*

Hatcher squinted in the scant light from the carriage lights. "Who's that you got there, Rolin? Looks like a female, don't it? Rather wet, ain't she?"

Emma, weary of hanging upside down with a sack over her head, pushed her hands against Rolin's back and lifted her upper body, putting the man rather off balance on the slippery cobblestones, as he'd been looking at Hatcher and wasn't paying quite the attention necessary to keep a determined young woman like Emma successfully held in his grasp.

She was free! Her feet were on the ground.

Emma yanked off the black silk that had covered her head, spitting bits of lint out of her mouth as she blinked, unable to see much after the darkness of the sack.

Rolin reached out, almost lazily, and grabbed her wrist, pulling her to his side. She kicked him, tried to make a break for it, but he held her wrist fast, now at arm's length but still holding her.

"Here, now, what do you think you're doing, Rolin?" Hatcher asked. He hadn't been born yesterday, after all, and he was fairly certain the young lady didn't wish to be here with Rolin, or go somewhere with him, for that matter. He put down his sack, the very last sack (he'd carried it down himself, while Wycliff nipped off to gather up his portmanteaux). Puffing himself up, he demanded, dredging up the words from somewhere romantic in his soul: "Unhand that woman!"

Then he took a step forward, tripped over the sack and fell against Rolin, who rudely pushed him off, releasing his grip on Emma to do so.

She could run, but now Rolin was hitting the older man who had tried to save her. She couldn't desert him.

Looking around for a weapon, she spied the sack at her feet, but it was too heavy to lift. She reached inside,

closed her hand over something about the size and shape
of a brick, and pulled it out.

"Emma!"

Emma, in the process of trying to sort out Rolin from
the two bodies now dancing around each other in the
downpour, each trying to land a punch, lost her concen-
tration for a moment as she yelled, "Here, Morgan,
here!" Which was a pity, because she was also bringing
down the heavy object on Rolin's—oops—the older
man's head.

Hatcher dropped like a stone.

"Oh dear," Emma said, wincing as the injured man
rolled around on the ground, moaning. "I'm so sorry…"

"Come on," Rolin said, grabbing her wrist once more,
even as he took out a purse and threw it up onto the box.
"Get us out of here, and there'll be another just like it."

Young Tommy neatly snatched the purse out of the air
and changed loyalties. "Yes, sir!"

Emma was being pushed into the coach, which was
already quite full of trunks, when Morgan reached the
mews, pulling Rolin away so that he could help her back
out of the coach and down to the ground.

He didn't make it, because Rolin picked up the
weapon Emma had so lately used to sad effect, and ham-
mered Morgan on the back with it.

Emma, still inside the coach, sprawled inelegantly
over the trunks, screamed.

Rolin slammed the coach door and bounded up onto the

box, brandishing the golden brick. "Off," he said succinctly.

Young Tommy, holding on to the purse (and not quite as dumb as he looked), obliged.

Rolin loosed the brake as he picked up the reins. He gave them a sharp shake, giving the horses their office to start, even as Morgan, down but not out, was climbing up the side of the box, not in the least distracted as Claramae and her magnificent bosom bobbed on by, chased by no less than two hundred assorted male and female members of the *ton*. Oh, yes, and Riley.

The horses, already made cranky by the rain, reared in the traces and attempted to break into an immediate gallop. Unfortunately, the rickety old coach, loaded down as it was by four large, heavy trunks filled with bricks, was not up to the challenge.

The back wheels collapsed, the shaft broke, and the four horses were off down the mews…followed, at least briefly, by Rolin, who had hung on to the reins just a tad too long, and had been catapulted into the air, only to land, facedown, in the middle of a very large puddle.

Hatcher got to his feet, goggling at the broken coach. His gold! His gold! He wrenched open the door, to be confronted by the resourceful Emma, who had opened one of the trunks and was now armed, both hands, with two more gold bricks.

The rain, as if in a hurry to be somewhere else, went away, all at once. The clouds parted, the moon and stars became visible. Some of them shone down on the glittery objects in Emma's hands.

"My gold! That's my gold!" Hatcher said. "Give it over, girl!"

Morgan, who had somehow managed to hold on to the side of the coach, turned to face a new enemy. "Get away from her," he said, nimbly leaping to drop between Emma and Hatcher.

But the older man wasn't listening or even protesting. He'd dropped to his knees to pick up the two pieces of gold that had so lately been one piece of gold, until it had made contact with Morgan's back. Now it was gold on the outside…and red on the inside.

"It's…it's—what happened to my gold?" Holding a half brick in each hand, he desperately tried to fit them back together.

Perry had sauntered into the mews behind the majority of the other guests, and just then had been peering into the disabled coach, opening trunk after trunk. At Hatcher's words, he lifted his quizzing glass to his eye and said, "Bricks, turned to gold? Ah, dear. Always knew there were a few slates missing from your roof, John. But think of this, there should be enough here to build yourself a lovely golden wall that will be the envy of all your friends."

Sir Willard elbowed his way to the front of the crowd—less well-heeled financially, and not so well dressed, and that crowd would be termed a mob, one who had assembled for a ball, but were now seemingly quite willing to watch a farce. "What's going on here?" he demanded. Perry stood back and waved for his uncle to inspect the interior of the coach.

"Curse me, I've been hoodwinked," Sir Willard muttered after a few moments, slamming the coach door shut.

"Tch, tch, Uncle," Perry said quietly. "And woe to me. Had it only been real, I would have one day inherited so much more."

"Shut up, you idiot puppy dog," Sir Willard said, and slammed away from the coach, only to add, "And be in my breakfast room at eleven tomorrow, boy. I've got a job for you!"

Hatcher dropped the pieces of brick and got to his feet, mud staining his once pristine hose. "Six thousand pounds. I paid six thousand pounds—for bricks?"

Wycliff, just then happily stepping into the mews, holding a large black umbrella above his head as he picked his way across the flooded walkway, stopped, looked, listened for a few moments...then turned and went back inside. To unpack.

A moan brought Morgan back to attention, as he'd been busy covering Emma's soaking wet and now rather diaphanous bodice with his jacket, and he passed her into Perry's capable hands in order to grab the back of Rolin's jacket and haul the man to his feet.

Rolin took a wild swing—the mud dripping from his

face rather impeded his eyesight—and Morgan countered with a more clear-eyed punch of his own, sending the man back down into the mud.

"Get on your feet," Morgan said, standing over Rolin, his legs spread, his fists jammed onto his hips.

"Don't, Morgan," Emma said, grabbing onto his arm.

"Don't what, sweetheart?" he asked, not taking his eyes off Rolin, who was once again struggling to regain his feet.

"Don't challenge him to a duel," Emma said. "That is what you were about to do, wasn't it? And you already know that a duel settles nothing. You said so yourself."

"A duel? Don't be silly, sweetheart. I was merely going to hit him again."

"Oh," Emma said, considering the idea, and not able to locate any flaws. "I suppose I should say that you shouldn't."

Morgan grinned at her. "Don't. Because I really, *really* want to."

But Rolin—scratch a bully and find a coward—wasn't going to give Morgan the chance. His broken nose gushing blood, he pushed himself backward on his hands and knees, keeping Morgan in his sight until he decided he was far enough away to get up, turn and run away.

"Won't stop until he's completely out of England, I'd say," Perry announced to the crowd. "Tch, tch, such a shabby creature, trying to lope off with his lordship's affianced bride because she snubbed him. Shabby, I say, and quite ungentlemanly."

He turned to whisper to Morgan, "Is that a word? Ungentlemanly? Never mind. Take your sweet but rather damp bride and be off, Morgan. I'll handle this. A pretty fib here, a whopping crammer there, and everything will be fine again."

"You're going to blame everything on Rolin, aren't you? That's what I'd already decided to do. All right," Morgan said, eager to get Emma away from all these interested eyes. "But what about him?" he asked, pointing to Hatcher. "What the devil was he doing?"

"Why, I thought that was obvious. Hatcher was making a jackass of himself, as usual. He's of no importance. Now, go on." Perry turned back to what he had decided to call his audience. "Fie!" he called out loudly. "Fie and shame on Jarrett Rolin!"

"Rolin? Was that Rolin loping off?" Sir Willard asked. "I didn't know. What did he do?"

Lord bless the man, Sir Willard always asked the right questions.

Perry struck a pose, now that he had everyone's attention, and spoke in a clear, carrying voice. "What did he do, dear uncle? Blister me, I thought it would be obvious. Jarrett Rolin is responsible for this *entire* debacle. And I hear he's under the hatches, as well. He planned to kidnap the marquis's affianced bride, ravish her cruelly, and compound his crime by holding the dear Miss Clifford for some enormous ransom."

Several ladies in the throng uttered small squeaks of alarm…but only small ones, as they didn't wish to miss a word.

"Indeed, there is no end to the man's perfidy. All but ravishing one of his lordship's maids earlier, loosing gamecocks as a diversion so that he could make good his dastardly getaway, hiring that horrid red woman to accost the Widow Clifford, who had tumbled onto his contemptible scheme. I tell you, there is no end!"

"Yes, yes, come with me now, dear boy," said Lady Jersey, with her maid behind her, doing her best to keep an umbrella over her ladyship's head, in case the night might once again turn wet. "That's enough for them to chew on a while. Tell me everything, and I will inform everyone else of the rest, do you understand? Of course you understand."

"Indeed I do, my lady. And you'll have told them all before the cock crows tomorrow morning." He lifted one brow a fraction as two brown gamecocks squared off right in front of the crowd. "Would you wish any cock in particular, my lady, or would one of these do? It appears we have plenty."

And Now, Good Night...

You have had enough fun, eaten
and drunk enough,
time you were off.
—Horace

THERE WAS NOT MUCH LEFT to be done before the evening was at last over.

Wycliff, wearily lugging his portmanteaux up the stairs, suddenly found himself backed against the wall as Sir Edgar Marmington—carrying a portmanteau and sporting a rather large "egg" on his forehead—barreled down the stairs, yelling, "Out of the way! Out of the way!"

The valet watched after the man for a few moments, then began climbing once more, convinced he needed to lie down, definitely with a cold, wet cloth on his head. He'd left clean water in his lordship's chambers, so he headed down the hallway, to avail himself of it. Then he'd call for a bath for his lordship, who certainly looked in need of his loyal valet.

"Good evening," Hazel Timon said as she approached down the hallway, smiling in a way that made Wycliff wonder if he'd forgotten to put his trousers on, or something. "Fine evening, isn't it?"

"Yes, Mrs. Timon," Wycliff said, frowning as he noticed the rolling pin tucked up beneath her arm…and then he saw the banknotes she held in her hand. "Rather…um, rather a lot going on downstairs. Some fuss, I'd say."

"I wouldn't know," Mrs. Timon said, walking away. He could hear her, counting: "Twenty…sixty…one hundred. Ha! And I only gave the eighty."

MRS. NORBERT, her wrists firmly tied behind her with a golden rope taken from the draperies in the ballroom, was led away by two stout footmen, on her way to the guardhouse.

Fanny Clifford watched her go from her seat on one of the couches in the drawing room. She sat with her feet up on the table in front of her, Daphne's shawl covering her rather tattered bodice but, remarkably, still wearing her purple turban, minus its feathers.

"Why did she want to hurt you, Mother Clifford?" Daphne asked, handing her mother-in-law a cup of tea that the woman, for once in her life, gratefully accepted.

"She thought I'd stepped in front of her on her way to true love, Daphne," Fanny said, then sipped the hot, sweet tea. "Ah, I was always one to put fear in other ladies, if they thought I was making a dead set at any man they fancied. I could tell you stories…."

"But you won't, will you?" Daphne said quickly. "Emma told me that you…that you…oh, dear. Just please say you won't."

Fanny smiled but didn't reassure her daughter-in-law. After all, a person had to have a little giggle now and again, didn't she? So all she said was, "Daphne? Do you think you could find your dearly beloved and ask him if he has any more of those strawberry tarts left in the kitchens?"

"MORE TEA, Miss Clifford?" Thornley asked, wringing his hands as he hovered over her in the morning room.

"Thank you, no, Thornley," Emma said, snuggling beneath the afghan Morgan had found for her. "I'm fine, really."

"Really," Morgan said, wishing his butler on the other side of the moon. "You may go, Thornley."

"Yes, my lord," Thornley said, bowing. But he didn't go. "Um...my lord."

Morgan looked to Emma, who smiled at him, then nodded.

"Yes, Thornley. Was there something you wished to ask me?"

"CLARAMAE?" Riley took two more steps into Mrs. Timon's private parlor, because he was certain he could hear Claramae in there, crying.

He'd searched for her, high and low, avoiding dark places, where she'd never go, but now he was sure he had run her to ground.

"Come in, Riley," Mrs. Timon said, her tone that of a command rather than a request.

The first thing Riley saw was Claramae, dressed in a horrible plaid bathrobe. The second thing he saw was Mrs. Timon's rolling pin.

"It's getting hitched we'll be, Mrs. Timon, Claramae and me," he said quickly. "Soon as soon can be."

"Yes, Riley, dear boy," Mrs. Timon said, all but caressing the rolling pin that had served her so well this evening. "I know."

IT WAS THREE in the morning, and most everyone was in bed, save for Morgan and Emma, who had stepped onto the balcony outside Morgan's bedchamber, overlooking the gardens.

Morgan had dismissed Wycliff, preferring to bathe himself, and for once the valet did not immediately take on an injured air, but had quickly bowed himself out of the room, smiling in agreement.

At which time Morgan had swept back the curtains and Emma had appeared, looking longingly toward the large tub.

"As I understand your lady's maid is otherwise engaged, and hopefully once again clothed, allow me to assist you, Miss Clifford," he'd said. "Perhaps even join you?"

"I don't know, my lord. Is it proper? The evening has come and gone, and you did not announce our betrothal."

"True," Morgan had said, helping her out of her sodden gown. "But I am assured that, between them, Perry and Lady Jersey have already taken care of the formal announcement. "

"Still, I do believe I would like to hear just what you would have said."

"Later, sweetness. First, let's get you into that tub. Your teeth are chattering."

And so, after sharing the tub and, directly after, the bed, Morgan and Emma were now on the balcony, having decided to watch the sun rise on the first day of their betrothal.

"Morgan?" Emma prompted, leaning her head against his shoulder. "Your announcement, please."

He slipped an arm around her and looked up at the faintly pink sky of dawn. "Lords and Ladies," he began in a clear voice. "Friends. It is with great delight and a full heart that I have gathered you all here to announce that Miss Emma Clifford has made me the happiest of men by agreeing to wed my sorry self. I love her more dearly than I do my own life, and I would ask for your blessing."

Then he tipped up Emma's chin, to look at her. "Was that soppy enough, sweetness?"

"Oh, yes," she said, and Morgan drew her close for a kiss.

Their arms around each other, lost in each other, neither of them noticed a flash of red race by below the balcony, or saw the bent-in-half figure following behind, arms outstretched, or heard Cliff Clifford calling piteously, "Harry! Oh, please, Harry! I didn't mean it…"

So...WHO ALL HAD COME to London? And what happened to them there?

The small but inventive staff has now quite dispersed; Thornley moving to his bride's home in the country; Mrs. Timon had happily shipped herself off to her newly rented seaside cottage; which left only Riley and Claramae, who had purchased a small shop in Piccadilly, where Riley kept a gamecock ring in the cellars, and Claramae sold hand-dipped candles.

The Interesting Family had also taken off in differing directions; Daphne now living with her Aloysius in the country house. Fanny had eloped to Gretna Green with Archie and was now a countess, Cliff was marching with his regiment in Dover (and hiding Harry in his rooms), and Emma, of course, snuggled delightfully at Westham, with her extremely happy and quite besotted new husband.

The two were picking out names for their firstborn, and hoping not too many of the *ton* had learned to count to nine on their fingers.

Perry, the "old friend," remained in London, studiously avoiding his Uncle Willard, who sent round notes twice a week, demanding his idiot nephew's presence, "At once, damn you!"

Olive Norbert, sad to say, escaped the two footmen on her way to the guardhouse, and was last seen running down a damp street behind a small man carrying a portmanteau, screaming, "I see you, Ed-gie! Ed-gie, you come back here with my money!"

Oh, yes, one thing more.

Six months later, while sitting at his ease in front of a lovely café in Paris, Robert Anderson, late of Mr. John Hatcher's employ, happened to espy a natty-looking older gentleman strolling down the flagway arm in arm with the wealthy and notoriously stupid Comte de Beauville.

The comte was hefting a small velvet bag, and smiling like the loon he was.

Robert Anderson, not one to allow Opportunity to pass him by, hastily threw some coins on the table, got up and followed after them....

*****

Watch for Perry's story, SHALL WE DANCE?
Coming in April 2005 from HQN Books.